W9-BLN-302

By Jesse Hill Ford

NOVELS

Mountains of Gilead
The Liberation of Lord Byron Jones
The Feast of Saint Barnabas
The Raider

PLAY

The Conversion of Buster Drumwright

STORIES

Fishes, Birds and Sons of Men

THE RAIDER

THE RAIDER

by

Jesse Hill Ford

AN ATLANTIC MONTHLY PRESS BOOK

Little, Brown and Company Boston/Toronto

FIRST EDITION
T 10/75

A portion of this work appeared in *Works In Progress*.

LIBRARY OF CONGRESS CATALOGING IN PUBLICATION DATA

Ford, Jesse Hill.
The raider.

"An Atlantic Monthly Press book."
1. Tennessee—History—Civil War, 1861-1865—Fiction. I. Title.
PZ4.F6983Rai [PS3556.07] 813'.5'4 75-17563
ISBN 0-316-288918

ATLANTIC–LITTLE, BROWN BOOKS
ARE PUBLISHED BY
LITTLE, BROWN AND COMPANY
IN ASSOCIATION WITH
THE ATLANTIC MONTHLY PRESS

Designed by D. Christine Benders

Published simultaneously in Canada
by Little, Brown & Company (Canada) Limited

PRINTED IN THE UNITED STATES OF AMERICA

To Lillian

Dulce et decorum est pro patria mori.
— Quintus Horatius Flaccus

BOOK ONE

The River

Chapter

1

Three creatures in the woodland rain. A man walking, looking about. A horse, browsing as he goes, hitched to the man by a long rawhide lead strap. A young dog, following of his own free will.

Judging by his pace the man is in no hurry. Like his horse he is burdened, a pack on his back too. And he carries a fourteen-pound rifle, now at his side, now at an angle over his shoulder — so much a part of him that he is hardly conscious how he carries his weapon. Shot pouch and powder horn ride on thin straps that cross his chest and pass over his shoulders.

Those moccasins he sewed himself by firelight squish with every step. Here is the low ground, West Tennessee, without mountains, a place of swamps and meadows and high forests, a vast and gently rolling wilderness.

In his pocket he carries a compass, that which the Indians call a landstealer. In his mind he carries a vision, as yet not entirely formed. Such a vision needs the right place in which to come alive. With such a place in mind the man leaves the road, making long excursions, now to the north, now to the south, but always from a westerly line passing straight through the ancestral homeland of the Chickasaws, a compass line, east-west, from the bank of the Tennessee River to the wide Mississippi.

That night, camping out of the rain beneath a ledge, what the Indians call a rockhouse, he discovers leavings of old campfires. He finds white skulls of deer strewn about. Flint chips, broken arrowheads, scattered bones, empty turtle shells. He sleeps, his dog beside him, his horse hitched nearby; his fire dies down to red-eyed embers . . .

Wolves howl during the night from deep in the far bottoms. Not so far away a panther screams. And next day, a flock of wood pigeons comes rising from nowhere and passes above the travelers, moving southwesterly, a great almost endless cloud of wings and life. Presently, after an hour's march, or just over it, he comes to the roost. The ground beneath the trees here is white, slick with droppings. Broken by the weight of that great, roosting multitude, limbs hang down like shattered arms, their green leaves drying, withering. A rank feathery scent of droppings reminds the man of sour milk. The scent hangs and follows; a wet, invisible mist.

The smell seems to trail and linger a long distance. When the dank, slick roosting-ground has been long left behind, the odor persists. The man plods on his way.

Before noon, an itch between his shoulders says turn off the road here. Head north. Many a time he's turned off the road before, yet never with quite this feeling, almost like a scent, as though at last he's found the trail of something.

Perhaps he smells a river; that small, tired, wandering sprawl of a lonely wilderness waterway hunting through this fastness, losing herself for long miles in flooded bottoms, oozing and slipping her way below cypress jams, sliding around smooth sandbars. Here rivers hardly move sometimes, pushing almost imperceptibly between thick columns of trees. The trees cast deep shade from bank to bank. Sometimes they bridge branches above the stream entirely. Has the man known the river was here? He unfolds his hand-sketched map, folds it away again, and plods on as before.

The horse smells something and sets his ears forward. He quits his lazy browsing and comes willingly now. The dog bays at a sudden racket. In tall woods ahead, three deer, tails flagging like three white handkerchiefs, go skimming and bounding out of sight. The man's heart thumps. "Here! Back!" he calls. The dog comes back and looks at him; a good young dog, his black face blunt as a hammer, his eyes willing. He's a fine young hunting mastiff and adores his wandering master. They move on . . .

Deer are a good sign; and that little rise straight ahead, what can be beyond it? They climb the rise . . .

When the man finally sees the river he slips his pack. He eases his burden to earth beside a poplar tree pushed down by wind. He sits and leans his rifle against his shoulder. His hands rest easily beside him. All about he sees forestlands in every shade, from darkest viridian to pale, pale blue. The little river comes winding between like a child's lost ribbon. Above it lingers a mist more delicate than smoke. Tall trees lean in along the banks.

Approaching the river he leads his horse across a clear, shallow creek. Three specks of life; three among the myriad millions of living creatures. A man, a horse, a dog, they descend the slope to the riverbank. In the trees, cicadas sing summer's deathsong. Fat grasshoppers leap and fly ahead, bending tall stems of grass in a little meadow. Mourning doves leap from the gray-white limbs of a tall dead willow and fly whimpering, whimpering away.

Pausing by the river, he shades his eyes with his hand. He sees fish. Suspended below a fallen sycamore log, they make promising shadows in the clear current which goes drifting above the white sand bottom. On the log sit round-shell turtles in a straight line, heads stuck up like thumbs. Leaving his master, the dog slides brace-legged down the sloping bank and pads over the warm sand to the water's edge. The turtles plop suddenly into the current and slide away into clear depths. The dog drinks, wading in a little, lapping, wading and lapping.

He unleashes the horse and hobbles him. He straps a bell to the horse's neck and gives him a slap. The horse goes grazing into the meadow, swinging and swishing his black tail. The bell makes a friendly *kling*.

Pink tongue rolling, black jaws dripping, the dog scrambles back up the bank. The man meanwhile is making a count of things. He counts his gun, counts his powder and flints, counts his few bars of lead, the bullet mold, the ax, the auger, the butcher knives, the tin cups, and some little packets of seed. He counts the dog and the horse and the compass, the oilcloth, and two stroudwater blankets. He counts every tool and container and little packet. He counts himself last of all. Elias counts one man alone in the world with these few possessions.

Thunder, meantime, makes a low muttering in the northeast quarter of the sky; a storm is gathering. But as yet it is far away, like a distant cannonade. God's artillery, afar off, and it makes Elias glad for a big sycamore standing nearby. He cleans leaves and sticks and rotten wood from its hollow and makes a dry place for this cargo of things. Here's room in the tree for himself as well. He's not the first to take shelter in a hollow tree. More thunder, muttering in the north. *Kling!* The bell in the meadow. And again: *Kling!*

Ignoring that distant thunder now his things are safely stored, Elias takes his gun again and with the dog following, begins a wide circle through the lonely woods. Soon he is counting again. Besides those deer he saw earlier and those fish beneath the sycamore log, he finds and counts a giant oak — a patriarch, a grandfather of trees —a tree such as makes a handy boundary mark. Not far beyond the mark tree, he counts another deer. This one stands stock-still, tame almost as horned cattle. It moves a little bit, but stops again and stands grazing. Only when the dog makes a rush, does it bound away. Elias hisses the dog back; as he does so a flock of fat wild turkeys goes mounting suddenly upward, scattering and flapping into the spreading tops of tall cathedral columns. A vast cypress grove stands downhill to the north. He counts the grove.

Where the ground rises again, more oak trees, straight poplars, tough shagbark hickories. Squirrels hidden high in the dense canopy of leaves drop a nut now and then or a cutting. Spiderwebs stretch from almost every dead, low branch. And a woodspider hangs like a chip in the center of each nearly invisible web. Here gnats dance the air. They bother the eyes and nostrils of man and dog alike. The dark woods drip little drops of moisture; here and there a sound, a drop striking and breaking the great, encompassing, all-silence. A way further along, the dog's hackles slowly rise. Sure enough, here's a den tree, home for a family of bears to judge by tracks and claw marks. And the bears are counted.

Thus, the man, Elias, makes a tally. Of things that creep, of things that fly, and of growing things rooted in the wild earth. He walks swiftly on now, so swiftly that before dusk he has circled clean back to where he began, to the sycamore; and the tree has a different look. It has a tame look and a look of home upon it that was not there before.

And he builds a fire. The first fire, and therefore not a fire like any other. Nevermind the storm's approaching grumble, nor a sudden breath of wind in the treetops, nor a riffle on the surface of the river. Nevermind the crash of a dead tree toppled and thrown to earth. Elias broils his last few strips of jerked venison. He sprinkles on gunpowder for seasoning; he makes his evening meal. Nor is this first meal like any other. He says a sort of grace, a thanksgiving, not aloud, but in his head and heart. He thanks God and feeds his dog what's left over.

Chapter 2

Winter. Indians pass that way. They come in a troop, mounted on short shaggy horses and leading pack ponies laden with deerskins and pelts. Come to harvest bears, it would seem. They've got a surprise.

Sliding off their horses, they note a snug shelter of poles built against a big sycamore. They count several bearskins already stretched. Close by, a man is felling trees and hewing logs, raising a cabin all by himself. And he's hewing his logs *square*. The man's ax makes a tireless sound the Indians have heard from afar. A black-muzzled hunting mastiff, meanwhile, goes barking and rushing, making the ponies nervous. Only when hissed back by the white man will the young dog hush. Turning back, he sets to gnawing a shank bone he seems proud of. But now and then he growls, as if to let Indians know he's still on guard.

A generous fire in front of the shelter invites cold Indians to warm. The white man, ax in hand, comes near. He speaks kindly. The braves stand and visit. They've come dressed for their long winter hunt.

"Square timbers?" says Pettecasockee. "Um."

"Yes," says the white man.

"Round logs make less work."

"Square timbers make a warm house."

"And bulletproof," says Pettecasockee. "See any bears?"

"Plenty of bears."

"Plenty of deer too," says Pettecasockee, eyeing a pile of skulls and several bales of skins.

"Yes."

Without appearing to, Indians have a way of looking and counting. They count a good horse standing in homemade harness to haul timbers. They count the hunting mastiff and other things. And a man — they count a man not easily frightened. He's a big man, built for heavy work. When he speaks they hear soft confidence in his voice. He is a creature of the woods, in no way awkward nor out of place here. His slow smile, his slow speech, the lithe, easy way he walks and moves make the Indians feel at home. Judging by bones and hides, he's a skilled hunter and a true shot, this fellow. Judging by his clothing, he makes his own shirts and leggings, sews his own moccasins. No soft, pale, city man.

"You stay here?" says Pettecasockee. The others look to him. They all have the deep features of the Chickasaw, the strong build of warriors, the stance of expert horsemen, and the good manners to leave their muskets in their saddle scabbards.

"Yes," said the white man. "Since late summer." And then: "Hunting?"

Pettecasockee nods. Silence like smoke. No man would square such timbers unless he intended to stay.

Pettecasockee seems satisfied. No bears for harvest here. The dog growls. First, Pettecasockee, then one brave and another turn away, leaping lightly into the saddle until the white man stands alone by his fire, his deerskin leggings tightly wrapped and bound against the cold, his ax in hand, on his open face the same serene look Pettecasockee has observed. A man well worn to danger.

Sudden as birds, the saddle horses spring away across the creek. The pack ponies scramble after. Hard hooves striking frozen earth, the shaggy cavalcade follows the curve of the river. Those earth-hollow sounds move on and on, farther and farther away, heading south.

The harnessed horse raises his head and neighs. Dog barks one last bark.

Then all was still. A cold hush settled. Weak sunlight slanted as before through the high, bare trees. A whistling drove of ducks splashed down upon the river with noisy clamor and quacking. Geese began honking in the distant, flooded bottoms. Swans made a shrill answering.

Then began the steady ring of the ax, with a pause now and then for the following splash of a falling tree. The same sounds continued straight through till dark. His hauling done, the horse was unharnessed, rubbed and had his bell strapped on. The fire, gray ashes now, was built up again and urged to a bright blaze. Man and dog divided a cold roast turkey between them. Owls hooted, calling to and fro across the woods, and made the wild ducks restless.

His back to the tree hollow, firelight on his face, Elias sits using his knife and awl. He sews new moccasins, the front of him baking, the back of him freezing, his lonely heart seized with thoughtful envy. Elias envies Father Adam created in a warm garden, naked in the midst of a bearing orchard. Not sitting half-frozen on a bearskin — not Adam, thinks Elias. Not out of whiskey, out of salt, no coffee, no pepper, Elias thinks. He halfway hates soft Father Adam for the easy time — the luck *that* fellow had.

Dog snuggles close to his master. Browsing near the edge of the canebrake, the horse moves. His bell rings in the chill bleak darkness. In the immense flooded bottoms for miles about, motionless water stands freezing tonight. Perhaps the river itself will freeze given a few days of cold such as this. The ground is hard as iron. Elias quits sewing. He puts awl and knife carefully away.

With a final look to the fire, piling it high with logs, the settler gathers himself into his tree hollow and beds down, sharing blankets and bearskins with his shivering dog. And they pass but one more in a long series of still, cold nights.

Wolves. Day and night they follow a trail of carcasses. So sure are the wolves of venison, they merely trot toward the sound of Elias McCutcheon's gun. It cracks day after day, splitting the silence of the curving ridge, booming again and again in the low ground, kicking forth a muffled thunder that echoes and carries for miles upon the flatness of the icy water.

Skinned carcasses lie one after another ready for eating. No more need for the wolves to busy themselves with hunting. They quickly grow sleek and lazy. Their young know nothing of hunting. Gunsound means meat here. The young wolves grow rapidly; gunsound is all they need to know.

Scents of horse, scents of dog, scents of man, sweetish scents of green hides — strange at first, these smells soon become familiar to the wolves. They trot through the familiar woods and openly show themselves beside the river. As bold by day as by dark, they make an increasing tribe.

But the panthers, never so many as the wolves and always solitary, now give up this territory. The panthers drift farther and farther away, avoiding the very scents and sounds which the wolves so eagerly follow.

The groggy bears that doze deep in the thickest canebrakes, sucking their paws and whining, are driven out by the dog's sudden raging rush and barking, and routed from winter lair, out of sleep, half blind, half raging, they lurch like drunken men. Thus goaded they go charging toward the trees and are knocked down and tumbled for fleece, that layer of golden winter fat. Working by night the man must render the fleece to oil. He butchers out the flesh for bear hams to be scalded and packed in ashes and smoked above the fire. The bear's paw is slipped under the ashes and left all day to roast. Returning to his tree at dusk, Elias removes the paw from the warm ashes. Outer hair and skin slip off as easily as a glove and the hunter makes his supper. Cooked thus and skinned a bear paw has a strange, close resemblance to the human hand, and gives the hunter food for thinking. Perhaps as Indians say, mankind is cousin to the bear; perhaps, thinks Elias.

And he packs home carcass after carcass, backs broken to fit the horse, and the poor horse laden sometimes to staggering. A fire-hollowed sassafras log makes a scalding trough. Stones first heated in the fire and dropped in the filled trough bring the water to a rolling boil. Thus is fleece rendered; thus is meat scalded.

Between bear hunts and deer hunting the ax does its loud work and the auger does its silent work. In the evening by firelight, Elias splits shingles. When split the dry poplar makes a special stink. The shakes are stacked and tied in bundles of fifty to be stored in the tree to wait for roofpoles and nails. The log house will have one room, a wide fireplace and a chimney of wattle and sticks. A stone chimney may come later. Whittled wooden hinges must hang the door for now and leather hinges hold the shutters. There will be a wait for iron hinges and glass panes. For now, auger and ax, knife and hatchet. Silent work; loud work. And a long list of things both waiting and wanting.

Chapter 3

A white man, alone and on horseback, stops by one day, having smelled the fire and heard the ax. He rides from the south following the curve of the river. He is wearing a fine warm woolen coat and a fine warm hat, neat gloves and new boots. He's got saddlebags and pistols. He rides a blooded roan horse with a white blaze on his narrow face. A gentleman stopping by, being just on his way north he says. "Gabriel French," he says, giving his name, "Gabriel French." His business he says is land. Timber. Minerals. Speculations.

Elias welcomes him. The visitor has a sharp eye. He sees cabin walls going up, several bales of deerskins, a field almost cleared, a legion of logs ready for rolling and burning.

French has a full face, muttonchop side whiskers and a happy laugh. He's seen other places in Western Tennessee but few so well chosen, he says. Indeed *none* so well chosen as this, he allows solemnly. He's plump, like his horse, and not nearly so big as Elias. Seems educated, speaking words fine as his clothing, turning compliments neat as gloves.

They "Mister French" and "Mister McCutcheon" back and forth a while, walking and looking. Then they sit on the log bench. Elias, not used to talking for so long a time, can't at first speak what he wants to say. Gabriel French seems not to notice. French talks for both of them. There's a settlement, he says, just go south to the military road and west a way. Consists of an old fort, a trading post, a rum ordinary, stocks, a whipping post, and jail.

"It's a stage post," Gabriel French says. "They call it Fort Hill and then first one thing and another, but mostly Fort Hill. A name hasn't really been settled on it yet. Drunken Indians, gamblers, a few soldiers fresh out of the army."

As it turned out, Gabriel French had coffee in his saddlebags, and pepper, and sugar, and salt. To go with these wonders, Elias furnished turkey, venison, and bear meat. The new friends made a feast in the winter dusk. The visitor brought out a bottle. Should discuss a few toddies, shouldn't they? he offered.

While Elias rubbed down and hobbled his visitor's horse, Gabriel French mixed the toddies — water, whiskey and sugar — stirred well in tin cups.

The "misters" and "sirs" dropped away. They began saying "Elias" and "Gabe." When came time to turn in, both crawled in the tree hollow and bedded down snug and warm with Dog between them.

Last thing, before they fell asleep, Gabe raised up and propped himself upon his elbow. Looking at Elias he said: "Fine place such as this should have a name. Have you named it?"

"Um, no. Not as yet," says Elias.

"How does Oakleigh sound to you. After that great old boundary tree, eh?"

"Oakleigh? Why, yes," says Elias. "Oakleigh."

And Oakleigh it was.

Up early, his bright face shaved slick as a pear, Gabe French is eager to be on his way north. Elias sees that his guest's horse is properly bridled and saddled. Gabe, meanwhile, lightens his saddlebags.

"You'd oblige me," Gabe says. "I'm freighted."

"Well," says Elias. And Gabe leaves coffee and sugar and salt and pepper and a bottle of good whiskey. "Well, thanks!" Elias says.

"A service to me." Gabe mounts. Elias is sad to see him go. The visitor smiles and tucks his chin down. "You've blazed good boundarics. Oaklcigh will bc a landmark."

Here was the first Elias knew that Gabe has seen the boundary marks on the trees while riding this way. So Gabe knows something of the size of the place. Gabe knows the dream Elias dreams.

They say their goodbyes. "I'll speak to the Indians hereabouts for you," says Gabe. "I'm known to them."

"Thanks again. That's a help," says Elias.

And Gabe French will be back, he says. He speaks to his horse and slowly rides away upriver, following that same way the Indians came down. All too soon he's gone.

Chapter 4

Pack-in-time. Five hundred and forty-six deerskins; twenty-eight beaver and three otters. Two otters and one wolf. Six raccoons. The bearskins can be left home and poor Dog must be left. It's his business now to guard things, but how can he know his master will come back? How can he know where these two — horse and man — are going and why? He can't. And he's tied to the sycamore tree with meat and water in reach of him. Man and horse walk away making the darkest day poor Dog has known.

Man and horse leaving, staggering away under all that cargo. But no, here they come staggering back! They leave some bundles off and start away again, this time with a lighter step. Dog grieves, he howls; he fights his tether; he mopes, finally he gives up. Horse and man cross the shallow creek. They disappear, fading into the trees.

Next day they return, and Dog leaps against the man licking and sniffing him, scenting strange new smells in his clothes. That night Dog wakes and lifts his blunt head time and again to make sure the man is beside him. And Elias is there all night, sleeping not as usual, but sleeping a hard, exhausted sleep.

Before daybreak the man is up. Poor Dog is tied. Man and horse walk off laden down. Another day of hopeless waiting, another night of shivering, with no smell of fire about. Howling wolves challenge all night long; they promise him dog-death, those wolves.

Then another surprise. Horse and man returning. Long before they appear, Dog begins to bark and whine and jerk the end of his rope. Again, Dog knows that miracle of his master's return. When the man actually appears and sets Dog free there is more leaping and licking and adoration, and this time some puppylike frisking about, some little fits of dashing and madness through ashes and into bushes and through the meadow and around the tree and down the river-bank and back again for more leaping and licking before Dog can finally settle down. It's more than he could hope, that the man would return a second time. He forgets loneliness, forgets wolves, forgets every sorrow. Dog's heart is full. For a long while, he lies very still and watches each move the man makes. The man is talking.

"Five hundred and forty-six deerskins," says Elias. "A hundred and thirty-six dollars and fifty cents." He's surely said it several hundred times these two days. But he must say it all again and again. "Twenty-eight beaver and three otters, thirty-three dollars and fifty cents." A pause. "Two otters and one wolf, four dollars." Another pause. "Six raccoons, seventy-five cents."

He's got a new red shirt and a new five-dollar blanket. His horse wears a new curb bridle. Here's a fresh supply of flints and powder. Eight pounds of tea (that came to two dollars). Here's whiskey, nails, cloth, tin cups, new butcher knives.

No handkerchiefs nor shawls, no combs and calico for Elias, however.

The storekeeper had held up a fringed shawl; next, an ivory comb. Elias shakes his head. *No.* No use for such as that.

The squaws exchange looks with the storekeeper. "Blue cloth?" asks one. She's a young vixen, first smiling and then giggling.

"No," says Elias and feels their laughter, how it follows him out the door.

The blacksmith's busy putting iron hinges on the fort gates in place of whittled wooden ones, although there has never been an attack here. Iron hinges, nevertheless. And a faction of newcomers has built houses downhill, outside the fort walls. Indian Town is a sprawl of shanties and hovels along the east slope, and down below, by the post road, the local bullies have gathered at the pond. They offer an Indian tots of whiskey if he will take a swim; the weather is freezing cold . . .

There was such a great deal Elias could tell. He was full to bursting. Restless thoughts were stirring, but there was no one to talk to but himself — not another soul. Ideas and plans went humming and thriving inside him.

Springtime crept out of the south.

More new things. A ladder against the wall; the man up on top of his house, nailing shingles. Elias totes shingles up the ladder a bundle at the time. He wears a leather nail apron that he sewed himself. He's fixed a loop at the side to hold his roofing hammer. Now and then Elias uses the high vantage of the roof to gaze upon his cleared field. There's bright sun. The wind is between cool and balmy, a young breeze not able to make up its mind. It rises sometimes to gusty wind. Behind on the riverbank, the willows have put out green. The maples drop purple-dark buds. Gnats and mosquitoes are venturing. Flies have begun to stir. Feeble wasps, stiff and cold each morning, feel warmed enough to go buzzing and hunting by afternoon.

Withal it's a lonely time and a man of small determination might ride to the fort and have a look. Inspect those iron hinges or discuss a dram at the ordinary? Listen for news, swap lies. But this man hates interruption. He hammers away.

And no sooner will he be off the roof than he must be building a fence. "Horse-high, bull-strong, and hog-tight," he mutters.

Between spells on the roof, he goes back a distance into the field and walks around slowly, admiring the roof. It's a wonder how tightly the fresh roof joins the mud chimney. When the roof is finished, he takes a look at the sky. He wonders why rain seemingly never wants to try a new roof. The sun shines far above. He and the roof must wait.

The very next day at dawn Elias begins "horse-high, bull-strong, hog-tight." And he puts special vengeance into beginning that fence, daring things to try to get through, under, or over *this* fence. Those rails and posts he split and cut last fall find use.

In the midst of vowing and swearing and laboring, Elias looks up from fencing to hear Dog greeting a mounted Indian. He is making both Indian and horse almost as welcome as he would make bear or wolf, panther, or the very Devil. Dog has to be called and tied before the Indian can dismount, much less state his business.

It's the same young Indian of last winter. "He will see you," says the young Indian. Just that: "He will see you."

Because it's no use ever to ask one Indian to tell another Indian's name, Elias ponders the invitation. Elias carefully says that as any Indian can see he, Elias, is busy building a fence. And more, planting time is snapping at his heels. Seed time . . .

"He will see you," says the Indian. The brave wears a red shirt and has a black silk handkerchief tied about his head. "He will see you."

"Who will?" Elias ventures, though it's no use asking, of course.

"Come," says the brave, shrugging and looking away.

"What's *your* name?"

"Pettecasockee," says the young man. "You are Elias."

"Gabriel French spoke to you?"

"Mister French spoke to my father," says Pettecasockee. "My father will see you."

While Elias makes up his mind, the young brave admires the house, approves the fence, and asks when Elias plans to have horned cattle and hogs. Thus Pettecasockee, who seemingly liked nothing he saw here last winter, suddenly likes what he sees now. Something has wrought a change.

"How long a ride is it?" Elias says.

"Not one sleep! You will be back tomorrow," says the Indian. "Come!"

Elias changes into his red shirt. He sets out meat and water for Dog. Then he saddles up and rides north with his new friend.

Pettecasockee's mount turns out to be a bright pony. Elias's horse, Rattler, is put on his mettle. Presently Rattler steps out and shows his long, tireless stride. Rattler's new curb bridle looks well on him. His big ears cock forward. Rattler has some fire in him yet.

Chapter 5

A brisk ride with Pettecasockee guiding him, and just before dusk Elias finds himself before a big house with outbuildings on every side. The place has barns and fine fences. Cattle are lowing. Mules bray. A plank bridge spans a shallow sandy creek. Plowland stretches on every side, fine, flat bottomland cleared clean and extending almost beyond the eye's reach in some directions. Closer by stand a wagon shed, a horse barn, a mule barn, a cattle barn — everything here is roofed and tight.

"Redleaves," says Pettecasockee.

Coming to take the horses is a Negro, a black slave with

flared nostrils. His hands look to be as long as split shingles. Flower beds and shrubs flank the well-set house. It has roofed porches high and low and windows set with glass panes. The tall front double doors have brass knobs and brass knockers bright as gold. The house itself, painted white, gleams like milk in the twilight. A late frost is falling, the air is turning cold.

They cross the porch. The door opens. Pettecasockee stands aside to let Elias enter first. Approaching him over the dark, polished hall floor, Elias sees a man in mid-life. He wears a black suit and a white starched shirt; he's an Indian by the dark look of him; he holds his hand outstretched. His skin is brown and wrinkled like a walnut. He smiles and says, "Welcome! Welcome to Redleaves. I am Shokotee. Shokotee McNeilly. And you'll be Elias McCutcheon! Have some whiskey, eh? Had you an easy ride?"

Abundance. Whiskey toddies. The household gives off a quiet bustle of secret movement. Women wearing full dresses go about quietly in moccasins. Now and again one of them peeps into the sitting room, giving Elias a glimpse of her handsome face, long black hair, and merry black eyes. It's a look he recalls from the day not long ago when he packed in his hides and furs to the fort. Saucy, vixen squaws — he tries not to notice. He tries instead to listen to what Shokotee McNeilly is saying, but Elias is conscious nonetheless of that secretive female moving about, that stirring in the back hallways. Such as that gives a strange, giddy feeling to a man so long in the woods by himself. Quiet laughter comes floating now and again — echoes now and then a shrill singsong voice rings out, gently scolding . . .

Presently candles are lit all around the room until it seems bright as day, almost. Elias is warmed by whiskey toddies, lulled by old Shokotee's incessant talk. Shokotee meanwhile smokes a black cigar. And he says:

"When I was a very young man I decided I would not carry

water and haul manure. I saw a great many Indians sold as slaves. Saw some married to slaves. Saw many die in the fields. I'd be shot first, I decided. Before *I'd* carry water and haul manure! Um. Cotton has been good to me."

An old squaw came shuffling in with a blue blanket and spread it upon Shokotee's lap. She tucked it about his legs. She shuffled away and presently returned with a brown woolen shawl bordered with an orange fringe. Carefully she put the shawl about Shokotee's narrow shoulders.

Shokotee meanwhile has a certain way of looking at Elias. He widens his eyes and raises his eyebrows, and stares at Elias as though waiting for the arrival of the next thought. And he puffs his cigar. "So I hunted and jacked around," he says. "Jacked around and hunted. And then I fell in with a priest? A Catholic father, and *he* convinced himself it was worthwhile to see to my schooling. Fancied he could make me a Jesuit? Saw in me *possibilities,* he said! So much for that."

The old man spat on the hearth and shouted something — Indian language. A second squaw, somewhat younger, brought fresh toddies. She carried kitchen smells of sherry and smoke in the folds of her calico dress. Elias was hungry. The whiskey had begun to go pleasantly to his head.

"Do you know Mister Gabriel French," Elias says.

"Ah — yessir! He spoke to me about you, yes! He is my friend. Yes, he spoke to me. He's a believer in land, wild unsettled, untitled land. He buys it, sells it, trades it, yes. Um."

The young brave, Pettecasockee, tossed off his black scarf.

He leaned back in his chair and propped his feet on the settle and gazed into the fire. Fireshadows moved upon his contented, handsome features. The firelight caught the reflection of his eyes. He too was smoking. Now and again he nodded, saying "Um!"— agreeing. Although he seemed to have heard all that his father now told, all of it many times before, he didn't seem bored. No, he seemed, rather, to enjoy a certain pleasant anticipation for what his father might say next. "Um!" says Pettecasockee, nodding.

All in good time they moved to the drafty dining room and sat down, just the three of them. There were meat and greens, fish and pickles, turkey and preserves, white and corn bread, Irish and sweet potatoes, pies and deep dish cobblers and pitchers of sweet milk. They pitched in, ate, and gulped cup after cup of strong coffee. Long after Elias was full, the Indians, father and son, were still eating. Endless eaters, they seemed!

Shokotee rattled on and on, meanwhile, talking and eating, eating great amounts of everything. At last peach brandy was brought around and signaled the end of feasting. Shokotee belched and pushed back from the table.

"Man such as yourself," he said, and belched again. "Such as yourself — I mean to say — well, what about a plow — cattle and mules? You have what you need?"

"Plan to rent them," says Elias. "Only a plow and a yoke of oxen at first, to begin."

"But rented cattle must have grain. Grain needs a wagon to haul it, eh?" Shokotee sips his brandy, smacking his lips.

"A wagon can be rented," says Elias.

Silence. The plates were cleared away. The men took their brandy back to the fire in the warm adjoining room. They sat down as before, in the same places. Pettecasockee propped his feet on the settle again. And again Elias heard those secret movements in the hall just beyond the doorway in the darkness. The fire had been built up and was hotter now. It popped and sang. A gray-muzzled hound limped in from the dark hall, his claws clicking on the floor. He sighed and slouched down, burped, and stretched out before the hearth. A mass of scars, he was. The candles were snuffed. The men sat smoking and sipping sweet peach brandy. The old hound, the favorite hound of the house, began to snore. His worn, gray eyelids fluttered now and then, his dark feet jerked, and his loose lip curled back and he showed his broken teeth.

Shokotee coughed and spat on the logs. He stuck out his smallish moccasined foot from beneath his lap robe and stroked the dog.

"Gabe French and I, we talked," he says. "It's our feeling that a man like yourself could use woman help. Had a man *servants*, he wouldn't need woman help. Could he buy slaves, a man wouldn't want woman help, maybe."

A pause, Elias was silent. What Shokotee said was true.

"There *is* a woman," Shokotee said. "White woman," he added. A smile came wrinkling from the corners of his eyes. "Name of Jane Nail." Leaning forward, over the dog, he spat into the fire again. "She came to me an orphan and's grown now. She was raised right here on the place. She's tamed and good and gentle — *she* might suit."

Elias is cautious. He neither says no nor yes. He *needs* help. Maybe here's a better place to find it, better than the fort, judging what he's seen so far.

"She's here?" says Elias. "Hereabouts you say?"

The smile wrinkles again about Shokotee's eyes. He nods. He puffs his cigar. He chuckles to himself. Finally he leans toward Elias. "If it might be as you're interested, why not let me ask her. See if she's willing? And if she agrees, then we'll send her. Try her! You don't find she suits? She's not satisfied herself? Send her back! Um?"

"That's fair," says Elias. Now more than anything he wants a glimpse of the woman. "Hereabouts, is she? Close by — ?" A broad hint.

"Yes, but — well, it won't do for you to see her. Not just now. She's shy. But now if she's *willing*, then . . ."

"I understand," Elias says. He's sure that he won't have a look at her first.

"Now upon the business of renting what you need to make your crop?" says Shokotee. "A man could take his chances at the fort. Wait his turn. But again, now he might be-shit himself."

"What? How's that?" says Elias. Is his mind wandering, maybe?

"Well, plant his corn late, using tired cattle behind the other fellow. Piss away his luck that way at the fort. Plant too late and the worms will eat the crop and cast down the stalks."

"That's true."

"But you could get *fresh* stock here. And a good wagon, good plow, good harness. Few barrels of corn. We could send it all down when we send the woman, make one trip."

"How much rent d'you want?"

"I'll see what they charge at the fort. Pay me that amount less a dollar?"

"Done, sir," says Elias. But his mind isn't on trading and renting, not just now.

"Um," says Pettecasockee. "I like you, sir. I'd like to see you do well. Gabe French likes you. We talked, yes. He spoke to me. You know of his speculations? No? He deals up in the thousands, the *hundred* thousands. Fear for him sometimes, I do. It's gambling, that's all! Call it speculation? But it's pure gambling! A roll of dice! Eh?"

"I'm not a gambler myself," says Elias. "Hundreds of thousands, you said? Well." Elias tries to pay polite attention, but his mind is wandering . . .

"Yessir! They live in a cold sweat, so much worrying. How they sleep nights — those fellows — is a wonder to me! Aye, Gabe, he's one of them. Land speculator. You play cards?"

"No, sir."

"Well," says Pettecasockee. The young brave stands up, stretches, says goodnight and goes off to bed.

"Checkers?" says the older man.

"Ye-es," says Elias, reluctantly.

"Sit still! I'll fetch the board!"

After a night's tossing sleep on a soft feather bed in a room with paned windows, stretched out between fresh linen sheets; after early breakfast with the two Indians (fresh eggs, hog ham, wheat biscuits, honey, fresh milk, pear preserves, and cup after cup of coffee), Elias finally says goodbye.

Old Rattler, grain-fed, rubbed down, and brisk as a colt, is led around to the front door by the same soot-black, long-handed servant. Elias mounts and turns off toward the bridge. Thus he goes away without a single glimpse of the woman. No sign of Jane Nail to be seen anywhere! All the way home from Redleaves he tries — he wrestles with his mind trying to imagine what she is like. He wonders and suffers that whole long way home. Then he reaches a clearing. What tiny log hut is this? And whose ugly dog jerking the end of his rope, yelling to be untied? What kind of unholy hacked-out ragtag place can *this* be, with those stumps dotting everywhere like black broken teeth, thick as tines, and that ugly sorethumb of a mud chimney sticking up like some blasphemy! Some poor soul, with nothing but a tree for his toolhouse, some poor devil hereabouts is trying to build a fence by himself. And the wretch hasn't a plow nor a wagon nor any horned cattle in sight!

Takes a while to come home sometimes, so it does.

Chapter 6

Waiting. Fools wait; wise men go about their work. The fool stops for a woolgathering gaze at a cool sunset stretching a faded sky. The fool stands preoccupied on the riverbank hearing fish slap and can't account afterwards where his thoughts have been.

Let the fool work; like a beehive he works daylight till dark; still he can't fall asleep as he once did. Because he's forever half listening for Dog to bark, to dash north aways and need calling back. Listening and trying not to listen, thinking and trying not to think, wondering and wanting not to wonder. Fools suffer a way the wise in this world never do.

The man's neck even seems to swell sometimes. Without warning, sometimes, his mouth goes dry. Fear? But what's to be afraid of?

True, the old wolf of an Indian called her a woman, but a woman to Shokotee? Could be a crone of seventy winters! A woman, then, yes, but an old woman with a wrinkled mouth, sagging tits, teeth half gone, cunt collapsed and hanging out for the world to smell. Trust an Indian? Trust a bear not to bite. Saddle a catfish. Black thoughts gather in; aye. That's an Indian for you, always looking to pawn some hag off on a near neighbor.

Yet, changes went forward around the place, about Oakleigh. For one, Dog was ordered to stay outdoors on pain of terrible, calamitous hurt. Dog must no longer sleep on the bed with the man. Poor astounded Dog, banished, cast out into the damp. Dews and mists become his night companions. Scratching the door only gets him a strapping. Finally Dog gives it up. He goes to the tree and sleeps.

The fence-builder meanwhile takes time to scrub and sweep. He starts considering a well and a little backhouse. And a barn will be wanted before summer's gone again.

Dog goes barking and dashing a little ways north. It's as though he hears something. Can't be anything, thinks Elias, and he goes on with fencing even while his heart pounds and his throat swells. It's a warm day at last. He goes right on sweating and hammering, digging, sawing, and augering on "horse-high, bull-strong, and hog-tight."

Dog slinks in home, barking. "Well, see what it is," thinks Elias. Dog is *facing* north all right. He's *facing* upriver and barking. Is somebody chopping wood that way? Was that an *ax*?

It's a sound too faint to be sure of, and Elias speaks kindly to Dog and goes back towards the fence, pausing betimes to look over the empty pen he built for the rented oxen, next eyeing the horse calmly grazing new grass by a stump. Old Rattler's bell rings now and then.

But — ah — now Rattler hears something! Up comes his big big head, facing north. Rattler's ears cock. He stretches his neck, he neighs, snorts, listens, and goes back to cropping grass. Still he looks up now and then, stops chewing, and listens.

An anxious man might saddle up and ride that way just to see what it can be. A fool *would* do that — ride out and make a bigger fool of himself.

But as steady men know, the surest way to make a thing happen is to tripledown devildog ignore it. A sober man goes straight on about his work without niggling nor fretting over noises. It's true Elias may step into his house and have a look in his little shaving mirror. If in doing that he happens to notice a certain red shirt hung neatly on its peg in the wall, then it follows, doesn't it, that he may look below the shirt and see his good new boots on the floor, mysteriously waxed and dusted and waiting? Is there harm to appear well dressed, maybe? But no — that could make him seem anxious when he wasn't anxious, not a bit. Still he takes time for a last look in the mirror and a shaggy fool stares back — a rough brute with sun spots on his cheeks and dark, thick eyebrows. The fool stares such a fierce, reproving stare that Elias turns suddenly and goes straight outdoors again dressed just the same — yes, Lord, bare to the waist, bless God, and brown as an Indian, and dripping sweat.

Elias ignores the silly horse and shuns the erring, misbegotten dog and is found thus deep at work, absorbed-like with fencing, when Pettecasockee rides in upon his bright pony and discovers him. Elias seems downright surprised! But that's Elias, after all, so busy with farming and building that he forgets all else — Elias does. Buried in work, Elias is — so much so that he needs a moment to gather his senses. Pettecasockee admires the progress of the fence — silently at first and then aloud.

"That? But it's only a few sticks propped up," says Elias, still confused. "Now how did you slip up so quietly?" And Elias shakes his head in wonder.

"I shouted across the field," says Pettecasockee, sliding down off the pony. "You didn't hear?" They step inside the cabin.

"Must be I'm going deaf," says Elias and pulls his earlobe. Confused and surprised — he's almost pitiful. Wiping his red face and damping the grime and sweat from his hairy chest. Pettecasockee stands quietly watching.

"Didn't hear your dog bark?" says Pettecasockee.

"Him? He barks at butterflies," says Elias.

Elias pulls on his red shirt and hauls off his old boots, slipping on his good ones. "Lucky thing there's water simmering for coffee," he says.

And Elias hurries outside with Pettecasockee in time to see the wagon appear, drawn by a team of big oxen, and just verging from the edge of the woods. He can't see a woman as yet, but there's the Negro driver on the wagon seat holding the whip and a group of Negroes walking beside with axes.

Having called in and tied the dog, Elias puts roasted coffee beans in a small leather sack and using a stump for a rest pounds away at the bag with the flat of his ax. Pettecasockee, showing his pony off, meanwhile, dashes away to the wagon yelling orders to *makase*, and *go ahead*, and *hurry*, just generally yelling and dashing about on his pony, every inch as wild as the woods, Pettecasockee is. Not a tame hair in his scalp, thinks Elias, pounding away.

The wagon arrives. The Negroes unload and store the barrels in the house. They take out the oxen, unyoke them, and turn them into the new pen. The bundles of hay and the plow are stored inside the sycamore tree. The wagon is backed up snugly under the pole shelter.

The Negroes have built themselves a little cook fire. Outdoors they begin frying fatmeat and corncakes, squatting at their ease now, resting, chattering, and laughing.

Elias and Pettecasockee return to the cabin. Elias pours the pounded coffee into the kettle and gives the hearth fire a stir of encouragement. Besides a bench against the wall, he's got two chairs now. Homemade things, they have rawhide backs and seats nicely tied and tacked. He's made a table of cottonwood plank. Inside, his walls are smeared with white clay from the riverbank — all new things since Pettecasockee was last here. The young brave is loud in admiration.

"Oh?" says Elias, as though he perhaps can't remember when it was he made these little improvements. He pours coffee like a man accustomed to coffee every day. Pettecasockee sups his coffee Indian style, with noise and smacking.

"So she couldn't be talked into coming?" says Elias, speaking calmly as he can. His heart has sunk below ground, cold as an egg buried in sand.

"Um?" says Pettecasockee, smacking and swilling like a hog. "She's in the woods."

"What? Jane Nail? What woods?"

"There," says Pettecasockee making a motion with his hand. It's nothing to him. "You don't see her trunk? See? In the corner?"

Elias sees the trunk. Now how could he be so busy looking at barrels that he would miss a trunk? Merely seeing that trunk his heart leaps. His arms tingle, a sensation like gnats drowning in his blood.

Pettecasockee has the grace to stick out his cup for more coffee. Elias pours. "She comes after we leave," says Pettecasockee. "Um."

"Ah — she's shy," says Elias, putting the kettle back on the fire, and suddenly starting to wonder why the devil Pettecasockee and his loitering Negroes must hang around! The Negroes outside give a shout of laughter.

"Ever give *them* coffee?" says Elias.

"During the big winter medicine," says Pettecasockee, meaning Christmas.

Elias grabs the kettle and strides to the door. "Here," he says. The startled blacks look up. "Bring your cups." They come at a trot. And so ends coffee, every drop.

Pettecasockee waits. Elias sighs and sets the empty kettle

on the sand hearth. Pettecasockee frowns into his cup and gives it a shake. He looks from the leather coffee bag to the ax.

Elias sits staring at the little trunk in the corner. His own cup, half full yet, rests forgotten on the table. Something apparently begins dawning on the Indian. He stands abruptly. "Goodbye," he says.

Elias starts. "Not leaving?" says Elias. He follows Pettecasockee into the yard. "Thought as we'd pick a bit of turkey later on and discuss a toddy?"

Pettecasockee can't hide a smile. "No. Goodbye!"

Elias follows, weakly protesting, but Pettecasockee leaps to his pony's back and gathers the reins, smiling his strange smile. His black hair shines in the sunlight. Sweat beads above his youthful lip. The Negroes struggle up and shoulder their axes. They go filing away like soldiers.

"Good coffee, Marse!" shouts one. The others guffaw like they know something.

"Step! Makase!" cries Pettecasockee. He raises his whip to Elias, a farewell gesture. His horse starts away, mincing and pawing, dancing — rider and horse — both like a single creature almost too proud to set hoof to earth.

"Tell Shokotee thanks!" shouts Elias, barely remembering. He has to run catch his own horse, meanwhile, and tie him securely. Old Rattler's wanting to follow that strange pony home. Rattler fights his rope, neighing and begging the other to come back even after the last Negro has disappeared into the woods behind Pettecasockee. Elias finally smacks Rattler a good whop on the neck for his foolishness. That whop serves warning to Dog who's been whining to be untied, wagging his tail so hard he moves his whole body. So Dog too subsides, but not Elias. He is plunged into a storm of wondering and fidgeting. And nothing stirs from the woods. What in the name of creation can be keeping her now? Didn't he run his guests off quicker than was polite? Isn't he dressed in his best shirt and best boots? Then a cold thought. What if she's seen me? *That's it — she had a look and saw the half-naked beast building his fence and changed her mind!*

Slowly, he circles the house, suffering. Next, he circles the tree in the same slow way, examining the wagon. He's trembling, cutting glance after covert glance at the distant edge of the woods. Nothing stirs there. Should he go look for her and make her know she's welcome? Find her and lead her in? The poor little silly cow! The drab old bitch! That was it — she was a crone so ugly and hide-worn, she was needing the cover of night before she could nerve it! The righteous anger of man betrayed makes a surge through his heart.

And now, he thinks, now she's seen me *worrying* and shivering about the house and the tree like a sick goat! "Devil take her!" He huffs back indoors and so *off* with the shirt and *off* with the good new boots. Had he really cleaned and waxed his boots for this? Should he pound up another little sack of coffee? "I'll die first and be buried!" he vows.

Flinging out the door with never a glance at the mirror, he falls straight to work. Not ten minutes later he hit his thumb such a blow it made him dizzy. Blood welled under the dying nail. He staggered and sat down. "God-God," he whispered. "God!" Pain struck him all but blind.

It was his punishment. For when his sight cleared there she stood by the house — slender, bewildered and shy. Dog was whining and wagging. The horse was looking. Elias clambered to his feet and stood still. His fears dissolved. She was a young woman after all.

BOOK TWO

The Raid

Chapter 1

"Mashed thumb?"

The man blushed. "It's nothing." Yet, he held it out for her to see. She took the wide calloused hand in both of hers.

"Looks fresh," she said.

He was pale and trembling. "It's nothing — nothing," he said.

At the sight of him, suffering, something moved within her. Her shyness suddenly vanished. She led him indoors, saying, "When it's been soaked and wrapped you'll feel better." And she sat him down on the bench by the cottonwood plank table and opened her brown travel trunk. "Good thing I brought fixings," she said.

Hurt he was, but not so badly that he didn't notice the inner side of her trunk lid. Pasted there was a picture of two young ladies wearing hats and ruffled silk gowns and holding parasols.

Jane put a cup by him on the table and poured in a little turpentine. Then taking his hand and guiding his thumb, she stuck it in to soak. That resin smell was a comfort. It reminded Elias of childhood. Now was a chance to look at Jane Nail — green eyes and dark hair, a well-defined widow's peak on her forehead . . .

"Virgin Dip turpentine," she's saying. "Draws pain and swelling, Virgin Dip." Jane was nothing like the tinted ladies pasted inside her trunk. Jane's hair wasn't twisted in curls, she didn't have rosebud lips and fat little cheeks. Instead she was lean of face. Her thin nose had brown freckles on it. When she opened her mouth to speak or smile he saw white teeth, pretty and evenly set. She was small-framed, still she had a look of strength. When she moved about, her light step stirred him. She set him to imagining. Now and again her green eyes captured his — a brief, direct gaze. What did she see? He wondered. And what did she *hope* to see? Something more than a simple, plodding man who had pitched here of his own free accord? Had she hoped he might be otherwise than he was? Perhaps, he thought, perhaps. He wasn't a beauty — no, and he didn't make pretty speeches, nor play the fiddle nor dance jigs nor sing in a high voice. No. Elias was tuneless and he knew it. He was only himself. No doubt she could do better! While his thumb soaked she filled the kettle and set it to boil. She found the cured meat where he had hung it in the chimney. She didn't have to ask — she knew her way about.

Might another man think her plain? She did have a wide mouth. An unkind person might say she had a narrow face. To men who preferred robust women she would seem too slim and slight. Nothing about her was full. Yet, Elias, the more he saw, the more he liked her.

The ache in his thumb began easing; the pain slacked. He counted carefully. Then he said, "Two barrels extra?"

"Meal and flour," said she.

"But that wasn't in the bargain."

"Meal and flour? But that's a gift from Shokotee, my father."

Bringing her lint she sits by him again. Tenderly, carefully, she bandages his thumb.

"Meal and flour," Elias says.

The moment his thumb was wrapped and tied off with a neat little bandage, he began awkwardly opening the barrels one after another until he found first the meal and next the flour.

"Is it all right?" she said. He saw those eyes again, that direct gaze. He turned away, confused by her beauty, and he looked first in the flour barrel, next in the meal barrel. Then as though he had not just looked, he repeated the inspection. Meal and flour. One after another, he smelled the ingredients. He thumped the barrels with his good hand. Finally, sure that she was watching, he picked the meal barrel up! Despite his injured thumb he raised it above his head — a dumb show of strength.

"Why!" she said. "Careful! You'll hurt yourself!"

Slowly, he lowered the cask to the dirt floor. "Um," he said. He wore a studious look, as though lifting a barrel told him something profound.

"I never saw such!" she said. "Lifting a barrel!"

Elias shrugged. It was nothing. He sat down again and let his arm rest on the table, his wrapped thumb cocked at attention. The thumb was throbbing and had its own little painful heartbeat. Lifting the barrel had made him dizzy, but he didn't want to show it. Now in the place of a cup of turpentine she served him a cup in which she had poured whiskey and hot water mixed with a little sugar.

"To ease your pain," she said.

He did not argue but sipped the toddy slowly.

The woman meanwhile set up her johnnycake boards in front of the fire and kicked off her shoes. Squatting barefoot, at work now in earnest, she tucked up her dress, showing her knees and the calves of her legs. The fire brought a blush to her face. In the uneven light her arms had a golden look. Wisps of fine hair clung to her moist temples. The man was filled with wonderment. This creature in *his* household!

What grand things she cooked. She had brought dried pumpkin and peas; dried apples. The more he smelled and saw, the longer he sat not wanting to leave the hearthside even to feed his animals. Yet he did feed them finally. Then, careful of his hurt thumb, he washed and came inside and slipped on his new shirt and sat down to the supper she had prepared. She — strange, new; how lonely he had been! She.

Each time Elias looked up from his plate, he saw her eyes. She blushed.

Then their first meal was over. She scalded the dishes. Elias left the table and went to the open door. He gazed out. The moon had risen. It made a rippling light on the river. Dog appeared wagging his tail. The man motioned to the animal, inviting him inside. Warily and with fearful humility in his step, Dog approached the fireplace. He sat down beside the hearth.

"The dog sleeps inside?"

"No, outside."

"Handsome dog, what d'you call him?"

"Um, Dog. That's his name. It's Dog."

"Dog?" And she says, "Such a dog!"

Whereupon Dog responded, his tail thumping the floor. And she says,"D'you like Jane?"

The dog stands and stares up at her face.

"He likes you. We both like you," says Elias. Then, quickly: "Bright moon tonight."

She blushed and went back to her dishes and johnnycake boards. When all was clean and put neatly away she took the homemade broom from the corner and swept the dirt floor smooth.

Elias called Dog outside and fed him the scraps. Leaving Dog to his supper, Elias went back in the cabin.

The door is barred. The fire is banked. Inside, two people alone. It was a beginning. He wanted her; she was willing.

Once, during the night, he struck his thumb against the wall. Half waked by the shock, he groaned.

"What is it?" she says.

"Ah — thumb," says he. "You awake?"

"Yes, here, let me hold it." She takes that hand in both of her own.

"Um," says he. "That's better." And then: "When I was hunting one day I found a cave."

"You did? A cave?"

"Yes. I lit a candle and crawled in and found two skeletons — bear and man. The human skull was broken, a flint spearpoint was thrust in the ribs of the bear. What made me think of that, I wonder?"

He touched her long hair and caressed her shoulder. He felt the soft thrust of her hipbone. Her lips seemed to know his lips.

Just before daylight he woke again. She climbed out of bed and fetched her gown from the floor where it had fallen. She slipped it on over her head, stirred up the fire, and set the kettle to boil. Then she came back to where he lay and let her hair fall upon his face, and kissed him.

Chapter 2

Following the instructions of Shokotee, his father, Pettecasockee had taken the Negroes a short distance north along the river. Then, having started them home, he turned back south again and lingered along the edge of the woods until nightfall before slipping down to the willow thicket near Elias McCutcheon's clearing. Pettecasockee lay and watched the cabin and chewed sprigs of green willow and spat them out and waited.

He heard the cabin door close. He heard the bar drop into place. He saw the light snuff out. He lay so still that not even the dog suspected his presence. He waited thus until the moon started down. So it was done. She was mated. She had taken the man.

Feeling a loneliness he left the thicket and found his horse, passing his hand over the gentle creature. He took the saddle from its hiding place.

Once in the saddle, having reined about and headed north again, he lay forward upon Shugganah's neck and slept until gray dawn seeped its way down to the forest floor. The horse went carefully.

He passed the Negroes, camped dead asleep about the ashes of their fire; not one of them stirred. They lay with their axes beside them. It came to him that he could spring down into such a midst and kill them all before the last should wake up.

Before noon Pettecasockee was home. He went straight upstairs and found his father. Shokotee was sitting in bed, propped upon bolsters. He wore a red dressing gown with a tassled sash and thick wool socks and new moccasins upon his small feet. His bed table covered his knees. Shokotee was at work on his ledgers. His eyeglasses were perched far down on his bent, beak nose.

When Pettecasockee entered, the older man did not look up at once. He kept scratching and scrawling in the ledger. His small brown hand, quick as a wren, fetched at the inkpot and went back to its scrawling. When he did look up at last, he removed his glasses and tipped the pen down longways into the mid-fold of the ledger, as was his habit. "Well?" he said.

Pettecasockee shrugged. "The door was barred. The light went dark. There was no more sound." Loneliness rubbed the young man's breastbone.

Shokotee sat very still, musing. "Good," said he. "She has taken him."

"Yes." Pettecasockee left the old man and went to his own chambers. He stripped off his clothes and climbed upon his high bed. He felt the memory of the gentle motion of the horse and fell almost instantly asleep.

When he woke it was nightfall. The woman, Leola, was squeezing his arm. She had deep birdtrack wrinkles at the corners of her dark, hooded eyes. Supper was ready downstairs, she said.

She spoke in a low, sad voice: "She took him?"

"Yes." Pettecasockee sprang down from the bed and went to the washstand. She was ahead of him and poured water in the bowl. While he washed she laid out fresh clothes for him.

Said Leola, as though mourning, "When she needs me I will go to her."

"And that will be soon," said Pettecasockee.

He thought of a dark-eyed girl in Fort Hill and admired himself in the wavy candlelit reflection of the mirror above his washstand. He turned his head first one way and then another. Dinner chimes sounded below stairs in the dark hall.

Chapter

3

Rows of sprouting corn covered the stump field. Bean vines pushed forth fragile tendrils. The pale squash blooms pulled their little fruit into being behind them. The baby squash lay fattening in the secret leaf shade, silently growing and swelling.

Now a woman works in the field beside the man. Their hoes fall, chopping almost in unison. They seldom speak. Sometimes without a sound they pause to rest. Their eyes meet and they kneel to earth. She draws up her dress about her waist and falls back. They mate. And after a while the hoes begin to fall again . . .

On one such day as they lay embracing on the dark clod ground, bathed in sun warmth, the man drew suddenly back. His seed, just rising to spill, sprang against the soft and secret undercurve of the woman's thigh. The man's seed fell into the ground . . .

In the last light of that evening, before the fall of the summer dark, when they had put their hoes away into the tree shelter, they went down to the river. Leaving their clothes on the sandbar, they embraced in the shallows. Rings and ripples on the river surface caught the last long rays of sky light.

Clean and dripping, they climbed the bank and stood by the sycamore. A soft breeze, like breath upon the skin, blew them dry. The stars appeared like scattered seeds cast upon a prepared darkness. Looking upward at those wanton stars, the woman drew a breath. Speaking close to the man's ear she said, "I must go to my father's house for a visit."

"When?"

"Tomorrow," she whispered.

Was he so changed? It was only bed-sharing, after all, sharing bed and board with another; but she was no sooner gone than he found no pleasure in anything it seemed.

Clearing and building by himself here deep in the wilds he had never before felt such loneliness. Every chore became heavy. He knew he'd never go back again to that independent person he once was. *That* self had walked away. Left behind was a settler who barred his door at night and slept on a bed. And Jane was gone.

She had gone away on a pony brought down by her stepbrother, Pettecasockee. Elias had watched them riding away, riding out of sight. With Jane went comfort and contentment. He sleeps fitfully and wakes often and listens. He misses the warmth of her body. He recalls a certain way she had of stirring in her sleep and speaking his name. Each early morning he waits for her to climb over him out of bed and stir the fire and fill the kettle, then realizes she is gone . . .

Elias hardly tastes what he eats. Dog must miss Jane too, for he comes inside and goes sniffing here and there as though seeking her. Not finding her his ears droop, his tail sags. It was she that fed him tidbits and praised him. He had only to stop beside her and she would pull away the cockleburs and search his ears for ticks. After sniffing and searching, Dog finally gives up the search and flops by the hearth and there he lies, and mourns.

Elias can hardly pass the table without wondering what it is she may be doing now. Visiting, no doubt, consorting with her Indian kin, talking woman talk, sewing small clothes. What's taking so long? Can it be he loves her?

Her little wall mirror gives him a pang. And he opens her small trunk for a view of those ladies of fashion pasted beneath the lid. He smells sweet scents of her in the folds of her dress.

Three days of doting and he realizes a need for hard, driving work. And, seeking exhaustion, he undertakes the heaviest tasks. Wrenching himself up before daylight, he jerks on his clothes. Out he goes and drives himself so, between sun-up and sundown, that red spots appear on his cheeks, above his beard and beneath the hollows of his gray, restless eyes. Twigs and earth tangle his hair. Elias is like an animal that was tame once but is going wild again. Clouds of gnats follow him.

One night, unable to sleep, he got up, took his gun, and went quietly into his cornfield and stood there. All about he heard the movement and rustle of that great, growing handiwork of God. As though in his own body he felt the growth and swell of the maturing corn. He felt the waxing of new grain. The corn was coming into the milk and was just ripe for roasting.

A sound then — something more than mere wind out there rustling the midst of his crop. He knows what it is. The knowledge is like vinegar dripping in his stomach. Deer — they've come raiding. He's killed so many of their tribe, slaughtered so many wholesale, he has, that now they're taking revenge.

For an hour and more he stalks up and down the dark rows. The rough leaves of corn graze his face and arms; the deer elude him. They are no sooner shooed away, it seems, than they come right back. The dog goes dashing and barking. It's no use. The deer elude him too. They've had a taste of corn and won't quit now until the crop is consumed.

Corn, thinks the man. Corn: life and survival.

How others may save their crops he hasn't the first idea. But with a plan in mind he fetches his ax, his wood saw, his hammer, his digging spade and a full two dozen of long spike nails.

At the edge of the cornfield midway along where the woods bulge into the cleared ground, he puts down his tools. Back he trudges and fetches the ladder he used to climb up on the cabin roof. If deer can work by night so can he! Easing the heavy ladder to earth he inspects the trees. He finds four that suit. Big around as his thigh they stand in a proximate square by the very edge of the field. Up comes the ladder against the first one. Up the ladder goes Elias bearing ax and saw. He tops that tree and comes down, moves the ladder, goes up again and tops the next one. Steadily he works on until he has four topped trees standing like posts. Now he's busy cutting saplings for joists and rafters. Doggedly, deliberately, he toils. Climbing his ladder with a joist pole he hammers a bit. He comes down and clambers up again carrying two more poles — more hammering — *whock! whock! whock!* He's driving nails with no more light to see by than a high quarter moon offers — but nevermind! If deer can see to raid he can see to drive nails! *Whock! Whock!* . . .

Joists first, rafters next, his platform takes shape, a raised floor six feet square, ten feet above the ground. Taking his fodder knife to the canebrake he returns with cargo after cargo of cane. This he totes up and spreads on his platform. Finally comes the hardest task. With a rope tied to a bucket, he goes up and down the ladder, up and down . . . filling the bucket with dirt, climbing the ladder, hauling up the dirt, dumping it on the platform . . . down and up again, a dozen, a hundred buckets full . . .

Stubborn. Single-minded. Sweat stings his eyes. Yet he seems tireless. Presently, he's got a thick layer of dirt packed on that sturdy platform. The night wears on . . .

Down he comes, finds his ax, and steps a little distance into the woods. Lighthearted now, he selects a tree. After so much dirt hauling, the ax is sweet rest. Down comes the tree. Soon he's staggering up the ladder, freighting up load after load of firewood and dry kindling and fire logs! He lays a fire, no less, on the dirt floor of his platform.

When it's time to light the fire, he stows his tools away and fetches his rifle. Standing beneath the platform, then, he watches. The growing fire casts longer and longer wings of light into the reaches of the cornfield. Here a bright gleam — over there two more reflections — eyes of raiding deer. Elias raises the rifle to his shoulder. He sights carefully. The slaughter begins.

In nights that follow Elias lies beneath the platform, Dog at his side, his rifle nearby. Half-dozing, the man guards the corn crop. He kills the raiders that would destroy his corn.

One daybreak when the fire on the platform had died away to ashes, Elias woke. The birds had begun to stir. First light had appeared. He stood, stretched, pissed, and walked to the river. Kneeling on the sandbar he washed his face and drank a long drink. Leaning over the calm, dark surface of the water he saw a reflection of his wild and tangled self. He smiled and thought: Well, but I'm saving my corn after all!

And presently he went to work on his fence. He was still at it, working away, when strangers appeared. It was after high noon when they came. Neighbors they were, two men and a woman, brothers and a sister, coming afoot, seeking a lost cow, they said. "Seen a horned cow?" says the one brother. He was skinny and had hollow cheeks and dark hair. The other man was like him, but taller. Both were pale.

The woman spoke then. She had long, slender arms and her hair was heavy and dark, red as copper, and she had tied it back with a white ribbon. Her wide lip trembled when she spoke, saying, "A horned cow about so high? And has a spot on her side?" She appeared to be on the polite side of thirty.

"No," says Elias. A pause, and then: "Didn't I pass your clearing — near that gravel strand by the bend in the river? Towards the military road?" He sees in his mind that hasty pitch, round-log cabin, a mud chimney. He had looked over that spot during his search and had found it to be cold ground and not well drained.

"Poor cow, my horned cow," says the woman in a low, sweet voice. Elias looks at her more closely. She's certainly well favored. Her dress is unbleached cotton, drawn at the waist by a little brass buckled belt of tanned leather.

"Fine corn crop," says the second brother, the tall one. He's Werdna, he says, Werdna Poe, and his brother is Andrew and their sister is Mrs. Ellen Ashe — Ellen.

Elias tells his own name and offers his own opinion as to cows. "A horned cow will rest all day in a canebrake, chewing her cud beyond reach of the sun, hiding quiet as grass. Might be as I could help find her. Surely she left tracks."

"Maybe," says Werdna Poe.

Elias brings out his horse and saddles him. "Your corn ripe?"

"No," says Werdna. "We planted late. And the deer, besides . . ." He trailed his words away to nothing, and seemed thinking of those deer, those raiding creatures.

Elias fetched a couple of baskets and filled them with roasting ears. He slung these over the saddle, one on each side, tied in the middle with rawhide thongs. For good measure he fetched a leg of venison from the cabin and tied it to the saddle.

"Now there's too *much*!" says Ellen, looking pleased.

"It's nothing. We've plenty hereabouts," says Elias.

"Live alone?" says Andrew.

"Me — I had woman-help a while back, but she's gone home now."

"Indian, was she?" Andrew asks. "Indian gal?"

"No — white."

"Some I know of as take on a *squaw* to help," says Werdna. He grins, showing small white teeth. His grin says he knows what those squaws are good for, all right!

"No, my woman-help was white," says Elias.

"Werdna wants himself a squaw," says Andrew. "He! He! He!"

"Wouldn't mind, I wouldn't," says Werdna. "Oh, no I wouldn't!"

"Hush!" says Ellen, blushing. "Such talk . . ."

The other three stood by the horse while Elias, excusing himself, ran to the cabin and changed his shirt. He dashed a bit of water on his face and ran a comb through his beard and his hair. Then out again he went. They set out walking, all four, with Dog following. Then Elias said Ellen should ride, and without waiting for what she would say, he lifted her straight up like she weighed a mere nothing, and so set her on the horse between the baskets. She blushed again . . . And it was the men walking now and Ellen riding and Dog, he came following as before.

"Your horned cow, had she a bell?" Elias asks after a while.

"Yes," says Ellen. "She wears a bell."

"Just at this season," says Elias, "with the mast gone, bears will call to a bell. Best not to bell anything at this season."

"I never thought!" cries Ellen. "Poor cow!"

"But it ain't a large bell exactly," says Werdna. "Tis only a small bell like."

"Not one of your big bells," says Andrew.

"Poor cow!" says Ellen again.

"At this season," says Elias, "I can take a bell and sit on a stump and ring it and call up bears more than I can skin and render."

Poor folk, they're new to the woods. Ellen's near to crying.

"Twas only a small bell," says Werdna, but his voice has gone weak.

The brothers are looking to Elias.

"Might be as we can find that cow and find her safe," says Elias, and he looks up at Ellen. He sees that she has taken hope. The sight of her stirs him . . .

The rest of the way down that trail through the woods Elias feels her presence. When finally they arrive at the Poes' hasty cabin what should be there waiting but Cow, a lovely creature with a spot on her side just as Ellen said. And what should be with her but a wobbly calf.

"She's found a calf!" cries Ellen. Elias lifts her down and Ellen goes running. The men follow and stand admiring that saucy little calf. A bull he is and will be an ox one day, says Ellen, a landbreaker.

"B'lieve I'd still remove the cowbell," says Elias. He's filled with admiration, for a calf is no mean gift here, so deep in the wilds.

Unstrapping the bell from the cow's neck, Ellen scolds Cow for wandering. In the same breath she praises her for finding such a fine calf. The calf, as though responding, wobbles up against his mother and begins to suck. He butts Cow's udder with his little hornless head. His tail switches back and forth . . .

Werdna and Andrew are just on their way hunting. They've not time, now that Cow's been found, to stand about admiring her, no. They ask Elias if he'd like to hunt with them.

"Thanks, not today," says Elias. The brothers fetch their guns from the cabin and untie a pair of droop-eared hounds. Tails up, the hounds charge Dog. Tail up, Dog waits for them. Dog makes five of them he's so big. He ends by letting them sniff him fore and aft. Then the brothers whistle, and the hunting hounds trot ahead of the men into the woods, stopping to sprinkle a tree and a post here and there as they go. Dog lowers his tail and sits down. Elias unties the baskets and empties the corn by the cabin door in a green plenteous heap. Slinging the baskets back on the horse he unties the leg of venison and takes it in the cabin and leaves it on the table by the hearth.

Ellen comes after him, a different woman altogether now her cow is found and safe. There is a radiance about her he has not seen before.

"Andrew and Werdna, they hunt a lot?"

"Oh, yes. And when there's so much else to do. When land needs clearing and crops need tending — they hunt! Too much, I think." She fetches two stem glasses from her cupboard meanwhile. "Blackberry wine?" she says, pouring it from a stone bottle. Her fingernails are white and well kept. She takes her own glass and hands him his. "This I made myself . . ."

He nods. "Thanks," he says.

They sit a while drinking wine. He hears her story. It's a familiar tale of land back in the east, worn out and washed away to gullies, of the furniture they tried to bring west, abandoned beside the road, and more. Of servants that had to be sold, a horse that went lame and well — here they were at last, in reduced circumstances but upon rich new ground. And finally she mentions a husband, Ashe, that abandoned her two years ago it is now, just when the family fortunes began to fail. Finally she draws a breath and seems to brighten. "I no longer consider myself a married woman," she says. Raising her glass she takes a tiny sip of wine and swallows. She gives Elias a sidelong glance. "More wine?"

"Thanks, I don't mind," he says. "Just a touch, if you please." Wine and woman mingle-like in his senses. They make a lingering warmness in his legs and arms. Sunlight slanting through the window strikes the dark opposite wall. Dust motes drift through the golden rays. In shadowy corners lie remnants of the emigrant journey — poleax and broadax, froe, mallet and maul, a foot adz, a battered travel trunk . . .

It's time to leave. Elias stands to say his goodbye.

"Shan't we look at the calf again? Cow needs a bundle of fodder," says Ellen.

She hands him the knife and he marches out to the canebrake and cuts one great armful and then another. He brings both bundles and drops them inside Cow's split-rail pen. He watches as Cow, wet-nosed, tosses her horned head to separate the tender stalks. Nearby, her calf is sleeping. He carries the knife back to the cabin. When he returns Ellen is watching Cow and admiring her calf.

Elias unloops Rattler's reins from the rail. "I'll be going," he says.

"But it's such a nice day maybe I'll walk a bit with you on your way," says Ellen. "May I?"

"Yes," says Elias, speaking slowly. "Yes . . ."

The horse and dog follow, the man leads the way with the woman by him. She's talking, but Elias hardly hears what she says. The baskets creak against the saddle. The sunlight filters through the leaves and casts golden freckles upon the shade. The man notices wildflowers for the first time, though they must surely have been here all along upon the floor of every meadow, at the foot of every stump. There's a faint fragrance of hearthsmoke on the air, a scent that seems caught somehow and contained in the woman's clothes — a sweetness that follows.

"See how deep the dust lies on the road," she says after a while. "It's warm . . ."

"Should we rest a bit?" He speaks timidly.

They leave the road and soon find a place with grass for the horse. Rattler goes browsing. He scatters butterflies and grasshoppers. Elias and Ellen sit down. She pulls up her dress a little way to see how the blackberry vines scratched her legs, little scratches . . . Her eyes are half closed. "Come," she says gently. "Come, it's all right."

Stretched on the ground they embrace, garments mingled beneath. He's fearful somehow. She offers reassurances. "It's all right."

"I hope — "

"No," she says, speaking softly. "Don't fear for me."

Nevertheless he's fearful, somehow. Is it awe or reverence, or fear of creation itself? Or can it be that a power seizes him and seems as though it wants to use him up entirely?

Her secret hair is dark and red as dry cornsilks too. And presently she cries out, saying "Ah!" as though somehow surprised, and overtaken somehow with so much rippling. She makes a sound then, a gorging sound. It dies and becomes breathing again.

Not until they're dressed and back to the road and he's walking her slowly homeward does she speak. She says,

"Your woman-help, Indian is she?"

"No, she's white. Reared in an Indian household."

"Where is she? Gone?"

"Gone home to visit."

"Will you come again?"

He nods his promise. Riding home he's not so lonely anymore as he was . . .

Chapter 4

And Jane came home . . .

She was feeling heavy and seasick every morning. She wanted a bite of hoecake and a sup of water when she first got up. There was a strange and full uneasiness behind her eyes. And it gagged sometimes at the back of her throat. She was taking on ballast, pushing out in front. Her calico gown was hiking up. Her back hurt, but she woke every morning before daylight. She pushed her legs from beneath the covers, her feet found the floor, and she gathered herself up for another day and was happy be it rain or shine. Jane was content whether the wind blew or was still; she felt constant, like the river beyond her dooryard. She was flowing-like and was headed somewhere. The stir and mystery of life and growth was in her body.

Jane and Elias, wife and husband by the Common Law.

"Should we find a preacher or go stand before the judge, I wonder?" says Elias.

"Seventy miles, Elias? Seventy miles to Dover?"

"I was only wondering," he says. It was a Sunday and he had washed and put on his red shirt. Here in the west work usually went forward on Sundays just as on other days;

churches hadn't come as yet, nor laws nor land companies nor preachers.

Folk found land, blazed boundaries, and built sheds and barns and cabins and fences. They yearned for horned cattle to graze the grassy meadows. They wanted hogs to feed and fatten on the acorn mast. When a man and a woman found one another and it suited them, they set up as partners.

"Nevermind formalities," says Jane.

And she was right, as usual. Work close to hand must occupy wise folk; loud and silent work. He took off his new shirt, put on his old one and went straightway to his tasks. He was his old self again, busy by day, busy after nightfall even, always with some task large or small to hand.

He pondered wondrous thoughts . . . where Indians came from; the continents being separated by vast seas; the blackness of Negroes.

No mystery where Negroes came from, of course. In ships, to be sure! An explanation of their color which Elias favored was that in making all peoples additional to Father Adam and Mother Eve, God told each manikin creation in clay what time to get in or out of the sunshine. As it happened there was one group that could not tell time. They therefore didn't move to the shade when they should have. No, they remained in the sun instead. By the time God got round to missing them (for God himself counted all His creatures, laying His finger upon the head of each one as He went), lo! — they were burnt black as lampsoot, their hair was shriveled to kinks. It seemed hard punishment to leave them that way for the rest of eternity, noses melted all over their faces, lips swollen six times human size, feet like huge pancakes. God could be as implacable as He was mysterious. Plainly He favored the white race above others on earth, God did, for — well, hadn't His white children come in out of the sun right on time? But the Indians in their laziness came in a bit later and thus were coppery red; the Chinese, coming in just ahead of the Indians, were bilious saffron. And Negroes, well, poor Negroes — they'd be there yet, still baking, if God hadn't finally mustered them in ranks and marched them into the shade.

Elias pondering. He discussed these thoughts with Jane. But though she was born white, she had been reared by Indians. Jane therefore had Indian reasons and explanations. It was Indian things Jane knew most vividly by heart.

In the place of God, for example, dividing the sea from the land, it was Jane's notion that a big bird performed this miracle of labor by flapping his wings above the mass of the earth which was at that time, in the Beginning, mud. And as he flapped his wings, land was drawn up into hills and mountains and dry plains. Spaces between became seas, she said. And rivers, of course. Rivers, too.

"Well," says Elias, "be sure to tell *our* child how God did all this in six days and not some great bird. It would be a pity to let a child grow up without the truth about matters." Thinking of children . . .

"Why not tell both versions and let him decide for himself?" says Jane, busy sewing. She sews while Elias sits splitting shingles.

"Well." Elias tries to think exactly why the child shouldn't be told God's truth and outlandish Indian things. "Only be sure to tell him that the accounts of God making the heavens and the earth and all things that crawl and creep and growl and moo and bark and cluck and crow — that God made these just as it's put in the Book. And herded them all on the Ark for Noah. Tell that."

"What about how the rabbit lost his tail?" says Jane.

"Well," says Elias, "that too. Only mind to tell him it's Indian nonsense and only fable."

"Why?" says Jane. "And what if it might be true? For his tail got lost some way, didn't it?"

Elias wouldn't budge. He was firm, the master. *His* child

must be told the difference between Scriptural truth and red heathen nonsense. Lately Elias had a way of ruling upon things, making things final, and accepting no arguments.

Jane liked his way of ruling upon things. Jane was content . . .

On a day when she was alone in the cabin with no one for company, a neighbor woman came calling.

She came afoot and brought two molds of butter and a little tin pail of milk. She was Ellen Ashe, and had fine, maddening ways about her. She spoke proudly of her cow and her cow's calf, and she asked if Elias were home?

"Elias? He's over in the fields and woods. Did you notice the corn crop?"

"Seeing *you* don't have a cow, I thought sweetmilk and butter might be welcome," says Ellen, ignoring Jane's question.

"You've a cow, you and your husband?"

"I'm not married. My two brothers and I have a clearing to the south. No — my husband abandoned me. Elias helped find the cow when she was lost. So I've brought milk and butter . . ."

"Thanks kindly," says Jane. "For milk and butter." She heard something. "Excuse me," she said, and went to the door and opened it.

She saw Elias leading the horse with a bear carcass loaded on. Elias leading, Rattler and Dog coming along behind. The mastiff's red tongue rolled first from one side of his mouth and then the other.

Jane ran out. The man folded his arms about her. She smelled sun and sweat, ox and dog, horse and rain. She leaned her head against his great, hard chest. "There's a neighbor here. She says you found her cow."

"Mrs. Ashe."

"Yes."

He followed Jane into the cabin. He seemed to fill it up. It was as though Elias brought in the woods and the wilds with him. His hunting clothes were bloody, his shirt was stained with his sweat. He stood his rifle in the corner, noticed the milk, smelled the butter, and thanked Mrs. Ashe politely. Then he said: "I'd best get skinning and quartering," and he went outdoors again.

Was it Jane's imagination, or did Ellen Ashe seem envious?

"Is he always so busy?" says Ellen.

"Always, yes. Plowing and building, clearing and burning."

"That's a fine fat bear."

"Elias never comes home empty-handed," says Jane, speaking carelessly. What does she care if Ellen has a cow? Jane has Elias — and more, she has his child stirring inside herself.

And finally Ellen went on her way home again, not empty-handed, for Jane gave her a bucket of wild honey, saying, over Ellen's protests:

"We've plenty! Elias carts it home by the tubful."

And that was true. He rendered the wax and strained the honey and this was part of his cargo when he drove the wagon into Fort Hill — hides and fresh meat, honey and wax, shingles and goose-down. He was busy laying money aside, bit by bit, coin by coin.

After Jane's return he had finally gotten around to making nets and fish baskets and live-boxes. He took nature's harvest from the river now. He was tireless, so he seemed, and something Godlike, what with so much energy and strength. She knew he would protect her all her life long, her Elias would.

And now another thing happened at Oakleigh, a momentous thing. Coming down from the north Shokotee appeared one day and brought with him a Negro slave, a gift, a living, human present, the property of Elias and Jane — their first servant. His name was Jake, and because he was the first servant at Oakleigh he was not a slave like any other.

Jake moved into the sycamore tree and made his bed where Elias had wintered. He was a big quiet fellow, black and strong and intelligent. He and Elias got along well from the first. They seemed more like partners than master and man.

Of an evening, after work, they made plans. They hammered with their minds over details, mapping the future of Oakleigh. Small things — a conch shell was needed to call them from the field and later it would be blown to wake the plantation every morning . . . *the plantation*, a bold dream. Great things. Says Jake, over and again,

"We have to have more hands. Just one nigger and another white man? We can't do it all alone by ourselves?"

"Yes," Elias agrees. "Yes."

But these two, black and white, they did the work of a dozen, so it seemed to Jane. The pace quickened; events began to march. She pressed her hand below her bosom when she thought about these happenings, when she felt the force and flow of these events. The weeks suddenly seemed to fly . . .

Chapter 5

When Jane was adopted into Shokotee's household at Redleaves Leola attached herself to the child. Jane was as flesh of Shokotee's flesh and since he had no natural daughter of his own it was through Jane that Leola had made secure her own place in Shokotee's house.

Leola was Shokotee's second cousin by marriage, his poor relation with skin like yellow smoke and dark eyes hooded like a hawk's. As a young woman she had followed a succession of white traders, serving them and bearing their children. They were rough fellows who went afoot through the Reelfoot Districts with packs on their backs. And one after another those "husbands" abandoned Leola, and it seemed each time that the next she fell in with was more hardhearted than the last. Thus her best years were spent. More than once she bore a child only to have its father twist its little head clean around and bury it on the spot.

Of Leola's sons, two had grown to manhood, but she didn't know where they were. Now, in middle life, Jane was her chief concern.

When Jane's child was due, Leola applied to Shokotee. He gave her a blue blanket and told her to pack her things and follow the river south. Following his directions she found the clearing and the cabin. Elias was gone into Fort Hill on the day she arrived. Lucky. It gave her time alone with Jane before the Master came.

A cot Elias and Jake had built for Leola had to be dragged out of the sycamore-tree shed. Leola insisted on bearing the whole burden herself. "Nevermind bringing your servant from the field just to help Leola," she says. "Working is he?"

"Working on the fence," says Jane.

"Like as not asleep under a tree with the Master gone. Want me to go have a look? Leola'll let him know he's being watched! Too busy to help with the heavy moving, is he?"

"Nevermind about him," says Jane.

"Nevermind about me," says Leola, "No, I can carry it myself," she says, picking up the cot and puffing. "Don't you touch it," she says. "Far away down the field at work on the fencing is he? Like as not he's snoring too, and working with his eyes shut."

Once she had gotten the cot inside the cabin she made a fuss, shoving the cot frame against the wall, moving and shoving it more than was called for, and then: "Oh!" And slyly, "Hadn't seen your floor was dirt!"

"Dirt," says Jane. "And good enough."

"Did I mean anything? Dirt's good enough. But if I had known it was dirt I'd have gone easier with the cot. Now look how I've grooved and dug your floor. I wouldn't do all that grooving on purpose just to call attention to a poor dirt floor, now would I? I'm used to wood floors, I am. And when does the Master come home? Goes away often to settlement does he, and stays away gone?"

"He goes away rarely," says Jane, "and always returns about nightfall. He took a load of shingles and beeswax. He's bringing a box for a cradle and some other things."

"Men," says Leola.

"What?"

"Nothing. Nothing at all," says Leola, a sagging figure with dark Indian features and wary, inquisitive eyes.

Leola changes her tack. "What a clean, fine house," she begins. "What a great strong fence they're building outside. How nicely the river flows here, and that clean little creek nearby with such white sand and all. Ain't I glad to come help? And why not? No man, no home of my own. Does your man — the Master — did he know poor old Leola was coming?"

"It seemed a sort of private thing. That you might come, that's all I said. He provided the cot . . ."

"Then he'll have a surprise. Maybe he'll not like me and throw me out," says Leola. "Like as not take a stick while he's at it and break my poor old ribs, unless men have changed their ways. And here I've walked all this distance — could have been eaten by bears! Could have been robbed and murdered and raped, maybe, sleeping on hard ground. All of that for naught but a beating." Pause. "Seems a month since I've tasted coffee. Seemed I'd starve for coffee. Can't we spare some coffee, or do you serve it in this house? I know this isn't as plentiful a house as my Cousin Shokotee's where there's coffee and sugar and salt and all good things to spare, and wood floors and so on."

So Leola must have coffee and be surprised how in Jane's house coffee beans are put in a leather bag and hammered on a stump with the flat of an ax instead of being ground in a proper coffee mill. "Not as I'd be one to expect you to have everything, mind," she says. "If my Cousin Shokotee had known he could have sent down one of the old ones from his kitchen." Meanwhile she's into the leftovers, eating enough for three. Having eaten her fill and drunk all the coffee she says she can't work lately without a thimble of whiskey for her rheumatism. Having tossed down half a cupful of Elias's whiskey she begs a pinch of tobacco for her pipe. When Jane shows her the tobacco Leola grabs a handful.

Leola looks at Jane as if to say: "Don't think you're going to get off free." Leola smiles a worn, crafty smile, showing black teeth. The wrinkles in her cheeks reach down like spiderlegs. She takes the firetongs, fetches a coal, and lights her pipe.

"Jane?" Making contented sucking noises, smoking her cob pipe: "Jane? Wouldn't have any worn-out clothes to spare Leola? Would you?"

Jane makes a discovery. Leola, she's woodsmoke and smells boiled-like. Indian. Here's something Jane never noticed before, though Elias has said over and again how Indians smell of sour skin and breath, queer and rancid. No mistaking an Indian!

Has Jane been too long away from her Indian family? Going home again to visit Shokotee she hasn't smelled any but comforting smells — of home, scoured floors, waxed halls, swept porches, sturdy odors of tar and hemp from the boat landing. But here in the woods, in her own house, Jane smells Leola's Indian strangeness.

The same goes for the mastiff. Dog, he must smell something too for something's made him uneasy. He goes grumbling and growling to his tree. He lies sulking in the shed. When the women have finished in the cabin and come out to the shed, the mastiff growls again, frowning and raising his tail and looking sullen. He marches away to the canebrake.

"That dog!" says Leola. "What right has he to put his nose in the air? Because I'm Indian? You'd think I'm a slave for life the way he acts. Where'd you get such an animal?" She doesn't wait for Jane to reply. "I've always yearned for a little fyce to follow me and rest by my feet while I snapped beans. To stay by me at night, a sweet little critter to keep an old body company . . . well, and let's clean out the shed. The servant sleeps here?"

"Dog sleeps in the hollow with Jake," says Jane.

"I'd not have a dog sleep with me!" says Leola. She shakes out the bearskins that serve for Jake's floor. She moves all his things about, and in so doing finds a book.

"Ho!" she cries. "A slave with a book!"

"Book?" says Jane. She can see what it is as well as Leola.

"A book," says Leola in a grim voice.

"Book sure enough," Jane admits. It was a small volume, well worn. Jane takes the book, but being as ignorant about reading as Leola, she can't make anything out of it.

"Ain't your husband's book, stolen from him?"

"Not as I know," says Jane. "I think not."

"Don't like it," says Leola. "A reading slave is a writing slave." She shakes her head.

Still shaking her head, Leola puts it back. "Here's trouble!" she seems to say. And back the book goes, into Jake's tote bag.

The women return to the cabin. They think over things to decide what there is to do and to see what will be needed. They search and sift through Jane's medicine chest and make it neat.

Next they search Jane's garments one by one, looking for knots — a knotted sash, a knotted belt, a knotted drawstring. Leola finds a mended moccasin thong, broken ends tied together. Her nimble fingers hasten to untie it.

"And does he sit with his legs crossed?" says Leola.

"Who?" says Jane.

"Why him — who else — your man, the Master, of course."

"Elias? I suppose. Sometimes."

"Ho! Sometimes! Sometimes can be once too many! Caution him about crossing his feet or sitting cross-legged."

They go through Elias McCutcheon's things. His shirts, his britches, his leggings, his linens, his hats, his heavy coat. Everything he wears or uses is searched. All knots are untied. All plaits are unraveled.

"I doubt he may be angry," says Jane.

"And why?"

"I doubt he believes such Indian stuff, about knots and all. And as for crossing his legs! He may make a fuss!"

"Never say *why*. Only say you've a mind to have manners and good breeding about your house. Tell him fine folk don't cross their feet and prop one leg over another like imbeciles. Tell him that."

"I'll seem silly."

"Better silly and safe!" says Leola.

"Never saw such a like of plaits and knots," says Jane.

"Nor I," says Leola. "Maybe he's a sailor. Has he belts besides these two?"

"Only one he's wearing."

"Um," says Leola, looking wise.

And Jane finds something, a packet tied with a faded ribbon. Letters, nothing less. And tied with them she finds a stem with withered blossoms — the remains of a rose and has some perfume still . . .

Leola notices. "A *fine* gentleman," she says. "With letters and all. He can read?"

"Yes," says Jane.

"And has ladies in his past. Letters and so on."

His past. Till now it has never seemed to Jane there was any past. Till now Elias always seemed to her as though created here, just as she found him, a worker toiling in the woods, a builder, building where nothing stood before; a big, kindly man rising each day to eat and to work dawn till dusk, and afterwards to sleep such deep exhausted sleeps that sometimes, waking in the night, she fears he may be dead — but no, he lies breathing. She holds him until she can go back to sleep and then, while it's still night it seems, he's up and stirring and so careful lately not to wake her, seeing as she's likely to have the baby before long now. She misses their lovemaking . . .

"Some I know about marry and move, marry and move," Leola is saying. "They leave clearings and cabins and women with fatherless brats at knee and breast. Men all have that wild itch. Between their legs they want a woman. When they've had her the itch moves into their feet and they walk away one night. Marry and move; marry and move. They're all the same, men are."

Jane feels a burning in her face. Her ears have a buzzing in them. "Not Elias," she says. "He's a settled man, you'll see." But her heart begins beating in her throat; her hands grow cold; she's still holding those terrible letters.

"Of course he's a settled man. Couldn't I see as much the minute I saw the door? Not a deerskin flap, but a wooden door? And such roof beams? But —"

"But what, Leola?"

"Well. It's only that wattle chimney. Nevermind a dirt floor. Dirt's good enough, but a mud chimney — mud and sticks!"

"Oh, Elias, he's building a stone chimney soon," says Jane. But she isn't a good liar. In her confusion she's almost retied the ribbon about those letters.

"Here!" says Leola, taking the ribbon and the letters herself. Jane is left holding the withered rose — small, dried, frail and fragrant — a little corpse — Elias McCutcheon's past.

"Only *wrap* the ribbon!" says Leola. She wraps it herself. "After all our work you'd *tie* a ribbon? Strangle your baby?" Then, perhaps seeing she's gone a bit far, Leola takes pity, that bitter, sagging woman. "There now, what do letters mean? Tracks in the snow and the snow melts. Does he love you, Jane?" She speaks gently.

"He's shy," says Jane.

"He's good," says Leola. "He's a good provider and keeps everything neat. Nothing starves here, does it?"

"I think he loves me," says Jane.

"Loves you! What's that sticking out and hiking your dress in front if he doesn't love you? Fallen on good luck, you have." Having quickly wrapped the ribbon back about the letters, Leola mercifully stows them away, out of sight. "Wasn't like he was hiding them," says Leola. "Merely old keepsakes like. Men all have a past, men do."

"Nor any need he has to hide them," says Jane. "Seeing I can't read!"

Surprise — Jane falls to crying! Leola puts her skinny arms about the girl and helps her to the settle and sits her there and then stirs about to make a cup of tea. Jane's only a child and like any child she needs mothering and comfortable gossip and someone she can talk to and someone to help her tend things.

"Crying? Ain't Leola here? You know the thing will go right. Haven't I come? Eh? Didn't your father, Shokotee, send me? There now, I've come! Here, mind the cup. It's hot. Tin cups — ah, but china follows tin. He's strong and stout, is he?"

"Strong? You should just see him lift and carry. Elias, he's a fright for strength."

"And his body — is he clean?"

"Yes, he's always soaping and washing himself. But hairy!"

"Ho!"

"Covered with hair, Leola!"

"He'll be rich one day," says Leola. "Hair gathers gold like a magnet draws iron. What about his teeth."

"Sound teeth."

"Does he droop or limp or have a sag in the shoulders?"

"Elias? He's sound as a horse."

"And look at yourself — crying? Give me such a man and I'd not cry. Tear my tongue out if I'm lying. Ah — but what will he say to find me in his house?"

"Why, welcome," says Jane, wiping her eyes.

Leola rattles — seeds in a dry gourd, on and on, mindless gossip, harmless, comforting talk. "The servant women at Redleaves have brought seven fine, fat babies. Slipped them out easy as swallowing eggs. Thriving and thriving, the whole plantation, nor is there a day can pass but someone will sigh and mention Jane Nail and wonder why you're so long between visits."

Jane smiles. "I'll go that way again before too long, Leola."

"The Sister hardly knows herself. Your saw her yourself, how she takes laudanum night and noon. The Brother's gone away to Fort Hill and stays drunk as a mop they say."

"My next visit I'll go with Elias beside me and the baby in my arms," says Jane. "He'll be a son, and we'll all go dressed in new clothes —"

"Have you seen my blue blanket?" says Leola. "See here, brand-new. From Shokotee, my cousin?"

Jane gives the new blanket a dutiful look, but she's thinking of that next visit home. "And P'-nache," Leola is saying, rattling on and on, "P'-nache makes a big drunk. He cut a face at the fort, he did, P'-nache. My cousin, Shokotee, your father, had to pay. He pays and says nothing. And Pettecasockee, he looks at the Frenchman's daughter."

"Chatillion's daughter? Which one?" says Jane, for here was something new.

"P'-nache and the Brother both say it. Chatillion's daughter, but which one Pettecasockee looks at I don't know."

Jane's heart takes a skip. She thinks of Henri Chatillion,

the mysterious Frenchman. She thinks how proud and proper he is, how the trading post is his, and all, and how it's claimed he's the first white man on Fort Hill, Chatillion. She hates him a little. And his Indian wife, a Creek, it's said, from a rich family of traders and has white blood in her. Chatillion's daughter, she'd have ever so many bonnets and slippers and dresses with silk flounces. She thinks of Petteca-sockee, so nimble and brave, with his clever tongue and his gently musical voice.

Leola says, "It's wars that took the men away from me and left me poor and lonely. War takes men away never to return them. Tap a drumhead, blow a bugle — the men, they disappear."

"Elias, he's peaceful, solid and sober," says Jane and again she smells Leola's wild Indian strangeness. She somehow can't quite get used to it.

"Wars took my men away from me," says Leola. "But Shokotee gave me that blue blanket. Life is never so bad as it may seem. Some I know may feel jealous now Pettecasockee's courting the Frenchman's daughter. Some may be jealous, but I think they shouldn't be, when they themselves have gone and married."

Chapter 6

Sundown. Elias comes home. He's brought the box Jane wanted and the flannel and other things. Carding combs and a spinning wheel and a spade for heavy digging. And something else — a Bible.

And although somewhat surprised to find his household bigger, he nevertheless speaks politely to Leola and quietly sits down to his supper. The women set up the spinning wheel. They lay out the flannel. They measure so much for cloth for a little cap and so much for a little blanket and so much for a little gown. Leola's hinting that should there be a scrap left she might like to have it. "Poor folk value the scraps," she says. "It's always been so. The poor must be content with the leavings of the rich."

Elias takes his candle lantern after supper and goes outside. The women hear him talking to Jake. They see the little dot of flame as it wanders far down the field where Jake has been fencing. The light comes briskly back and again the men, master and servant, can be heard talking.

The women see to the box. Boring a little hole and hitching a rawhide string at each corner, they hang the box from the rafter poles and make a cradle. Elias and Jake come have a look.

"Well," sniffs Jake, "we gonna need a proper cradle directly, won't we, with rockers on it?"

"This is good enough," says Jane.

Meanwhile Leola is snuggling herself into bed on the cot by the wall, showing off her new blanket. She stretches out and begins to snore. Jake leaves. The door is closed and barred.

Climbing into bed beside Jane and looking up, Elias sees the cradle. By firelight and moonlight it gives him a queer feeling. It hangs in the air like a boat without cargo, empty-like and demanding — strange. And though he tells himself it's nothing but a stout box just brought home by himself; yet suspended and hanging thus it gives him half a fright. And the old woman on the cot is still snoring. Elias sees her in his mind's eye, walking about with her long plaits hanging at the sides of her head, muttering and sucking her pipe. Jane turns. Her stomach rests against him. What's inside there kicks now and then, swimming-like and kicking, then moving against him, making soft contours. The banked fire pops, winks and pops. As banked fires will, it licks its lips with a now-and-then tongue of flame. Jane's fingers push into the hair in the middle of his chest.

"We have stone on the place, do we?" she whispers.

"Stone? Yes," Elias replies. "Sandstone by the bluff."

"Then we can have a chimney? Can't we? A stone chimney?" Her fingers move, twining the hair in the hollow, between his chest muscles. The fingers stop, waiting.

"Yes," Elias says. The fingers move again. And he says: "I'd thought of it. And a large dressed stone for the doorstep outside. But the chimney still draws, doesn't it?"

"Draws? Yes — but I just thought if there's stone on the place and well, wattle chimneys, they sometimes catch fire."

"True," says Elias. "They've got a way of catching fire on the coldest nights. No, I never liked a mud chimney. They don't look solid nor settled-like."

"Why I hadn't *thought*," says Jane. "But it's true. They don't look settled and solid, mud chimneys . . ."

"Oh, yes," says Elias. "But your stone chimney says folk have landed to stay." And he thinks again of that thick door slab, solid stone, a foot thick and red, and dressed square and smooth. "And a wood floor too," says Elias. "A real wood floor."

"But one thing at a time," says Jane. "There is something else though."

"What — ?"

"That Bible."

"Place needs a Bible. What of it?"

She makes a sorrowful sound. "I can't read. Nor write either."

"Is that all?" says Elias, turning and taking her in his arms. "Won't I teach you to read? A little effort every day? You'll read the Book cover to cover."

"How good you are! Now I can sleep." She turns away from him on her other side. For a while he holds her gently. She seems so soft and fragile. Jane wanting to read God's holy word. She was coming around to see things his way after all. She was sloughing off Indian ways and Indian thoughts, sure enough. And he closed his eyes and sank towards his slumber with the comforting thought that he had not suspected so much depth of ambition in this woman when first he saw her not so long ago.

Chapter 7

Evening. The sun has gone down below the high hedge of the forest. Yet it is still light. A sunset glow spreads over an immense stretch of sky. It lights an advance of towering thunderheads that march in a long skirmish line from north to south. The clouds approach, silent soldiers in search of a fugitive sun.

The air is clear, the light is crystalline. Every stalk and leaf seems chiseled, awaiting the slow approach of the clouds. The corn stands in ranks, a motionless army awaiting inspection or battle . . .

On the far bank of the river nothing moves. Even the tireless sawyers are motionless, for the level of the river has fallen, the current almost at a standstill, and the surface like a narrow lake, holds a calm reflection of the luminous sky on its patient surface.

The ageless moment between daylight and dark. Day creatures are still. Night creatures have not yet begun to stir. And still the light continues . . .

Leola has come out of the cabin to watch the approach of night. The men have been fed, the floor is swept clean, the dishes are scalded. She looks to the river. The men are there, minding the nets and fish baskets, but Leola sees no movement. Seemingly, Elias and Jake have been swallowed by the crystal air. All about Leola the world is stillness.

Witnessing this sky, the world stillness enters her. She thinks upon dreams she cannot remember. (Her body contains a young heart.) Her eyes look out upon a young world. Folding tired hands into her apron she leans against the solid strength of the cabin wall and continues to look upward, to the realm of the eagles, to the swan trail. Finally, lowering her gaze she sees gnats, dancing a myriad swarm on the warm air. Jane comes out. She too stands watching the sky, her hands folded upon her abdomen.

Movement from the river. Two men. One brings a sack of fish. The other a basket of turtles. Leola takes the turtle basket from Elias. Jake walks away to the creek to put the fish in the live-box. Hefting the turtle basket before opening it, Leola makes a pleased sound. "Hum!" she says. Lifting the basket latch she peers inside. Five turtles, alive and quick, struggling and pushing to come out of that basket. "Turtle," says Leola. Flickers of lightning lick the sky in the northeast. Lick-lick! Leola laughs. The men move briskly, Jake returning from the creek with the empty sack, Elias striding to the cattle pen with a load of fodder. A breeze springs up. Dog follows close upon Elias's heels. The breeze comes fresh, then fresher still. Jane, as though anchored, as though latched somehow by what's in her high belly — Jane stays just as she is, leaning against the wall, her face up, her eyes closed . . .

Thunder comes rolling down. "Eh?" says Leola. "Jane has something in her basket that wants out, eh? Turtles?"

Jane does not move.

"Having pains?" The old woman waits for an answer. Getting none she turns and enters the cabin with her basket. "Before bedtime I must mind to put in wet leaves and grass.

Cover the creatures and keep them." No answer. "Else one might come out! He! He!"

More thunder — it rumbles like a heavy cask rolled on a gravel bar.

Morning. Jane lies abed, her pains upon her now. Pain comes; then goes away.

And what was it like to be dead? Was it like sleep, or what was it like? Was it peaceful rest? Jane wonders, for all too many die in childbirth.

The ground. Only grub a little ways, and it was cold, winter and summer alike, ground was cold. And sometimes at work in the fields with Elias, the two of them working side by side, chopping weeds during summer, gathering corn during the butternut days of autumn, she had wondered about that final sleep.

During that first winter it seemed that the world slept. Now the second summer. How slowly and yet how suddenly everything seemed to happen.

Now it's too late. The baby will come. The life force will have its way with her. She lies very still, not wanting to move, as though somehow that final moment will be postponed — but no, she's sweating and Leola has noticed.

"Pain?" says the old woman. She stands by the bed, yet at the same time stands as it were outside of Jane's trouble. And how wonderful *she* must feel, thinks Jane. For this thing is not about to happen to her; no, I am the one to whom this is about to happen. "Another pain?"

Jane slowly nods.

Leola has a wet cloth which she presses to Jane's forehead. "Don't think," says Leola. "Thoughts bind."

As though something is stepping on her stomach, Jane feels herself suddenly seized. "God!" she cries.

"Now. It's all right. I'll just have a look. Let it go. It's like a boat and the current wants to pull it. Cut loose and go downstream! Take a breath, that's it. Breathe! Cut loose! Go with the current. Try not to think about it."

A shadow rose in Jane's vision. She gave a hoarse cry. "That's the way," says Leola; the shadow rises again.

Something is being asked of me, something over which I have no control.

"That's it — you're strong," says Leola.

"No. It's wearing me out," says Jane.

Closing her eyes she sees a field of cabbages. She goes drifting. The cabbages are blue-green. A voice is saying: "Put your knees up, that's it. Let's see. Yes! Now, try! It's time to try, Jane! Push."

Opening her eyes she sees Elias, stained with dirt and sweat. He puts his hand out to her. Jane takes his hand.

"Out! Out with you!" Leola is saying. "No need of men here. No need. We've women's work here." Nothing she says can budge Elias.

Closing her eyes Jane sees a spinning quilt and the quilt is a sound she makes and she feels water and the water tugs her body down and down towards a field in which yellow flowers stand quietly blooming. Something very hot makes her scream again and when she opens her eyes there stands Elias, his hand gripping both her hands.

"Out with you — out!" Leola cries.

The baby is coming. The baby is moving and Jane pushes with all her strength. Inside her that enormous force has begun moving downward and is leaving her behind it. "Ei!" says Leola. "Ei!"

Leola snips something with the scissors. She walks away from the bed, carrying something. "A man," says Leola. "See how calm he is."

"Not crying?" says Jane. And she's anxious and empty.

"What need has he to cry?" says the old woman. "He's

breathing and taking it all calmly. Here, see what a fine one he is!" And Leola holds the baby for Jane to see. He's wrapped in his little blanket now, and has a smudge of blood on his face. One tiny hand moves beside his cheek.

"Did you count fingers and toes, Leola?"

"And why not? Perfect as perfect," says Leola.

"A boy," says Elias.

And Jane closes her eyes. She goes drifting again.

"Isaac," she says in a sleepy voice. It's the name they've discussed, Jane and Elias. "Isaac," she murmurs.

Chapter *8*

When Elias goes away to Fort Hill not many days after Isaac's birth and comes home leading a cow, Leola decides that no one may milk the creature but herself. She takes charge of Bossy just as she has taken charge of Isaac. The cow and the baby are Leola's, and nevermind that Elias frowns.

Each evening after milking Leola sings Indian songs to Isaac, she sings to him of the month of the seven cold days, and the pairing month and the month of the wild geese. She sings of her half brother, I-Hear-Somebody-Coming, and of what a famous thief he was, who bathed his eyes in a secret spring and made himself invisible.

Elias was heard to mutter some Goddamns — which made Leola happy. She festered the stubborn man. Still he did not send her away, even though she made him surly.

Leola gets a Goddamn from Elias and Jane says: "But it's only lullabies, Elias. She's a help, she is."

"I'd sooner be married to seven old women," says Elias.

Leola must bathe Isaac and rub him with bear oil, all by herself. Only be the child's mammy and see how close she'll stick and stay here.

"How will he speak English when all he hears is grunts?" says Elias.

"But it's only lullabies," says Jane, lying abed.

Presently Jake comes in from his tree and hints after coffee. It's nightfall now. Jake and Elias sit smoking by the settle. They slip sweet potatoes under the ashes and drink tin cups of boiled coffee sweetened with honey. Leola can't help but raise her voice such that Jake must hear, Leola holding the baby and rocking him, and saying to Jane lying abed, saying: "Niggers that live in trees, and have books and beg tobacco. That's some strange niggers the like I never saw before. Such I never saw — eating roast sweet potatoes like the master himself."

Then Jake: "I'd know how to stop lullabies. Lullabies need a stick laid on 'em. I'd put the cowhide to squaw songs. Hang old gummy-gums to the whippin' hook one time and watch squaw songs take off down the river. Wake some mornin' and our hair all gone off our heads — I won't need three guesses what took it."

"Um," says Elias.

"Is he 'sleep?" says Jane from the bed.

"Aye," from Leola. The rocking chair creaks. "My little man sleeps," says she, in a softer voice.

"Wake some mornin' with the raw head," says Jake.

"Haul that biggest stone tomorrow for the doorstep," says Elias.

"Got it dressed today," says Jake.

"Haul it while the ground's yet slick for the sledge to run on. Set the doorstep, then bring along the chimney stones."

"Yes, sah, Marse Elias. That's what *I'd* do," says Jake. "Tomorrer." He puffs his pipe. "We'll do it." Everything is possible to hear Jake. He makes big medicine with words.

When the men raked their potatoes from the ashes baby Isaac stirred against Leola. He opened his dark infant's eyes and gazed peacefully into the old squaw's wrinkled face. Leola carried him to his mother and laid him to her breast, propping her up a little, the better that she might let Isaac suck.

The potatoes made a sweet smell in the cabin. Dog, having hesitated a while just outside the door, took this occasion to walk quietly in and ease down by the hearth. No one bothered to scold him. Elias reached out his moccasined foot and rubbed him on the head. He'd been hurt lately, after all. "About healed where the bear caught him," says Elias. "Thought he was killed sure."

"Can't kill him," says Jake, the all-knowing Jake. "No bear gonna kill him. He's too much dog for that. I keep a little grease rubbed where we stitched him up. You can't kill him." Jake took a bite of sweet potato. His lean jaws moved.

Leola sniffed. She went to the southwest corner where her churn stood with a cloth over it. She drew away the cloth and leaned down to smell. The milk was soured. Fetching the lid and the dasher and the stool she sat down to churning. She noticed that the Master, Elias, was watching. Now what is he thinking? she wondered. Isaac's mammy, I am, she thought. And will be so much help he'll never send me north again to Shokotee. She looked toward the bed where Isaac lay with Jane. Isaac's mammy, Leola was. Her heart was full of him.

"That rain I hear?" said Elias.

It was. Leola held her breath and listened.

Chunk, went the churning. *Chunk-a-chunk . . .*

Chapter 9

A visitor at Redleaves, "Gentleman Bob" Chatwood, comes calling on Shokotee, with servants and closed coach and his saddle mare hitched behind. He's come all the way here from his lair in Missouri. Part highwayman Chatwood is, and has for his partner a half-breed, Sim Hornby by name; these two, Chatwood and Hornby, rule the roost at the Horse Pens across in the Missouri bottoms.

The first afternoon they sit upon the high porch, Chatwood and Shokotee and Pettecasockee. While Chatwood spoke Shokotee lit a cigar. Thunderheads blew out of the north. Thunder crump-crumped and the pale undersides of the leaves were turned by the wind and flashed silver green. The air went suddenly cooler. Chatwood sat leaning back, bracing his small, booted feet against the iron balustrade.

"But I read about all that in your note," says Shokotee,

interrupting. "My note was to *prepare* you," says Chatwood, speaking shortly. He's a foppish Virginian with pale hair and blue eyes and a high forehead. "Now wait a minute!"

"A fool's errand," says Shokotee. "Damn-fool notion," he says.

"Hold now, hear me out," says Chatwood, lifting his hand. He tilted his head to one side. He raised his thick eyebrows. "Just hear me out, if you please! I come to you with a sure thing, a sheep shearing proposition, the money already counted, thousands for the taking, a sheep shearing . . ."

"Sheep *shitting* more like," says Shokotee. "Um."

"Now *wait* —"

But the old man would not wait, not Shokotee, though Chatwood's voice rose higher and higher. Shokotee shook his head and waved his hand through cigar smoke. He turned to Pettecasockee who had remained speechless this whole while. Said Shokotee: "Bring it."

Pettecasockee leaped up as if waiting for this. He disappeared through the green porch door.

"Bring what?" says Chatwood.

The hinges groaned again. Pettecasockee was back with a coil of rope. He handed it to Shokotee.

"I give you rope," says Shokotee. He leaned forward and tossed the coil into Chatwood's lap.

Chatwood looked at it irritably. "You're only an Indian," he said.

"And you," said the old man, "are only a thief."

"You don't understand," Chatwood went on. "The land companies are asking fifty cents an acre here. Two acres make a dollar! We know every settler has the money about him now — and it comes to thousands! The hell with this rope. What's meant by it?" He lowered his feet from the balustrade. "I made you a fair proposition."

"You towhead," says Shokotee, shaking his head.

"What?"

"You'd only get them up in arms, that's all."

"Them? *Who?*"

"The settlers!"

Chatwood laughed. "The *settlers,* is it? The settlers! Me and my boys and Hornby and you and your bunch. The settlers are sheep. . . ."

"They are too many now," the old man said gravely. "Give it up, I tell you."

Chatwood appealed to Pettecasockee. "The old man off his oats or something? Off his feed, is he?"

Pettecasockee looked at the floor.

"You back him up, Petty? Eh?" says Chatwood.

Still looking down, Pettecasockee nodded.

"Well, I'll be God damned. Bless me if I won't be God damned to *Boston* and home again! I thought you were men!"

"Careful —" says Pettecasockee facing him. "Careful!"

"Then make him take his rope back and be sensible. Thousands for the taking, a sheep shearing . . ."

Shokotee sucks his lower lip and pulls his brown woolen shawl close about his shoulders. He plucks at the bright orange fringe on the shawl. Jane Nail made it from a piece of wool she got at Chatillion's last year — that brown shawl. Said Shokotee,

"Five years ago, do you remember? I told you five years ago that I was out of the trade, getting out for good. Told you I wanted nothing more to do with the confederation. To count me out and never again to mention *anything* to me. Remember?"

Rain was sweeping heavily down. It was like a curtain of gray gauze beyond the porch. It roared on the roof and the porch began filling with flies driven in from the wet. Water poured a stream down the trellis and splashed through the vines of the climbing rose at the end of the porch. Said Chatwood,

"Now, Shokotee."

"Five years ago I told you I was through and I meant it, Bob. The settlers are too many. They won't stand for any foolishness. This side of the river the trade is over and done for. My answer is no. Forget the idea. I forbid it."

"Now, Shokotee. Now wait —"

But the old man would not wait.

"You have spoken?" says Chatwood.

"I have spoken," says Shokotee.

"Very well then, but this *rope* wants an apology!"

"And shall have it if you aren't hanged," says Shokotee.

Chapter 10

The Snail felt trapped.

Timothy Laird, T. Laird, the Snail.

Trapped by the wind, trapped by the rain lashing the north walls of the house on the slope of Fort Hill. Whipping down like grapeshot, a volley of hailstones cracked on the roof.

"Gentleman Bob" Chatwood had come to Fort Hill — he had come and gone. He had left the Snail's nerves raw. "Gentleman Bob" had renewed his demands.

Objecting, the Snail had said: "It's too dangerous!"

Chatwood, smoking a cigar, had smiled his lupine smile and helped himself to the brandy. Whereupon the Snail had tried again:

"Information on freight wagons, passenger coaches and the mail, now that's one thing, Bob. But what *you're* asking is another bill of goods entirely. All I'm saying is that when you get that many people churned up, that many folks that have sweated and busted their guts to get up fifty cents to the acre, and here you come with your bunch and take it from them, rob them blind. I'm just saying there is nothing in God's *world* to save you then. And when they discover it was me that got up the list and slipped you the information — why they'll God damn well boil me in bear oil, don't you know? *Fry* me!"

"Yeah," says Chatwood. He could be like a razor when he chose — merciless. "Don't disappoint me. Don't disappoint a gentleman, Snail. Do so? See if we don't know how to handle that, Snail old boy! Eh?" And he poured himself another pony of brandy, helping himself again. Then he produced the coil of rope from inside his coat. He had tossed it on the floor at the Snail's feet — rope. And moments later he had gone, riding his saddle mare, his coach and servants following. Fear, from that moment, had folded about the Snail like a dark, smothering wing. The storm, the second to gather in as many days, finally broke out after Chatwood's departure. Thundering in just at nightfall it came, shaking the building.

The Indians told it that Fort Hill was sacred ground, protected from whirlwinds by the storm god himself. The Snail put no faith in the legend and lived in fear of storms . . .

Now this storm shook and it shook his fears. It rattled his misgivings. When he sat down to supper the image of his terrible misgiving appeared in the candle shadows like a skeleton sitting opposite. It took away his appetite.

Aunt Tio, his servant, went to and fro from the kitchen, waiting on him. And by now Chatwood, halfway to Missouri, would have his feet propped up in some crossroad tavern, cigar in his mouth, brandy bottle by him on the table, and not a care in his head.

The Snail looked at his food. Fried steak, buttered rice, pole beans, pickled beets, corn muffins. The Snail pushed at his meat with a fork. Thunder, straight overhead. He dropped the fork. It clattered on the plate. Tio brought him a goblet of wine. He tried a sip, but his hand trembled.

"Wine for your nerves," she was saying in her soothing voice. "Wine . . ."

"God damn it!" He glared at her. "You worry about my *nerves?*" If I'm found out can you guess how long it will take them to hang me? Be practical and worry about my *neck!*"

She stepped back to the kitchen and said something to P'-nache, a mumbled sound. P'-nache would be there eating. And when he had eaten he would take his blanket to the hay mow and sleep beneath the stable roof. The Snail took another sip . . .

The village band came to mind. Two days ago the band played for a hanging: and two days before the hanging it played for a whipping: the day before the whipping, for a funeral. Today, before Chatwood's arrival, they had assembled to serenade the mail coach. Because it somehow seemed that none but an honest man would serve as Fort Hill's drummer, the Snail was deemed honest in the eyes of his fellow citizens. Being a mulatto he had to be careful in a way whites, like Chatillion, the trader; like Cork, the blacksmith; like Wall Stuart, the horse trader, didn't have to be. Those others more or less openly did business with Chatwood and Hornby and none of them stood in the way of being hanged. Though they bought stolen goods, swapped stolen horses, worked stolen slaves, decked wives, daughters and mistresses in plundered jewelry and dined daily upon stolen plates and drank hourly from stolen goblets, carving roasts with stolen knives, wearing suits tailored from stolen broadcloth — they had naught to fear. They wiped their noses on stolen handkerchiefs, and were considered respectable. Not so, the Snail, a free man of color . . .

Tio came back. "For your own good," she said, "furnish what he wants, what he commands," she said.

"How many turnouts between here and Missouri?" he said. "D'you know how many?"

"I know trees fall across the road, yes," she said.

"A tree will *never* fall any other way than across a road. Just fetch the hot water — just shave me if you don't mind. If it won't put you out too much."

"You won't eat anythin'?"

"No." He got up and went to his bedroom and sat down in the chair which was faced so he could observe himself in the mirror. He watched while she steamed his whiskers and lathered his face.

The rain ceased while she was shaving him — the wind died. Courage stirred in him again. He thought of the road and the turnouts but it didn't bother him so much anymore. Chatwood's plan was fatal folly. He drew the list . . . While he sat writing she laid out his travel clothes.

The Snail arches almost flat against his mare's neck; he rides balancing upon her shoulders. He moves upon the distance. The storm's aftermath has left still-damp, swollen essences such as make men restless and leave them lonely. The Snail's uneasiness gathers back of his breastbone like shoaling minnows.

Alone, I'll die alone, he thinks. He remembers and sees P'-nache, leading the mare beneath his window. He sees Aunt Tio filling his wooden canteen, tucking meat and biscuits and hardboiled eggs in his saddlebags, him saying: "So by God you want to weigh me down? When you know I couldn't eat anything even if I was paid?" And the walls had given off their wet-weather smell of straw and moistened dust. The Snail had set his hat snugly, smelling the damp smell of the walls, the green smell of floors. He had had a farewell glimpse of the parlor and the white cat bunched beside her bowl of cream in the corner by the spinet. Then he was outside where P'-nache waited, holding the mare. The whiskey reek of the Indian's breath had been like spoiled berries. T. Laird, the Snail, had grabbed the stirrup and swung himself suddenly astride the light saddle. Aunt Tio hands up saddlebags and pistols; pistols ride holstered snugly, forward on either side of the saddle and covered by the bearskin flap. P'-nache and Tio stand back. T. Laird clucks to the mare and reins down. He crosses himself and so doing shifts the reins to his right hand and speaks the mare a word of encouragement.

The fist that knots his stomach eases somewhat after the first turnouts, the first miles, and as he passes north the road dries and leads out of the track of the storm.

They had made the journey many times, man and mare. Thus without pausing to ponder crossroads, horse and rider bend through without stopping and shoot swiftly, with no hesitation, past lonely taverns and way stations. They breeze into the tunneling gloom of deep woods. Leaping tree trunks, edging miry wagon tracks, their fluid progress peels away layer upon layer of the time and distance lying stretched between them and the Missouri shore and Bob Chatwood.

Silent and veiled, distance drops slowly behind with steady fading — white to gold to red to dusky purple, and next moonrise, a glabrous radiance scattering brittle patches of chalkish light. The mare goes suddenly skittish. The Snail sweetens her with spurs and a gentle pressure on the reins and she is again one creature with him, his legs riding deep and secure in leather husks. They breast, mare and man, odors of dried bark and winged seeds, all converging from the vegetable night. The road unrolls, a spotted skein, turnout to turnout, a snakeskin, turnout to turnout, in dripping dew, and all leading to that sudden twist, that precipitous wrench where the road ascends the ancient riverbank and meets, finally, the crest of these ravine-cursed bluffs. Down then, to the floodplain. Once on that flat, after twisting and plunging down, the distance becomes like a good poison, rapidly absorbed, slowly eliminated. The Snail sees cottonwoods and finally the ferry landing, and beyond the trees, the river, where it waits and holds the dark shadow of the between island. Here the continent divides; the Mississippi. Behind him the sky had turned pink.

Bill was waiting for him. "Oh, yes," says Bill in a sleepy voice. "The Governor said to expect you." Tall and very thin, cranelike, and a very paragon of loyalty to Gentleman Bob Chatwood, this young ferryman. The Snail knew nothing more of him than that. "Ain't you the Snail?"

"I'm called that, yes," the Snail said, speaking stiffly, somewhat hoarse.

"Oh, yes," says Bill. "Just let me have her reins. I'll put her aboard. Don't I remember her? Wouldn't be for sale, would she?"

"No," said the Snail. "She wouldn't be for sale. No."

Bill shoved, using a pole to push the ferry away from the landing. The Snail stood by the mare. The oar began to chunk. "Nobody else like the Governor for a gentleman to wear clothes the way he does. 'Look out for the Snail, Bill.' That's what he says. 'Don't worry about me, Governor,' I says. I save the little ones for him, the fiddlers. The Governor don't like a large catfish, but favors little ones. Fiddlers. 'Got any fiddlers for me, Bill?' I'd do anything he asked, nevermind. If he must to ask me, 'Bill, knock the Snail in the head, gut him and sew rocks in his hollow and drop him deep,' which is not to say he asked me anything on that order. But wouldn't I do it? I'd be glad to and so would you, wouldn't you? They call you Snail or what do they call you?"

The Snail nodded.

"Free nigger, ain't you?"

The Snail nodded. He saw the western shore revealed by the dawn. They were dropping down below the between island. The island, like the far shore, was a morass of trees, each with a twisting tangle of grapevines, each vine seemingly larger than the last.

"Something's up," says Bill. "I believe it's always better not to know, don't you?"

So it had gotten so even the boatman knew. Had gotten so that everything Chatwood planned was known ahead of time. The Snail thought: *They don't lack anything else but a newspaper to let the public know what they're up to. And they want me to furnish them their intelligence, maybe so they can publish that too, because of course nobody will think anything of it except to hang me, that's all.*

"You take the amount of land down around Fort Hill district that's going for fifty cents an acre," Bill says. "That comes to something, like the Governor says. That *really* beats tanbark. Oh, yes!"

By the time the ferry grated on the shore the Snail was feeling dizzy. He felt dry and hollow, gourdlike, as though if something should shake him he would rattle. He looked upon the tangled vines and smelled the peculiar combination of swamp and shore, forest and human habitation. The mare coughed. He mounted and rode her ashore and up the bank. The road here was rutted. Wagonloads of contraband, herds of stolen horses — all came this way.

Four turnouts and he rode into the Horse Pens. Chatwood came down the steps from his high porch. Dogs were barking. The Snail followed Chatwood up the steps. They went inside. Sim Hornby was there, a low-built Louisiana half-breed, grinning and one-eyed.

"Not a little weary is he?" says Sim Hornby. "He's tuckered is he?" Hornby laughed. "Damn me ain't he tired?"

The Snail took out his watch and opened it. Without looking at it he put it away again, automatically. He sat down. Beyond the window was laundry day. He felt in his waistcoat for the watch. Brown chickens scratched at the base of a bell-bottomed cypress. Not far from the covered well, three cabins down, a woman tended a fire built under a black washpot. A child struggled towards her carrying two buckets of water. The Snail felt shoaling minnows again behind his breastbone. He took out the list and handed it to Chatwood and turned again to the window. Blue smoke came puffing from beneath the black washpot.

Hornby was dropping a dirk point down on the hewn log floor. *Chunk,* like the ferryman's oar. *Chunk . . .*

The Snail would have to sleep soon. Weariness was rising out of his legs. He thought of his pistols. But someone had taken the mare and whoever had taken her had taken the pistols, and was keeping them. He glanced at Hornby.

"Why don't you lay down a while?" the half-breed was saying. *Chunk* — the knife again. "Bite to eat? Drink of whiskey?" Hornby was trying to be kind.

The Snail waited for the sound of the dirk. When it didn't drop he looked Hornby's way. Hornby held the blade end now, not the handle, as before. He rubbed the blade with a slow, caressing movement. There was a dreamy look in his face.

The Snail went outside. Hoping somehow to shake off his weariness, he stood a while on the stilted porch. He could hear the knife again. It struck the floor. He went down the porch steps. A mule-drawn freight wagon passed up the street to the storehouse just opposite, and was backed to the lading dock. Three Negroes began unloading it, taking off casks and crates.

The Snail walked to the sheltered well. It stood in the center of the Horse Pens. He dropped the bucket and drew it slowly up again. Taking the gourd dipper from a nail above him on one of the supports, he took a dipper of water and moistened his handkerchief. The water was cold. He pressed the wet cloth first to his face, then to the back of his neck. He knew people must be watching him from the high stilt porches of the little houses all about. The river flooded here. A mound of earth was pushed up inside the horse fence. That way animals could crowd together on that patch of high ground and not drown during a flood.

He took drink from the dipper and threw the last drops on the damp ground. He set the nearly full bucket on the well rim and turned away, feeling dizzy again. Pressing his damp handkerchief to his closed eyes, he seemed to feel the mare's motion beneath him again . . .

Chapter *11*

For a month Fort Hill had had a school-educated physician. The whiskery young fellow had rented the loft over the rum ordinary for rooms and offices. He kept his horse in the stable behind. His name was Cargile Parham.

Henri Chatillion had no further information concerning him and witnessed, for the time being at least, no decline in his own practice. Until Parham's advent Chatillion — self-educated — had been all there was. He had done a brisk trade in powders and tonics, herbs and laudanum, medicinal whiskey and a salve which he prepared, called mull. Mull was a compound of salt, bear fleece, sulphur and hog lard. It sold steadily and well.

On a day, clear and sunny, his old friend, Shokotee, came calling at the trading post. Chatillion received the Indian in his office with that silence for which he was famous.

And what made Chatillion this way? He had grown up hearing French, Creek and English but until his fourth year had never spoken a word. Then, having given proof that he was neither deaf nor dumb, he developed a brisk intelligence. In a family of traders, he soon mastered bookkeeping, money-changing, trade, barter, and the symptoms of biliary calculus. As he grew, his silence brought him attention. By the time he had settled on Fort Hill, opening the territory to Indian trade, he was given out to be a wise man; it was said he could be trusted absolutely to keep secrets. He became a receiver of information. Steadily, year to year, he prospered. The log structure which commanded the crest of the hill was bit by bit enlarged to contain not only his wares but his womenfolk — wives, daughters, slaves, and maidservants. (He had no sons.) His was the oldest building of any; Indians had helped raise the structure on that charmed spot where no twister or whirlwind had touched. Before memory the hill was a campsite for parties on the long hunt. And here Henri Chatillion lived and traded, as silent as when he first emerged from the woods, on foot, toting a peddler's pack.

First the trading post, next the fort, which for a time sheltered a few soldiers; hardly more than a single company, rowdy fellows for the most part. They had nothing to do it seemed but sit at cards and play at dice and dominoes. A few died of camp fever and were buried in the sloping graveyard, in gravelly earth beyond the stockade wall. A drum tatted. A bugle echoed. Once in a great while a soldier would be shot for desertion, but never in battle.

But no more. The soldiers were gone. The stockade walls were rotting. The parade ground was covered with tents and wagons and campfires of migrating settlers, a constant file heading west. On the hill by the abandoned military graveyard lay Indian Town — tilting backyards, mud huts, petticoats and blankets hung to dry between fenceposts. And Indians. Staggering, they wandered up and down or they sprawled asleep by the mud walls.

Shokotee and Chatillion sat a while in the office in Chatillion's trading post of peeled logs. Below and opposite stood Stuart's blacksmith shop, and next the livery stable.

"I now come to the point," Shokotee said.

A nod from Chatillion. His dark eyes shone.

"Pettecasockee, my son, admires your daughter, Denise."

A nod from Chatillion. Then a quick smile . . .

"If you favor the match Pettecasockee will come for her, if she is willing. Or you may send her to him, as you wish. Shall I send Petty?"

A nod from Chatillion. Yes.

"Then I will send him next month." Shokotee put his black hat upon his head again and smoothed the brim down level with his walnut eyes. He stood up. Black coat, starched white cuffs, stiff collar, black tie, as befitted the solemnity felt by them both, Shokotee stood. "Then our blood will be mixed. I'm glad."

A nod from Chatillion, and a glisten in his eyes. He took Shokotee's hand.

For a long time after Shokotee had gone, Chatillion stood looking out the window, at the vast trees beyond and on beyond the Fort Hill clearing, stoic wilderness, green and dark green, far as mind and eye could reach.

His heart was moved. He turned back to his desk, sat down, and penned a swift note, pushing his ledger aside.

"Next month, my child," he wrote, then dipped the pen: "I have given Shokotee my permission. Chatillion."

Pettecasockee had been her heartfelt wish these six months past. Chatillion sighed. He was pleased to reflect upon his child's happiness. He lifted his brass desk bell and rang it. A dark, fat, barefoot woman-servant wearing calico came in. She stood waiting. Chatillion held out the note.

"Denise," he said.

The woman took the note and went back downstairs. From below came a cry; footsteps clattered on the wooden stairs. Denise ran to him where he stood by his desk. His long arms were outstretched.

"Papa! Papa!" she cried. "Next month!" She hugged him. She kissed his cheeks, laughing and crying. "Next month! Oh!"

Chapter 12

Ellen Ashe sat churning. Because yesterday's rainstorm had so closed in upon her, lowering her spirits, she had moved her churn outdoors when the sky came clear again. She sat churning in sunshine. Presently the butter would rise — if she didn't think about it . . .

Elias was on her mind. She had told him not to worry for her sake. How many? she wondered. How many fall into so foolish a trap?

For when her husband deserted her without giving her any children she had thought it was herself to blame. Ashe had thrown it up to her, saying: "Well, and if it weren't enough you're barren to boot. Barren besides all the rest of it!" And that had hurt more than anything else. He had known right away that it did. "Barren!" As for the real reason Ashe had ridden off, it was failure, barren crops, not barren bride. It was land worn clean out and washed away to ravening gullies. It was two crop failures, then a third, and a fourth; they had begun selling their Negroes. The way pointed west but Ashe could not, as he said, bear up to the ignominy of an auction, nor stand and see what was left loaded in a wagon. He would not, he said, leave North Carolina like a common immigrant, him saying: "I had thought you were rich and that we might have children. And you barren!"

And having so said upon a Tuesday he was gone away with his horse upon a Thursday. When she was satisfied he would never come back she had consoled herself with thinking that at least she didn't have to make the west journey with a nursing baby tugging her teat. The very last thing any abandoned woman needed was a child. Thus had she thought . . .

And had come here with her brothers. And Cow had wandered off one day. Poor Cow was only a poor dumb creature. When Ellen and her brothers took alarm they even imagined that perhaps that fellow to the north of them had found Cow — even stolen her! But they had gone to Dutt and Fancy Callister's clearing first. Not finding Cow there they had gone to seek Elias with anger in their teeth. They found him all alone and hard at work and with no sign of Cow anywhere about his place. And in his gentleness he had shamed them with roasting ears. In his gentle kindness he had gone the whole way home with them and Cow was discovered, safely back home with her bull calf. It had seemed to Ellen that Elias was owed something. But what? She could have sent a gift of butter by the boys. But no, she had thought of something else, something she hadn't found use for those months past, something he might take kindly and gently. Not as she thought at the time exactly what. She didn't let herself think that far. She wanted to feel respectable after all. She had merely thought that here was a kind and gentle man, as good and generous and so much better than most and *if* . . .

If. She hadn't let herself get beyond that *if.* Herself, her private self was free and offered no kind of danger so long as she were not found out. Hadn't she told him not to worry? Giving her secret self, she had invited him to second helpings and more. "Come anytime." Take what he would, there was plenty, and did no one harm, and he had been terribly gentle — and grateful. She had felt a new warmth and a new pride in herself. She had felt as people feel when they do their duty — their pleasant duty and then some. And it had pleased her for some time afterwards to realize that she was good for something beyond milking and churning and feeding and boiling clothes, for something beyond molding butter and sweeping and scrubbing and sewing. Dawn to dusk.

But oh, she hadn't *known*. What she hadn't known now served to bring her to the very steep edge of herself. She hurt — hurt every time she thought it: "Feel so wise, discover a fool."

Elias had his own wife, his own child. He wouldn't have room for another of each. Her brothers would be bound to guess. For a *growing* secret, the saying is, can't be kept . . .

Elias. Lately now he was nearly all her thought. Fathered a child in her, he had. Guiltless — with no pleading, no guile, no force, no urgency from him. Would have been all the same with him if she had given him a kiss only, and nothing more. For he was the very soul of sweetness, was Elias . . .

She had invited him and had thought nothing else but how full she felt. "No worries down in the west," she had thought. Afterwards she had asked herself what there was about this same business of breeding, of lying with her husband, that had seemed so unpleasant and wicked.

Elias. She had thought herself free. She sat now, churning, with new life in her stomach and no earthly idea what to do.

She thought to look in the churn. The butter had risen.

Chapter 13

Fanny Chapleau was a little drunk. Last night's rain had made a puddle on the floor. During the storm water had leaked through the walls. The girl was on her hands and knees sopping a rag on the floor and wringing it out in a pail. Seated by the game table, sipping wine, Fanny watched her.

"Fated to hang will never drown," said Fanny Chapleau. She considered herself as she had lately begun to do. In the late bloom of her beauty she lived exiled from pleasure and luxury, from the New Orleans she had taken for granted until she had made that mistake — murdering her husband Aaron Chapleau. Why had she murdered him? Hadn't Aaron been generous? Hadn't he loved her, given her jewels and gowns and carriages? He had, he had, he had . . .

But he had also nettled her. Cotton, as he tirelessly explained, came down the river to New Orleans. Aaron bought it. From New Orleans pale Aaron's cotton went to England and New England all in ships which Aaron and his friends and their English partners owned. The ships, like good creatures, returned with finished goods of fine European manufacture, with everything the heart could wish from needles to music boxes, from playing cards to chess sets to game tables to brandy decanters; glassware, chinaware, silverware, paint, varnish, stoves, boots, hats, lamps — !

"What do I care for that?" said Fanny. "What a bore he was!"

"Ma'am?" said the poor girl. She had a fine enough figure but a plain face. Indeed, thought Fanny, her face was ordinary. Yet she was a mixed breed and that made her exotic to men; she was not intelligent. "Did you speak, Miss Chapleau?"

"Get the water up," said Fanny. "I've already stepped in it twice."

"Yes, ma'am," the girl said. "Such a lot seeps in, don't it?"

Sunlight flooded the window curtains. Not a tree had been left on the hill for shade. As in all backwoods settlements the first thing done was to murder all trees in sight, and nevermind how raw-muddy, how bald-dusty, how nude the effect might be afterward.

Fanny Chapleau sighed and filled her little glass again. She was bored and she felt sorry for herself and she was about to enter the third decade of her life. Had she remained in New Orleans to stand trial and live down the scandal — but why risk imprisonment?

Fanny had come away up the river, and reaching Memphis, had journeyed east by mail coach until she couldn't stand her fellow passengers any longer. Something told her besides that Fort Hill, Tennessee, was a safe distance. And here she stopped. And having no better way to hide her past and disguise her purpose she had set up a modest bordello. That much Fort Hill district folk understood well enough. Tender truth the district folk spurned. They didn't care about Fanny Chapleau's dreams. The district folk cared about nothing but cotton.

"If only something would *happen,*" Fanny Chapleau heard herself saying.

The poor girl only looked at her and asked if she were hungry.

"Hungry? Ah — yes, hungry! But I don't want anything to eat!" Fanny said.

"Ma'am?"

"I want to die, can't you understand?"

The girl didn't. She looked down, embarrassed. She had no poetry in her, the poor little scullery trollop.

"Nevermind," said Fanny. "Finish your chores."

"The sun's shining today, ma'am."

"The sun? And what's sun to me, pray?"

"It's only that it rained so hard last night, ma'am."

How little it took to make a poor wretch happy. Fanny pitied her. She would never know real happiness, poor girl. She'd be laced mutton her whole life, she would.

A knock at the door. The girl hauled herself up and opened it. It was, Fanny saw, only the same slave that always came peddling. He brought fresh vegetables and dressed game. He came often and was always clever about selling something. Out here where money was scarce that fellow and his master were always grubbing for it.

Fanny always watched. She had plenty of time for watching. The loaded wagon, drawn by the same solid span of oxen, would appear, master and slave walking alongside. Sometimes it was a load of wood shingles. Another time it might be deer hides. Today it was vegetables and dressed meat, peddled door-to-door.

The man was a hunter. He had a family out there in the woods somewhere, to judge how he bought things to cart back to his clearing.

Fanny, still a little drunk, sat by the game table watching the street. The man and his slave and the ox-drawn wagon passed on down the hill. The man was leading a cow. His servant rode in the wagon. The cow's udder wagged back and forth. The wagon jolted through miry holes in transverse agony, like an open boat driven headfirst into dashing waves. The oxen sometimes miring to their bellies, moved somehow. As though swimming, they always managed to rise again. The man was urging the cow. When her udder dragged Fanny felt a curious tingling in her own teats.

What powered that fellow? What had brought his like here? She wondered. Something beyond necessity, she thought.

"That man, yonder, Jake's master. Who is he?" Fanny asked.

"Elias McCutcheon, ma'am."

"They fling themselves down here for no other reason than to defy all reason, don't they."

"Ma'am?"

"Nothing," Fanny said. "Where does he come from?"

"Back east they say — Middle Tennessee maybe."

"Where does he live?"

"In the woods," said the girl. "So they say. He's industrious and . . ."

"And what?"

"Well, gentle and handsome-like," the girl said. Having finished the floor she was heating her irons and preparing to iron Fanny's ruffled gowns. "Settler folk like Mister McCutcheon are tied to the land-like."

"The townfolk welcome me," said Fanny Chapleau. "Like they long for a Jew, they welcome a curtesan and want a bawdy house. They all talk the same thing — the glorious future. But townfolk haven't any real feeling for this or any other place. You observe as much?"

The girl nodded. She licked a finger and tested her iron. The smell of ironing and laundry filled the room.

"It's his sort, him yonder — what's his name again?"

"Elias McCutcheon," the girl said in her low numb voice. "Elias . . ."

"Accumulating in the woods. His kind will *be* here. D'you wonder what he goes home to?"

"His fambly I suppose."

"I wonder," said Fanny. She got up from her chair. And surprised how unsteady she was, she went to the window, and watched Elias McCutcheon down the hill, a pioneer, a settler; a stolid figure in a red shirt leading a cow . . .

Chapter 14

Leola woke. Dog had been baying. Now he was barking. His defiance rang against the wall of the night. Inside the cabin only bleak silence, only darkness. Reaching from beneath her blanket Leola braced her hand against the wall and listened. Closer and closer came Dog's urgent barking and Leola heard something else — horses now, no doubt of it, horses all right; then a strange voice:

"Hello!"

"Who's there?" says Jake beside his tree.

"Preachers. A bad accident."

"Sah?"

"Horse threw him. Brother Cole's leg is broke. McCutcheon clearing?"

"Yes, sah, that's right."

"Where's your master?"

"The cabin. Have to wake him, sah."

"Tie that dog, if you don't mind."

"Dog! Hyar!" Jake calls. "You, Dog! Hyar!" Silence.

Then: "He's tied, sah. Come on up."

Leola stirred herself. Standing up on the cot she pushed the curtains aside and peered through the little window. The night was black and moonless. Jake's lantern was approaching. She watched three figures materialize in the feeble light. They came three abreast, two supporting the third, the injured — . He was groaning.

"All right, Brother Cole. We're nearly there," says the strange voice.

Knocking, then loud knocking at the door.

"Elias?" says Jane, from the bed. Little Isaac wakes in his cradle and begins crying.

Stirrings then. The bed ropes creak. "Coming!" says Elias.

But he mustn't open! thinks Leola. She gets up, making her way to the table. She finds the candle and lights it.

"Master!" she hisses.

"Eh?"

"Careful!" says Leola.

"Who's there?" says Elias. He stands at the door stuffing his nightshirt into his trousers. He's barefooted.

"Preachers, sah," says Jake's voice. "One got a broke leg."

"Mister McCutcheon?" calls the strange voice. "It's Brother Barker! Brother Cole with me! Fear his leg is broke."

Raiders! thinks Leola. So thinking she moves swiftly to the far corner and takes up the heavy rifle leaning there. She cocks the hammer and leans against the wall in the shadows.

Elias is unbarring the door. "Bring him this way," he says.

Jake and the stranger enter with the injured man between.

"This way. Put him on the table —"

The injured one groans. Leola's heart goes out to him.

She lowers the rifle, thinking to help, but as she does so she hears a sound. It's a doom-dealing crack and comes as an arm flails. A pistol strikes headbone. Down goes Jake, dropped without so much as a word from him, felled by the very man he was helping.

"Reach!" says a voice. Two strangers stand pointing pistols at Elias, all unaware of Leola . . .

She brings up the rifle — a heavy weight it is — she steadies on the outline of the nearest robber and pulls the trigger — *wham!* The crash is enough to break her ears. Gunsmoke fills the cabin. The nearest robber sinks down, screaming. Elias grabs the other, snatching him like. Leola is squatting to peer beneath the smoke. She's looking to see the effect of her shot. That nearest one is screaming his lungs out. She sees how Elias grabs the other, snatching and heaving him bodily into the solid wall by her cot, throwing him like you'd hurl a cat, then snatching him up again and throwing him a second time, flinging him like a rag doll. Headforemost he goes into the wall with a shock that shakes the cabin. It sets little Isaac's string cradle swaying.

On the floor the one Leola shot down is still screaming. Won't hush it seems. Leola clubs the gun, gripping the business end of the barrel in both hands. Deft as a snake she moves to the wounded man. Up goes the heavy gun over her head, held in both hands like an ax. Down she swings, aiming her blow. She breaks his skull. She cuts his scream short. Again she strikes, one for good measure. Blood spatters her face and arms.

"Die, pissant!" Leola cries in a cracked voice.

She sags, victorious. But then, like a torrent, more men poured through the door. They came bursting from nowhere, materialized as though from some night substance. She saw Elias go down. Then she herself was tumbled.

So, she thinks. Death finds me. In her heart she saw the end of a dark abyss of waiting. Calmly, as though from a long mile's distance, she saw the end.

Did she swing the clubbed rifle at her nearest attacker, or was it a dream? She smelt rum. Aye, must be his breath she smelled. He was wrenching her arms from her sockets, trying to jerk away the gun, but she was holding. She held on with a deathgrip, she did.

Then she came around. She was tied hand and foot and propped on the floor, leaned back against the wall beside Elias. He was bound the same way.

She moaned . . .

Elias turned his head at the sound. He saw Leola, that it was she who made that sound. Her head was moving. Side to side it wagged, waving her iron-gray braids. Like dangling snakes they seemed in the candlelight. For what seemed the hundredth time he looked up and tried to count his enemies. Seven — ? Nine — ?

Too many. He had been beaten and gouged. They had come sudden as wings. Just when he had bethought himself to look to Jake, to see if poor Jake were still living, to help him, these others had entered and struck him hard. A roaring was still in his head, like distant rainfall . . .

Now a fellow with a half-breed's face seized Elias by the hair. One of the fellow's eyes was white and blind. He wore a black hat of the same style favored by Shokotee, wide-brimmed. Tightening his grip in Elias McCutcheon's hair he slammed his head against the wall behind. Elias heard roaring again, that rain-sound roar in his ears. Dog was howling outside . . .

They brought Jane from the bed. They knelt in front of Elias. Behind somewhere Isaac was squalling. Jane's eyes were closed. One held her hair, another her arms . . .

"The money, McCutcheon?"

"Under the sand. Left side of the hearth," says Elias.

Silence. Then: "It's here," a voice from the hearth.

"Sack it," says the half-breed. "The trunk?"

"Nothing but scissors and some other fixings."

"No false bottom, you sure?"

"Just scissors."

"Hand 'em here."

"Scissors, Sim?"

"You heard me! Hand 'em, God damn ye!"

"We got his *coin*, Sim."

"But Kettle and Striker are nipped!" says the half-breed, taking the scissors. He clicked them, Jane's scissors.

"Got another hidey-hole, McCutcheon?"

When Elias shook his head the half-breed thrust his hand between Jane's breasts, into the bodice of her white cotton gown. He ripped straight down. A savage jerk and her gown was torn clean away. She moaned. A white bead of milk appeared on one nipple. The half-breed put the point of the scissors to the nipple, he took Jane's milk; he raised the scissors to his lips and licked. His single eye fixed on Elias. "Another hidey-hole?" He grinned.

"No!" says Elias. "Leave her be!"

"Come on, Sim!" says another, standing behind.

"Shut up!" says Sim.

"Kill 'em and have done!"

"What if I slice off your brat's ears, eh?"

"Get it over, Sim! Let's move!"

"Hold her head! Hold it good!" says Sim.

He slipped one scissors blade into Jane's mouth. She screamed. Her body thrashed. Though she went limp, as though dead, Sim worked on and on, snipping . . . When he was done he had opened her cheek from the corner of her mouth almost to the eye above. Her jaw sagged. Her cheek flap fell aside, revealing teeth. From her chin down she was bathed in blood.

"No!" cried Elias. "No!"

"Let's go, boys!" Sim, the half-breed, said. He had stood up and was wiping his bloody hands on Jane's gown. She lay limp at his feet.

The man leaned down and spat in Elias's face. "Settlers!" he hissed. He stepped over Jane and stopped, drawing his knife. Seizing Elias again by the hair he pushed the blade to his neck. "Beg!" he whispered. "Sheepfucker!" he hissed. "Beg!" Removing the point from Elias's throat and releasing his hair he pinched the loose skin above his eyebrow and drove the point through, twisting, scraping bone. Blood flowed into Elias's eye. Elias felt his breath go out. He groaned. "That's better!" says the half-breed. "Now —!"

"Sim!" The voice called from the night beyond the door. "Sim!"

"Aye." As though reminded of something the half-breed stuck the dirk back in his belt scabbard. Giving Elias's head a final slam against the wall, he straightened up and was gone . . .

Again Elias heard rainroar in his head. He drifted inside himself. He woke to see Jane. She was on her hands and knees, whimpering. Slowly she swayed to her feet. With one hand pressed to her bloody cheek she made her way to the door, closed it, and dropped the bar. She came back then, bloody to her knees, blood on her belly, blood in her secret hair. She found the scissors, dropped them, picked them up again, and on hands and knees, she rolled Elias forward face down, and cut his binding thongs. Blood came again to his arms and legs. He lay a moment helpless. Then he could move.

Leola was speaking in a cracked voice. "If you hadn't opened the door! But no! He had to open it!"

Elias stood trembling. "Wet cloths, soot and cobwebs," he said, speaking to himself. He pushed Jane to the table, lifted her bodily, and laid her gently down, face up.

"You let them in — you!" Leola cried.

He snatched a blanket from the bed and covered Jane. Leola, meanwhile, had dragged her own blanket off the cot, the blue one given her by Shokotee. This blanket too Elias spread over Jane. She lay shivering, as though cold. Leola fetched more candles and lit them and put them in bottles which she put on the table by Jane's head. She brought cobwebs from the corners and soot from the fireplace. She wet pledgets of cloth. Elias pressed the soot and cobwebs into Jane's cut cheek. He packed on the pledgets of wet cloth, staunching the bloodflow.

"See to Jake before we stitch her cheek," says Elias.

Leola kneels by Jake. "Alive," she says. She dashed a dipper of water into the Negro's face and slapped him hard. "Up!" Jake stirred. "On the cot with you!"

Jake groaned.

"Blood! Bodies — what a mess!" she said. Elias helped her and they lifted Jake between them and put him on Leola's cot and she wrapped a wet cloth about Jake's damaged head. Jake gave a croak.

"Scald my curved stitching needle," says Elias. "And bring the stitching thread."

"I'll not! Sew her with a dog needle? I'll not have it!" But Leola knelt at the hearth, nonetheless. She blew on the embers and set fire under the kettle and soon brought it to a simmering boil. She scalded Dog's suturing needle, grumbling as she did it, but it was only noise, after all. She's cool-headed when things get snug, thinks Elias.

She poured hot water in the washbowl and he scrubbed his hands with soap and water and wiped them dry. Then he threaded the suturing needle and lifted the packing away from Jane's cheek. What he saw made something move in his head. This wasn't Jane at all, but a ghastly grinning Thing instead. "Going to stitch you now," he said softly.

That Thing, blood matted in its long, dark hair, nodded.

He began. In the corner of her mouth — the first stitch. He felt her wince. Tears came coursing from Jane's closed eyes. She whimpered.

"Here, wait," says Leola. "Bite a bullet!" The squaw fetched a rifle ball. "Open!" she said. Her lean, dirty fingers thrust the ball between Jane's jaw teeth. "Bite now!" says Leola.

Stitch and tie. Snip with the scissors. Stitch and tie, sponge blood away. Snip the thread. Slowly and steadily he worked, with no thought of anything but the work itself, until all was done. That was the way of him. He drew the edges together neatly as he could. Now he sponged the length of the wound with turpentine, Virgin Dip, of that same lot Jane had soaked his thumb in that day he smashed it.

Leola washed Jane head to foot, put a fresh gown on her and helped her to bed. Jake roused. Elias poured him a cup of whiskey and stirred in a few drops of laudanum. Jake drank it all, coughed, and after a while got up by himself, like a horse that's been stunned. And he said: "Wellum."

They dragged out the corpses. Daylight came quietly filtering out of the forest. While Jake and Elias dug, taking turns with the spade, a chill gray light crossed the river and silently created the opposite shore. Red dawn appeared, a dawn like any other.

Chapter 15

To Jane, suffering in the midst of preparations, it seems someone once had lived here. And had that cot yonder dragged inside and placed against the wall so an old squaw woman, Leola, might snore on it at night.

That same Someone, that young woman, had a string cradle made from a packing box and she hung it from the rafters. There stands the broom in the corner. Curtains the young woman sewed herself by firelight adorn the windows. While a child grew inside her, a child planted in her by the man, she had sat evenings by the firelight sewing. And the man had split shingles to sell in Fort Hill. She had sewed those curtains that blow now, that move a little now and then when the breeze rises from the river.

Quite another person she seems, that sewed those curtains. Not at all like this Someone stretched on the bed, her face swollen, one eye nearly closed, and fever talking endlessly in her head. Turning a bit she sees that Bible the man brought home, still in its place on the mantel. The young woman had even begun to read in it a little before . . . before she died that night; and woke to discover she was someone else, someone damaged.

Beyond the river on the far shore crows have discovered an enemy — hawk or owl. Cawing, they fly to the attack. Closer by meadowlarks whistle from the green land. Screaming and cawing in the distance, placid whistling close by, and wind rising to stir the curtains.

A near neighbor, Dutt Callister's wife, Fancy, she's here. Come to visit and help and to look at the cheek if it's anyways possible to see it, maybe? Leola's saying that as it's now the fourth day today, the bandage might come off. Elias, in the midst of so many preparations, nonetheless agrees. With some soaking the bandage comes away. Jane has no need for the mirror. Only see the look on Fancy Callister's face and know what your own face must be . . . Fancy has plump cheeks, red and healthy; maybe the woods have done her a deal of good since she came down to West Tennessee with Dutt and their many children.

Elias begins removing stitches. Jane closes her eyes. Snip and pull; snip and pull. Jane has watched him take Dog's stitches out the same way after a bear has mauled the poor faithful critter and he's been sewn together again. Snip and pull — from the corner of her mouth to the corner of her eye.

"Don't mind a little drooling," says Leola. She wipes Jane's tender mouth. "Whole of her face droops on that side, don't it?"

"It does droop," says Fancy. "Oh yes!"

Leola wipes Jane's mouth again.

Then Elias is finished. The last stitch is out.

And Leola is saying: "Leastways my little man's milk didn't dry up on us. His Mama Jane can feed him and his Mammy Leola can rock him to sleep."

"And you've got a cow, I see," says Fancy.

Jane nods.

"And a sandstone step in front. It's not a cabin anymore, but a house I'd call it." Looking down at Jane, Fancy sighs.

"What a terror for us all. Robbed stark poor, every last family in the district. The Matthews, the Poes, the Stones. Ellen Poe Ashe's calf is growing up to a strong young bull. That was to be the next thing for me and Dutt when our land was paid for, a cow." Fancy's voice trails away and she sets her lips as though holding pins in them. "That baby of Ellen's, he's looking fat and she's named him Edward. But none I know ever saw his father. Oh, she's brazen all right, Ellen is!"

Leola comes with the hand mirror. "See how it's grown together again?"

Jane turns away on her side.

"Don't want a look?"

Jane wants to lie facing the wall, but can't. Her face on that injured side is still too sore and swollen, too tender. So instead she lies turned halfway and looks upward at the joists and the braces and the undersides of the shingles, trying not to think, staring upward. Damaged, she is, in ways she cannot understand as yet. It's as though she's somehow fallen in upon herself.

A hand squeezes her shoulder. Turning she looks into the expressionless face of Shokotee. He's wearing his hat as he always does in a crisis. He takes a close look at the cut and shakes his head. Pettecasockee appears and has a look. The young brave's face darkens with blood and anger.

Neither speaks. Bustle and preparation, meanwhile, go on as before, in both cabin and yard.

Leola comes to the bed and says to Shokotee, "He had a bad eye and was called *Sim* by the others."

Shokotee nods, expressionless as ever.

Fancy comes holding little Isaac, cuddling him. "Such dimples and dark hair! Um's fat as a butterball," Fancy croons. "Did um's mama get her face all sliced and has an ugly scar and can't hardly speak?"

Elias comes, a jagged black scab over his eye. He takes the baby from Fancy. The men follow him outside.

Jane wants to be up. Fancy and Leola help her down from the bed and seat her in the rocking chair. Leola tucks a blanket about her. Jane feels uneasy behind the eyes. Does she see something others don't see? Fever visions . . .

Pettecasockee and Shokotee step in for a word with Leola. Both go outside again.

"What is it they say?" asks Fancy. "Indian talk?"

"Only that they leave soon," says Leola. "Shokotee says the wrong face was cut, that's all."

"Makes a body uneasy, Indian talk!" says Fancy, taking the chair beside Jane's. "But not you, I guess," she says, turning and looking at Jane, "being as you were raised with it!"

Leola goes to the doorway and receives the baby from Elias.

Shokotee comes in again, his hat firm as ever on his head, his face blood-dark. He speaks to Leola, and stands looking at Jane.

"Now what?" says Fancy.

Jane could tell her, could she speak, that her father says the same thing again, that the wrong cheek has been cut. It is all he says. "The wrong cheek has been cut!" It is Shokotee's way, when angry, to repeat himself and wear his hat.

Fancy cranes about for a look through the doorway at the assembled horses and men, shaggy ponies and Indians in buckskins. While she's having a look Elias comes in, gives the baby a kiss, and turns to Jane, reaching for her hand, giving her hand a squeeze.

"What's all this, Elias?" says Fancy. "What's going on yonder?"

"We're leaving. I'll ride down and see Dutt."

"Dutt? Why would you want to see Dutt, Elias? What for?" says Fancy, her voice rising. "What's going on yonder?"

"A hunt," says Elias.

"What kind of hunt?"

"A little hunt, that's all," says Elias, speaking grimly.

Fancy looks away. "Dutt shan't go," says she in a snappish voice.

"I expect he shall. Wasn't Dutt robbed?" Elias gives her a look.

"No reason Dutt must go," says Fancy.

"He's needed." Elias fetches his guns.

"Jane?" says Fancy. "You won't let Elias go —?"

Jane's swollen, sagging face doesn't change expression. Elias is needed. Elias will go. Jane nods *yes!*

Fancy takes Jane's arm. "Jane! What if they kill him?"

"Elias is going," says Jane in a flat struggling voice, with a hiss that leaks about the edges of her words.

"Calm as that! And you with a baby and you'd let Elias be killed! You with a baby boy! No!"

When nobody speaks, Fancy leaps up from her chair as though stung.

"Indian nonsense!" cries Fancy. "Bring my horse — no, I'll fetch him myself. A body can't stay about with all this Indian nonsense. A body can't even come and visit quiet-like without Indian nonsense!"

She storms out, her eyes squinting tears, her fists clenched at the sides of her head, her lips drawn back in a queer grin of grief, and crying.

Elias follows her out the doorway. "Fancy! Wait —! Jake! Help with Mrs. Callister's horse!"

Jane stands up, trembling. She holds to the unsteady rocking chair. A moment later Fancy gallops away. Slowly Jane sits back down. "Elias —?" She calls, her voice hissing.

The cabin, the clearing, the river, the woods — everything is in a queer calm and silence. "Elias?"

He appears in the doorway. Her heart struggles like a fish. "Elias?" He comes and takes her hand, kneeling beside her.

"All they took was money, Elias. So many to go, so many to die and be hurt. Nevermind my face. I need you here. Dutt's family needs him. Elias, please?"

"And next be murdered in our beds?" says Elias. "But I'm leaving Jake."

"If you go, take him," says Jane. "It's wrong of me to ask you not to go. No — go along. And Jake must go help. We'll manage." She squeezes his hand in both of her own hands, not wanting to let him go. Just the same squeeze she squeezed when Isaac was on the way. "If Dutt goes, tell Fancy I said come here and bring the children if that will help. Tell her —"

He will, says Elias. He'll be careful and not get hurt. He'll be home again, he promises. But he must be leaving now, and he kisses her. She knows she may never see him alive again. Goodbye, Elias. She must let go. Goodbye, then. Nevermind about us here at home. We'll manage. Only look out for yourself! Kill them — have no mercy on them, Elias? How can she tell all she wants to say? She must release him.

She lets go and follows him to the door. "Goodbye!" she whispers. So strong and live, so erect, and his face fierce. He's up, his horse under him now. They leave, Jake close behind Elias on an Indian pony. Pettecasockee is looking stern. They raise a shrill shout. The entire little band starts away south, across the creek. Jane watches, no longer sure which one is Elias. Their shrill keening rings in her head. It joins the fever and swirls there . . .

Leola helps her to bed. "Lie down. Didn't I say wars take men? Tried to tell you, I did. Will you stay awake?"

"Yes," Jane says.

"Then only Isaac will sleep," says Leola.

Thus begins the watching. For should the women sleep the men might be caught unawares. Leola busies herself. She's pointing every knife and tool and needle northwest, including Jane's scissors, *northwest*. Can she know the enemy is there? She turns every edged and pointed thing in the cabin to the west and north. Can she know something?

Jane struggles not to sleep. Thoughts swallow the tails of thoughts. Leola sits by the bed, whispering. Night comes, and with it the chorus of night creatures; wild voices from river and forest.

Chapter 16

From the instant he left Redleaves with his father Pettecasockee wondered every moment what might come next.

And because he had never taken part in any sort of fighting, everything seemed wondrously new. All things appeared in sharp contrast to everything that had been before. The grass by the road was a paler green than he had ever seen it. His horse, Shugganah, went more eagerly. Even Shokotee was changed. He was both younger and livelier than Pettecasockee had ever seen him. He knew that his father had killed men, but until now he had never realized it.

At Oakleigh they no sooner said farewells to Jane and Leola and little Isaac, than it seemed they were riding into Dutt Callister's clearing. There, at a word from Elias, Dutt made short work of saddling his horse and fetching his guns. Andrew and Werdna, the Poe brothers, were gathered the same way. And meanwhile this volunteer and that one dashed to Elias, who headed the column (for such it had now become) and offered to gallop ahead to other clearings and scour along the creeks and gather neighbors living off the distant byroads and cart tracks.

Pettecasockee strove to make sure he did nothing to betray the full extent of his own eagerness and energy. Although he was one of the best riders and had, in Shugganah, perhaps the fastest horse in the district, he made no move to volunteer to ride away and gather men from distant clearings. For him it was essential that he remain where he was, with the main body. Otherwise he might miss something.

Their number steadily increased. By the time they reached Fort Hill a feverish, mysterious momentum had seized them. The volunteers felt disdain for everyone who could not or would not be a part of the expedition. Any man left behind was to be pitied!

Riding into Fort Hill Pettecasockee hoped that a certain girl might see him. He was just harboring this hope and savoring its fullness when he realized that his father had spoken.

Shokotee offered him the choice of going with the other volunteers to requisition powder and shot and firearms from the merchants, or of going with him, Shokotee, "to call upon someone."

"Chatillion?" Pettecasockee asked.

"Not Chatillion," Shokotee replied.

Partly because he was curious, but mostly because he feared coming face-to-face with Henri Chatillion, his father-in-law-to-be, if he went requisitioning, Pettecasockee said: "I will go with you."

"Come then!"

Leaving the main body Pettecasockee felt a stabbing thought. Had he made a right choice? Would he miss something after all? He was on the point of riding back up the hill to rejoin the others when Shokotee reined in before that bleak, oblong structure which Pettecasockee recognized as the Snail's place of business and living quarters. Dismounting, Pettecasockee tied Shugganah's reins to the hitching rail alongside his father's big gelding. Following Shokotee into the building, he observed how abruptly his father opened the door, and how, after Pettecasockee had entered, he slammed the door violently shut.

The crash startled a dignified mulatto woman. She dropped her sewing and stood up from the table where she had been sitting. Her mouth was open. Her tall, full figure stooped in a curtsy as Shokotee spoke, saying:

"Fetch him here." Quietly, just that, no more.

Leaned against the south wall flanking the window were six coffins — four large, two small. The woman hurried to the back rooms, heedless of her sewing crumpled on the floor. Pettecasockee suppressed an urge to pick it up for her.

Then the Snail appeared. To Pettecasockee it seemed that he should have known the Snail was the "person" his father must come to see.

To judge his appearance, the Snail was ill, for he spoke in a strange cadence as though just waked from a deep sleep. "Gentlemen? Please sit down!"

They sat, all three, in straight chairs the servant woman brought from the north wall. As quietly and as swiftly as she had brought the chairs she picked up her sewing and left the room. A long silence intervened. Shokotee sat very still, his hands folded upon one knee of his deerskin riding britches. The Snail's childlike hands moved down slowly to the sides of his chair and took hold of the seat, gripping it. His eyes wavered back and forth as he looked from one of his visitors to the other. His suit was pale yellow and his brown vest was adorned with a thin gold chain.

"He carries a watch," thought Pettecasockee, whereupon, for the first time, he heard the watch ticking.

"The wrong face!" said Shokotee suddenly. "Cut!"

"I know," said the Snail. "I know!" He swallowed then, and licked his lips.

"Eye to mouth!" said Shokotee. "Cut!"

The Snail was trembling. Loosing a hand from his chair seat, he slowly wiped his trembling mouth. "Ah —!" he began. He drew a breath.

"Her blood is my blood. You helped. You as much as made the cut yourself."

"Shokotee! Not true!"

Shokotee stood up slowly. His pocket derringer, as though by magic, appeared in his hand. Like a soldier jumping to attention, the Snail popped to his feet. Shokotee fired point-blank.

Trembling and grunting the Snail hunched inward. He clutched his middle, covering a dark, spreading stain. Then with a queer, mechanical movement he sat down again. His large head rolled back and then came forward. His pupils were large and dark and he stared at Shokotee without moving.

Shokotee meanwhile reloaded, tipping a powder charge into the derringer's muzzle from a tiny silver flask. Without a quiver he seated the ball, primed the pan, and deftly thrust everything into the large pocket of his black riding coat. He smoothed his hat brim.

"Why did you shoot?" grunted the Snail.

"Because you'd have ridden ahead of us and warned them. Why deny it?"

Chapter 17

The wound scab above Elias's eye broke open. He tied a cloth about his head, cutting th strip from his shirttail. On he rode. Blood dried in his eyebrow and his beard, and a pain, where Sim Hornby's knife had scraped his skull, made him squint.

While resting and letting their horses drink it was decided that they should elect a leader. Dutt spoke for Elias. Shokotee seconded the choice.

A show of hands. Elias was leader, with blood in his beard and squinting wrath in his eyes and a rag covering the crab-shaped cut Hornby had given him. It pained him to wear his hat and he carried it tied to his saddle. And hatless he was shaggy and terrible, bearlike in his anger. His rage seemingly was communicated to Rattler; big, ranging Rattler with rolling eyes, now a war-horse, yet the same old horse Elias brought along when he came to settle.

Leading Rattler out front where both he and the horse could be seen Elias stood silent at first. His head was sore, his nose was skinned, giving it a certain prominence. His open shirt revealed a powerful neck, the swell of big shoulders. He cleared his throat.

"Any son of a bitch won't fight, I'll personally shoot him dead. I want the six best horses and riders for scouts. The rest stay with me. Dutt Callister and Shokotee McNeilly are my lieutenants. Question?" There were none.

He turned, stepping his foot in the stirrup, swung up, and let old Rattler step out. "Forward!"

Pettecasockee rode alongside and offered for a scout. Then others. The six best took their orders. "Watch for ambush!" They rode ahead of the main column, on out of sight.

Shokotee drew in beside.

"They believe you," he said.

"Good," said Elias.

Dutt Callister, the husband and father who but a few hours earlier had been promising his wife, Fancy, that he would not leave home, waited in darkness. He stood in a mosquito-ridden thicket less than a mile from the east bank edge of the Mississippi River. Like the other volunteers he awaited the return of Pettecasockee. The young brave had ridden ahead to scout the ferry landing.

In his mind's eye he saw Fancy counting and naming the neighbors on her fingers. She had seemed comforted that so many had been afflicted. "Isn't only us — it's everybody," Fancy had said over and over again. Then: "You won't go, will you, Dutt?" And he had given his solemn promise. He would stay home where he belonged. He had solemnly said that since the same thing had happened to so many others, there would be no need after all for himself to be up in arms over it.

Thus had he spoken and reasoned with perfect logic until Elias had knocked on the door and called to him. Try as he would, Dutt couldn't remember what Elias had said. Almost nothing, yet more than enough; for Dutt no sooner saw others in his clearing, mounted and dressed for the expedition, than he knew he too must go. Those reasons why he must not go suddenly evaporated without a trace.

Elias McCutcheon exerted a power over men. You didn't tell him no.

As for Fancy, she had seemed almost glad to see Dutt break his promise. It gave her all the excuse she needed to raise her loud voice and predict to the children that their father, who of his own accord and for no earthly reason was going away, would never again be seen alive by any of them. And much more:

"Tell your father goodbye. He's going away of his own accord to be killed," says Fancy. The older ones tune up and start crying right away. The girls cling to his legs. "Don't go, Daddy! Don't go! Please!" they shriek. And now the younger ones tune up. "Don't go away to be killed!"

It had been a fine scene, such as Fancy always enjoyed, a scene to remember. Fancy had wanted it and she had gotten it and wouldn't let Dutt so much as give her a kiss goodbye.

"If you want to go away and be killed why should you want a kiss from me? No, go on, be killed. But don't expect me to kiss you for it. Go —! Don't try to kiss me now that you're going!"

"Not even on the cheek?"

"Go! Leave us. It's what you've always wanted! Go!"

And the children made such a shrill cry it had hurt his eardrums. He had ridden away feeling cursed. That was Fancy's way, to put a cloud over him when she got a chance.

Long since, Dutt Callister had come to conclude that marriages were created in heaven for the punishment of creatures below. God's special slavery.

When Pettecasockee finally returned he brought word of three boats and five boatmen and a campfire and a pushed-down cottonwood. A second scouting party went now to capture the boatmen and the boats while the main body prepared to follow at a slow pace. Dutt tightened his saddle girth and mounted his horse and prepared to ride with the main crowd to the river.

By the time they reached the camp and saw the pushed-down cottonwood everything had been put in order there. Four were hanging by the neck from another cottonwood, the fifth was a captive. He would serve to guide them. A stork-like fellow with a large Adam's apple and a long stride, he had somehow been spared. Somehow he was not like the other four who had been members of Chatwood's gang. No, this guide, Bill was his name, Bill was different. He knew everything about the defenses of the Horse Pens, where guards and sentinels were posted, how every house stood and who lived there, how many were sick and how many were well, how many horses there were. "Just above two hundred and eleven head," says this fellow, Bill, and his eyes narrow a little as though he's thinking to make sure there is no mistake, proud of his accuracy in every department. "Now we can't go for them over the main road," says Bill. Wonder of wonders, Bill's joined the volunteers. Maybe those four things hanging by the neck from the cottonwood helped Bill make his decision. "We can't land on the other bank in the regular place. Need to drop us down to another place I know." Bill was the soul of willingness, ready to do anything he could to help. Perhaps it hurt his feelings a little that he was not trusted with a gun, but if his feelings were bad hurt he didn't show it.

It occurs to Dutt that one in five will be like Bill. One in five will be able to make quick decisions and leap to the winning side before it's too late.

The horses had to be put over. Dutt went with the first boat as a horse holder. Bill took them below the tip of the between island and then let them drop a way downstream before he whispered for oars. Presently all three boats made the dark shore and the horses were quietly unloaded. The boats were shoved off again and Dutt with two others was left to wait. They had been warned not to talk. The river lay terribly quiet beside him and beyond in the woods there was too much silence to suit him. Perhaps he should have stayed at home after all, he thought. Anyone can hold horses. He waited. The other two must have been as uneasy as he was.

"Wonder would it be all right to smoke?" said one at last.

"No!" said another.

Silence.

They had put all their trust in Bill. They had ridden all this way until now without mishap. They hadn't needed Bill to find their way the entire distance to the ferry landing and now they had put themselves into the hands of an enemy, Bill Somebody, and he had got the horses over at a spot nobody but himself could ever hope to find again, even if he could do it. They only had his word on it that he knew what he was about. It seemed to Dutt that he would never see his family again. Then it seemed to him that he would never again see those others Bill was supposed to be bringing over. Ultimately Chatwood and his gang would walk out of the woods and take the horses for themselves and treat Dutt and the two with him to a taste of greased rope. Crow bait, Dutt was thinking, when I should be at home. Haven't a damned bit of business being here, I haven't!

More silence.

Then a noise in the woods. It was men, no doubt. It was something creeping in the woods — human footsteps. Closer and closer. Then nothing. Surrounded, thinks Dutt, cut off from any hope of escape. He begins to sweat. His fingers cramp he holds the reins in such a grip. He's begun thinking that if he merely wrapped the reins on a limb then he could slip quietly into the river and drift down aways. He's thinking how to save himself when in the edge of his vision he sees something on the river — a dark shape. Then it divides — three dark shapes. The boats! They come steadily on, larger and larger. Who but good, reliable Bill could have done such a thing? They land precisely where they landed before and the men step ashore. It takes a while for each to locate his horse. They mount then and ride a while, until it seems to Dutt that they must be heading for California. Bill, thinks Dutt, must have done the same to a dozen expeditions before, winding them around until they are lost in the Missouri bottoms, at the mercy of Chatwood's merciless bandits.

At last they stop. The plan unfolds. Seven of the best riders will take the high ground to the main road leading into the Horse Pens. The main body will wade the swamp, leaving their horses here, and will form a skirmish line on the high ground behind the Horse Pens. At a signal the mounted men will dash into the village for a feint, a demonstration, a frontal attack. Then the main body will make the assault — going it afoot — upon the flank.

Just how Elias's plan unfolds is not something easily known. It seems, almost, to unfold itself. Perhaps Shokotee has had something to say about it. Pettecasockee is to lead the mounted assault upon the main road. Perhaps that young man, despite all his youth, has had a say in it; who's to know or care? The plan, as unfolded, makes sense. Surprise is the key. They all know that much. The seven are shown to the main road over the high ground. More waiting. The night is wearing away. Now the horses are left in the company of two men, and Dutt, like everyone else with the main body, must sling his powder horn high up under his chin and hold his guns over his head for the walk through the swamp single file in utter darkness. Dutt wished that it had fallen out so that he might have been one of the horse holders waiting now behind, back in the woods. They were wading now, and the swamp got deeper and deeper. It gave up bubbles at every step. Floating tree trunks had to be pushed aside. Anyone unlucky enough to step into a stump hole would be over his head. "Bit more to the right! Hole ahead! Shhh! We're near the road!"

When it seemed that Bill had made terrible miscalculation and was about to drown them all, the word whispered down that the high ground was finally located.

Just when it seemed to Dutt that this must be a rumor, the ground rose a little and a little more and the water became shallower and shallower until all that remained underfoot was a fetid mire. Then they touched leaves and dry ground again. Presently the skirmish line was formed, all done in darkness, and Dutt like the others was obliged to endure more waiting. Gave him a chance to wring out his socks and pour the water out of his boots. While he sat he felt his clothes begin to dry a little. He made sure of his shot pouch and powder horn. At last there was nothing for him but the waiting itself.

Fancy would be sleeping now. The kids would all be asleep, perhaps wondering in their little dreams if they'd ever see Daddy alive again. As for Fancy, she wouldn't be bothered. She knew well enough Dutt was coming home again. Otherwise she'd have no victim to torment.

And as to how she tormented him, he knew it all too well. She got herself pregnant, that's how. Pregnant and pregnant again and some more pregnant and always pregnant, always whining, always ready with a complaint. As time went it seemed to Dutt that she tried to make herself ugly as possible. And she talked in a loud voice, pointed her finger when she talked, and made her eyes swell and roll in their sockets. "Tell your father goodbye. He's going away of his own accord to be killed."

Chapter 18

Jasper Coon, he was a Free-Soiler and had not wanted to come along. Had claimed his horse was lame. They had loaned him a horse. Had said his gunstock was broke. God damn, they loaned him a shotgun!

He lived in the woods between the Poe, Callister and McCutcheon clearings and didn't bother trees with his ax very much, no, and he'd hollowed him a log which he kept in his cabin for a bed so as to separate him from his dogs when he slept. Six dogs to leave and none to feed 'em, he'd said, and God damn they sent one of the Callister kids a-running, half-growed little shaver he was, and pledged he'd feed the God damn dogs, so he would, and water 'em too.

So Jasper didn't have shit for luck, no. And was a Free-Soiler himself and didn't want no kind of nigger about him and there Elias McCutcheon had brung his nigger along to rub it in, maybe, on such as didn't own a slave, aye, rub their noses.

Jasper had done a hitch in the artillery and here on this raid they hadn't no guns along, so why make *him* go? But God damn they wouldn't take *no* and here he set aslapping mosquitoes, God damn and saddlesore as a widow's boil for it was not his way to go a-straddle of his horse, his horse was too God damn old for one and too God damn mean for two and for three wasn't no count but for packing in venison or bear or what-have-you, was *his* only good, except only to kick the buttery shit out of the very soul that fed him. Retired artillery nag that's all he was but he was enough and would bite to boot. Bite wasn't no word for it!

"God damn my ass is raw," he whispers and wonders what in Cooty Brown that God damn little Indian peckerwood can be a-doing so long there by the river. Then it happened that his horse, the one he'd been a-riding and suffering on — his horse shifted and stepped on his foot. He yelped and here come Elias hisself out of the black dark of nowheres and jerks him back and forth and breathes on him right heavy and says the next one to let out anything — let alone a *fart* — gets his head blowed from between his God damn shoulders!

Aye, so his foot was sore and would of been broke sure but that the mud was soft and he thought, hating the horse: "Wouldn't I beat your ass off could I git you off by yourself, wouldn't I take a limb to your head!" He give him an elbow then and the horse grunted and stepped on somebody on the other side of him and that fellow only groaned and mentioned in whispers how he thought his foot was broke, maybe, and God *damn* couldn't whoever was holding that shitkicker, couldn't he let him place his hoof somewhere's else but on somebody's feet?

When he stopped his groaning and whispering Jasper Coon whispered and asked:

"How's your foot?"

Silence.

"Hope your foot don't hurt!"

Silence.

"I'm sure sorry about your God damn foot. Now you know by God how mine feels, don't you? Yes, by God. I never ast to come along in the first God damn place I never. I was in the artillery, you know that? Well, I was. And I can tell you I know something and ever God damn one of us is bound to git his head blowed off or cut off by this bunch of cunts — sure, you think they ain't the meanest worst batch of piratey cunts ever smelled shit?"

"Cunts?" A whisper.

"Cunts —" whispers Jasper Coon. "Anything mean as them devils I call 'em cunts, I do. Cunts — wait and see if they ain't and never a single gun do we have if I had a gun, by God damn wouldn't I show you some real shit, so I would!"

"Shut up, can you? What's your name, anyhow?"

"Nevermind my name, asshole!" whispers Jasper. "You'll not remember your own name onct we cross that God damn river and mind my words we have to cross it by God or git blowed down by Elias McCutcheon? *Wisht* I'd a-never heard *his* name!"

Silence. Mosquitoes. Cunts, thinks Jasper Coon. His foot gives him a slow pang. Cunting horse, he thinks.

Then he's thirsty. "Hey, thar, asshole? Got a canteen?"

Someone passes a canteen. He takes a long swig.

"How about a breast and a drumstick? Piece of bread? Pone of hoecake — anybody? Hssst! Ain't none of you bastards got *nothing* to eat?"

Pretty soon he had all he could eat and more. He dropped his leftovers in his leather foraging bag. He was by God not short on experience when it came to a campaign, no he wasn't.

He'd have laid hisself down for a nap then, Jasper Coon would. Had some other poor bastard hold the luckless cunting reins and had him a nap, but he sensed it wasn't time enough remaining for a nap, no, and besides he didn't want his head blowed off by Elias, no. One *look* and you knew by

God *he'd* do it. He wasn't no paper officer, not him, he was a cob, he was, and he wouldn't need him no God damn firing squad to get the job done, no. Do it his own self, pow! Elias would, quick as spit, and no matter if a man was a Free-Soiler and Elias has hisself a God damn nigger on his place, you had to like McCutcheon for the fact that he was gonna kill you he'd God damn well pull the trigger hisself . . .

Chapter 19

Elias kept Jake near him. Master and man sat resting their backs against the same tree, facing the Horse Pens. They knew the direction by the sounds of a restless dog. Now and then the creature barked.

Presently, as though touched by a mysterious hand, the whipoorwills which had made ceaseless chorus, suddenly hushed. The bullfrogs that had burbled deep notes from the bottoms far and near on every side, went silent.

Thus they knew the approach of day. They waited. Now begins the owl talk between Pettecasockee and his mounted volunteers and Shokotee with the foot skirmishers.

*Hoo-ah-hoo-hoo!*Close and querulous, an owl sensing day. He calls his mate. Let's seek the deep shade?

Hoo-ah! The lofting answer from beyond the Horse Pens. Then silence.

"Didn't I know it was men I'd be *sure* it was owls," says Jake in a whisper. "What do they say?"

"Shokotee tells them wait yet a while. Isn't light enough yet. Pettecasockee is too eager. Wants to ride in too soon."

"They say all that," whispers Jake. "All that." And then: "How did *you* learn it?"

"My daddy. He knew the talk. In his day you knew the difference between owls and men or you didn't live long to get old."

More owl talk. Silence.

"Now what they say?"

"Pettecasockee finds no sentinels nor outposts, no pickets nor lookouts. Shokotee says we have found none. Pettecasockee wants to ride now. Shokotee says not yet."

"I never been in a fight," said Jake.

"Aim low. When we first started hunting together you shot high — remember?"

"Yes. My arm trembled."

"Make yourself crack down."

"Crack down."

"Stay by me. Minute you shoot, fall down. Crawl to a tree. Kneel behind it to reload. Twelve buckshot each barrel."

"My arms tremble," said Jake. "What they say now?"

"Not long to wait," said Elias.

"I see houses," said Jake.

Below them, beyond high trees, the little cluster of houses had emerged veiled in the damp first mist, in first light. They saw peaceful, rude habitations with honest mud chimneys. Black washpots stood in the yards. A covered well was in the midst, between the surrounding houses. The freight wagons stood in the sheds, shafts down. Beyond was a long building, a warehouse perhaps, much like Chatillion's trading post, with the same long look and the same high porch. The houses were on stilts and a mound had been raised inside the horse lots.

Owl talk.

"Here it comes," said Elias. "Stay by me now." Elias stood and whistled. He waved his arm.

"You'll be all right," said Elias. "Stay close to the trees."

They went forward. From beyond the cluster of stilt houses came a stir and commotion. The restless dog began barking excitedly.

"Here they come!" Jake shouted. "Crack down!"

When Shokotee's permission came Pettecasockee signaled "Here we come!" He leaped to Shugganah's back.

Like himself the other six were small and wiry, none above a hundred and sixty pounds, most nearer a hundred and forty. Every one was mounted on his own horse. "Full speed! Kill everything that moves!" Two were braves like Shokotee, the rest were young settlers. Their lives had been horses and guns, shooting and riding. Now at last they would shoot and ride at something besides stumps and blazed trees.

Their horses bunched together and boiled forward in a braced leap. From standstill to full gallop they went, racing for the clearing. Pettecasockee bent forward, low upon Shugganah's neck. Before, while it was still dark, the riders had made a promise between them that if any were hit or lost his horse another would bring him out. If need be all would ride back to bring out another. Capture would mean torture first, death afterward. So they had agreed — no one would be left behind. It had seemed proper and exactly the right thing to make that pact. Nothing else, as Pettecasockee saw it, would have been proper. Nothing else could have given each man such a full measure of exhilaration. Pettecasockee was sure that what he felt was shared by the other six. Turning his head so as to listen, putting his ear to the wind of his progress, he heard the dog barking. He put all his trust in Shugganah to take him in and bring him out again and to keep the road. The dog barked on, the final stretch of the road swung into view and with it the entire little village of wet, stilted cabins, wattle chimneys, and packed, naked yards. He flashed past the horse lots and smelled the kept odors of livestock rising from those low-lying sheds. Then as though in a vision he saw everything about him all at once, and everything was quiet and clear and precise as the green grass by the roadside had seemed when he had first taken the road to come here. The weeds at the corners of the cabins, the roofed well in the middle of the compound. It was just as Pettecasockee had imagined it would be and at the same time it was entirely different. Expectation and reality instantly fused; everything about him was at one and the same time both larger and smaller. He was so absorbed with the newness of the experience that it came to him, too late, that he had forgotten to yell. The other six, holding back perhaps on his account, had not yelled either. As a consequence they had made one complete circuit before the houses and about the well without having seen a soul and without firing a shot. Then Pettecasockee yelled, the long, shivering sound was taken up by the other six.

And at that moment a figure in white appeared from a doorway and stood out upon a cabin porch. Pettecasockee saw it was a woman raising a rifle to her shoulder, taking aim at him. Riding dead on at the porch Pettecasockee raised his shotgun a trifle, pulled the trigger, and blew her head off, knocking her backwards, headless, through the dark doorway. This he saw all in a split instant as he swerved through the blue gunsmoke, almost brushing the porch steps in his passage. He saw a half-naked man with a bald spot making for the rail fence, running barefoot, a long gun in his right hand. When Pettecasockee pulled the trigger the man was in the midst of vaulting the fence. His arms flew outward, his gun went tumbling away. His back, blackened by powderburn, was torn open between the shoulder blades. As he fell Shugganah veered to avoid the fence.

More people were on the porches now. Pettecasockee took the reins in his teeth and as he pushed the empty shotgun into one saddle scabbard he withdrew the loaded one with his left hand. Still clamping the reins in his teeth he charged a porch on which three men were standing. He let go both barrels and, emerging through the gunsmoke cloud, he saw that the charge had cleared the porch. Buckshot had cracked into the logs leaving white scars beside the doorway. The three on the porch had been hurled flat. Between the crack and roar of guns he heard the shriek of a woman and the insistent crying of a child. And as he pushed the empty shotgun into the scabbard beneath his leg a big fellow with a red beard leaped from behind a cabin square into Shugganah's path. Raising an ax with a blade as bright as new money, poising it high over his head, he prepared to strike the horse. His mouth was open, his blue eyes were wide and bulging. His thick lips were drawn back to show stained, yellow teeth. Snatching a pistol from his belt, Pettecasockee leaned sideways, giving Shugganah a nudge which broke his stride. Surprise was reflected in Redbeard's face. He swung his ax too soon. It bit nothing but air. Pettecasockee shot him in the mouth, the ax fell, the man toppled backward, and Pettecasockee let go a shrill yell.

Turning for a glimpse behind him he saw the other six, firing from their saddles. Bending down, Pettecasockee spurred Shugganah and made a dash for the leaf-framed tunnel of the road, the others bunching behind him. They flew bucketing back into the gloom from which they had just emerged, skimming the low, misty ground. Then with a sudden movement they leaped down and pulled their horses into a thicket and tethered them. Reloading, they stationed themselves by the road, stretching prone in the grass to make ambush. With each hard breath Pettecasockee saw the grass move in front of him. The dew beneath held a cool, drenching quality. The ground seemed to welcome his body. He was sweating.

"Don't see him," said a voice.

"Nevermind, he'll come. I seen him saddling."

"Mind and don't shoot too soon."

Pettecasockee saw three mounted men.

"Him," he whispered. The three drew even with the ambush, and there was a burst. Two slumped out of their saddles and fell. The third went by but caught a charge of buckshot from behind. Lurching to one side his foot jammed the stirrup. His body struck the ground and went flailing up again and down until he was dragged out of sight. The two horses with empty saddles stopped and after a brief pause they began cropping grass at the roadside.

The man who had fallen nearest to Pettecasockee was not quite dead. He struggled, twisting around. There was blood on his tow-colored hair. His head bobbed unsteadily. Up he came up on all fours. His bloody arm moved. Finding his pistol, he pointed it straight at Pettecasockee and he cocked the pistol and pulled the trigger — it snapped. Pettecasockee, meanwhile, drew his own pistol. Without taking aim he pulled the trigger and shot Bob Chatwood dead.

Ponselle, Sim Hornby's woman, she heard owls. They waked her with talk back and forth. She pushed Sim's shoulder. She said about the owls. He said God damn a no-count nigger *would* wake him, didn't she know he was asleep? Since his return he had been into the rum every night and he stank of it. Was it some reason, he wanted to know, she couldn't let him get his nap out without all time waking him by God to listen at owls? When but in the middle of the night were owls supposed to talk nohow?

And Ponselle, Sim Hornby's woman, she slept again. But the owls were still talking. She slept but she was uneasy and he was on the rum again with the bottle on the table by his side of the bed where he could reach it and he stank of it and in her dream she smelled it. Something struck the porch steps. She woke and heard horses galloping and knew it was dirt striking the steps — thrown by the hooves. She got up and looked out and saw them and went to the bed and pushed his shoulder. She said to him about the horses but his answer was he hit her twice before she could get away from him, on the breast and on the neck and would have come after her except that the yelling commenced and then gunfire. It dawned on him that it was something more than just owls and horses. Dirt hit the steps again. He looked out. "Indians," he said.

She was gathering the children and pushing them under the bed. Fetching the gun from the corner, she tried to shoot through the window. She tried for one of the horses as it was bigger and looked easier than trying for the rider, but the gun snapped. She cocked and it snapped again. It was unloaded. She saw Red McQuiddy with an ax, barefooted, trying for the horse himself. Then his head was in smoke and he fell down out of the smoke; the ax dropped and Red lay where he had fallen while the last of them poured back into the road that crossed the swamp to the landing, into that leaftunnel; they flew like creatures sucked away, quick as thistle; gone. A man, she could not tell who, stood in the grass sagging against the fence, supporting himself, both hands on the fence. Beyond him she saw the garden where just yesterday she cut cabbage sprouts. The bean vines stood peaceful and undisturbed. The children started to moan because Sim was yelling at them to shut up and she turned around and saw that he had gotten one boot on and couldn't find the other. It was on the floor, plain in front of him. Turning again to the window she saw movement down at the horse lots. Some had gotten bridles on and were cinching their saddles. Soon as foot hit stirrup they went riding out, full speed through the gate and making a leaning turn, sucked into the road, swallowed out of sight. A fourth hit the stirrup and was not quite even in the saddle good, heading for the road opening when he backed on the reins and dug his heels into his horse's flanks. He brought the horse up on two legs in a rearing stop. She heard guns from the road and guns from the high ground away to her right, a rolling crackle of guns. The rider turned his horse and dashed back towards the well. His horse sank, as though floundering in mud. Its forelegs buckled. It rolled against the wall of the well, head struggling to be up, legs thrashing . . .

Sim found the other boot. He was stomping into it. Through the door and down the steps he stumbled while she was screaming at him not to go. He tripped near the bottom, fell and broke his gunstock. His cap fell away. He got up, first hobbling, then sprinting, dropping the stock-broken gun, and going clean across the compound to the storehouse. Rabbitlike he dived under it, out of sight. Something hard, like gravel was striking the outer walls of the house. She knew it was rifle balls. She stayed where she was. She saw skirmishers running and stooping, tree to tree, log to bush. She saw blurts of smoke where they fired. Converging, they came in a thin line, making a coil of little squatting, moving figures. Into the garden they sprang, stooping and squatting among the bean vines. Others were hiding in the corn. She found the squirrel gun and, though trembling, loaded it. She stepped out on the porch. Her shot went wild. No use, she was thinking. No use. Garden ruint anyhow. No use . . .

Stillness. Silence.

"Everybody out on the porches! Come down slowly! Hands over your heads!"

She went to the back door thinking to take the children and leave that way. Below she saw a man with a shotgun, waiting on the ground, on guard.

She knelt by the bed and pulled the children out and started them to the front door. Pushing and herding them ahead of her onto the high porch, she started down the steps with them. They clung to her legs so she could hardly move.

When finally they reached the bottom they sat down on the step as they were told. Beside the dead horse lay a man with his lower jaw shot half away. He moved, making sounds. He raised his arm. On steps nearby, below the next porch, sits a man with his arms folded about his middle. His entrails are spilling. In the weeds by the fence, pink blood bubbling from a hole in his lung, every breath making a sucking noise, lies the man who had been leaning against the fence.

Blood drips from the porches into stillness, into silence. Smoke drifts sideways, wafting, ghosting towards the river. The captives — the wounded and unhurt men and boys — are gathered and herded in about the well. Their faces have a stunned and stony look. The man with the shattered jaw makes a struggling effort. He stands up, waves his arms, and falls drunkenly, backwards over the dead horse. The prisoners seem not to notice. They look upward instead at the crabwise progress of the smoke. The wind marches it slowly and easily into the trees. The smoke is moved away.

Mounted men appear behind the ones on foot. Each rider has a shotgun in his hand. They trot out of the leaf tunnel and make a semicircle. Two horses with empty saddles follow, bridles dragging the dust. The stiff-eyed prisoners stand helpless beside the well, waiting . . .

A searching party stoops for a look under the storehouse.

The shouts of the searchers can be heard in the woods. Others are searching the pens and the sheds. "Come out! Hands up! Out before I shoot!" She watches while they fetch Sim from under the storehouse. They drag him out like a doll. He finds his feet. Then she sees that he has his boots on the wrong feet. The children press close to her, watching, clinging to her skirt. Sim seems not to see her. There is a stiffness about his eyes. Sim does not look her way. The other prisoners also seem stiff about the eyes, the same as Sim.

The children, staring at the horse, push one another. "Dead horse," they whisper. "Horse is dead."

Beyond a way she saw ropes being thrown up over the low limbs of trees. The ropes flew snaking through the air and came coiling down again. The nooses, one by one, were tied. From the woods now and then came more sounds of shooting as though hunters were hunting there. Hunters, she thought.

When they came for Sim they bound his hands behind him. He didn't show anything. The stiff look reached into his eyes. He was silent, and his boots on the wrong feet. They marched him to the nearest tree and put him face backwards astride a big, brown horse. An Indian rode in and slipped a noose about his neck. When the brown horse was led from under him he quietly dangled, kicking. She tucked her head down and could not look.

A Negro stood before her, a slave he was, like herself. He demanded her name. She told him. The children shrank against her.

Jake. He was Jake McCutcheon, he said. Then he spoke kindly. "Walk for me." Her oldest girl took the baby from her lap. Ponselle walked. "Run back and forth a little," he said. Next he asked to see her teeth, smelled her breath, asked to see her tongue. "If I can manage it I'll get you and these chillun for my master's portion. That way you won't be separated."

"Who is he?"

"Elias McCutcheon. He's a kind man. In the huntin' shirt there."

"Wearin' a beard, the big man?"

"Yes. Your husband was Sim Hornby?"

"Yes."

"Let me see what I can do," he said.

She looked at her feet, thinking that the garden was trampled, remembering what hopes she had held for it.

She looked up. They had opened the storehouse and begun the inventory — bags of coffee, hogsheads of sugar, quarter-casks of rifle powder, kegs of rum, barrels of whiskey, cases of crockery . . .

Hornby, he was hanging dead. The storehouse had been his pride. Her man; his pride.

They were making a list. Each box, barrel, bale and crate was brought into the sunlight. Everything was being sorted.

She heard the voices. "Still in the cases, two and one half thousand muskets with accouterments . . ."

"Very well," says a man. They've set him up a table and a chair. He sits and writes. "Very well," says he, now and then — writing, scratching the silence. "Very well!" in a singsong voice.

She can see a green fly trying to light on his cheek.

"Item. Quartercasks of rifle powder, three hundred . . ."

"Very well."

A strongbox was brought and broken. A wiry Indian, older than the others, supervised the counting of the money. He wore a black hat. His eyes squinted now and then.

More crates from the storehouse. "Knives, six- to nine-inch blade, good quality, two thousand."

"Very well."

"Flints, four thousand."

"Very well."

"Lead, independent of ball for muskets —"

"Very well —"

"Two thousand pounds."

"Three thousand bushels of corn." Pause. "Saddles . . ."

The servant man, Jake, was talking to his master. Both were looking at her. Jake came to her again. "Get first in line when they call for darkies."

"Tobacco, twelve hogsheads . . ."

She drew a deep breath.

"*Very well*!" cries the clerk.

"Be ready now," says Jake.

Shooting ain't over till Jasper Coon makes himself a little fire and scours up some bacon and a skillet and a basket of eggs, and he's frying bacon and then frying eggs and downing captured coffee and captured whiskey — quick as that. Eats him his meal and next drags him a pallet of captured blankets to a shade tree opposite of where the hangings are taking place and there lays him down and sleeps like a babe and everybody else so busy either counting or looting or hanging or hunting or haggling over how many head of niggers this or that one deserves, that nobody bothered with Jasper, not waking him nor trying to put him to work, but letting him sleep like a babe. Things he had learned in the artillery came handy to him now. He knew, by God, that drinking and eating and sleeping had to be accomplished the minute there was a chance for it. He knew to cook and to drink up and eat up all he could and to set back some things in a bundle for later.

After his nap he wipes his mouth, has him another pull of whiskey, wipes his mouth again and sidles like, skirting the edges of things, and looking about with a practiced eye until he sees what it is he wants next. Mayhap she's not the prettiest of the women captives, no. She's cross-eyed and red-nosed and her front teeth were knocked out — her yellow dress is spattered with blood, somebody else's blood though, not her own and she was a-setting on a keg apart from the dead horse looking down at her big bare feet that was resting in the dust. She had a chaw of tobacco in her mouth and she spit now and then just like a man. She was bareheaded, without kerchief nor bonnet neither one. And her brown hair blowed frowzy in the breeze. It's hellfire hot even so and she's a-sweating.

"Hello," says Jasper.

"Howdy," she says, not looking up at him, not moving, still all of a sudden.

"You a married lady?" says Jasper.

"Was." Still looking down.

"How's that?"

Pointing her finger in no particular direction she says as how that corpse-body hanging yonder had been her man. He was dead as a hammer now, wadn't he? Never was no count, though, she says. Always she knowed it would come. Herself she never expected no different.

She taken up with him in the first place, says she, knowing all along that Alfredo was bound to have the shit shot out of him on account of his meanness if it didn't happen first that the law would git a rope on him and hang it out of him as he was wanted far down as Natchez and far up as Ohio. Never stole if he could rob, never liked to rob unless he could kill along with it. Alfredo.

Jasper listens sympathetic until she stops, then says:

"Take me, I'm a Free-Soiler? Forced to come along with this bunch. Had a hitch in the artillery —"

"How's that?"

"Minded the big guns of which this bunch hadn't any, not a God damn one, so it was a case of we had to sneak. Taken to the bushes. God damn if we didn't bag the whole bunch and make a slaughter pen. But I tell you —"

"What?"

"Whole shebang, and you ast me, it was for the sake of niggers. Slaves. That's all they want. But not Jasper!"

"Who?"

"That's me, Jasper. Maybe you wouldn't like to go with me. Go somewheres and lay down and rest a while, would you, dearie?"

"With you."

"Got dogs and a cabin and a clearing. Guess I'll have a share of this shithole if ever they git it all divided."

"You go fast," she says.

"Fast is best, yes or no, finger or dick, I say. Only make up your mind. That's my best offer — yes or no?"

"See the storehouse?"

"Yeah."

"Come behind and crawl under. I'll be waiting," she says.

"All right, dearie," says he, and walks away, back to his blankets and picks up one and folds it. He knocks off the dust and the wood trash. Then he steps towards the storehouse and rounds the corner in behind it next to the woods where it's shady. Stooping down he peers into the cool, under-building darkness. "That you?" says her voice.

"Yeah."

"Come on before somebody sees you."

He crawls under.

"Promise me you'll ride me back to Tennessee with you?"

"Ride you over this blanket first."

"Hop when you feel froggy," says she, stretching down on the unfolded blanket, her breath sweetish with chaw tobacco.

Unbuttoning, he followed his appetite's direction, mounting her, cuntfucking her mindless of anything else, same as they did it back when he was in the artillery, that same deep way, by God. Having done, he allowed himself a rest before he buttoned up. "Bring the blanket when you come," he says.

He crawled into daylight, out of cool cavelike dirt darkness into blink-eyed brightness.

Rounding the building, heading back towards the compound, he saw Elias. Shaggy and sunburned, he was, a black scab like a beetle above his eye. Elias filled Jasper with a fear that was like his fear of God . . .

Chapter 20

The Pendletons, the Wrays, the Alstons, the Turners, the Dyers, the Stannards, the McNeillys, the Musgroves, the Pitts, the Humes, the Goodloes, the Loftins, the McCutcheons, the Stirlings, the Kieffers, the Hedgepaths, the Coons, the Baggetts, the Malones and others . . .

Families that settled the vast district that had been the land of the Chickasaws, fighting clans that protected their holdings. Hot bloods and raiders? Maybe.

They had wiped out a whole village beyond Cottonwood Point in Missouri — burned it and brought home every valuable thing there. Everything. Including slaves and women and children and thimbles and thread; all of it — including chickens and churns, puppies and kittens, duck eggs and rolling pins, horse collars and candlewicks and withal some coin. They divided among them some silver and gold.

But beyond everything brought home they brought an intangible something more valuable still. They brought the beginning of law and order. That fight was the beginning. Law and order appeared down in the west.

And as though this beginning made it needful that all things be made new, Fort Hill got an official post office name, "Somerton, Tennessee." The place became Somerton.

While these events went forward Elias was called to Redleaves, to appear in his best clothes, and to ride into town with Pettecasockee and Shokotee to fetch the young bride, the beautiful Denise, Chatillion's daughter, and bring her to Redleaves as Petty's wife.

It was a mixed-bag wedding, with half the territory in attendance so it seemed — black, white and Indian, with a priest brought from somewhere by Gabe French, for yes, Gabe was on hand for the wedding. He had not come visiting for some time. He recalled how it was to sleep with Elias and Dog in that tree — that sycamore. Just traveling this way from Kentucky, he said, with a twinkle in his eyes, and "happened" to have a priest along with him!

There was just time in the midst of so much excitement for Elias and Gabe to swap a few words back and forth.

"That was quite a raid, old fellow! Men are talking of nothing else, and not just here in the district but beyond as well! D'you know you're spoken of in Kentucky? And always favorably! Maybe you should go into politics, Elias."

"No," says Elias.

"So it's to be farming, the same as ever?"

"Yes. We're planting cotton. Now as I've got slaves I can

raise cotton," says Elias. "Not as I approve of slavery —" And Elias seems not to know what else to say.

"Jane's getting that slash was the devil's own luck," says Gabe. "But that raid of yours will bring prosperity such as hasn't been dreamed of in this district before. Cotton and slaves, law and order, eh?"

"We're planting cotton," says Elias. "Will you be down for a look at the place this trip?"

Just then the fiddles began to scrape. "We'll see!" says Gabe, and away he goes to the dance floor while more and more folk appear, crowding the rooms. They came by boat and mule and oxcart and on foot — a vast gathering at Redleaves. Some would sleep in barns, others in guest rooms. Some would wrap in their blankets and sleep under the wagons.

Besides horse races there was a shooting match and a wrestling competition and a fiddling contest. The women, Jane Nail included, brought extra dresses for the dancing that went on in the house and down on the threshing floors. When one gown was drenched with so much perspiring the woman would retire upstairs to a room set aside for that purpose and change. On and on the dancing went.

Jane, a patch over her cheek, dancing a reel with Elias at her brother's wedding; Pettecasockee dancing with his dark-eyed little bride; Gabe French dancing first with one and then another, dancing with Ellen Ashe and Fanny Chapleau. Dutt Callister danced with Fancy, but not for long. He did a turn or two, and then disappeared and Fancy went calling and looking for him, gazing at heaven like a goose and honking his name, her eyes popping out of her head, but he wasn't anywhere to be found. There were too many hiding places at Redleaves and too many girls after Dutt, for he was a handsome fellow and was rich besides, since the raid on the Horse Pens.

Elias, on the other hand, though he had gotten a larger share than Dutt, seemed not much changed. Not fancy in his clothes, Elias still dressed like a woodsman, and though he had servants now, he still worked in the fields alongside his hands. Jake was his slave driver and saw to discipline. Jake was a good driver and they were making crops at Oakleigh. They made every day count, night and morning.

The talk at Pettecasockee's wedding was of crops and rain, of cattle and slaves, of plans and seasons. It came to Elias that without his quite knowing it the country round about him had been settled. Men like himself, armed with axes, had made fields and plowlands. It came to him that a year, even five years, went like nothing when people were busy as folk were here in the west. It was a revelation brought on by much drinking at Petty McNeilly's wedding. Elias saw that time was strange, and had a way of passing behind one's back.

Chapter 21

The Snail, day by day, calls Doctor Parham's attention to the hole in his side. Contrary to the doctor's predictions and expectations, the little mulatto's wound has refused to close and he has refused to die. And instead of getting smaller the hole has sloughed away at the edges and enlarged.

But day after day the doctor puts off the Decision as to what must be done. Parham has a way of sticking that Decision into another part of his mind.

After fits of postponement, the doctor, urged on by Fanny Chapleau, finally decided on Tuesday following the wedding that he must operate. He allowed himself until the following Thursday to prepare.

Thursday came. The doctor found the Snail lying abed like a saffron shadow. The patient, long ago convinced that removal of the bullet would effect a cure, was even now laboring under that old illusion. By the Snail's utterances it was plain that he was sure that the quiet rituals of preparation going on in his bedroom were one and all concerned with "fetching the bullet." Said the Snail: "I'm bound I'll be damned glad to see that bullet." His eyes were large and luminous, the eyes of a man who has lain dying a long time. The doctor knew that look too well.

"Hot water," said the doctor.

"Here," said Aunt Tio.

"The basin of cold water."

"Here," said Fanny Chapleau.

"And the pitcher of cold water," said the doctor. He was checking his list the third time. "Carbolic acid, one pair curved scissors, one pair straight scissors, scalpel, blunt curved hook. Six needles threaded with catgut sutures. Aunt Tio? The bullet?"

Aunt Tio handed a bullet to the doctor who in turn motioned the Snail to open his mouth and take it between his jaws.

"Now what?" rasped the Snail, talking around the bullet.

The doctor frowned. "I must tell you that this will hurt badly."

The Snail only nodded his agreement.

"Now," said the doctor in a stricken voice. With a trembling hand he took up the blunt, curved hook. Slowly he thrust it into the wound, trying as best he could to effect the "slight, rotary, oscillating movement from side to side" which he had just studied last night again in the pages of his surgical textbook. The Snail gave a loud groan. The doctor let the hook rest a while and held his breath. At last the Snail seemed better. Breathing again, the doctor pressed the hook deeper. Somehow he must get the hook over the loop in the bowel. A tug, a lifting motion, told him he had hooked something. Hoping desperately no vital organ was in the way of the hook, he very slowly drew the instrument up towards the opening. The hook appeared, and with it, to the doctor's considerable relief, he saw the bowel. Drawing the loop slowly through the opening until he found the cut made in the bowel by the bullet, he placed a roll of bandage between the loop and the opening in order to hold the bowel and keep it from slipping back inside. Now he picked up the curved scissors. He began snipping away the puffy, ragged edges about the cut. Sweat was pouring from the Snail's face. He made a sound.

"Nearly done, sir, nearly done. Can't stop now," said the doctor, speaking nervously.

Fanny Chapleau handed him the first of the curved, catgut sutures. One after another the doctor placed six stitches in the bowel, tightening each stitch alternately so as to fit the fresh edges closely without puckering. Then, having drawn all up tightly, he wet his sponges in hot water and bathed the bowel, removing blood clots. Then, with a large syringe, he washed out the cavity itself, removed the roll of bandage, and let go the loop. It needed only a push to drop back inside. After snipping away the proud flesh about the hole in the Snail's side, the doctor began to suture that wound also. Six more stitches satisfied him.

"The operation is finished," he said.

"I'm almost dead," the Snail said. He held out the bitten bullet. Aunt Tio took it. "What am I to expect?"

"If you live until the onset of cold weather, you will recover," the doctor said. "If there is no change."

"And if I die before cold weather then I will die, won't I?"

"Yes, I was about to say just that. If there is no change you will live until cold weather. I'll call by tomorrow."

"In other words I need a miracle," said the Snail.

"Most wounds of the bowel are considered fatal. Your case, however, has admitted of treatment and responded. I'll call by tomorrow."

"Did you fetch the bullet?"

"No. Too dangerous to remove it."

"Then what did I go through this for?"

"Let's see what happens, shall we?"

"I don't have a choice," said the Snail. Then in a weak whisper: "No choice!"

Fanny Chapleau and Aunt Tio, meanwhile removed the bloody sponges, cleaned and emptied the syringe, washed the bloody instruments, took away the bloody towels and bandages, and made the patient comfortable on his bed. Without a word they went about this work. They kept at it until no trace of the operation remained.

The doctor meanwhile washed his hands, rolled down his sleeves, fastened his cuffs, and slipped on his coat.

"No choice," whispered the Snail from time to time.

Chapter 22

Autumn. Elias witnessed the springing breeze at day's end. He watched the coots, tipping above the coves by the river. Suddenly wheeling they went folding down all in a flock, with a movement graceful as a woman's hand. No sooner are the coots hidden in the feathery grass than the cranes go rising, making long, forlorn cries. Upward they drift in soft spirals until the light of the vanished sun strikes them. In a straight line, the sun polishing their wings, they sail out of sight like angels. Flock birds settle, cheeming in the cedar thickets. Blue dusk in the woods, yellow dusk quivering above the autumnal fields. The light fades and hangs curtainlike above the river surface.

The last leaves snatch from their limbs and branches above the river and spiral down and land on the water. Touching the man's beard, that cool wind is a caress upon chin and cheek. The wind has a taste of wine in it . . .

Leola comes to find him. She interrupts his musing. An old prattle-wagon. She demands more and more, does Leola.

"What is it?" he says.

"Why nothing. Only my little Jane's going to need that cradle again."

"What?"

"Just as I figured. She hasn't told you."

And the old woman left him and went back to Jane and Isaac.

Jane's scar was ruining her life, robbing her youth. It had taken all the joy out of her. Another child coming, and she hadn't even told him. Worse yet, somehow he hadn't even noticed. No matter if the Horse Pens raid had put him ahead. No matter if that raid helped him build Oakleigh faster. Jane sat suffering, and nothing there was he could do for her.

He'd throw his gold in the river and free every servant on the place. Burn all to the ground again, so he would, and start all over again if only it would make Jane whole.

He wondered. Was he punished for what had gone between himself and Ellen? If he had not had to do with Ellen, perhaps Jane's face wouldn't have been split like a fish! It was a notion that haunted him from time to time.

As for Ellen Ashe, she herself was having to bear up. She had a son now, nearly big as Isaac, and had named him Edward. Ellen Ashe was having to face people down and say Edward was her husband's child. Mister Ashe had come to see her and then he had gone straightway off again, she said . . . to the west on business.

When it seemed life was nearly too burdensome for him, Elias would throw a saddle on Rattler. And no matter what the direction he rode, it always seemed he wound up at the Poe clearing. Ellen was there. And now she had her son, Edward; she was more beautiful than ever, for being thus fulfilled. It seemed she had sucked the beauty out of Jane and taken it all herself. To Elias, it seemed that way . . .

Not a month ago during cotton picking, he had left his labors for a day and ridden to Somerton to call on Parham, the doctor, who was famous in the district for the operation he had performed on the Snail. The Snail was alive and on his feet again, though he went stooped forward, a little bent over. He was active again nonetheless.

But the doctor, though he received Elias politely, offered no hope that Jane's face could be repaired. He explained that he had only stitched up the Snail as a last, desperate resort, a *daring* measure. He'd not touch the cheek of anyone in good health, nor would anyone else he knew. Not even if Elias took her to Philadelphia, would he find a surgeon to attempt such an impossible task. The doctor had been firm.

"She's well, isn't she? Has a good appetite, has she?"

"But it's the scar, and her spit drains to the outside."

"No," said the doctor. "That fistula can't be helped. Repaired it yourself, did you? That's best in these cases. Immediate repair."

"Aye, but it's spoiling her looks and her life. Spittle on her cheek day and night and it droops, the cheek does, and her eye sags down."

"Severed nerves. Um," says the doctor. "Lucky she didn't die. Maybe she'll accommodate to it in time. How long ago is it now? Years?"

Elias nods.

"She must live with it, sir," said the doctor, speaking sternly. Then in a kinder tone he said: "But if you'd like me to have a look? Perhaps if I spoke to her it would bring her out a bit."

Elias nods. "If you would," he said. "Were it a matter of money I'd give all I have to see her well."

"But it isn't a matter of money. It's plain, cold fact — nothing can be done. Still I'll ride out and speak to her one day. I've a patient with a broken leg nearby your place."

"Who?"

"Coon. Shiftless fellow. Tumbled off his own roof repairing a leak."

BOOK THREE

The Wolf

Chapter 1

Dog — what of him?

He got old and venerable. He had his wives. His descendants lived in the kennels at Oakleigh and made up the pack. Dog had his run of the place. During cold winters he was let in the house and allowed to dream before the fire at Elias's feet. Though his black muzzle had turned gray, Dog seemed as fierce and strong as ever. He was the lord of the plantation.

Did his vision fail, and his judgment too, perhaps? While seeking bears during cold February, Dog tied in with a huge black she bear, what the West Tennessee settlers call a sow. Deep in a dirt den she had lain, whining and sucking a paw, awaiting springtide and the birth of cubs.

Poor Dog, that would have driven her forth with hardly a scratch to himself when he was younger; somehow he joined too close this time. The sow bear caught him. She raked him. She hit him awful blows and bit him deep . . .

Elias carried Dog home in his arms. Jake helped and they sewed him up. Sitting up that night Elias nursed him before the fire while Dog fought with the enemy over which no creature wins the final victory. Growling and rattling in his windpipe, Dog fought his final fight, breathing bubbles of blood from his nose. He made such a fierce fight that Jane and Leola and even little Isaac left bed and came to the fireside to watch the struggle. And Leola said:

"Aye — Dog. He's dying."

"No," said Elias.

"Oh, yes," says Leola. Little Isaac began to cry. For Dog had been a friend and had watched over him. Dog had been so tender towards the child that Isaac could take bones from his mouth and bite his ears. Dog endured it all and followed the child everywhere to keep him safe.

"No!" says Jane. But her tongue swelled.

"Oh, yes," says Leola in her hard, cracked voice. "Dog, he's breathing his last, he is. He's in his death dreams — see how he kicks?"

But the others knew Dog would win — the others knew he would. Jake comes to the fireside and puts on a new log. The sparks fly up. Jake squats on his heels and rubs his bootlaces and looks across at Leola as though to say he too knows what it is. For once Leola doesn't rail at Jake and scold him.

A violent trembling, a final warning growl, and Dog seemed to discover contentment. His breath came easy — but each breathing was spaced farther apart than the last until it seemed he did not breathe at all anymore . . .

Leaving the fireside Elias returned with a blanket — and not an old blanket either, but a new one. Lifting Dog he placed him gently down on the blanket and removed his collar and laid it on the mantel. The wintry wind fluttered in the chimney. The new log popped. More sparks flew up. Kneeling by the fire Elias used his iron punch and his hammer and made a hole in the center of a bright silver dollar. Such extravagance made Leola shake her head. Elias fastened the dollar to Dog's neck, using a bit of wire.

No one spoke. Little Isaac whimpered.

"Now!" says Leola, taking the child on her lap. "Now, now!"

They all knew the reason for the dollar, all but Isaac. They knew that if earth someday should give Dog up, whoever should find Dog's bones would know he was loved, and no mere cur.

Thus was Dog buried in winter in a new blanket with a dollar wired to his neck — Dog that came to the woods a half-grown creature, little more than a puppy. Others would come after, but none would have his place nor mean so much.

Leola even, that never liked Dog much, it seemed, even she would sigh afterwards and say: "Doesn't seem right without him. His place by the fire seems so empty. Jake should never have sent him in that hole after so great a sow."

"Hush," says Jane. "Wasn't Jake that sent him, nor Elias. Dog charged in of his own accord."

"Nay, we should have kept the old fellow by the fire, home as he deserved," and Leola sighs. "He'd still be with us. Now he's gone to the long hunt and won't be seen anymore."

Elias was restless for a long time afterwards. He'd leave bed at night sometimes and go outside. Jane followed once and found him kneeling by Dog's grave.

Warm weather again. Jane took to her bed before noon on a Friday. She wouldn't let Leola call Elias from the fields. No need she said to have him stand about the yard to wait and wonder.

Leola took little Isaac to Jake's cabin and left him with Ponselle and her children. When Leola returned Jane's baby was already born. Only the cord needed cutting.

"Did he slip out easily? What a fine one he is — another man!"

But Jane only turned her face away and stared at the wall.

It was the scar that made her so. She got up after a while and asked for her writing case and when Leola fetched it she scratched a note to be carried to Redleaves. Then she lay back down.

A note, thinks Leola, when word of mouth would serve as well. Proud of her reading and writing, *she* is, thinks Leola, recalling how many seeming endless fireside hours the Master spent teaching Jane to read the Bible and make those crazy bird marks with a writing quill.

Now lately Jane has begun teaching Isaac, with chalk and a slate. Elias helps too, teaching Isaac to cipher and do sums in his head.

"Call the Master now? Fetch Isaac home?"

"After while," says Jane. "Not quite yet."

"Not quite yet," Leola repeats. "Shall I give the note to one of Ponselle's brats and start it to Redleaves?"

"Yes, do that," says Jane in her flat voice. And she decided aloud then that this child's name would be Willy.

Chapter 2

The school in Somerton being too far away, Isaac learned what he could from his father, Elias, from Jane, his mother, who spent a great deal of her time talking to him, and from Leola, who told him Indian things, and from Jake, who knew black African things. Bible stories and Indian stories and African tales of the mumbo-jumbo, of Raw Head and Bloody Bones. Jake told stories to give a body shivers and make a boy hide his head beneath the covers at night.

Thus Isaac got an education good enough for settlers. For playmates there were Ponselle's children and the children in the slave quarters. There was Edward Ashe and the Callisters' children. Willy tagged along. He was sometimes a burden, Willy, for he was just beginning to walk.

Then there were the animals on the place, Old Rattler and the other horses, the mules and the oxen and the gentle cows that Leola and Dotty milked. There was the fierce-looking Tom Turkey, and the cat in her basket by the kitchen hearth, nursing her soft, squirming kittens. The geese on the pond came out to be fed and one in particular would give the boys chase were they not careful. There was a red rooster that got mean and flogged Isaac and was put in the pot for his crime. Yet no sooner was that rooster removed than another took his place as lord of the flock.

And there were adventures and dangers, never to be forgotten, things that gave Isaac food for reflection and taught him the mysterious truth about the world, the sort of truth that can only come from living and can't be merely told or explained.

A wolf walked out of the woods at Oakleigh. In full broad day the creature circled the millpond and might have eaten Willy up, or so Isaac thought, had he not dragged his little brother away to the house as fast as he could fly with him, meanwhile shouting for Leola.

Out comes Leola, half disbelieving. Does she think this is some of Isaac's nonsense? Just look then! Leola's little dog, Chutt, her fyce that sleeps with her on the bed and follows about at her heels all day, Chutt spies the wolf before Leola can think and he sails off after the wolf, yap-yapping straight for the millpond. Nothing Leola does can call Chutt back to her. Chutt bites the wolf and drives it away into the woods again. The fyce comes back with blood on his neck where he's been slashed.

Father and Jake have a look and decide Chutt is no worse for it. The place heals over in time, but when Father speaks of the incident he seems to be uneasy over it though Chutt wasn't hurt. Father worries and looks strange when he speaks of that day.

A short while after the wolf adventure, a black bear breaks into the hogpen. He's killed two of the innocents that live there and is devouring a third, eating the third poor old pig alive, guts first, when Father and Jake run up with their guns and kill the bear.

Thereafter, whenever they can, Father and Jake go to the woods with cowbells and guns and mules and horses and come back with dead bears, for otherwise the bears would kill all the hogs and destroy all the horned cattle — and who knows if a bear, crazed by hunger in such a season as this with no acorn mast left on the ground — might not such a bear attack a child and eat him too, guts first?

Following along the creek, beside the narrow banks above the millpond, Isaac spies sun perch in the shallows and snakes that lie twined together like pieces of rope on the dead trees that lie half submerged — and turtles, and snake doctors (which Edward Ashe calls dragonflies) and simple wonders, such as the ripple and pattern of the current where it passes a sandbar, the clear, sweet peacefulness of the water itself and the gentle bending of the willow limbs when a warm wind blows.

No sooner was the plague of bears controlled (the carcasses broken in the back and packed along home on horse and mule, to be skinned and quartered and the meat butchered and pickled in casks and the oil rendered and stored in stone crocks) than the bottoms dried out sufficiently for logging.

It was August, the fourth day of the month. Isaac stood that morning with Jake, who was head man over the slaves, and Elias. They were looking over the work. It was early and they stood near a cookfire when suddenly from nowhere Chutt, Leola's fyce, came running. Leaping on Jake, who was squatting down, Chutt bit the Negro in the back of the neck, nipping him good.

Chutt was gone again. Before anyone can think what it is, Chutt's vanished . . .

"What?" says Jake, taking his hand away from his neck. Isaac sees Jake's blood. "What?"

"Mad dog," says Father. Words to make Isaac tremble!

"*Mad* dog?" says Jake.

"It's just as I've feared. Lie down flat. Quick! The bite has to be cauterized."

Face down Jake stretches out on the ground. Isaac watches while his father swiftly cuts a little green stick and splits it, making tweezers. This he uses to capture a coal, a red, live ember from the fire.

"Great God!" Jake screams, for Father has just put that live coal to the bite on Jake's neck. Jake's blood sizzles, his flesh smokes.

Leola's fyce, meanwhile, before it can be found and shot, bites nearly every animal on the place.

But of humans it bit only Jake.

There was nothing for it now, as Father said, but to wait and see what would happen. The fyce has bitten horses, mules, geese, cattle. The mad dog has done terrible work at Oakleigh. Lucky the fyce could not get into the kennels or the entire pack, Dog's descendants, would have been destroyed too. "Lucky the pack wasn't running loose," says Father.

Jake loads the wagon and puts in the seat of an early morning. Now that the roads are dry he lets Isaac go with him for the day into Somerton. They haul fresh vegetables and eggs and butter and barrels of flour and meal. And bundles of wood shingles, hides, bear oil, beeswax and honey. Jake never leaves Oakleigh without a cargo. He rarely leaves Somerton without stopping to visit Aunt Tio.

He stops by T. Laird's place on Fort Hill in the afternoon, since it is known to him that the Snail sleeps every afternoon. It's a deep and soundless slumber that overtakes the Snail. He's never been quite the same since Isaac's grandfather, Shokotee, shot him in the gut once long ago.

During the Snail's long sleeps Jake stops by and visits Aunt Tio in her kitchen. Jake never fails to give Aunt Tio eggs and honey and fresh vegetables.

"Why, look who's with you!" Aunt Tio cries. She gives Isaac a kiss and serves him a slice of cake and a glass of milk. While Isaac eats he counts the coffins stored by the kitchen wall.

This trip Jake shows his neck, where the fyce bit him. "Wadn't I bit by a mad dog and you didn't know?"

"What? *Mad* dog?"

"Leola's fyce."

"Bad luck," says Aunt Tio.

"Spang on my neck what I mean."

"Um!" she says, taking a look.

"Marse Eli put the fire to it — raw fire."

"I'll say."

"Yeah."

In a lower voice she says: "Don't you know I miss you? Been feelin' empty. Get to thinkin' about New Orleans and my heart begins gettin' heavy. New Orleans girls I knew when I was young? Now they ride in carriages and wear silk every day. Here I stand barefooted. And look forward to what?"

"Same as me," says Jake.

"Milkin' that man's cow, churnin' his butter, bakin' and cookin' and cleanin' and doin' his laundry. Daybreak to dark. For what?"

"Me too," says Jake. "Bit my neck, didn't he?"

"When I think to myself about what life I have left! Life ain't somethin' to let go of easily. Young folks say as how they'd as soon die young and leave a handsome corpse. They don't care if they throw life away like slops. It's old folks that value life. No matter how many miseries they got, the old ones cling to what remains."

Jake sits at the end of the table opposite Isaac. Neither Tio nor Jake pay Isaac any notice beyond Tio slicing him another piece of cake and filling his glass, Jake saying: "I miss my home country too, back in Maryland." She serves Jake coffee and cake and buttered biscuits. "Yes'm, mindin' my own business in the woods and that little somebitch bit me spang on my neck. Yes'm."

"I'm called to slave harder than you," says Aunt Tio. As always happens she eases herself onto Jake's lap while he continues to eat biscuits, having put away his cake first. He picks up biscuits like money and puts an arm about Aunt Tio's waist. "And him, sleepin' in yonder, what if he caught me and you like this? Huh, Jake?"

"I'd say to him 'Have a biscuit!' " Jake laughs.

"Hush! But he's hard, though."

"Sho. A free nigger he's always gonna be hard. Feels like he has to be." Jake downs the rest of his coffee and looks at Isaac. "Finished?"

Isaac nods. What comes next is the price of a ride to town

with Jake. Isaac follows Aunt Tio into the front room. She sits him down at her sewing table with the dinner bell by him.

"If you hear Mister Laird get up or see him, please ring the bell?" she whispers.

"I will," Isaac promises.

Back to the kitchen goes Tio and into the pantry with Jake. Isaac waits. What transpires in the pantry is a thing he knows and doesn't know. Isaac is aware that the Snail is sure to be mad as a wet hen if ever he finds out about Jake and Tio in the pantry.

There's something special about Aunt Tio. She's prettier than other servants, has lighter skin, and she hums a waltz when she clears the table. She tells about the military bands serenading in New Orleans. That New Orleans life of hers wasn't so long ago as she can't remember it, she says. Sometimes she will lift her skirt and look at her ankles. And it's a fact that she has slender ankles still. All this gives Isaac food for deep thinking.

Presently the pantry door opens and Tio and Jake come out again. Isaac takes the dinner bell back to the kitchen.

Says Tio: "Wasn't so long ago as a body can't remember how it was in New Orleans, waltzin' with a soldier, wearin' a hat, walkin' about and all!" She speaks so sadly and wears such a wistful look on her handsome face, that Isaac can't help but feel sorry for her.

Back out they go, Jake and Isaac, to the wagon then. But Aunt Tio can't send them off empty-handed. She hands them a tote-pack — meat and biscuits and blackberry pie. The jolt wagon begins to move in a filtering jingle of trace chains, through dust and towards a slight and lingering sense of desolation, and a lonely tingling at the back of the heart. Nevermind, it all passes; and one day Isaac will be old enough to understand and take part in grown-up adventures himself. Still it gives him such a left out feeling, being so young, knowing and not knowing . . .

If anything bothers Jake on the other hand, or affects him in any way, he never shows it. Never a sign or a hint from him. Isaac envies him the bite and the burned place on his neck and his way of saying "Great God!"

He's never sick, Jake isn't. He rarely complains. Alone with Isaac he rarely speaks.

Turning for a look at the south wall of the Snail's house, Isaac sees the window by the sewing table. He thinks of the Snail, sleeping deathlike in his bedchamber. He remembers the coffins against the kitchen wall. Beyond, by the stable, he sees P'-nache currycombing a red horse. The Indian wears a rag about his head.

Chapter 3

Willy McCutcheon has been to Somerton. He rides on the horse behind his daddy. He's got a big brother, Isaac. Isaac reads.

Leola's fyce, Chutt, that slept on Leola's bed. Chutt went a mad dog. Daddy and Jake shot Chutt and Chutt was buried on Wednesday in the dog graveyard. Chutt has a wood marker and has gone to heaven but Leola cut her hair and took it to the kitchen and put it in the fire and didn't say anything and wouldn't tell stories at bedtime. And she went out to the dog graveyard and Willy went with her. She put her hand upon the dust covering where Chutt's asleep but he's gone to heaven and was Leola's fyce that slept on the bed with her. Isaac says. Leola says.

Chutt went a mad dog.

Mama's face.

Leola burned her hair in the fire. It made a smell in the kitchen. But hair grows back.

"We'll go down to see the geese," Leola says. She puts Willy's shoes on him. Isaac can tie his own shoelaces. Isaac is big.

They go outside. Leola holds Willy's hand like it's the steamboat but it isn't the steamboat and it isn't Chutt's grave this time because it's the geese.

See the geese long before we get to the pond. They walk in a circle. *Honk-ee! Honk-ee!* They talk to the sky and look straight up and walk in a circle, around and around. Chutt bit the geese.

"Let's go see the mules," says Leola.

"He bit the mules," Isaac says. He's a big boy.

Willy holds Leola's hand like the steamboat but it isn't the steamboat because it's the barn and she holds Willy up and lets him see the mule. It's a black mule and bites the skin and the meat out of its shoulder. The blood. The hair and the hide and the meat in the straw and the mule makes a sound. Willy screams.

Then they go out where the hands are digging the ditch for the mules and the horned cows and the horses and the geese and Jake doesn't have his bandage anymore and Jake didn't take mad because he was lucky and Father burned his neck. Leola says. Isaac says.

Jake has the pistol. It's Daddy's old horse he never rides anymore. Poor old Rattler. He's old anyway. Isaac's crying.

"Crybaby," says Leola. Isaac hits her but she grabs his fists. "Crybaby."

Jake shoots. The old horse rolls down on his side. Father looks strange.

"Poor old horse," says Willy.

"Hush, don't say that," says Father. "Hush, Son."

"Why?"

"Just don't say that. Take them to the house! Why did you bring them down here anyway? A cannibal would have more sense!" Father shouts at poor Leola.

"Um," says Leola. "Um." That's all she says.

Jake is sweating. "She likes it," says Jake. Sweating. "She can't get enough of it. If it was my horse and her dog bit it, I know what I'd do. How come you to cut your hair. Say?"

"Um," says Leola.

"That all you can say for yourself? Just a savage, that's all you are. You know that?"

"Hush," says Father. "Hush," Father says. He's got something in his eye and has to wipe with his handkerchief. Wiping his eyes.

"Damned old savage," says Jake.

"Um."

Back to the house. We go upstairs. Leola tells Mama.

"I died that night," says Mama. "I died that night."

"Poor old Rattler," says Isaac.

Chapter 4

A project that had been months in the making was completed at last. The river that flowed past Oakleigh was opened to navigation. A steam packet henceforth would stop to take on cotton and leave off goods. The trees that blocked the way had all been cut, the snags had all been blasted. A steam launch with a crane on the front had helped. The planters along that way, Elias especially, would profit.

Werdna and Andrew, the Poe brothers that Elias had thought so shiftless were not so shiftless anymore now that they had gotten slaves. Named their clearing Riverside, they did, and soon proved what cotton farmers they had been all along. Using their share of the prize money from the Horse Pens they, like many another, had bought slaves, and more slaves . . .

With every season Elias observed new works at Riverside. The Poe brothers cleared more and more land. They gained a reputation for being hard on servants. They had hired an overseer, a Mississippian named Tug Chambers. He fed a brace of bloodhounds and rode back and forth on his horse through the fields carrying a cowhide lash. He went armed with a pistol and a bowie knife and stayed to himself in a separate dwelling house, without a wife — alone but for an old servant woman who cooked for him. It was said the Poes paid him four hundred a year and furnished his vittles and fed his dogs. He was the first overseer in the district . . .

Taking a special way through the woods to avoid the road, Elias had been calling on Ellen more and more. Each visit was like the last.

Climbing the stairs he enters her bright room. Closing the door behind him he turns the key. For a moment he looks at her where she sits, hands folded in her lap, her beautiful head held high. That look she gives him makes the blood beat in his neck.

This day he appeared at Riverside in answer to a note she sent him secretly by a servant: "Come today."

"Sit down," she said.

He sat on the sofa beside her.

"Not only is Edward older," she said. "But there is Jane, disfigured for life."

Elias looked away. The breeze through the open windows stirred the blue bombazette curtains on Ellen's bed, and pushed the white mosquito bar. He remembered when she had gotten her mattress. She had had it stuffed with Spanish moss imported from Louisiana. And he remembered when she had bought other things one by one — two red settees, four carved chairs, the rosewood table she used for her desk, the étagère by the wall, the bowl in which fresh flowers were kept, the little bronze statuette of a nymph in flowing bronze robes, the white vase with peacock feathers in it.

He was thinking: the work of cotton. It buys all this — it's cotton, slaves, and the downriver trade to New Orleans. Elias was more comfortable when Ellen lived in a cabin surrounded by stumpfields.

There was a new oil painting on the wall. In it was a bridge, some trees, a riverbank; soldiers in red and black uniforms were firing cannons at a city across the river. Each building had a red roof. Clouds of smoke stood in the air above the blue surface of the make-believe river.

Coming here on horseback today Elias had seen how the land all about was touched with drought. Sorghum fields were fading from green to sickly yellow. Back at Oakleigh Leola has already hung the gourds to cure.

A lean year, all in all, he thinks, but he takes consolation in that the late peas have made a passable crop. The peas are being brought from the fields in cotton baskets to be shelled. The pea vines are being piled for fodder.

Ellen put her hand on his. Turning his head, he looked at her again.

"You do understand, don't you?" she said.

"Ho!" he said. "Ho! By God —!"

"It's best. Now I've thought hard about it and it's no good for you to get angry. That won't help."

"No? So you're the boss now and you tell me, *me,* by God, you tell *me* it's over! Ho!"

"Now — now, Elias! *Elias!*"

But he was furious. He picked her straight up and took her to the bed. He'd have her, so he would, whether she liked it or not! But she stopped him. She merely gave him a look and moved her head, imperceptibly almost from side to side. Her mouth shaped the word. *No,* said her mouth, making no sound, and it froze him. He took away his hands.

"All right," he said. He nodded, and then, in a choked voice: "I won't plead, by God!"

And somehow he feels older, whereas on his way here through the woods just now it seemed to him that he had found his prime of life. All he knows now is a bitter wish. Suddenly he wants another crack at youth and like a gambler he thinks: *If only I could have another chance at the wheel.*

Aye, he'd win the next time around. And he considers how it would be to have another turn, nerves dancing in his fingers, sweat standing cold on his brow. Just now he'd give everything to be allowed to hazard it all again.

All these years past it's been only because life comes but once that he's called on Ellen and loved her. He's loved her dearly and truly and has never wanted anything but what was best for her. Can he say anything now she's decided to send him away forever and for good?

"Aren't you going to kiss me goodbye, Elias?"

So now was the last time he'd ever hold her. He held her gently as one holds a child, feeling how she breathed, observing the delicate blue of her closed eyelids. The last kiss between them then, and therefore not a kiss like any other. His mouth feels dry. His throat has a hurt in it.

"Goodbye, Elias," she whispers.

It was time he left. It's a queer feeling. He's detached inside. What was a bright world has gone gray as twilight. What things he'd stored up to tell her, what inner thoughts he'd not tell another person in the world! They've flown away, those thoughts, every last one. They've left him thoughtless and a little numb. His hands feel cold and empty.

Trying not to show any sign of what he felt, he found his feet and made for the door.

Ellen had rehearsed beforehand. When the door closed after him and his footsteps sounded on the stairs, she pushed him out of her mind. Thinking: "There was Edward. I must see to Edward. Now Edward is older I had seen no other choice than to send Elias away for good."

Voices below in the driveway. She lay full length on the sofa, clutching a silk pillow against her stomach. It was Ellen's intention to lie thus until all the hurt she felt went away. But at the sound of hoofbeats she sprang up. She rushed to her balcony doors and flung them open. She looked out.

He went at a gallop, already beyond earshot. She had a last glimpse of his strong back, his big shoulders, and his hair reaching below his wide-brimmed black hat. A cry stopped in her throat. She stood helpless, powerless to do anything but look.

"If he should turn and come back, if he should wave farewell," she was thinking. But he didn't. Then he was gone and she felt a giddiness in her ribs.

Never again would she know the full feeling of him. "Never," she thought.

She looked down and saw a red swollen face, cruel lips and a wide neck. The face was leering at her.

It took a moment to realize it was only Chambers, the overseer. The man coughed and turned away. She went back in her room and closed the doors and lay down again, clutching the pillow. From time to time she held her breath, determined. She would not think of Elias.

Chapter 5

Gabe French comes visiting. Not so elegant as he once was, he comes walking this trip. He says it's for his health. But did the doctor tell him to wear old clothes and worn boots and not to carry silver in his pockets?

Elias is too considerate to ask questions. And Gabe, he's as welcome as he was the first time, when all Elias could offer was a tree hollow and a bed of bearskins facing an open fire.

"Everywhere I hear Oakleigh is the wonder of the district," says Gabe. His muttonchop whiskers have some gray sprinkled in and his forehead seems higher. His face has gotten thinner, as though he may be worry-worn. Still he's bright and cheerful, or appears so, saying: "And to think all this began as a clearing in the woods. Now it's the wonder of the district!"

He walks about with Elias and doesn't miss a thing. The mud chimney on that cabin Elias built himself has been torn away and a stone chimney put there instead, and the big house, Oakleigh, has chimneys of brick, the bricks having been made by hand and fired right here on the place. Clay from the earth and wood for fuel; kilns and brick chimneys for every slave cabin, and brick walks, and bricks sent to Somerton by ox-drawn wagons and sold for chimneys in town. For all the improvements, and for all the proud white columns of the big house, there is still a rustic air, a pioneer flavor, an evidence of individual toil. Elias may be the master here, but his hands are calloused too.

Gabe French has something nice to say about every new thing that has been built since he was here last time, saying:

"That seed in your mind — it took root, sprouted, leafed out and now begins to bear fruit." He speaks thus, grandly, turning fine phrases. Gabe is the same as ever.

To some it would seem this all sprang up suddenly — but Gabe, that longtime friend, knows better and he *remembers back when,* as the saying goes. Aye, what's here had taken years of toil. Dawn to dusk and after dusk. What's here has taken sweat and blood and has made as much sorrow as happiness.

And now, from Gabe: "Is that a boat landing?"

Gabe goes with Elias to inspect the new landing. "So they've opened the river to navigation. It was bound to happen one day," says Gabe.

"It's only a small landing. Yet the boat comes and takes our cotton," says Elias.

"Boat?"

"A packet steamer," says Elias.

And Gabe: "Aye — it was *bound* to happen. I knew this district would be rich one day. Men like yourself have made it so. New barns?"

"Mule barn and cattle barn," says Elias.

"Slave cabins? A full complement of slaves, almost?"

"I don't favor slavery," Elias says, uncomfortable for the first time since Gabe's arrival. "Never have favored it."

"But we couldn't produce cotton without them. Progress on every hand. When did you dam the creek and set up the mill?"

"Last year — no, let me see. It's two years now — or three."

"So much going you forget, eh? Give this country another hundred thousand fellows like yourself, I say. Your own mill . . . Self-sufficient. A boat landing."

Down they go to witness the mill humming and clacking at its work. They stand a while and watch the water thrust and churn through the race. Gabe stands still a long time, witness to the quiet calm of the millpond stretched behind the dam, flat and shining. White geese glide upon the surface. Muscovy ducks go grazing the shore rim. Grain wagons rumble on the stout timbered bridge. The planks are dusted white . . .

"Who was the millwright?"

"I saw to the setting of the stones," says Elias. "Myself."

Their thoughts turn to graver matters — North and South. For a cosmic mill is humming and grinding in America — South against North; North against South.

That greater mill is like to make flour for a very bitter bread. Elias is strong for the Union. "An America without all the states together would be like a separated family, half gone one way and half another."

Gabe shakes his head. "But we cannot condone the North's incitements to servile insurrection," he says.

Servile insurrection — it's only a fashionable phrase, but it strikes terror in the Southern heart, especially in Deep South districts where black slaves are the majority. The term covers every sort of slave trouble, from simple runaway to mutiny to outright revolt. Servile insurrection has been talked about by the South's white population for a decade.

Servile insurrection . . .

"I'll not say I haven't given it thought," Elias admits. "There was Mister Porter Bean poisoned by his slaves last year. His place lay south of Somerton in the bottoms near the Indian mounds. They served him calomel in his tea and he died. Three were hanged, two escaped."

Gabe nods and rubs his chin. "An entire family was murdered in South Georgia not two months ago — throats cut ear to ear. Six souls murdered in their beds."

Gabe asks about Jane and those two boys, Isaac and Willy.

"Jane has her separate room. She sees folk less and less. Her happiness has been killed, Gabe. The fault was mine for I unbarred the door that night. Spit leaks through that hole in her face. She keeps the blinds closed, the curtains drawn. She talks to herself and says: 'I died that night. I died that night.' "

"Her mind may be touched, and no wonder," says Gabe.

Elias waits in the kitchen while Gabe goes upstairs, shown to Jane's door by Leola who knocks three times. Entering Jane's dim room Gabe finds a chair and sits down.

"You recall Mister Gabe French," says Leola.

"Yes," Jane replies. She sits in her rocking chair, slowly rocking.

"I've been in Georgia settling matters for my wife's family. It's taken years."

"Wife? Never knew you had a wife," says Jane, her voice flat and hissing.

"Oh, yes. Back in Georgia. They'd made such a fix of things. It took time, but finally I got things set straight. Now it looks likely my Kentucky land may be worth something. How've you been?"

"I died — that night," says Jane, slowly rocking. "I died . . ."

"You remember Mister Gabe French, don't you?" says Leola. "This is who he is. Want me to wipe your face and get you a clean towel?"

Leola moves between Jane and the washstand, back and forth, waiting on her, wiping the hidden cheek.

Devil of a thing. Devil of a come-up, thinks Gabe. Presently he excuses himself and goes back downstairs to the kitchen where Elias sits. Elias seems tired. There's a weariness in the man's voice that Gabe has not heard before. His big shoulders seem burdened by invisible weight. Elias is getting older.

"If it happens you're short of funds you'll do me a favor to let me advance what you need," says Elias.

Gabe feels himself blush. Can Elias be remembering how Gabe left off a few supplies once long ago?

"My saddlebags are freighted," says Elias. "Eh?"

The friends laugh. Tricked fate, they have, so it seems.

"Whatever you need," says Elias.

Says Gabe:"More than anything else . . . I need rest."

Now follows a season of visiting. Winter comes with a hard breath. First the millpond and next the river itself freeze tight. Both go white as a put-out eye. The ice is so thick folk can walk up and down and back and forth on it. A rare, hard freeze in West Tennessee.

Gabe walks on the ice. Back and forth and up and down he goes with Elias and the boys, Willy and Isaac, and the servants. Even Jane comes down, wrapped against the cold and her face heavily veiled. Jane too walks upon the ice and seems to enjoy the miracle.

More wonders. The trees freeze. Now and again one explodes during the night, with a crack sharp as a musket shot — a tree exploding.

By now Gabe has been a guest so long that his room is called "Mister French's room" by the servants. He's bought a few clothes from the packet steamer and replaced the threadbare suit and those worn boots he was wearing when he came here. First he bought summer clothes and boots, next winter clothes and boots, and gloves and hats, of course, and linens, soaps, brushes, toiletries, combs, teethbrushes, suspenders and a whalebone riding crop — all put down to Elias McCutcheon's account.

Before the freeze the packet steamer has taken Oakleigh's cotton and left off shoes and shirts and trousers and blankets and much, much else. Wines and spirits and Christmas fireworks; candles and tree ornaments.

Jake, Oakleigh's slave driver, oversees the shooting of wild ducks and geese by the other servants. The women pluck the feathers for feather ticks and pillows. Wild goose and duck are served smothered in rice, with gravy and apples — Gabe's favorite fare, he says, sitting down and taking up his napkin and bowing his head while Elias says grace. "Lord, make us truly thankful . . ." There is also roast beef, venison steak, chicken, turkey, quail, wood pigeon and bear — such a multitude of good things to eat, and many bottles of good wine chilled in tubs against the wall. Gabe raises his glass:

"To the Union."

"It must be preserved," Elias replies.

"May it prosper forever."

After midday meals Gabe reads his newspapers and takes a glass of brandy in the library. Smoking a fragrant cigar, he sits thus, reading. Everything in those papers is far, far away. North and South . . .

Presently he falls asleep in his wing chair, facing the hickory fire . . .

Then spring came walking north again in green shoes.

Shokotee comes visiting. Elias, Gabe and Shokotee take long, orderly rides about the place to see to the planting. Gabe no longer worries so much about walking anymore. His face has filled and the lines of worry have gone. He may be a few pounds heavier than he was. Riding is all the exercise he wants.

As to news, Shokotee says that the quack has married the whore — meaning Doctor Parham and Fanny Chapleau.

"But he operated on the Snail and made him well," says Elias.

"Ho," says Shokotee. "But that was years ago and what has he done lately?"

Where spring has walked, the woods are leafing. Songbirds drown human conversation with musical calling back and forth. Bees make a sleepy buzzing in the orchard. The cows have calved and the young calves spar with one another; stiff-kneed and frisky, they butt heads and push . . .

Sundown and bonfires. The servants sing and dance. Children shriek and leap through the flames. Yellow fire reflections play on the river surface. The night birds begin crying . . .

The gentlemen sit on the high veranda. Suitably weary after their day's riding, they sit, talking and smoking. Ten o'clock chimes below in the hall. They go indoors to the dining room and sit down to late supper.

"To the Union," says Gabe.

"Death to it," says Shokotee.

Going to the top of the stairs, Jane stands listening to the voices of the men below in the dining room. She stands holding the little bell in her left hand. She hears voices, but not what is being said. She rings the bell and goes back to her room and out to the high porch. The porch rocker is dewy damp to the touch. She sits in the dewy chair. Below her the bonfires have died to embers.

"Did you ring?" It's Leola.

"Sit with me a while," says Jane.

Leola takes the other chair. "Did you dream again?"

"Yes. I saw Fancy Callister's children. And I saw the scar and the hole and my cheek and the hideous drooping. I felt my mouth sagging and leaking at the corner and Fancy's children ran away hollering like scared puppies."

"Um," says Leola. "Don't think on it."

But though she puts away mirrors and tries to brush her long hair so as to let it fall loosely and conceal the scar, nothing helps. Nothing but darkness such as this, thinks Jane, and dark fires such as wink below where, only a little while ago, the children were leaping and shouting.

"Not think!" says Jane in a bitter voice. She remembers sitting in the darkest corner of the cabin before this big house was built. She remembers herself as she was before, settler folk and not plantation people. Had she thought it would help when Elias planned a big house with columns and verandas? Would a new house somehow take her out of her reclusion?

Him saying: "Why, this clearing will be a plantation — think of that!"

She had watched his hopes slowly fail when she would not answer. Yet Elias, all along, had believed that when he had created a plantation here she would be happy again . . .

"Leola, how can I ever tell him what it is that's happening to me, when I don't know myself what it is?"

"Hush," says the old woman. "You must teach yourself not to want what you can't have. As for men? They ride you like a horse and throw you away."

"Not Elias."

"All of them. Doesn't the Master spend more and more time with Jake? Don't I see him going to Jake's cabin more and more? Makes himself at home in Jake's household. I see it. Time was when he rode away by himself now and then and came home happier than he was when he left. He doesn't ride off alone anymore. He goes with a new sadness. Have you noticed?"

"I'm not going to think about it," says Jane.

"The packet is due any day," says Leola.

More than anything else Jane looks forward to the visits of the packet steamer. Should the river run low it makes her melancholy to think that the little steamer won't be coming, for it brings a world to her doorstep. An hour ahead of its arrival almost, the hoot of its whistle is heard downstream — a faint promise that grows steadily louder.

The captain of the packet jokes and says that as to low water he wouldn't be one to brag and say his boat's got a shallow draft. He won't go that far, he says, for she needs a *heavy dew* to cross the fields, and that's the truth! Jane hides her scar with a silk mask and puts a black veil about her hat before she goes down and walks aboard to make her purchases.

On that boat she's "Mrs. McCutcheon. Yes, ma'am! Right away!"

Leola stays by her to help and they buy buttons and cloth, gowns for Jane, clothes for Elias and her sons; shoes for her servants, orange marmalade, a music box, coffee, tea, and sugar; candy, perfumed soaps, silks, lace, hats — and just this last trip a parlor organ. No end of wonders come up the river now.

"When is the packet due, Leola?"

I died that night.

"Soon," says Leola. "Isaac goes about, Isaac does, reading everything on the place — even labels. Can so much reading be healthy, I wonder?"

Jane listens to the crying of the night birds.

"Leola, my pores are about to bleed!"

"Bleed? You won't bleed, not with Leola here, no. Aren't you a matron with keys on your waist? Leola's here, never-mind!"

"Could God restore my mind, Leola?"

"Leola will make some sassafras tea. Only be still and try not to think."

"But yesterday I dreamt God removed my scar. Could he restore my mind if I prayed to him? Could he, d'you think, Leola?"

"Now —"

"Where is Elias?"

"Why below in the dining room with your father, making their farewells to Mister French. He's leaving tomorrow, bound for Kentucky he says. Or they may be in the kitchen now or out smoking on the porch. Only be *still.* Leola will fetch some tea. It's springtide, that's all. It makes me dizzy too, for it tries to stir the blood about but the blood's too thick after so much cold winter. Wait, I'll bathe your wrists."

"I died that night, Leola!"

I died . . .

Chapter
6

Ponselle, Jake's wife. He would not let her touch the scar on his neck. Where the coal had been laid to it long ago after the fyce had bitten him, she was not allowed to touch it. The flesh about it puckered proud, then slowly wore away until the scar alone remained. Jake's neck. He was touchous.

She dreamed now and then, Ponselle. In dreams she was Ponselle, Sim Hornby's woman. She lived at the Horse Pens in a house upon stilts and her children were small and clutched her knees. Yet in her dreams Sim was Jake McCutcheon, and Jake McCutcheon was Sim. And both had the mad-dog scar upon their necks where the fire was laid to it.

In dreams she reached to touch the scar only to find it not there. And she smelled Sim Hornby and was his woman again.

Then sometimes she woke and walked outdoors at night, barefoot down beside the river. Then it was as though she did not know who she was, Ponselle.

She had been proud of the geese. It had been her pride to feed them and to see how they swam the pond. The first went mad and died. More geese were brought, the second flock was not the same. She didn't care about geese anymore.

"Put his shoes on backwards, his boots," she thought sometimes. "Wrong foot."

Should Jake hear her, as now and then he did, he would ask, "Who?"

And Ponselle would say, "Nobody."

"You Ponselle, lucky you," says Jake. "Lucky it was me caught you. Else you'd been sold to Louisiana with all your kids. Stay by me — Jake's *lucky*!"

Her children grew and went to the fields. Isaac and Willy and their friend Edward Ashe, that has the red hair, all three came to the cabin and Ponselle gave them coffee and was proud that they came to the cabin. They sat down and spoke like regular visitors, Isaac, Edward Ashe, and Willy.

Isaac asks Ponselle to tell how it was across in Missouri where his father and Jake went. To fetch her away and shoot the outlaws. How they hanged Sim Hornby that fathered her light-skinned children — tell that, says Isaac.

And she tells it. Edward Ashe and Willy get quiet as stoves. They don't move. They don't twitch. She tells it all, one drop of blood at a time. She makes them hear how the blood dripped off the high porches — *drip*, and *drip-drip*!

Says Willy: "Pettecasockee, he shot a woman's head clean off her shoulders." And: "He's my uncle."

"That was Aunt Fronnie got her head shot away off her shoulders," says Ponselle.

Says redheaded Edward Ashe: "He's my uncle too."

"No, he isn't your uncle," says Isaac, speaking solemnly.

"My uncles went to Missouri too," says Edward, who hasn't got a father and comes to Oakleigh to play when his uncles will bring him. Marse Elias will take Edward up behind him on his horse and carry him home. Edward Ashe, his red hair.

Presently all three grow up. All three get large enough to spit and smoke and tote pistols and to ride away galloping and hunting by theirselves. Presently. They begin to take their horses into Fort Hill and race. To bet on cockfights and follow hurly mischief; except Isaac doesn't take so much part in that as those younger two — as Willy, that's got the devil in him, and Edward Ashe, that's got a double dose of devil. Redhead.

Isaac sometimes brings his book and reads to Ponselle; and in the big house it's said he also reads to his mother, Miss Jane, in her curtain-dark room where she lives with blinds closed. She comes out on her high porch sometimes, gray streaks in her black hair . . .

Three times late of a moonlit night as Ponselle walks by the river barefoot, she sees Miss Jane on the high porch in her chair, *rocking, rocking, rocking.* Wearing a white gown, her dark hair streaming down like blood. She's like a ghost up there, alone. In the moonlight, all alone.

Look away, do you dare? The wind will blow a season by. Blink your eyes, the years sneak and steal behind your back. Dream, and it's long, long ago; wake, and it is now. The river goes talking beside you and sobbing.

The river is a woman and sobs at night. Only walk beside her and listen; hear her sobbing and sighing?

Chapter 7

Dutt Callister, all the years since first he settled in West Tennessee, had a plan. Call it a dream. He would, one day, simply leave Fancy and these brats she was constantly birthing. He would disappear. Over the river into Arkansas and on beyond. There he would melt into distance. Every trace and memory of life back here would vaporize. Prairies lie yonder somewhere; vast stretches of sky and grass. The buffalo graze thick as fleas.

But he wouldn't go west to take up land, Dutt wouldn't, no. No more would he break his back on iron toil. He would sleep by campfires. The silent song of the wilderness would bless his dreams. As it happened he found a place and wanted to remain a while, he would. When he wished to move again? He'd move! Beholden to nobody, and none to answer to or for. He would live his own life and be himself.

Meanwhile here's Fancy. She's a regular breeding factory. One at her breast, one clutching her knee, another on the way and for some reason, only God knows why, she's all the time scolding. She's so pale a creature it seems to him sometimes he can damned near see clean through her. And in quieter moments of stepping down the seemingly endless stairway of years, Dutt tries to recall what it was like, back before he married, way back when he was free — he tries to remember but he can't. So many things tear at his mind. Lord, help.

Debts. They came after him like that mad wolf that caused Elias McCutcheon's trouble, but with a difference. The wolves of debt came in packs and droves, never singly, never one at a time. Dutt wasn't lucky with money like Elias. Dutt lost at dominoes. Dutt lost at cards. Dutt lost at dice. Dutt lost . . . From time to time he hoped Fancy might somehow take terribly sick. Get down with an awful spell of illness and die. Leave Dutt with the young'uns.

Then a pretty young gal would hire out to help him and presently he'd — ah! But hellfire, wouldn't that put him straight back where he was now? Hadn't he sense to see that all women — even pretty young gals — meant kids and kids meant complainin? There was no end to it this side of death, unless something happened . . .

Thoughts can make a dark world. Thoughts can sink him so low he's not above basing his own hope for happiness upon the death of poor Fancy. And she loved him once. She puts her trust in him now to care for her always. And she scolds . . .

More and more, to make life a little bearable, Dutt takes to collecting newspapers when he can. Like another would take to whiskey, Dutt takes to the news. It's a way to keep his mind off bad luck and troubles at home.

The more unhappiness, the more he reads. Fancy's milk fails. It's happened before. Dutt must boil the cow's milk himself and stopper a bottle with a rag to feed the baby. Fancy's done it again. She's come down puny with milk fever. She has sores on her teats where the breast baby nursed. She's down flat on the bed, flushed and hot. She leaves Dutt with the chores, saying how dear and sweet he is to put up with her this way. "Do you want me to die?" she says. "Wouldn't you be better off if I would just die and get out of your way and then you wouldn't have to go through all this?"

"No," Dutt says, pious-like, "Don't talk that way. I just don't see why we have to have all the bad luck, that's all."

He takes the breast baby, offering him the rag-stoppered bottle, offering the rag to suck, trying to feed the poor little devil. Dutt tries to bury his thoughts elsewhere. He thinks about the newspapers, the war fever. The baby doesn't like the rag. It squirms like a dog. It fights his grip, spitting the rag from its little mouth. Fancy's calling from the next room.

"Dutt? What's wrong with the baby? Dutt?"

"Huh?"

"What's ailin' the baby?"

"He don't favor the rag," says Dutt.

"Go gentle on him, Dutt."

"He don't like me. Maybe I'll lay him down in his box and let him hungry up 'fore I try him again."

"Mind and don't heat his milk too hot, Dutt," says Fancy.

"Little fyce dog, ain't you?" Dutt says quietly, under his breath. He puts the squirming baby down and goes outdoors where it smells good. Taking his newspaper with him he walks deep into his cornfield. The sun is there. It smells sweet. A breeze comes off the river.

Hidden in the quiet corn Dutt feasts his mind. He reads news and opinions of the oncoming war. He reads speeches in Congress. He reads how violent feelings run wild in South Carolina. Rabid war fever. Dutt's on the side of secession. He dreams of a South no longer married to a whining, complaining, self-righteous, sickly North. He dreams of a free South, without damned tariffs. Were it not for tariffs Dutt Callister might be a big slave owner himself. As it is he's lost those slaves he once had. Bad luck and the North are the cause.

Here the North is stealing Southern slaves! Dutt wishes God's curse on the God damn North!

After reading his paper (he's read it twice before) he gets his hoe from the barn and returns to the corn rows. He begins chopping weeds and vines. He works carefully, chopping about the thick green base of the cornstalks. He tries not to think of Fancy, down and feverish and can't nurse her own baby! And the baby hollering his head off. The older children jumping in and out of the house. He comes on a little snake. He chops it in two pieces and then chops each of those pieces into two pieces and goes straight on about his work, mindless of the little serpent, mindless of anything.

While he worked a mass of clouds piled up out of the southwest. A stiff wind came gusting on the heels of a gentle one. Birds skimmed the sky, playing on the wind. Trees about the edges of the clearing began to bend. Their limbs tossed up and down. Leaves, twigs and dust came sailing. The corn seemed to kneel, a reverent army called to prayer. The sky went brown, then gray, then black. Rain fell. Big, warm drops scattering in the corn. Then small drops pushed by the blowing wind.

Dutt's choice was either to leave the field for the house, there to be cooped up with Fancy and the kids, or to saddle a horse and ride into Somerton, rain and all.

Dutt ran for the barn. Ain't been lucky like Elias, Dutt thought. Still, a pole barn was good enough. He slipped a bridle on the startled horse, saddled him, mounted, and galloped out of the barn straight into the rain. South he galloped, to the Somerton high road. Trees had toppled across the way here and there. The road turned more and more to slop. In places it was flooded. The rain was blinding . . .

Dutt didn't mind. No more than he minded getting wet to the skin. He had a reason for riding to Somerton after all. He was anxious for news. And while he dried out he'd have a drink or two at the hotel, as protection against the wet. He might sit down to a table of dominoes. The South was going to need her loyal sons before long, or he was badly mistaken.

Chapter 8

Some called him Bad Jasper, others called him Common Jasper — Jasper Coon, but for young men like Isaac and Willy and Edward Ashe, he held a fascination for he squatted in the woods, devoted himself to sleeping and drinking and hunting when it pleased him and he didn't give a good God damn.

Pore white. He fucked his cow. He was so vulgar he was poetic. He could move back and forth between the purity of the woods and the campfire and the sluts on the slope behind Indian Town. He was a gold mine of iniquity and had an old woman he'd brought home from the Horse Pens. She was better than a mean dog, he said. A plug horse and a gun and a jug and he was ready for anything. She was a cross-eyed thing with big feet and worshipped the ground Jasper walked on and never talked back to him.

He'd served a hitch in the artillery and he could cook anything. He knew everything about stealing and gambling and he could light a fire in the pouring-down rain and live a week, two weeks in the woods or on the rivers. He hated a bath as much as any boy and he hated niggers and hated slavery and hated the ways of the planters. Scratch him and he hated just about everything there was, yet he would give you the shirt off his back. He could eat anything, he could sleep anywhere.

Fond of roaming and riding at night, of listening at dooryards and peering through windows, he taught the boys those stealthy arts; they'd ride into Somerton and creep in among the tents of the camping Irish, those brutes that were building the railroad, tenting in the woods and swamps, gambling and swearing and fighting with knives and pistols and clubs, murdering and dying of fevers and the tents moving through the countryside like a sudden migration of moths. Laying and spiking the rails by day, fighting and roistering and singing by night — the Irish. Their stew kitchens marching down through the west beside the line of the telegraph poles, past the new yellow depot building where the telegrapher sat hunched beside his key, putting Somerton in touch with the rest of the world.

There were fires on Fort Hill. The livery stable was licked down, leaving a black mark. Chatillion's came next, and made a red glare against the sky that was seen for miles about when the trading post burned, for it was on top of Fort Hill. And the walls of the old stockade rotted and were dangerous and had to be torn away and burned until only the gates and the iron hinges remained as a reminder that the wall had been there.

The rum ordinary which had a dirt floor at first and felt cool and solid underfoot, got a wood floor and planked walls and a steamboat picture was hung behind the spirit counter. Log walls weren't good enough anymore, scowls Jasper. Nor dirt floors, and as for steamboats don't everybody know the way those boats blow sky-high and bring scalded God-damn doom to every critter on board?

The best time to be hanging about town was when the coach came in with the blinds drawn.

When the cry goes up in Somerton, "Coach coming, blinds drawn!" dominoes go asunder, playing cards drop, cider spills. The populace goes dashing for the post tavern and sure enough the coach appears below the hill, blinds drawn, with the driver stuck out front naked as a thumb. He's given a blanket and swaddles himself, looking gray-faced as he draws the coach to a stop before the tavern and sets the brake and slinks down off the seat and stalks inside wearing the blanket.

T. Laird appears with a cotton basket and begins supplying naked arms with random articles of clothing kept for these precious occasions. Once the clothes have been fed inside, the coach commences to rock and squeak, as though in a queer process of digestion.

At last what Jasper Coon and Isaac and Willy and Edward have waited to see, happens. The door opens. Down come the passengers, ladies first, gentlemen next, looking like what they are, proud strangers who've been robbed and stripped naked and now wear old clothes. They alight without watches, jewelry, canes, stovepipe hats, bonnets, pistols, flounces, capes, parasols. They've ridden miles in jumbled nakedness.

"Be a God damn pity if the railroad must to do away with the coach," says Jasper. He feared it would. It did, finally.

Nevermind, other pleasures remained to them. One and all they chewed tobacco and spent long days beside the river spitting, and shooting the heads off round-shell turtles with their rifles. They charged on horseback through the stumpfields firing pistols and yelling.

They disassembled Dutt Callister's wagon for him and put it together again on top of his barn.

Then one cool and early morning the cannons began firing in Somerton. One biting thump followed another. It was a signal the entire district had been waiting for and half expecting and half dreading. It didn't have to be explained, no. The thunder was man-made and those mad bites of sound rang in the woods and touched every clearing and Jasper Coon stood outside barefoot and wearing his long johns and as he pissed the thumps continued, one biting the heels of another.

"I'm be God damned if they'll make me go this trip," he said aloud. His lean hounds rattled their leashes, stood up, faced the direction of the sounds, and began to bay.

Chapter 9

Some might content themselves to live and die in the woods and never see the world. Not my Isaac, thinks Jane. He will see the world and live in a city one day.

His reading and schooling and his association with his mother and his grandfather, Shokotee, had given Isaac a look over the wall, as the saying is. Isaac was bound beyond the district one day into the great world and would make his mark there, Jane was sure.

Willy, on the other hand, her youngest. Willy, he will stay in the woods and farm and be like his father, thinks Jane.

Elias and Willy and Isaac spend more and more time only sitting in Jane's room with the fire blazing, her three men, staying close-like, for soon they'd all be gone away.

Because the going-away was a thing they all knew and all regretted, they seldom spoke of it but sat instead before Jane's fire and kept her company. They spoke of the old days when the McCutcheons lived in a cabin. Those were good days, and Jane liked to hear that talk and stir in a word or a story herself now and then.

Presently the boys, two grown-up men, stand and stretch and go off to bed and she has Elias to herself.

She hadn't wanted more children after Willy, and now with Elias leaving soon, she wouldn't want to be left to carry and bear and raise another one. With him leaving. But she wants a child all the same, another of his children, a little girl maybe. She'd dress her in white dresses and brush her hair and tie a ribbon in and call her Geraldine, after Jane's mother that was long ago killed by Indians.

But no, she took those precautions Leola had told her of; she didn't want a baby with Elias gone away. (Yet she did want one!) Strange, how these last days of lying together, these last moments of love-making, seem so terrible. She holds him a long, long time. After all, death is a door we all enter, but it's awful when a woman must hold her man so long, for thinking he might be hurt and torn. To think of something piercing him — it's all too vile and awful. If she holds him long enough maybe such won't happen, not to him. Jane puts her body between Elias and those hurts.

A strange thing too, that she never really worried about him when he rode away to the Horse Pens. No. That time she sent him with her blessing and wished him well to kill all of them and leave behind nothing but ashes and graves. She'd have asked him to sow salt on the place had she thought of it. Was it because she was so young then, or because she ached so with wanting revenge upon the scum that cut her cheek? All, and all of that, it was.

She holds him, protecting him with her body. No harm will come to Elias, will it? No harm will come to her man. He'll not go away in the first place because he has no sympathy for such war as would divide the country and make little nations where one big one had been and let the powers in Europe — "Let them," repeats Elias, "come along and gobble us up one by one!"

Isn't so long ago as that, says Elias, that his own folks and Jane's own folks fought the British at New Orleans to keep the foreign heel from Southern necks. Break up the Nation? Do that and when the British come calling again things might not go so well. The Union must be preserved . . .

Aye, if she but holds Elias long enough, it may be the whole danger will march away and be resolved. Bless him, but he's deserved better than he's had, something more than a wife that's touched with lunacy pushing him away sometimes in the past and all because she's been vain, that's all, over a split face and a drooping eye and a sagging mouth.

He'd like a bit more light to see by, he says.

"No."

"Why?"

"Because in the dark maybe I'm better looking."

"But it's me, Elias; that's always been the same. Couldn't we have the light? A candle maybe?"

"No!"

Darkness. Blind love-making. And holding him afterwards, so close and so fast that he will never go away and never be harmed. And wanting his baby but taking precautions all the same.

He sleeps while she lies sleepless, hearing the cries of the night creatures — wolves and foxes, hoot owl and screech owl, whippoorwill, panther and wild cat; strange, mournful sounds that seem human sometimes. *Soul Birds, says Leola. Never seen by the eye of man, but Soul Birds cry at night all the same.*

But peacocks cry and yelp, thinks Jane.

It's only the peacocks, Leola.

Nothing like, says the old woman. It's the Soul Birds that cry like peacocks. Have him rid the place of those peacocks? See if the Soul Birds cease crying!

Wolves then, Leola. And screech owls. It's screech owls that make me shiver, Leola.

Put shoes upside down on the tongues. That will hush a screech owl, don't I know? Leola knows!

Jane slept. When she woke Elias was gone. The conch was blowing. Horns made from seashells and she would never look upon the sea except in pictures, but those sounds, like the soft gray moan of a dove, put her in mind of sea and mists. For leagues in every direction, from the Atlantic shore to the Mississippi River and beyond, conch shells call forth the people on every plantation, on every farm of any size at all; dawn sounds of beckoning launched upon the wind, from here all the way to the Gulf.

She went to her east window and looked down into the yard and saw him. It was as yet only barely breaking light in the sky beyond. Elias stood with the conch to his lips, his hair like wet moss, and the sound of the horn came, beckoning daylight. She smelled his seed where it had slept within her.

Chapter 10

Elias and his boys were backwoodsmen. It would be worse than wrong to think of them otherwise. It would be sinful.

They looked at the world with a backwoods eye. Nevermind city foibles and books and styles and fashions. When the corn was shelled down, the West Tennessee district was a backwoods district and Elias and Isaac and Willy were part of its backbone.

The unwary might be fooled, by Isaac especially, by his growing whiskers and reading the Waverley novels. But so did Elias read those novels and Willy too, only they read rather more privately than Isaac, who would sit up in the library at his reading.

New books came regularly to Oakleigh, for books were entertainment here in the backwoods. But often as a McCutcheon said "plantation" he'd say "clearing" in the next breath.

It was a clearing, after all, Oakleigh was. They'd hewn a clearing here in the woods and they still wrestled with stumps and sweated about the burning in the new ground and split rails for snake fences.

Of the three, Elias, Isaac, and Willy, Isaac had more veneer of civilization about him, but it was only veneer, paper-thin and glued on and subject to curl and swell and fall-away if exposed to even a few drops of rain. Veneer of any sort hates the outdoors and can't stand the direct heat of the sun nor the wind from the north, and for all his big words and his high notions and ideas, Isaac underneath was a backwoodsman and rough as a field cob.

Like a well-bred young gentleman Isaac made it his business to be at the First Presbyterian Church on Main Street in Somerton every Sunday. He listened to sermons telling how God had smiled upon the South and upon Southern slavery. He was told how traitorous and trashy the North was. He learned that slavery was an adjunct to the most perfect civilizations ever devised — to Ancient Greece and Rome.

But Isaac had his own notions about slavery, even if he kept quiet. Privately he agreed with his father that slavery was wrong. It was wrongheaded and wrongminded and no backwoodsman would ever think otherwise, no. A backwoodsman knew the difference between right and wrong; he lived day by day his whole life long and looked wrong and right both in the eye and knew one from another. Wrong had an evil smell and its eyes were red, did you only look. But right had clear eyes and right had a smell of sweetness; a backwoodsman knew the difference. No amount of fancy preaching would blur Isaac's vision.

And though at times it might seem that Isaac's every friend came originally to West Tennessee from Virginia and was delivered by a physician and raised by a nigger mammy and had a father that fought duels, the truth of it was that those friends were a trifling few. Some came down to the western district in spring buggies marching with a full complement of slaves and built big houses right away, but they were a pitiful damned few. They only seemed numerous and that, perhaps, because it was they who spoke so vociferously in favor of war.

Isaac had only to see Leola to remember who he was, Leola dozing in a corner of the kitchen and a favorite hunting hound or two asleep in front of the hearth and the cat in her box with her kittens beneath the stove — and Isaac knew. Waking, Leola scrubs her gums with snuff and takes herself a dram of whiskey. Like many of her tribe she confuses "good spirits" with the "Great Spirit." She it was that brought Isaac into the world and taught him the rain song and made cornshuck dolls for him. Isaac was a backwoodsman delivered by an Indian midwife and he never fought duels. Well, almost never . . .

Sometimes Isaac and Willy sat down to meals with Leola, taking meals in the kitchen with the servants; and why not, where the servants were close as kin almost?

But once Isaac took the steamboat to New Orleans with Jake along as his gentleman's servant. Isaac carried a sword cane and had a brass-bound steamer trunk and in a fanciful way he thought he was having fun, taking a little wine in the mornings and going back to bed again, after the French fashion. But the role hadn't suited him, exactly. He wasn't a rake hellion after all and he couldn't spend money without feeling certain pangs. It was hard-gotten money and represented the sweat and the pain of labor. It was moreover, honest money, and was therefore not so easily spent.

For all of Jake's urging (for Jake knew all about the bright world or imagined he did, which is the same thing) Isaac couldn't bring himself to plow a wide furrow. He was Elias's son, after all, and there was a quietness in him and a dignity. It was the backwoodsman in him, the true bone of his being and it gleamed beneath the veneer.

In the most expensive bordello he visited his adventure with a young woman was not fairly begun when cries of female distress from behind the heavy doors of a large chamber just across the hall made the young man spring up and rush to the rescue in spite of all his pretty companion could do to hold him from it.

Cracking through the doors he beheld a nude girl tied to a low bed and a great blackheaded fellow in a blue silk robe in the act of burning his helpless victim on the thigh with a lighted cigar.

Isaac sprang on him with a roar, stuck a thumb in his eye, loosened his teeth, butted the wind out of him and was in a fair way of breaking the man's neck when he was finally hauled off by main force and given to understand that the gentleman he had just assaulted was none other than Colonel Watt Hickey of Natchez, who owned above a thousand slaves. Watt Hickey, Esq.

Isaac left the address of his hotel and went straight there and woke Jake and told him everything.

"Now the fat's in the fire," says Jake.

And the next day at ten in the morning Colonel Hickey's second called on Isaac, presented the colonel's compliments and said the colonel demanded satisfaction. The second, a Dr. William Foreman, confessed that he hadn't expected to find Isaac so young and he offered further that it was the colonel's pride that was bothering him most, that and his shame. Isaac could leave New Orleans before sundown if he wished or . . .

A week to the day after the incident Isaac went by private coach to a plantation eight miles in the country. He slept in the guest room and was waked before daylight. The last leg was accomplished on horseback. An enemy of Colonel Hickey's, one Pierre Labry from Mobile, rode with Isaac and was his second.

"I'm afraid the colonel's a crack shot," says Labry.

"Um."

"How's that —?" says Labry.

"Just thinking. I'll have to let him shoot first I suppose. I'm not quick."

"Well," says Labry. And after a little while: "Well."

The dueling ground was a pleasant swale of grass beside a bayou. Heavy beards of moss hung from the live oaks. Stakes were driven twenty paces apart. Isaac chose a pistol and Watt Hickey took the other. Watt's face was long and pale beneath his shock of black hair.

The agreed-upon stipulations were read and explained. Now the seconds took a pistol each. Foreman stood behind Isaac who stood behind one stake and Labry stood behind Watt Hickey who stood opposite, facing Isaac across the interval of ground from his position behind the other stake, dangerously near!

"Ready!"

He's going to kill me, thinks Isaac.

"Aim!"

He'll kill me sure. There, he's taking aim.

"Fire!"

At the word *fire* Isaac felt a shock. He had not raised his gun. I'm hit, he thinks, swaying a little. A numbing pain had begun in his right side and seemed to be reaching through him into his left breast.

He looked at Hickey, who stood open-mouthed. "My God!" cries Hickey. "I know he's hit!" So saying Hickey took a step backward.

"To the mark sir!" says Labry, raising his own pistol and cocking it with a distinct click. He aimed it at Hickey's head.

As Watt Hickey stepped again to his position behind the stake Isaac raised his pistol, took aim, and pressed the trigger. His finger met iron resistance. He lowered the pistol and looked at it. It was on half-cock. He cocked it full and raised it again. Something warm had moved down his side, meanwhile, beneath his clothing, and was running into his right boot.

Isaac held his breath and fired. Colonel Watt Hickey dropped with a groan. Holding out his pistol to Labry, Isaac turned and made for his horse, gritting his teeth.

He was just mounting when Labry caught up with him. "Is that blood on your boot?"

"Yes, sir," says Isaac. "I believe he may have pinked me."

"Then let the surgeon attend you."

"No," says Isaac. "I don't want the son of a bitch to know I'm pinked. I don't want him to have the satisfaction. Nossir."

At the plantation Isaac was given brandy, the bleeding was staunched, and he was put to bed.

Labry meanwhile went to see what he could find out about Hickey. When he returned Isaac was in pain but resting and taking a sip of brandy now and then.

"How is he?" says Isaac.

"He's gut shot. They believe he's dying. He's suffering horribly."

Labry poured himself a pony of brandy and walked to the window and looked out, a big fellow with sleepy features and a pouting lip. "I wish I'd done it."

"So do I," says Isaac. "I wish you had!"

About sundown Labry returned to the house where Hickey lay. He returned after nightfall.

"Well?" says Isaac.

"He complained of the room being dark not an hour ago. He asked who it was that had removed the candles."

"Is he —"

"He's dead. They've started back to New Orleans with him. Dead as a hammer," says Labry. "Wish I'd done it!"

A dark moment for Isaac and a shadow to follow him the rest of his life. He wasn't a duelist after all, no; he was only a young man from Tennessee's western district, a quiet young man.

Elias had heard it all from Isaac, first in a letter which Jake took home, and later from Isaac himself who came home as soon as he could travel.

Had Elias thought out in advance what he would say to Isaac? He had, and he'd rehearsed the speech a thousand times, or so it seemed to him. Half speech it was, and half sermon, and Elias's text was threefold. First: "Lie down with dogs, get up with fleas." And next: "The wages of sin is death." And finally: "A live dog is greater than a dead lion."

Elias hammered it all together in his head like a blacksmith. He spoiled for the moment of Isaac's return. He'd tell him to go cut a stick and bring it. "Yes, whip me. Isaac! Beat me with it, Isaac, for plain as cake I didn't raise you right! Brawling in a whorehouse, getting yourself shot. Is this the example you set your brother? Dueling? Killing a man!"

Yet the father no sooner laid eyes on his oldest son again than he put his arms about him. Near to weeping, all Elias could think was that Isaac was home.

"Isaac, Isaac," says Elias. "My son, my son."

Isaac was shocked one early morning. He had been sound asleep. Then someone shook him. It was Willy.

"Lincoln's been elected," said Willy. "So I thought I'd better wake up everybody. It's war."

Willy had his mother's direct, green gaze. He stared straight at Isaac. Without replying Isaac opened the drawer of his bedside table and reached in for his watch. He opened the case and looked at the time, closed the case and put the watch back. "Did you wake me at seventeen minutes after six o'clock in the morning just to tell me that?"

"It's war, I tell you," said Willy. "Open your window,

Isaac, and you can hear it. They're firing the cannons in Somerton. Open your window and listen real close.

"I'm telling you, Isaac, it's war sure as hell. The minute that son of a bitch gets in the White House . . ."

"Willy, it's very early . . ."

"Isaac, I'm serious. This is war. God damn, don't you know they wouldn't shoot the cannons if it wasn't?"

"It isn't war," Isaac said. "It's just those blockheads that shoot the cannons every time the telegraph key clicks, in the *hope* of war. It's Dutt Callister again. That crew."

"My friends."

"Your friends and some of mine too. I expected Lincoln would win the election. I feared it. It's just the same old *talk* of war. The South would lose, Willy! We'd get whipped if there were a war."

Willy smiled. "What about England? You think they don't have to have our cotton? Think they won't come in shoulder to shoulder with us, Professor McCutcheon? Think you know everything don't you because you lay around and read so much? And grow hair on your face? Have to stay up here and hide until you get it all growed. Ain't thought about England have you? Tell the truth!" Willy smiled. "Got you, don't I?"

Isaac shook his head, self-consciously he felt his new beard. "England isn't coming in, Willy. Take my word on it."

"I'd like to know how you can say that? How come you think you know so much more than everybody else? Father thinks England *will* come in on our side but then he's against the war too and I don't know why. He's too old, I guess. But why are you so much against the war?"

"Why are you so much for it?" Isaac said.

Willy thought a moment. "Because it's fun," he said.

"*Fun*!"

"All right, but you yourself heard Petty McNeilly tell how he shot that woman's head off at the Horse Pens. I tell you

Isaac, it's war! It's gonna be fun! And if you keep laying here in the bed and sleeping all day you're gonna *miss* the God damned thing! Be over before you get there."

"Waked up," said Isaac. "Wide awake."

"You gonna go bear hunting with us?"

"I might."

"Then get dressed."

Leola appeared, bringing Isaac his tea. He touched his beard and yawned.

Rance came in. "Somebody's up early," he said. He was a house servant.

"Going bear hunting," says Leola.

"Um," says Rance. "Marse Isaac? Want me to go too?"

"Yes, get my horse," Isaac said. "Hurry now."

Breakfast was boiling on Leola's hearth and stove — grits, eggs, bacon, biscuits, ham. She served the young masters first, then handed Rance his plate. Rance ate standing aside. He rested his elbow on the cat stand.

Willy said it was time they bathed their feet. It was a custom Elias had taught them. If a hunter bathes his feet in icy water then they will feel flowing and warm when he puts his socks and his boots back on his feet. And if his feet get cold along the way he has only to dismount by an icy stream, and bathe his feet again.

Outside the day was clear. Frost had fallen. They went down the bank below the millrace. Isaac took off his boots and his socks and made a face when he put his feet in. He left them in until the ache of the cold made it seem to him as though his feet would drop off. Then he dried each foot carefully with a cloth and pulled on his wool socks. His feet began to warm instantly and when he pulled his boots on they felt as though they had been warmed overnight on a hearth.

He took care then, before he mounted his horse, to check

everything over, beginning with the bridle, the bit, the reins, the chin strop, the breastplate, the saddle girth, the gun scabbard, the gun itself. When he was satisfied all was in place he put his foot in the stirrup. He let his horse go the first mile in an easy walk. Five hounds made up the pack and they began the day by going ahead of the horses and sniffing the weeds and the grass. The females squatted. The males lifted a hind leg. When they had pissed all they would they started, one after the other, to shit. They wanted themselves empty in preparation for the bear and they worked at this and left little marks of steam in the frost.

Drawing a deep breath Isaac felt the horse, he felt the land beneath the horse, he felt the gun scabbard beneath his leg. The cold pushed through his gloves trying to get at his fingers. Away in the distance the oak stood upon the frost-covered ground with no other trees near about it to challenge its size and authority and age. "Why haven't I hunted more than I have?" Isaac wondered. He felt the old pleasure and desire that had been a part of him for as long as he could remember, his whole life long. "Hunting is better than anything," he thought. "And everything else is false and anyone who does not hunt is false." Then the sun began to sparkle on the fields. Isaac's entire self felt the sun as it touched the outer layers of his clothing. His body reached eagerly to take in the warmth where the sun touched. His horse began to break through the crust of the plowed land. The dogs had strung out ahead in a line, going at a steady trot.

Far in the distance beyond the cleared ground the north edge of the bottoms stood out from the horizon. It was there they were headed, edging and crossing the ditches that bounded the cultivated fields. They passed the oak. It seemed to be reaching to embrace the early sunlight. "Oakleigh," thought Isaac. "Have I been out of touch with myself so long as to have forgotten what all this really means to me?" The tree shamed him a little. And so did Willy's lithe figure and his sunburned face, for Willy hadn't forgotten anything. "He's been in touch with this all along, while I've cheated myself," thought Isaac.

He promised himself that he would hunt every day henceforth until the last day of cold weather. "Every day this season," he promised himself. "And henceforth after this, every winter of my life. Amen."

When they had crossed the last stretch of open ground and entered the woods the cold came back at Isaac's fingers again. His body drew down against itself, seeking warmth. The air had a cold smell here in the woods. Isaac was just thinking that he would reach for his flask and have a drink of brandy, when the dogs struck a trail and belled into a chorus. At the first bellow the horses broke into an abrupt gallop. Willy led the way with Isaac close after him, breakneck through the woods, leaping tree trunks and skirting the edge of a slough.

After a while the dogs lost the trail. The hunters stopped their horses. Waiting at a standstill they listened for the dogs. The guns were still firing in Somerton. The sound was dull but intrusive and seemed closer somehow.

Presently the dogs found the trail again. Isaac began to sense that he would see the bear. They galloped dead on, dodging vines, swerving to miss trees and drawing closer and closer to the beckoning sound of the pack.

Isaac saw the dogs first, then the dead tree. But when he had ridden in under the tree the bear was nowhere to be seen. Yet far up the gray side of the tree was a hollow and it was into that hollow that the bear had gone. Noses up, the hounds continued to bay. They wagged their tails.

"So," says Jake. The Negro got down from his horse and untied the ax from his saddle. He put his coat aside, rolled up the sleeves of his calico hunting shirt, spat in his calloused hands and began to chop. Rance meanwhile gathered wood and lit a fire. Isaac sat down on a log and watched.

"Now you try him," Jake said after a while. He handed the ax to Rance. The younger Negro laid his coat off, rolled up his sleeves, and exactly as Jake had, he spat his palms and attacked the tree. He made a show of striking harder licks than Jake had struck and he grunted after each blow. The day, until that moment still, began to blow a little and the sky was a bright deep winter blue and the trees, except for the dead den tree, were very black in the trunk and the small limbs were mottled.

The bear appeared. Bit by bit it backed its way out of the hole until it was clinging to the side of the tree, very far up, and wagging its head back and forth.

Seeing the bear the dogs began to bellow and leap. Rance left off chopping and backed away from the tree. Isaac went to his horse, took his rifle from the scabbard and stood back a way to see what the quarry would do.

Willy carried his rifle in his left hand; now he loosed the reins and took his horse to the other side of the fire and tied him there, all the while looking where the bear was.

The bear moved, as though decided to climb back into the tree. Isaac and Willy both shot. The great, black beast leaned slowly away from the dead trunk and fell in a long somersault. The carcass crashed into a pile of limbs on the ground. The dogs flung themselves on it. Jake and Rance seized the dogs and leashed them one by one and tied them a little distance away. Now Jake, butcher knife in hand, moved in cautiously and cut the bear's throat. "Big sow," he said, and he stood back a moment. "Big old sow."

Rance drew his knife. In a moment the guts were on the ground, purple and crimson. Jake unleashed the dogs. They began eating the guts and whining. Using the ax, Rance cracked the spine in the middle, breaking the back so the carcass could be tied to his horse. He chopped off the head and threw it aside. Then he chopped off the paws one by one.

Jake brought the paws to the fire and buried them under the ashes, laying on more wood above them. A gust of wind made the smoke billow up into Isaac's eyes. At the same time he heard what at first seemed to be a shot. Then he saw the tree and he saw that it was already moving, already falling, and he knew what had happened without needing time to think about it. His legs felt like lead stumps. He leaped away from the fire, turning and scrambling, stumbling out of the way.

The length and shadow of the den tree converged with the ground and sent up a splash of lesser limbs, of loam and leaves and ashes and when this had settled Willy's horse lay dead beneath and the fire was gone and the tree trunk lay like a giant gray bone not far from the headless carcass of the bear. The hunters stood astonished. The dogs began baying, then stopped, and began to whine, making that uneasy sound they make on a cold night . . . then they began to lick at the entrails again.

Isaac followed Willy to where the horses had been and saw only the velvet nose of the beast that had brought Willy here. Clambering over the trunk to the other side they saw no sign of the horse at all.

"Dead, buried." That was all Willy said. He looked away.

"God all mighty, God all mighty," says Jake. He stood on the great trunk, ax in hand, looking down. "God all mighty." His hair shows a little gray at the temples. His arms tremble.

Chapter 11

Now and again, since the guns fired that day, Elias has a horse saddled and rides away from Oakleigh as though seeking something. He rides into the woods like a man exploring backwards into the past and going his way thus has conversations with himself. His dog, a young hunting mastiff, follows . . .

"Yes, God," he begins. And everything comes back to him as though it were yesterday. What fine company was that Connecticut clock upon the mantel in the cabin he grew up in back to the east a way in Middle Tennessee where he had his birth and beginnings. A clock is fine company in the woods, ticking and striking the hours. Seems he hears that clock again. *Kling*! Or is the sound but the striking of bells about the necks of horned cattle with notched ears, cattle browsing in the nearby canebrakes? *Kling!*

And he remembers how the hogs crowded under the house during a storm. When visitors stayed all night they would say, "Hogs too, with all else you have?"

And Elias's father would say, "Hogs? Yes, a few, but I don't know how many." Speaking carelessly as though they did not count every one of those creatures every day.

The stage passed four times a week on the high road and went through Pistol Creek passing to and fro between Louisville and Nashville. And land taxes were paid in meat delivered to the military stations . . .

In Pistol Creek there was a tanyard and a rope walk. Then came a saddlemaker, and finally, wonder of wonders, a carriage builder. Those were great moments, going into town with the whole family to observe progress and count the new buildings there.

Then came cholera and death — whole families taken down with chattering teeth and black vomits. "Yes, God."

The people everywhere were beyond the powers of medicine. Guards stood in Pistol Creek and made the coach pass straight through without letting off passengers. People died in the fields. They fell dead on the roads. In the clearings whole families were found dead . . .

Still it raged and created a condition in the minds of men which was against God. Those who hired out to nurse robbed the sick. Others were drunk for days on end in the expectation that it was the end of the world. Houses were burned to destroy the plague.

Of the McCutcheons near Pistol Creek only Elias survived. Like many others he began wandering, as it were seeking his God again in the woods, with naught but a dog and a horse, a gun, and what few things he could carry. He came to love grass, how it stood bent before the wind, and the sun, the heavens and the firmament. He came to respect everything wild. Given time, he found, everything passes, and everything comes back again and the tired man can sleep on the ground with his arm cradled beneath him for a pillow and he will not miss the dead so much, nor dream so often of the Connecticut clock on the mantel, nor remember the dreams he's had and how his teeth chattered, nor the terrible cholera cramps. The rain washes him, the sun warms him, the wind speaks a special language and the woods feed and clothe him. His creatures are his companions.

There had been a blue-eyed girl sent away from Pistol Creek to a school for young ladies in Nashville. She and Elias had written letters back and forth.

When so many were sick, her own family included, she had come home to help nurse and she too was buried. Mary Fetridge . . .

Aye. He had kept those letters. Not as he read them over again and again, no, for that would have made him a madman, and well he knew it. No, he merely kept them, with the blue ribbon from her golden hair tied about, in respect for the fond, sad memory of one he had loved, of one that loved him.

Rough fellow that he was, he wasn't without sentiments, Elias McCutcheon. And never did a season change that he didn't have some thought of Mary Fetridge and ponder a little bit over what might have been. First love, if it's true love, leaves that mark in the breast; invisible, but real as real . . .

Wandering from Oakleigh, deep in thought, he finds himself in Riverside. But instead of reining about and going home again, this time he rides in.

Ellen is walking beside her rose beds where the last of her late, white roses are in bloom. She sees him and stops. Her black dress shows pale, white skin at the throat. Her red hair is longer than when he saw her last. A servant takes his horse and she waits standing just where she stopped. He approaches. Barn swallows, swooping in from the fields, make patterns in the sky back and forth.

He takes an interest in the roses. "Beds must be covered and the plants trimmed back," he says. He looks at her. She smiles.

"Your beard — it's thicker," she says. "Your dog, he looks just like the other one."

"Yes. He's descended from Dog, the first one. And Edward, how is he? I see him sometimes at a distance, riding with the boys. He sits a horse better than Isaac."

"But not so well as Willy," says Ellen. Pause. "I was just going down by the river for a walk. Will you go with me?"

"Yes, thanks."

Friends again, as easy as that. They cross the road, a couple, a big man, and a slender woman with long hair the dark red color of dry corn silks. The restless barn swallows pattern the sky above the river. Elias and Ellen talk a long while. After such a separation there's much to tell and say. But comfortable silences fall between.

Jealous, the young dog fetches his head up under Elias's hand. Elias is reminded of Dog. He lies buried now near the first cabin on Oakleigh, behind it like, with a neat white-washed wooden marker and a mound with grass growing. Graves . . .

"Jane, does she still sit by herself?"

"Sometimes," says Elias. "Buried almost, it sometimes seems."

She changes the subject. Edward, she says, is yearning for war. "He can't understand why I'm so opposed to it."

"They all three think I'm a rough old fellow fit for nothing but work — farming. They don't know why I'm against slavery. How is it I'm a slave owner and against slavery? That's what they ask and I don't have any answer." Pause. "I never wanted slaves."

Friends.

Seeing a mounted man passing on the road Elias looks to discover who it can be. He recognizes Dutt Callister on his fine horse. Elias waves. Dutt passes. Even though he seems to look straight at Elias, he gives no sign. What can it mean?

"Who was that?" says Ellen.

"Dutt Callister," says Elias.

"I thought so," she says, contempt in her voice.

"Why, what about him?"

"Nothing," she says. Yet her tone of voice makes Elias wonder if she is telling the truth.

Later, riding home, he feels much improved.

Chapter 12

Passing Riverside on the road to Somerton Dutt had seen Elias. Elias it was, and no one else. No mistaking the way the man stood, nor the lightness of his step. Like spring steel, Elias was and the sight gave Dutt things to ponder as he rode the distance into Somerton. Elias with Ellen Ashe walking by the river . . .

It was known that Elias opposed the war, yet who had profited more from the plantation system than Elias? In the circle of Dutt's acquaintance, no one had made a greater fortune than Elias. Yet the man professed himself to be flatly unwilling to go forth to defend the system that made him rich. He was willing, Elias said, to give up his slaves without a struggle, without a murmur, without a fare-thee-well!

Yet Dutt, who was a ruined man for the fact of his having pissed and trickled everything away somehow (what with bad luck and worse investments and Negroes that wouldn't work as they should; he'd sold his servants, every last one), yet he, Dutt, was willing to lay down his life for the Sacred Cause and the Sacred Soil.

Not liking to feel like a ruined man and not wanting to remain home and confront his misery, he rode to town to take a few hands of brag at the tavern. He had some cash left from the sale of his Negroes, after all. But no sooner did he sit down to cards than he sensed the game was crooked. Certain ones seemed to win every hand. Nevertheless he stayed in until he had lost a hundred dollars. That much accomplished, he excused himself, and strolling up the hill he entered the rum ordinary where a rough crowd was playing keno at twenty-five cents a card.

The place was full of smoke and a man had to shout to make himself heard above the roar. Land auctions had brought a new bunch into town with money. Cranked by the caller who wore a greasy apron and a slouch hat, the keno cage whirled and clacked. The balls in the cage danced and tumbled. Taking out the next ball the caller held up a hand for silence and bawled out the number. Dutt shouldered his way to the bar.

The counterboy was solicitous and called him "Mister Callister," and fetched him a keno card and a large whiskey punch and found him a chair, treating him just as though he were still the prosperous fellow who had got great loot from the Horse Pens raid.

He lost three games in a row, drinking three large whiskey punches. But the fourth game he got three buttons in a row and only needed an eighty-eight.

The caller held up his hand, squinting to read the number on the little ivory ball just drawn. "Eighty-eight!"

"Keno!" cried Dutt in a mellow voice. Men nearby turned on him with envious looks. The capper came squeezing between the tables. One by one he checked the buttons on Dutt's card and so confirmed his win with a nod to the caller. Dutt took his winnings — twenty-three dollars — drank off the last of his whiskey punch in a gulp and turned his keno card in to the counterboy.

"Leaving, Mister Callister?"

Dutt gave the boy a wink and nodded. Taking a cigar in his teeth he lit it and strolled carelessly towards the door.

"G'night, Mister Callister!"

Dutt waved a hand in reply and stepped outdoors, away from the smoke, away from the noise. The night was crisp and clear and the stars seemed very close and very still. Puffing gently on the cigar he let his feet carry him downhill. He turned in at Fanny Chapleau's. Her place was the only building in town with a silver doorknob. Her Negro groom wore a tall hat and white gloves and drove a red-wheeled carriage drawn by matched thoroughbred trotters.

He let his hand rest lingeringly on the knob before reaching for the knocker.

A Negro girl answered and ushered him down the hall to a little chamber where two damask chairs sat facing, with a small, carved table between them. On the carved table's marble top were two stem glasses flanked by a decanter of wine. On the chimney wall a large, polished sideboard stood beneath an oil painting of a reclining nude with plump breasts and rosy nipples and a dark furze of hair just showing beneath her hand. No matter where a man stood in that room the reclining nude seemed always to be looking at him. Her eyes followed you. An oil painting on the other wall was of dark woods where three nymphs in flowing, gauzy garments were running and playing beside a river. And there was a framed mirror in which a man could look and see himself and know how well he looked and how handsome in such surroundings. In the gilt mirror Dutt saw himself framed as it were in gold. He cut a flattering figure.

Madam Chapleau, the girl said, was away visiting in the country and had not returned as yet. Indeed she rarely worked here anymore. Hardly ever at all. Nothing like the old days. A new girl now served as hostess, Miss Teenie Queen. "I'll call her."

Miss Queen herself appeared, beautiful and gracious in black silk, with hair and eyes as dark as Fanny Chapleau's. Dutt seated her in the chair opposite and sat down again himself.

"Well, well!" he said. "Dutt Callister, Miss Queen!"

Her reply was an ever-so-slight inclination of her head and a smile that showed little white teeth. She poured the wine. As she poured, it came to Dutt that the stuff was costing him a dollar each glass. Total: two bucks. But looking at Miss Queen and raising his glass for a toast to her health and her beauty gave him the distinct feeling that he could not be a ruined man as he had imagined himself to be while riding this way on the cold road.

Here was a place Elias never came. Thought Dutt: He's never seen the gilt chamber pots nor the bedrooms with lace hangings, nor how snowy the linens are, and all for a mere ten dollars with breakfast next morning thrown in to the bargain.

When Dutt dressed he would find that his boots had been polished and his clothes neatly pressed.

Miss Teenie Queen poured their second glass of wine. "Your pleasure, Mister Callister?"

Dutt felt a husky heaviness in his throat. "The Indian Princess, is she taken?" Deep in his mind he saw the Princess and her golden skin. Nevermind the subterranean suspicion that she was a mulatto.

"The Indian Princess is free. You want a jolly time?"

"All night," said Dutt, feeling his throat thicken.

"My, my!" Miss Teenie Queen's voice tinkled. "My, my!" Her tiny laugh went straight to his cods and gave his pecker a stir.

"The Indian Princess, yes," he said.

Before discovering the delights at Fanny Chapleau's Dutt had slept at the hotel, or the inn as it was called. He'd slept only to be waked by gamblers quarreling below stairs in the bar, and by bedbugs tormenting his flesh. As for Elias, did he come to town and stay the night, *he* took his blanket to the wagonyard like any farmer and slept on the ground. When he could afford the hotel, when he could afford Fanny Chapleau's, Elias kept his old ways. It remained for Dutt, who could ill afford any of it nowadays, to continue to enjoy the refinements and advantages of Fanny Chapleau's.

Miss Queen poured the third glass of wine and went to fetch the Indian Princess. Dutt savored the last puffs of his cigar slowly, and laid it aside in the round silver ashtray. The Indian Princess appeared. Dutt stood. He bowed. The Indian Princess curtsied. She wore white. She led the way down the dim hall and up the narrow staircase.

Fresh linens were stacked behind the glass doors of the armoire in the upper hall. Following into her boudoir, Dutt's heart gave a jump. A basket of dried wild flowers was hanging from the tester of her bed. The maid who had answered the door came bringing a bottle of wine iced in a bucket. Dutt opened the wine and turned to see the Indian Princess stepping out of her petticoats.

As she took off her chemise he saw again the dimple on each nether side, above her buttocks. Her small breasts were sharply pointed. Shivering, she helped him out of his clothes and put everything neatly away in her own little cabinet.

Kissing, Indian kisses. They were on the bed. She began writhing and wrestling and uttering soft little savage war cries. She grabbed his member and squeezed it and guided it straight to her little cunt cleft with its exquisite adorning triangle of black hair. When he was shoved all the way inside she bit his shoulder a hard bite. Her legs gripped and her open mouth pressed his with tastes of tongue and wine. Her heels cupped behind his knees . . .

"Love me?" she whispered.

"Yes!" Breathing hard. "Yes!"

"Love me!"

His cares, his worries, all his disappointments spilled and flowed away.

Leaving Fanny's house at nine next morning he was pussywhipped, drained and happy. The cold sky was a clear, clean blue. There was no breeze and the dusty streets had a clean dry-wintry look. He made a fist. His fingers were tight. Going to the hotel he entered the bar. "Whiskey," he said, with a look at the stranger who stood nursing a drink of his own, a traveler by the look of him, and no native of these parts. Cocking an eye at Dutt the other man drew his coat aside and stuck a lean thumb in his vest.

"What sort of country is it between here and Memphis, sir?" he asked. He had a Yankee accent and he spoke through his nose, through close teeth.

"Big plantations, sir. Nothing else. Rich plantations." Dutt took a sip and let the bourbon warm his mouth. The fellow was a spy probably and should be strung up at the nearest crossroad as a warning to others like him.

"How rich are these planters?" said the Yankee.

"How rich? From a hundred thousand to several millions."

"Nothing worth less than a hundred thousand?" The stranger's eyebrows rose a trifle and he gave a snort.

"Any sort of plantation is worth that. Negroes alone would sell for that."

"How many Negroes are there on these plantations?"

"Rarely more than a hundred. Fifty to a hundred mostly."

"No? Why is that?"

"When they've increased to one hundred they are divided to stock another plantation. You'll see three and four plantations joined, an overseer for each, and all belonging to the same man."

"Who would your richest planter be, I wonder."

"Elias McCutcheon, if I had to hazard. Or Shokotee McNeilly."

"Shokotee?"

"Indian name."

The Yankee was quiet. And then: "How many acres will a hand tend here?"

"Ten of cotton, five of corn."

"And the usual crop?"

"Bale and a half to the acre on fresh land and in the bottoms."

"How much upon old land?"

"Old land isn't worth bothering with," said Dutt. "What brings you here, sir?"

"To the South? Well, sir, I'm from New York, and it has been my ambition for some years to see the South. With things as . . . how shall I say . . . as they are."

"The hostilities?"

"The hostilities, yes. It came to me I'd best skip down this way and have a look-see before it's all destroyed. Understand, I mean no offense, sir?"

Dutt breathes through his mouth. "Destroyed?" said he, choking on the word. "Destroyed?"

"Destroyed, sir," said the other. "Utterly, totally destroyed."

"Why you *son* of a bitch!" Dutt stood trembling. "Are the rest where you come from as big a god damn fool as you, thinking you'll destroy us down here? Where the hell do you get such an idea as that?"

The other man looked at him coolly. He cleared his throat. "The fact is that you don't have a chance," he said briskly. "But everyone I speak to down here seems to react as you do, sir. Really I mean no offense, but *you* asked the question. Your entire region is gripped by a sort of mania. And understand, we in the North don't want this war and we haven't asked for it. I oppose it. I'm dead against it but the fact remains that the Union will be maintained. May I buy you a drink, sir?"

"Why, yes. Why not . . ." Dutt was too shaken to refuse.

"And you, sir, are you a planter?"

"I am," Dutt said. "I cursed you. It was wrong of me, sir, I offer my apology."

"Don't mention it, sir."

"I don't mind saying you'll be safer if you keep your opinions to yourself," Dutt said. "Others down this way might not be so tolerant."

"I'm beginning to see what you mean. Boy? Here! Whiskey!"

Dutt gave up trying to talk. The Yankee rattled on in his nasal staccato. Dutt left him after another drink and went to the livery stable and got his horse. During the cold ride home he could not shake that terrible word from his system. *Destroyed. Destroyed.*

When finally he entered his own cabin Fancy was waiting for him, waiting to pounce. Where on earth had he been? Hadn't he scared her half out of her wits? Couldn't he at least send a note home when he must stay gone overnight on business? And what kind of business was it anyway?

In the next room the baby was crying.

Chapter 13

Goodbye to Edward Ashe — and others — youngsters snatched from the bosom of the western district in which they were born, young boys — and bound away to Virginia.

Goodbye to a hundred and a hundred more, bound for Virginia in the expectation that if they do not hurry this war will be clean over before they can get to it.

Letters come from training camp. The new soldiers want boots and trousers and books and pencils and paper and a bit of money and a ham, if you please, *anything* edible. Comfits and cookies and spice cakes. The railroad does a fine business in freight sent the boys in camp from their folks at home.

Some gentleman privates even take along a servant or two. The Snail, meanwhile, has opened his front rooms to provide military tailoring and alterations. He has also put in a stock of supplies essential to soldiering. Surprise —! Depend on the Snail to find such a cache at a bankruptcy sale in New Orleans, to buy it in for a few cents on the dollar and bring it to Somerton. At least that is what he claims . . .

A gentleman no sooner has his uniforms and begins to drill

and practice military evolutions than he loses twenty pounds. His uniforms must be altered or discarded.

Meanwhile he will want some percussion caps, waterproof, in oval tin boxes of 250 and some percussion cap boxes with spring covers. The Snail has a good buy on copper powder flasks, India rubber powder flasks, brass bound; fine English horn powder flasks, India rubber drinking cups for the pocket, and gent's Britannia drinking flasks with Britannia cups.

He has pocket compasses in wood, brass, and German silver cases, and thermometers in japanned frames, warranted correct. Also several garrote rattraps, another item much in demand by the boys at camp. For cavalrymen he has sporting whips and riding whips and whistle whips and whalebone whips, rattan whips and rawhide whips and India rubber whips. Also pocket teethbrushes in various sizes, nail brushes in various patterns, and lather brushes of nearly every description.

His entire supply of patent blacking for making boots and shoes waterproof is sold out within a week along with all the Chinese teethpaste and every last bottle of Glenn's Strawberry Teeth Wash.

His shaving soaps disappear almost as fast as he and P'-nache can open the cases — Creole Military shaving soap, Worsley's Military shaving soap, Rigg's Military shaving soap; and when all that is gone he sells out of Bazin's shaving cream and Guerlain's Cream Saponine pour la Barbe. Paper knives and pencil sharpeners, envelopes both plain and cloth-lined, envelopes extra strong for mailing bank notes; pens and penholders, black and blue ink; and ruled letter paper in white and blue; playing cards, chess and backgammon boards, dominoes and dice . . .

Portable writing desks in rosewood and mahogany; razor strops and hones, shaving boxes and Sheffield razors, snuff-boxes, segar cases, tobacco boxes plain, fancy and painted, in German silver and morocco and heavy calfskin. Wax matches and German waterproof matches and Clark's friction matches and meerschaum pipes and fancy German pipes and French gorsewood pipes and green glazed Moravian pipes and Powhatan pipes and Burn's Scotch Cutty pipes, plain, stamped and carved. Also leather cases containing one meerschaum pipe, one segar tube, tobacco pouch and match safe. The entire stock of pipes is referred to by the Snail as "military pipes," just as the watches are *military* watches and the compasses are *military* compasses and the watch guards and watch ribbons and steel tweezers and nail files and the steel key rings — all are described as *military*, even including pocket tape measures, three and five feet, with return springs.

Pens and penholders, black and blue ink in stands, porcupine quill holders, superior Holland quills, common cedar pencils, gold and silver pencil and pen cases . . .

Chatillion and his son-in-law, Pettecasockee McNeilly, mutter some dark words. Maybe there wasn't a bankruptcy sale in New Orleans as the Snail claims and advertises. Might be as some helpless merchant ship was taken by a Confederate privateer of war and the Snail got in on the prize maybe?

However, the Snail had got the stuff and no matter where it came from, it was welcome in the district and soon sold, and when it was all gone, down to the last violin string, the Snail still had his military tailoring and alteration service and a new enterprise as well — the making of daguerreotypes for the soldier going away and the loved ones remaining at home; he made pictures — daguerreotypes of the living and daguerreotypes of the dead, and of the living soon to be dead . . .

Goodbye to sons from every family in the district.

Goodbye, Mother, for I'm bound away to war. Not for long, though. It can't last a few weeks at most.

Goodbye! Goodbye!

Chapter 14

Leola named her new fyce puppy Trish and fed her tidbits of whatever she liked best and made her the queen of the kitchen. The cats slept upon their stand as before.

Jake's oldest daughter by Ponselle was brought to the big house quarters to live. She was a large girl and slept on a cot in Leola's room and helped in the kitchen. Her name was Dotty and whatever Leola told her to do she did. One day, if she did well, she might wear the keys and be in charge here, Leola promised.

Leola was proud of the keys at her side and if she pretended to be harsh with the house servants, saying she was going to have this one whipped and that one hung up in the barn by her thumbs and another one sold down the river into Louisiana, she nevertheless always managed to relent at the last minute.

And Dotty, little by little, made herself as much like Leola as possible. She dressed the same way, spoke the same way, and ended by being as spiteful to Jake as Leola herself ever was. And Dotty promised Leola she'd look after Trish if Leola should die.

That was a comfort. For Leola felt her age more and more. She thought more and more of her younger days and it seemed that those times had really been happy. Her life hadn't been such a tragedy after all.

"Oh, yes," she told Dotty one evening. They had scoured the kitchen and left it bright and were getting ready for bed. Leola was tying her nightcap and peering in the mirror at herself. "I was loved in my younger days more than some people might think. You'll be loved in your turn, Dotty."

"Yes'm, Miss Leola. I believe so."

"You will," said Leola. "Is my bed warm, Dotty?"

"Some, Miss Leola."

Dotty always filled the warming pan with coals from the kitchen and brought it to warm Leola's bed. And to warm it faster she got in herself and lay shivering. When Dotty's teeth stopped clicking Leola knew the bed was warm.

"Get in your bed then," said Leola.

"This here bed ain't all the way warm yet," said Dotty.

Leola turned on her. "Out of my bed! And say 'Yes, Miss Leola' when you speak to me! Well, say it!"

"Yes'm, Miss Leola."

The girl was sulky and slow. She got out of the bed and Leola got in it. Dotty pulled up the covers to Leola's chin as she had been taught. Leola glared up at her. "I don't like that look on your face," said Leola.

"Yes'm, Miss Leola." Dotty crossed to the dresser. Leola raised up her head to watch. The room fell dark.

"Dotty!"

"Ma'am?"

"Light that candle and blow it out again! And this time mind you blow it out right. You think I didn't see? You think I don't know sass?"

Dotty lit the candle. "Now," said Leola.

Again Dotty blew the candle out, but this time softly and respectfully.

"That's better," said Leola. Trish, the fyce dog, was snuggled against her leg. Leola smiled at the darkness.

"Miss Leola?"

"What, child?"

"Is it true that the slaves will all go free?"

"What on earth put that in your mind, I wonder?"

"They say that's what the guns mean."

"The guns? They mean war and the men all riding away. The men, they like it, even if they don't say so — but as to setting all slaves free — I've heard that gossip all my life."

"Then you think we won't be set free?"

"What makes you ask?"

"Because it scares me, Miss Leola. Where would we go and what would we do? It scares me, that's all."

"Even if they set you free Leola will be with you, Dotty. I'll not let you come to harm, I won't. Come, kiss Leola good night. There's a good girl."

In darkness Leola received the kiss on her cheek. Dotty went back to her own bed. "Goodnight, Miss Leola."

"Mind you don't fall asleep till you hear me snore," says Leola.

"Nome, Miss Leola, I won't."

I've been loved, thinks Leola. *Loved more than some know. Here I've a house in charge and my own servant who loves me so much she's afraid of freedom.*

And presently, though she could not know when, Leola fell asleep.

Chapter 15

Winter.

It gathers down in earnest, but isn't a winter like any other, for the telegraph clatters in the yellow depot in such a way as to keep folk fearful as to what the next dispatch will be.

As a means to keeping up spirits, the band marches and serenades in front of the tavern, thence to the rum ordinary for refreshment, and then down Fort Hill past the depot and so to Main Street. T. Laird, the Snail, bent forward though he is, plays rat-tatting on the drum. The fields and the woods resound with his drumming.

The militia meets Saturdays with Dutt Callister in command. Calling themselves the Sligo County Volunteers, they march to the drum and parade to the music.

Beneath all, the Snail has yet another new business that is like the old one was, in that he keeps it to himself. He helps runaways that come through Somerton on their way north. He's dug a hiding hole below the floor in his back room with a trapdoor above. When the rug is over the trapdoor and a trunk has been placed on the rug just so, the room looks very natural.

Thus by day the Snail beats the drum for Southern Independence. And by night he angles away north driving his spring buggy towards the Missouri line where he meets a tall fellow named Bill, who's a ferryboatman. Bill will put the runaway across the river and will share whatever he has to eat with the poor slave. There is no profit in the runaway business, what folk call the underground railroad, but there is profit in another sort of business the Snail conducts, so much profit that even P'-nache has money, P'-nache, Shokotee's kinsman and Snail's groom, servant, handyman and what-have-you. P'-nache that never before was seen with money now goes about Somerton wearing a hat in place of that rag that used to be tied about his head. He gets drunk on a finer grade of whiskey than before and he owns four blankets now instead of one. He does a lot of digging in the woods near Somerton. He digs at night, burying and digging up, back and forth in a wagon, hauling heavy packing cases. By day he's rusty about the gills from so much digging. He sucks the dirt from his fingers.

Sometimes he goes with the Snail on night journeys, always angling away to the northwest over roads as bad now nearly as ever they were in the beginning down here in the west. The destination is always Cottonwood Point. "Knows the way almost as well as the horses," says the Snail.

"Shame," says Aunt Tio. "You know he's got more sense than a horse and him so faithful to you."

"In a pinch I'd choose a horse," says the Snail.

Winter dark outside, and indoors Aunt Tio helps the Snail out of his band uniform. She hangs up his drum and helps him into his working clothes — a black broadcloth suit, a tall hat, a heavy cape, gloves and a woolen muffler. She brushes his cape and follows him out the front door into the cold. Around comes the buggy with a runaway already loaded in behind the seat, upon straw and under blankets. Up climbs the Snail and sits by P'-nache, taking the reins from him. P'-nache draws up and adjusts the bearskin robe over both of them. Down the hill they go. The rest of Somerton is asleep.

"Warm enough back there?" asks the Snail.

"Yassuh," says the cargo.

"Freedom bound, then," says the Snail. "You start getting cold you just think about your freedom. It will warm you."

"Yassuh, I do think about it. I have."

In silence they went a distance on the road where it entered the woods. There was one turnout and then another. The road went winding. After a while the Snail passed the reins over to the Indian.

"You hardly ever spoke before, but now that you wear a hat you speak more seldom than ever, or is it less seldom?" says the Snail.

Nothing from P'-nache. The Snail leaned back. "Warm enough?"

"Sah?"

"You want to push your head out now, you can. I see a piece of moon now and then to look at but nothing more. Where did you start from?"

"Coldwater, Mississippi."

"Good to you down there?"

"Might nigh kilt me. Had me a bad master. Might nigh died before I got away, yassuh."

The Snail wondered why he took such risk, when he owed them nothing. Why had he become a station on the underground railroad when he kept a slave himself?

"How do you feel?"

"I feel good. Like what I dreamed all my life is about to happen."

The runaway offered nothing else. He volunteered nothing. The Snail sat in cold contemplation of the breathing horses frosting the air in patches of broken moonlight and the sound of hooves cracking the iced puddles and striking the frozen road; the creak of the high wheels, the moan of cold, steel springs. He must have dozed for he was waked by P'-nache. The Indian was lost at a crossroads. The Snail took the reins. He spoke to the horses, urging them into the proper turning. Just now he had been pleasantly dreaming. He could not remember the dream. Handing the reins over to P'-nache, he leaned back.

"Asleep?"

"Awake, yassuh. I sleeps by day, travels by night."

"Have a wife?"

"Had one."

"What happened?"

"She got sold."

"Children?"

"Two chilluns, sold with her."

"Ever expect to see them again?"

"Not in this life, sah."

"Know who I am?"

"Naw, sah."

"Know where you are?"

"Wid friends, that's all I know."

The Snail dozed again and woke as they began to twist over the old riverbanks. They reached the crest of the bluffs and began snaking down the road, descending to the flood-plain. When they were on the flat the going was swift. The road here was straight and the horses, perhaps smelling the river, began to stretch their stride and didn't need urging.

"We're coming to a river. On that other side and just north aways you'll be free."

The road went straight as a gun barrel. The frozen fields went turning, spinning out on either side under the moon-light and falling away behind. The Snail again took the reins from P'-nache whereupon the Indian almost instantly fell asleep and began snoring. His head sagged to one side, he swayed a little on the seat. His placid face was lost in the shadows below the dark brim of his black slouch hat.

"I see the river," said the runaway.

"On the other side you can rest," says the Snail.

The cottonwoods loomed like pickets. The revealed river lay down beneath the moon. The fields all about were covered with a white rime of frost.

The Snail smelled smoke and saw the smoldering campfire and the white smoke rising cold and straight in the windless sky. He gentled the horses to a halt not far from the fire.

"Bill?"

"Hello!" Bill's voice came from the darkness. Then Bill himself appeared by the wagon with a blanket shawled about his head against the cold, like an old woman. "Good trip?"

"No trouble," says the Snail.

"The cargo?"

"Anxious to be on the other side."

"Not sick?"

"Sound and well."

"You can get out now," says Bill to the runaway. "I'm going to put you over the river."

The runaway picked up his bundle and climbed out of the buggy. "Very grateful, sah," he said to the Snail.

"You can trust this man," says the Snail.

"Come," says Bill. "Boat's this way."

Still shawled in his blanket Bill helped the slave into the boat with his bundle and then came back to the buggy. "Need two wagons tomorrow, big, freight wagons," says Bill, swiftly and quietly.

"So they got here."

"The boat's in the slough on the between island."

"What have they brought?"

"Two thousand guns," says Bill.

"I'll start on back then. Goodbye," says the Snail. He spoke to the horses and slapped the reins. The sky seemed to wheel about and then go straight again.

Chapter 16

Mother and son, Edward Ashe and Ellen.

He was bound away tomorrow-like, and set on it since that day the guns began firing in Somerton. "It is my intention to defend the South's liberty," he had told her.

"But I'll hire someone to go in your place and you can stay at home with me, where you belong," she had said.

He had coppery hair and luminous eyes and pale, pink skin. He was wild, she knew that; and he suspected who his father was and suspected who his father wasn't. Or in other words he knew and yet he didn't know he was a bastard. Kings had been bastards though, hadn't they; and proud to be what they were in another age? He was proud and was all she had and was so precious to her that she had never been able to refuse him anything he asked to have. Edward was spoiled, but when one never expects to have a child in the first place, and then has one . . .

She finds him in his room oiling his favorite shotgun. She enters quietly. And Edward, he's particular about his guns and particular about his boots and particular about his horses. He loves cockfights and dominoes, cigars and toddies. When she wants to talk to him she must find him when he's interested in something at home. Otherwise he calls for his horse and leaves when she tries to speak to him. She got no help from her brothers with Edward. Werdna and Andrew were afraid of the boy and only recently he had gotten one of Ellen's house servants with child.

"Edward?" In her softest voice.

No answer. He's absorbed with his oils and solvents and gun rags.

Looking at him she's reminded of Elias McCutcheon. What a blessing, Ellen thinks, and no terrible mistake. It's hard now to remember how she felt when first she knew she was pregnant. How the rumors had flown, what the neighbors had said; Dutt Callister in particular had seemed to know something. Dutt had come sniffing, asking as to the whereabouts of Ellen's husband, saying:

"He was *here*? I missed seeing him. Where is he now?"

"Gone away to the west, on business."

"Expect him home soon?"

"In a few months, yes."

"Fine baby," says Dutt. He couldn't quite keep from smiling. He dropped hints. Should she ever need him, says he, just send for him and he's at her service . . . *He! He! He!*

She had gone to Doctor Parham as soon as she was sure she was pregnant. Wanting to believe her, the doctor had pulled his whiskers and marked his calendar and given her a tonic to take four times a day.

"One level tablespoon," says the doctor.

The worst had been yet to come. Werdna and Andrew had wanted to know who the father really was.

"Twas Ashe," says Ellen. "Who else?"

"Ho!" roars Andrew. "Ho!" A soreheaded bear, that Andrew. "Ho!"

"Then why didn't I see him?" says Werdna quietly. "Why didn't Andrew see him? He's been *here*, d'ye mean?"

"And why not?" says Ellen. "He came one night and went away before morning and the two of you were away in the woods hunting."

"Ho!"

"And you never thought to mention him to us?" says Werdna.

"Didn't think of it. May be as I forgot to mention it. Wasn't important after all."

Andrew looks at Werdna; Werdna looks at Andrew. Both have accused the other one. Looks that drive deeper than words. They spring at each other, those uncles-to-be whapping and mauling.

"No!" screams Ellen. "Elias! It's Elias!" she says.

"Elias?" says Werdna.

"Ho," says Andrew, weaker than he was.

"Elias McCutcheon. Tis my fault, not his."

"Best we say it was Ashe that came for a visit and then went on his way west and stick by it," says Werdna, making a shrewd face.

"Shame on you both to suspect one another! Shame! Look at you! Bloody as pigs!"

"We're sorry, we are," says Werdna. "If you'd only said there was to be a bastard in the house and it was Elias McCutcheon's —"

"Shame on you both!" cries Ellen.

Andrew is not so mad anymore. "What's done is done. Long as it had to be, leastways Elias, he's the chief man in the district. Makes him kin to us like! Ho!"

"Aye," says Werdna quietly.

"The neighbors are but envious, that's all," says Andrew, a philosopher with blood on his shirt. Ellen melts. She binds their wounds and makes a pot of tea . . .

Thus had her brothers backed up her story about Ashe. And they hadn't been shy afterwards about asking Elias for help, which he always gave, and borrowing this and that from him. Elias, he had helped them manage things along. And therefrom had they set foot again on the road to prosperity. Ellen's mistake became the founding of their fortune.

"Edward?" she says again.

He sits at his table. The balcony doors behind him are shut against the winter chill and damp. Spring and fall those doors are opened to give Edward that serene, uncluttered view of the river and the road beside it and the winding drive. Winding road and silent river and purple distances in the forest beyond . . .

"Edward! Son?"

"Here I am," says Edward. He's bound away to volunteer for service in Virginia, to go as a gentleman private in the cavalry. Bound away early, so as to miss nothing.

"You must not leave me. You must stay here." She stood by the wing chair.

"We've been over this. It's settled. I'm bound away and that's all there is to it." Edward was neat. By nature he was meticulous and clean. He has put down newspapers on the table first.

"But I've spoken to Doctor Parham. He assures me that you may have an exemption."

"That won't do!" says Edward. He concentrates ever so fiercely on the gun, cocking and clicking and oiling and rubbing. Besides the shotgun Ellen counts eight revolvers, brand-new Navy sixes bought just last week.

"Doctor Parham tells me that in such cases where there is but one son in a family and the mother is widowed, or where a place has more than thirty able-bodied Negroes and needs managing — these exemptions are being discussed and put forward, if only you'll wait a bit. For my sake, Edward?"

He replies in that deep voice, too deep a voice for one so young, and says: "If you can't leave off this subject, please leave me alone."

"Edward, while I promised I wouldn't tell your uncles about our little problem with Betsy . . ."

He looked at her in that certain way. Seeing those large eyes of his, her world seemed to stop. It was a moment before she could go on. ". . . I'm just saying that I've kept that promise. And I want a promise from you in return."

"As for my uncles, whether they know or don't know about Betsy makes no difference to me. Werdna and Andrew don't scare me. What happened with Betsy is a common, everyday thing. It's the hazard of slavery that there will be proximity. There will be intimacies. I wish you wouldn't throw her up to me. It makes me melancholy. How is she?"

"She's well."

"Where is she?"

"Sold," says Ellen.

"To whom?"

"Sold," says Ellen again. "If you promise me something I might tell you where she is."

"Too bad. I was curious to see what my child would look like. And you've sold her. Did she bring more for being fresh?"

"I have sold her," Ellen says weakly.

"And your grandchild with her."

"Promise me, Edward. Then I'll send for her. I'll buy her back."

"Promise what?"

"You *know* what! Promise you'll stay home. Promise you won't serve even if they should send for you."

He gives her a look. "I'm damned well going," he says.

"Men!" she cries. It bursts out. She's lost control. A hot dripping terror spreads under her breastbone.

"Mother, this war will be our deliverance," says Edward. "From Northern tyranny."

"Edward! No!"

"I can't sit this war out," he says. He picks up the rag again, caressing the gun with it. She sits watching. He puts his cleaning tools back in the wooden case. He carefully rolls up the newspapers, puts the gun and the pistols aside. He goes to the washbowl. She hears the splash of water and sounds of lathering. She smells the perfume of his soap. When he has dried his hands and rolled his sleeves down he slips on his shooting jacket. Very handsome, Edward is.

"Someone has poisoned you against me," says Ellen.

"No one has poisoned me. I'm just me, Mother, and I cannot be anyone else. I can't be a cowering fool. Accept me for what I am. That's all I ask."

"But Edward, I do!" She holds her breath a moment. "Going somewhere?"

"To town."

"Why?"

"For news. You'll tell me where Betsy is before I leave," he says. He looked at her fixedly. "I'm bound away tomorrow. Where is she?"

"Sold," says Ellen, quick as that. She watches him leave. She hears him call for his horse, then hears him riding away. Sitting down, she rests her face against the wing of the chair and closes her eyes. She feels a chill in the room that she has not been aware of before.

Ellen, Edward, Elias. She sees the tree together, a family under one roof. Ellen sees what might have been, another world. But this room is cold, this house is cold, this world is cold. Ellen sleeps in a cold bed, wasting away, all alone.

After a while she goes into the hallway, calling Pompey. He answers from the hall below.

"Build up the fires," says Ellen. "I want the library warm for Mrs. Parham."

"Yes'm," comes Pompey's reply, sailing up from below.

Fanny Parham, as dark and beautiful as ever. She visits often and works needlepoint before Ellen's fire, and always knows the latest gossip.

"Miss Ellen?"

"Yes, Pompey?"

"When she due here?"

"Midafternoon," says Ellen. She goes to her own room and sits for a long time at her writing table.

If a note would come from Elias, if only he would appear from the woods on his horse and come striding up the stairs and take her in his arms. Elias could comfort her. His embrace makes her know everything will work out for the best. Heart and soul she loves him. Blood and bone she adores him.

Opening her writing box she takes out a sheet of blue stationery and composes herself to write, dipping the pen:

> *My dear Elias – Edward is bound away tomorrow for Virginia unless he can be stopped. Please come at once, my darling. My heart would break should anything happen to him. Please come.*
>
> *Faithful until death,*
>
> *Ellen.*

She slips the note in a blue envelope and takes it downstairs to Pompey who's in the library supervising the servants called in to build up the fires.

"Send this to Mister Elias McCutcheon at once, by the fastest horse."

"Right away, Miss Ellen," says Pompey. Taking the blue envelope, he goes out with it. A moment later one of the stable grooms goes flying out the drive on a jet-black horse with mane and tail flowing and the little groom perched forward, head hard against the neck of the horse, elbows down, buttocks high.

Leaving the window she goes back upstairs to her room and climbs upon her bed, drawing up her feather comforter and stretching out beneath it. She feels a tingling in her loins and nipples such as comes over her upon waking from a dream in which she is mare and Elias stallion. Her breath comes short, hissing between her teeth.

"I'll have him someday. I'll have him all to myself!" she whispers. "I will! I will!"

The slow surge of feeling comes first to crest and next to overflow and gives a faint scent of musk. She's left weak, as though drained of marrow, and drifts to sleep . . .

Waked by Pompey she sits up as though drugged. Mrs. Chapleau and Mr. McCutcheon both are here, says the Negro.

Elias appears from the hall wearing high boots and a great coat and holding a whalebone whip.

"Leave us," says Ellen to Pompey. "And tell Miss Fanny I'll be down directly."

Pompey turns away, and with a nod to Elias, he goes out, closing the door. Elias turns the key after him, shrugs out of the coat, and throws it with the whip on the nearest settee. He comes to the bed and takes her in his arms. He smells of man and horse and the cold air is still in his clothes.

Unfastening the hooks in her dress behind, he helps off her gown and her petticoats and her chemise, kissing her mouth and her breasts, kissing her belly, him, all rough and shaggy, but gentle, always gentle.

"Do it! Do it!" she whispers, feeling the soft surge and

swell of him, the prick and the slow, smooth plunge, stuffing her, filling her. "Do it!" Bathing her with his shooting warmth, the explosion and spring of his seed. "Do it!"

She puts out her tongue to touch the circle of gray hair in the midst of his chest, that gray in the midst of his bosom, and the rest, all about it dark, touching with her tongue and tasting until he comes large again and she holds her breath then, full of him and no longer afraid.

Gone away all loneliness, gone away. Hold him yet a while to feel the beat of his racing heart, yet a while, and falling then; she fell tumbling all the distance down; dying, yes, delicious dying and bedwhirl and deathswoon and floating and him battering and riding and herself clinging and breath shooting out of her and him crushing down upon her, driving and crushing. "Do it!"

Warmed by him and rested, she lies beside him talking a while and then sits up and he fetches her brush and she sits with her knees folded, heels pressed to her inner thighs, brushing her dark red hair while he kisses her two high breasts like a gently grazing beast in a far green pasture.

And Edward, he's bound away tomorrow, that's true; but she has strength now to say a mother's goodbye and wish him well with a level look and firm mouth and a kiss upon cheek and brow without trembling. It's giving him up to that in which he believes, after all. So says Elias, who opposes the war himself and is resolved not to go for either side, not being willing to fight against his own friends and neighbors, nor yet being willing to fight with them in a cause which he feels to be both foolish and wrongheaded, and *wrong* even. To break up anything so hard won as the Union — tis wrong and wrong again to think of it; aye, tis abomination! he says.

"But my Willy, he feels just as Edward does," says Elias, kissing and kissing again. "They won't be talked out of it now. None of them will. Nor you yourself . . ."

"I'm for Southern independence, yes," says Ellen. "My

brothers too, and everyone I know but yourself, Elias. Help me dress. Fanny Chapleau's downstairs waiting all this while. What will she think?"

"That we've lain together," says he. "And done this . . ."

"You!"

"And that I did this, and this, and this!"

"You!" But she drops the brush aside, holding him again. "You . . ."

And she's thinking, *Someday I'll have you. Someday.*

He's playful, huge and childlike now, with his smile and his friendly crinkle about the eyes and his face so bright with innocence. And not looking so old anymore, no; now he's like a young god, thinks Ellen.

Chapter 17

Dutt's chest swelled. His body went taut inside his new gray uniform.

"Gentlemen of the Sligo County Volunteers! Parade rest!" he cried.

The ranks obeyed. The clatter of muskets was brisk and the early sun above Fort Hill shone upon them like wintry gold.

After a pause he called them to attention again and then

ordered: "Dismiss!" The men fell out of ranks and the little crowd of citizen folk that gathered now on Saturdays to see what the Volunteers would do next, began slowly to disperse.

Dutt was considering his need for a drink in the ordinary to warm him when Tug Chambers stopped by him. The Riverside overseer hadn't missed a single Saturday drill. He had been elected sergeant at the same time Dutt was made captain.

"Shan't we have a drink?" says Dutt.

"Need a word with you away from the others first if you don't mind, sir," says Tug. His gray uniform, his bulging neck, and his red face made him the picture of a sergeant. His voice was a hoarse, high tenor. "Walk aways down the hill if you don't mind, sir?" he says.

Side by side they headed downhill towards a desolation of shacks that was once Indian Town. When Dutt first came into the district these tattered dooryards offered a cheap tumble with a squaw and a glass of raw whiskey, all for fifty cents. Now it was all dead weeds and brown grass and overgrown pathways. Old blankets that had served as doorflaps stirred here and there in the cold wind. From the corner of his eye they seemed to beckon — Aye, ghosts, thought Dutt.

And Tug was saying: "Been deputized, or appointed you might say, so I have, to take a *matter* up with you."

"Yes?" says Dutt. "A matter?"

"On behalf of the rest," says Tug. "Ahem!"

Dutt stopped. They were standing in the midst of the old Indian street. Here the way was scarcely wide enough for three horses. Dead thistle and ragweed thronged both sides. The wind stirred a plum tree. Its branches scratched the shingles of the nearest shack. The day, already cold, was getting colder. "Spit it out," says Dutt.

"We need us somebody for major that will be able to undertake to *lead* the organization —"

Dutt nodded. He considered a thicket of yellow stalked pokeweed bent double and broken by the rains. War, real war, that smelled of heat and horror even at this distance, had put them all, Dutt realized, in a new frame of mood. They could march, they knew the manual of arms; but they were not really trained, not really equipped, not really armed. In such short time as remained to them there was small hope they could have all that was needed.

"Elias," says Dutt. "Elias."

Tug looked relieved. He nodded. "Got to have him, Dutt."

Dutt looked at the weeds again. Up to now it had been a frolic. From here on it was a cold question of fact. Either they went forth jaybird-naked to die in their own shit because they hadn't the gumption to admit when a ramrod leader was wanted, or they faced up to truth. They need Elias.

"But he's a Union sympathizer," says Dutt.

"We need him anyhow," says Tug.

"I know."

"He's made hisself terrible unpopular but by God . . ."

"I don't know how we'll get him," says Dutt.

A drum beat the long roll on the parade ground above them. A cheer was lost against the cold emptiness of the blue indifferent sky. Horseplay again — the Volunteers taking a few drinks, passing the jug. Every Saturday was the same, after drill . . .

"It's like this here," says Tug in that high, thin voice, with its husky pitch, "We got to have Elias . . ."

Dutt reached down to scratch himself between the legs. So much worry over the predicament was giving him the itch. He'd have to remember to apply Chatillion's mull to his crotch rash. He scratched savagely and at the same time made up his mind, saying: "Make them fall in again, that's what, by God. March the whole raft out to McCutcheon's place!"

"Now?"

"Now," says Dutt. "We'll all march out to Oakleigh!"

Together they went up the hill. It took some doing but they finally cleared out the rum ordinary and sent to the tavern for stragglers. They gathered the entire bunch save those few that had already ridden for home. Forming a column of fours they marched off down the hill, past the land office, past the pond, alongside the railroad until it veered away. East out of Somerton they went, with the cold wind at their backs and some grumbling in the ranks.

"Next mumble I hear I'm gonna whip somebody's ass!" Tug shouted. Silence then. They marched on . . .

Elias lay sleeping. Last night he had been on the river with Jake, minding trotlines and nets. Fires had been built and iron pots had been set over the fires on tripods. Lard was thrown in, and as fish were brought ashore they were gutted and skinned, dipped in a salted batter of eggs and meal, and thrown into the pots and sizzled brown. The slave women and children attending the pots had diced onions to mix with meal and water. The dough was dropped in with the fish to make hushpuppies.

There had been feasting and singing through most of the night, and when the pots were set aside the children had leaped back and forth across the fires, uttering shouts almost as shrill as bird cries.

Thus today, after dinner at noon, Elias had lain down in his room to rest on his high bed. And sleep had overwhelmed him such that he dreamed he saw the fires again. He seemed to feel his cold wet clothes and cold fish slime on his hands.

Hearing a commotion below, in front of the house, Elias came awake, feeling refreshed and the dream had been so real he looked at his hands, expecting slime, and at his clothes, expecting dampness. Going out to the porch he saw

Leola's fyce, Trish, running towards the road. The little dog was barking fiercely. A moment later he saw the gray file of the marching volunteers coming out of the woods. On they came in spite of the dog's rushing and barking. They assembled in gray ranks on the lawn. An officer was approaching the house. Elias went down to meet him and recognized Dutt.

"We need you," Dutt says.

"I'm for maintaining the Union," says Elias shortly. "You know my sentiments, Dutt."

"We want a commander," says Dutt.

Elias felt a rush of fever mount to his head. He clamped his teeth together. "God damn it! You brought this bunch here on my land? Me — a Union man? And you —"

"They're your neighbors," Dutt says. "The South is invaded, Elias!"

"I'm not for it!" says Elias. "Nobody with any common sense —"

"You favor the Abolition movement?"

"I don't disfavor it."

"We're scared," says Dutt. "We're asking you."

"You know my sentiments!"

Dutt stood quietly. There was dust on his boots, dust on his hat, dust on his uniform. He'd gotten an old dragoon saber somewhere. There was a pistol in his belt. He looked Elias straight in the eye. His voice was barely audible.

"All right," he says, almost whispering: "By God you ain't for it? All right! Maybe *we* ain't. But here it is. Maybe *we* ain't all for it. But if you're so God damned opposed to it then why ain't you joined the Yankees? You ain't too old. And another thing. Some people have a short memory. You came after me one time. Forgot that? Have you? And maybe I didn't want to go and Fancy, she sure's hell didn't favor me going but when you called on *me,* what did I do? These are your neighbors and their sons. Take a look. I just want you to see 'em, that's all. I don't doubt but you can call the name of every one."

Elias felt himself hesitate.

"We need you," says Dutt. "All right, you refuse? Tell *them* that. Look *them* in the God damn eye and tell them! Do that and I won't bother you again. Tell 'em you're on a side different to what your own boys are, and to what all your neighbors are. Don't stand here and cuss me. Go tell them you're against your own sons!"

"I —"

"Tell 'em it was all right for them to follow you to Missouri but you can't help them now that we're invaded. Tell 'em you don't care about the women and children. Their homes — tell 'em that don't concern you. Big Union bastard! Tell 'em! I want to watch!"

"Elias?" Jane, above on the high porch. "What is it?"

"The militia. Dutt —"

"Tell her —" Dutt whispers. "Well, you going to? *I'm* not going to do it for you!" He stood glaring, breathing hard.

"Elias?" Jane was calling. "Elias?"

He went down the walk alone, crossed the drive and made his way down across the field. He recognized Tug Chambers, the Alstons, the Wrays, the Musgroves . . . "Elias?" Jane was still calling. The men in ranks stood quiet. Elias read an expectancy in their faces. He saw that they were poorly equipped. "Elias?"

"I hear tell you want an officer," says Elias. They broke ranks, cheering. The shrill cry came as though from a single throat. They took off their hats and began to slap at one another, stamping, raising dust.

Jane watched the militia column wend back into the dusty road. Elias returned to the house. He came to the high porch beside her.

"The boys and I will be leaving," he said. "Soon . . ."

He wore his winter boots and work clothes and smelled of dust and tobacco. The little scars on his hands and the larger scar above his eye were pale marks on his sun-weathered skin. His dark-gray eyes looked in the direction of the retreating column. His jaw muscles twitched, his nostrils flared.

"When?" She heard her awkward speech. "Elias?" From her mouth his name was a hiss and slur. She put her handkerchief to her cheek as though to wipe all that away.

"You'll have to manage." he said.

She sat down in the rocker. "Yes — we'll manage here. Nevermind."

He leaned down to kiss her but she turned her face. "Don't" she said. "Leola and I, we'll manage."

He crossed the porch and went back into the house. She heard his heavy tread in the hall . . .

She sat rocking. She gripped the arms of the chair, her eyes closed. Isaac came out and she opened her eyes as he kissed her on the cheek. He smelled fresh and sweet. He took her hand.

"Look after your father," she said. "Please, Isaac?"

He nodded. She studied his blue eyes and his lean, serious face. He was not the horseman nor the hunter his father was. He compared in no way to Willy, who was such a daredevil. Isaac had grown up thoughtful and studious and had taken time, ever since he was a little fellow, to help his mother with her reading and writing. He was a natural scholar. Teaching was pleasure for him and he could recite poetry. She had hoped he might make his way to fame somewhere in a faraway city where gifts such as his would be appreciated and she had secretly put money aside for him, little by little over the years. He'd never be much help on the farm, and as much as he spoke of one day minding and owning and living on a plantation of his own, she knew in her heart he wasn't suited for it. Isaac was meant for something finer than his father had known, for a way and a world that Somerton would hardly understand. He had fought that duel, it was true. . .

She caught herself inside. I must be brave, she thought.

Isaac kissed her again. She was reminded of those wet little kisses the boys gave her long ago and of how they came and climbed in bed with her on early mornings. Those sweet times when they were little fellows came back at her again. It had never mattered to them that she was scar-faced. In their eyes she was always beautiful. Now Isaac and Willy would leave. She would have neither of her sons by her. Foreboding was gathering about her like a cold sea.

Isaac was gone then, packing. Rance and Leola were helping. Dotty was clacking back and forth, up and down the hall. Jake called from below.

The geese sang out from the millpond. Trish, Leola's fyce, was yapping. The wintry, evening sky was bright and clear, clean and calm. A pale quarter moon was visible, like a white crescent cloud. Night fell.

She held herself in and though she felt strange and almost disembodied, she stood up, and went into her room and lit a candle and without thinking opened a certain drawer. She saw her man's letters with the pale, stained ribbon wrapped about them. *His past* . . .

Why not unwrap the ribbon and read those letters one by one? She picked them up. She felt their fragility. Years had turned them brown long since. She put them down unread again, carefully closed the drawer, and climbed upon her bed. Those letters were his. She had too much respect for him to read what another had written to him. She didn't have Leola's prying Indian curiosity, no. Jane could respect her man, honor his privacy, and leave wrapped ribbons in place . . .

The withered rose told enough besides.

But Leola had said, "Leastways if you won't read them you could cast them in the fire! Keep them about to let him see them maybe and be reminded of another? I wouldn't! If you *don't* burn them it will be your sorrow, mind my words!"

"They are his," Jane had said. As often as Leola brought up the subject of burning those letters and worried and babbled about it, Jane made that same reply. And always, afterwards, Jane felt the stronger for it, somehow.

Chapter 18

Farewell to the land, farewell to Oakleigh, to Jane and Leola, to Jake and Rance, to servants and fireside. Elias says his goodbye. He takes a last look over everything as though he may not see any of it again. Time comes at last to leave.

It is like dying. You say goodbye to a place and you hear in yourself a whisper thought which says: "You must give it up. You must leave all of this and give it all up, house and pond, dam and barn, fences and cattle, river and landing, creek and bridge — every field and fen — all of this which you know as well as your tongue knows your teeth."

Goodbye then. Jane he embraces last of all. It is not just a raid into Missouri, no; something larger this time and may take longer. Surprising how strong her arms are and what a squeeze she gives in return.

They've talked, between themselves, as man and wife. She's got the management of the place from here on in till the war's over. He's to move into Somerton and stay at the hotel with the boys to manage his recruiting campaign and take his orders from there — his marching orders: they can't be long in coming, no, for there's a Northern army on the way and it dares Southern men to fight.

Her long arms hold him. The boys, Isaac and Willy, have gone along into Somerton ahead of him. When Jane lets go she finds a piece of lint on his gray uniform coat and plucks it away.

"I'm going to be well, I promise," she says. "Nevermind. Don't worry about us here. Only see to your own business and have this thing over quickly, Elias?"

"Yes, quick as can be, but it may be long . . ."

"I know, but have it over quickly for my sake?"

"Yes."

"I've loved you all my life, I think. Maybe I haven't said it."

"Nor me, I've not said it either," says Elias. "Still I've thought the same, that I've loved you since that first day."

"Ugly face and all, Elias? I only wanted to be pretty for you and well . . ."

"I'll be home often as I can."

"Go now," she says. "I'm all right."

"Well —"

A Northern army coming and himself all but forced into uniform with his commission folded away into his inner breast pocket and his saber hooked on behind his cavalry saddle with his blanket rolled behind and his pistols holstered forward and his steed hitched and waiting by the stone mounting block. His caped overcoat gave emphasis to his arms and shoulders; his eyes were grim and gray and wintry when he pulled his hatbrim down. The beard was trimmed somewhat but still wild, a wilderness beard with streaks of gray at the chin.

"Be fierce!" she says.

He grinned, swung himself into the saddle, waved his left hand, encased in its fringed, military gauntlet. For luck he wore a crimson silk handkerchief tied about his neck. It was Jane's gift for his going away, and he wore it.

She went back up the porch steps and stood there waving and then folded her arms as he cantered slowly away, sitting well back in the saddle. The pond to his left, the river on his right hand; he clattered over the bridge. Down the road then in that same slow canter past his fences and fields, but he was already a stranger to them. His thoughts were elsewhere, ahead of him somewhere like a darkness, and he was moving, entirely in control of himself, moving upon that distant, inner darkness.

His gear was waiting for him at the hotel. He moved in and that day ordered handbills printed for distribution. He wrote advertisements for the district newspapers. He sent word to private individuals that money must be had, both subscriptions and letters of credit for purchasing arms, supplies and ammunition. He was resolved to act first and send for authorization afterwards, either to Nashville or Montgomery.

To Dutt and Tug Chambers he said: "Given so many good horses and riders it seems a shame to fight on foot. We'll organize as mounted rifles."

"What about artillery?" says Tug.

"For the present none. We'll take it from the other side, maybe."

"But who's to manage it then?" And Tug looked at Dutt.

"You, maybe?" says Elias.

Dutt cleared his throat. "There's a man in the neighborhood that knows guns. Served in the U.S. artillery."

"Who is that?" says Elias.

"Jasper Coon."

"We're needing Jasper Coon," says Tug in his high, hoarse voice. "The son of a bitch."

"He was in the artillery," says Elias. "Seems I heard him say so himself. Send him word to report for duty at once."

"We have," says Tug in a dry voice. And he gives Dutt a dry look. It was late and the room was close and beyond the windows was the darkness of the street and beyond the closed door a hall and the outside door. Horses were moving in the street and men were arriving, entering the hall, and asking hollow-voiced where it was a man reported to sign on? They came from Texas and Mississippi and Alabama and Kentucky, singly and in pairs and sometimes in squads of ten and platoons of twenty. Tug turned and knocked his pipe ashes into the fireplace, at the same time opening his tobacco pouch and treading fresh tobacco into the pipe bowl with his fingers, fidgeting after a match, and lighting the pipe then. "We have."

"I don't understand," says Elias. "Jasper didn't come when sent for, you mean?"

"He's a Free-Soiler. Opposes the Confederacy. He's in sympathy with the damned Yankees," says Dutt.

Voices in the hall from the recruiting desk: *"Sign here. Your pay is eleven dollars a month."* Pause. *"You looking for the fight? Sign here. Pay's eleven dollars a month . . ."* Footsteps and more voices.

"Want to send out a squad and have him arrested and brought in?" says Dutt.

"No," says Elias. "I'll fetch him myself. Leave Jasper Coon to me — I'll fetch him."

Elias also has doubts about the Confederacy. Elias too opposed slavery. Didn't do, he thought, to arrest a man, no; and besides, when he rode that way there would be time to stop by Riverside and see Ellen.

Was Dutt looking at Elias as though he knew something? Did Dutt wear a wise look? Maybe, thinks Elias.

Isaac, meanwhile, had read the artillery manual. He was clever, that Isaac. He read that book until he knew it backwards by heart. He was determined to be a gunner.

Still it was Jasper Coon that knew the practical aspect of gunnery. Without Jasper it was all words for Isaac, naught but sounds in the young man's head.

And Elias, presently, rode out to Jasper's clearing as he had said he would. He had a quiet word with Jasper while the man's big-footed wife and his cross-eyed children stared from the cabin door and peeked out through the windows, the woman barefoot, and the yard bare but for an old seine and a boat turned bottom up and a sow wandering back and forth with her ears forward, as though listening to Elias McCutcheon. The sow cocked her head and stood still.

Jasper, wearing galluses on his trousers and long underwear, stood in the yard barefooted, and nevermind that the day was cold. He scratched his sides.

"Isaac's read the manual," says Elias.

"Isaac? I like Isaac," says Jasper. "I'll be along and report for duty this afternoon, but mind now — I'm agin the Confederacy. I'm doing this much for you and Isaac and not them God damn planters!"

Elias nodded, mounted his horse, and rode away without another word. He took his way through the woods to Riverside. He found Ellen at home.

"Edward," Ellen said when she saw him. "Edward's been

wounded in Virginia! Shot in the hand. He's in the hospital. Oh —!"

"If he's bad off they'll send him home, nevermind. His hand, you say?"

"Yes. Here's the letter . . ."

Elias read it, then handed it back to her. "Maybe it will get him out of the army altogether and bring him home for good."

Ellen seemed to take hope. She nodded. And then: "Is my overseer a good sergeant?"

"Yes."

"Poor man."

"Poor man, why?"

"He wants to marry me. That's all."

"Tug Chambers? He asked you?"

"Yes, why not? Seeing I don't have a husband. He's done a good job."

"Did you refuse him?"

"For the time being," says Ellen. She was in her bloom, with her full, pouting lips and her red hair soft and heavy on her neck; she made Elias jealous with her talk about Tug Chambers. "The war and him going away and all," she said. "He asked me . . ."

"I never knew there was anything between you," says Elias.

"There isn't — not yet."

"I make no claim on you. You know that."

"Nor I on you," says Ellen. "Want to kiss me? D'you have time to lie down a while?" Her fingers played with the crimson handkerchief about his neck. She shut the door to the hall and locked it. "Werdna and Andrew, will they make good soldiers?"

"Good enough," says Elias. "About Tug . . ."

"I only wanted to make you jealous," she said. "Hold me?"

"Then he didn't ask?"

"He asked all right," she said.

"Then maybe he'll find himself in the forefront of the fighting for all his asking!"

"You wouldn't! Would you? Get him killed all on my account?"

He smiled. "You know I wouldn't."

Yet such a feeling came on him as made him wonder at himself. It was a hot sensation and crawled like into his arms and legs. Ellen belonged to him. "My Ellen," he whispered, holding her. "My Ellen."

"Yes!" she whispered.

BOOK FOUR

The Hawk

Chapter 1

Autumn. The bees feed on goldenrod and wild azalea. Choosing a balmy day Leola goes to rob a hive. She carries her cedar pails and her bee smoker and wears her gloves, her leggings, and a veil of cheesecloth on her hat. The veil puts a soft mist about everything she sees. The hives stand in a row down in the orchard meadow. One after the other she inspects them. The odor of goldenrod is heavy and she talks to herself:

"There you are, eh? Everything sealed? Ready for winter?"

She takes the bottle of diluted carbolic acid from her pocket, opens it, and drips a little of the dark stuff on the cloth underside of her robbing lid. Placing the lid cloth side down, tin side up, on top of the hive she's chosen, she lets the sun warm the tin. (Just yesterday, in preparation, she painted the lid with stove blacking.)

She stands very still. She thinks quiet thoughts. Soon now, when the season has advanced a bit and forage has become scarce, the creatures will be mean. But on a warm autumn day such as this, with goldenrod still in the fields and the white and purple asters plentiful, bees are tame as cattle. When the lid is warm she lays it off and harvests the dark, rich layers of sealed honeycomb. There's hardly a movement from the bees that haven't left the hive to escape the fumes of the carbolic. No need to light the smoker, even. She replaces the hive top and gathers all together and goes wending her way to the house with two full cedar pails of dark honey and yellow comb. She's marked the other hives that are ready and noted those that are yet lean; the smell of goldenrod follows after her skirts, a bitter, saffron scent. It reminds an old woman of so much, stirs certain tinctures and brings back young memories. A mockingbird sits in the low branches of a crabapple tree, softly warbling.

"Everything sealed and ready for winter," chants Leola, climbing the back steps and entering by the kitchen way. She puts off her bee togs. Dotty holds the big kettle in both hands, scalding the stone crock:

"Yes," says Leola. "Mind you do it right!"

"Yes'm, Miss Leola!"

Taking a bowl from the cupboard Leola spoons in a serving of honeycomb. Then with this on a tray with a small spoon and a napkin, she climbs the back stairway to find Jane, muttering as she goes: ". . . all ready for winter."

She finds Jane sitting on the high porch beyond her sunfilled room. Jane sits rocking. She holds those letters in her hand, from her menfolk — Elias, Willy and Isaac, from the menfolk gone away to war.

Hadn't Leola told her it would be thus?

Seeing the bowl, Jane shakes her head.

"No?" says Leola. "But it's fresh and cold from the hive."

Jane only shakes her head.

"Um," says Leola and sits down in her own low rocker. Not wanting dark honey to go begging, she takes a spoonful for herself. Once inside her mouth it tickles and makes her tongue want to dance. Its sweetness softens a place behind her eyes. She holds the tray on her bony knees and feels the sun in her clothes.

And she says: "Seven hundred pounds of honey in the hives alone. To be gathered and strained and the wax put up in cakes. And much more than that wild in the woods if only the black rascal will hunt it out and cut the trees. It's time, you know? Just smell the goldenrod!" Leola sniffs and looks across at Jane. "The black rascal — want me to tell him?"

She never speaks of Rance other than to call him "the black rascal."

"Remind him, yes," says Jane. By her tone of voice Leola knows Jane's thoughts are elsewhere.

Her heart is in Kentucky, by the river where the men are camped, thinks Leola. "The Master was never backward at this season. He had the honey home by now and wasn't too proud to smear his hands. How it dripped from his beard! He'd take the comb in his bare hand and bite and dark honey would come dripping from his beard. He'd come home from the woods — remember? Like a burdened beast, himself carrying as much as the horse and the horse staggering."

"Don't speak as though we'll never see him again," says Jane.

"Did I speak so? But that ain't how it's meant, no. I just doubt I'll ever again see him pick up honeycomb that way with his bare hand. He was wild then, and young like an overgrown boy, with his gray eyes and the warm way he smiled . . ."

"That's so," says Jane. "When will he come home again, I wonder?"

Leola took another bite. She held it on her tongue. Closing her eyes she saw something. "Three won't come," she said, and opened her eyes.

"Don't say that!" says Jane.

"I knew we'd miss those days when the cabin was our house," says Leola, soothingly. "Dirt floors were good enough. And such a man as your Elias was — I wouldn't wonder if your heart has a little ache now and then."

"Please — just hush, Leola."

"Now what did I say?" Leola spoons the last of the honey and the last of the comb into her mouth and stands up with the tray in her knobby, bony hands.

Jane sits as before, staring straight ahead, clutching those letters, still as was.

Going into the hall, and back down the kitchen stairs, Leola thinks of the sealed combs. In her feet she detects the approach of winter; a tingling coldness flows about her ankles.

Chapter 2

Pettecasockee.

He went to war and left behind him a wife with an ivory comb in her hair. The day of his departure she sat quietly by the hearth fire wearing a dress of blue cloth.

He said: "I am going." For it was now at the edge of cold weather and he had known throughout the last days of summer that when the autumn taste was in the air he would go. He rolled some few things in a blanket and tied it and walked slowly outside where his young horse, Tenasse, stood already saddled. He secured the blanket roll behind the saddle.

Pettecasockee wore his red shirt. He wore his tin cup hooked to his belt behind, as though for hunting, and his butcher knife stuck in his belt. To Tenasse's saddle he had strung two spare gunstocks and a small ax and two leather scabbards with a shotgun in each.

Shokotee appeared on the porch with his brown shawl with the orange fringe pulled over his shoulders. The old man stood a moment as though sniffing, then he came slowly down the steps one step at a time, and on towards the horse. He stopped, twining his brown fingers in the fringes of the shawl, and regarded the horse.

"Nigh on to going," said the old man. "Eh?"

"Yes."

"The long hunt."

"Yes." And Pettecasockee got busy with the saddle. May be as the reins need a bit of adjusting too . . .

"The long hunt," the old man repeated, as though tasting the words. "I'd go too. I'd have gone with Elias. Where is he?"

"Kentucky."

"You tell me but I forget."

"Yes."

Pettecasockee left the old man standing beside the horse and went back inside the house. She sat by the fire just in the same attitude and position that she had been sitting before. He saw the ivory comb and the blue of the dress. The folds of her skirts would have a warm smell.

She was warm-skinned and a comfort in winter to share his bed. And his longing for her had not diminished with the years but had remained upon him, for she took such pleasure in their love and would have him take her in the morning just after waking when her dark almond eyes were quiet and sleep still lay upon the beauty of her face. He did not like to think that he had remained by her all the summer not wanting to leave her side and that because of her he hated the notion of his having to go away to war. So he had postponed it all he could with excuses. This and that about the plantation needed him. He was not for the Confederate cause; he was Indian and had no interest in the white man's fight. The summer long he had wrestled with excuses that put off his departure, lying meanwhile long abed with her sometimes, pressing his cheek to her naked shoulder, smelling the sweet warmth of her skin. Waking early he had lain very still and watched her face as she lay in morning sleep as the light of the sky crept in at the windows and the gamecocks began crowing outside from their cages. He saw the first flutter of her lids, and the opening of her eyes to full wakefulness and the slow smile of pleasure that came to her lips when she saw how still he lay and with what quiet patience he had been waiting for her.

"Well, I am going." And the words made his mouth dry.

"Goodbye. My love. My husband." She spoke in a whisper.

He was not in fear of dying for any reason other than it would mean leaving her. She needed him. Since that day he had brought her here to his father's house they had hardly once been separated.

Hearing voices and footsteps he looked back into the hall and saw Anda. She and others were gathered there, waiting. Anda coughed and looked away and said something in a whisper. She and the other women and servants were waiting to tell him goodbye and the old man, no doubt, was still outside, waiting beside the horse.

He looked at the comb. "Goodbye . . ."

Outside then, into the hall. They followed him to the porch, young and old. He hardly saw them. Out of respect for the old man they stayed on the porch.

Pettecasockee gathered the reins. Shokotee stood as before, regarding the horse and waiting, his hands still. Perhaps they'd not see each other again, father and son, they might not.

"Goodbye," said Pettecasockee.

"Yes, goodbye," said the old man. "Good luck and all."

"Yes, thanks," said Pettecasockee and he mounted Tenasse.

The old man looked away to the river for a moment as though he saw or heard something there, but the river was still . . . too still. He looked back at Pettecasockee. "That stirrup," he ventured.

"This one?" said Pettecasockee.

The old man took the stirrup in his hand. "Mite low is it? I'll take up a notch, nevermind." His shawl fell away to the ground. He ignored it. Using both hands he took the stirrup up a notch, his thin shoulder leaning a bit into Pettecasockee's leg. "There. How's that?"

"Much better. Thanks."

"Well, on your way! Tell Elias howdy, don't forget. And nevermind things and folk here. We'll manage."

"All right."

With a final wave Pettecasockee rode away, down through the gate, and down along the worn, familiar road. He didn't let himself look back. He knew she was on the porch by now. She would be there and the old man would have picked up the shawl and presently he would turn and go inside again and she with him, those two.

Both by woods and road, fording and bridge he went. Three days. Three camps. Three sleeps.

And he spied the tents where they had been pitched upon a parcel of high ground at the narrowing of the land between the rivers. As it was morning he rode straight in, asking after

Elias and found him, meanwhile seeing both Isaac and Willy as well as Jasper Coon and Tug Chambers, the Wray brothers, the Alstons, father and sons, Dutt Callister, Andrew and Werdna Poe, two of the Musgroves, the Van Velzen boys, Aard Lindgren and others . . .

Elias was eating fat bacon and pone bread and had a map before him. Eating and studying . . .

"So you decided to come along after all," says Elias. He was leaner than Pettecasockee remembered him and his hands were weathered brown.

"Yes," says Pettecasockee. He was hungry, but he said: "Killed any?"

"None as yet," says Elias. "You'll want a uniform."

"No — because I'll ride as a scout."

"They hang spies." So saying Elias offered a tin pan of corn pones and fried bacon. Pettecasockee helped himself. The bread was just warm and the bacon was salty and crisp to the rind.

Pettecasockee swallowed. "Scout, spy — what's the difference?" He took another bite of bread and bacon and unhooked his tin cup from his belt behind. Elias poured from a brown jug. It was cider, just cold, like the autumn air at night, and held a sweet, sharp taste of winter.

Pettecasockee drank, closing his eyes.

"Very well," Elias was saying. "A scout then."

Presently, after a second cup of cider they took their horses and rode about the encampment.

"My father says howdy."

"How is Shokotee?"

"The same . . ."

Below the bluffs on the riverbank an artillery piece was fixed in ambush for boats. Above on the flat were ditches dug as fortifications.

And Pettecasockee wondered if he had come this distance

to die in a ditch. He had expected more, hoping to fight on horseback. Instead seven hundred were assigned here to watch the rivers.

"A dog could watch a river," thinks Pettecasockee. "A one-eyed dog."

Chapter 3

Since October when they had marched into Kentucky and occupied the high ground between the Green and the Cumberland rivers, Isaac had made progress.

Calling at the headquarters of General Tilghman at Hopkinsville with Jasper Coon to back up his story, he had represented himself as an artillerist and come away with a four-pounder. The gun was hidden on the river in point-blank range of any boat that should pass and Isaac enjoyed the rank and privileges of his lieutenant's commission, and for a few weeks his command went swimmingly.

The younger officers looked up to him. He had killed a man in a duel, after all. That seemed important now. Perhaps it meant that Isaac was steady and could be counted on when things got "snug," as the saying was.

But then, only a few days after Pettecasockee's arrival

(an event which the Mounted Rifles, rank and file, took for a good omen, remembering the Indian's reputation as a raider) the skies closed in and it began to rain. For with the rain it somehow came to Isaac that nothing had happened. The fortifications were finished. The contingent of slaves that had done the heavy digging were long since marched back to Hopkinsville. Isaac and his gunners had built a hut with timbered walls chinked and plastered with mud. Pleasant work it was. They had covered the edifice with a tent roof. While the weather continued fair Isaac and the young officers had played cards outside while the watch on the river, day and night, came to nothing.

But it rained and with the rain came a cold snap and there was complaining because blankets and boots were in short supply, and worse yet, with the Negroes all sent back to Hopkinsville there were no servants anymore. Elias, the old man himself, had laid down the law as to servants. Henceforth every man would look after himself.

And as though to add emphasis to that dreary ruling the cold rain fell with an enduring relentlessness, a wintry rain, and it wet everything in such a way as to tell Isaac that he had never really known what rain was before now.

It wet clothing. It wet toilet articles and playing cards. And somehow it put horsehair on bread, plates, forks and in coffee. It made horsehair stick to a man's fingers.

After a few days walkways became mud sluices and a trip to the shit ditch became an expedition. Nevermind an oilcloth or a rubberized poncho. This rain honored neither. Invariably, before a man could make it to the ditch and relieve himself and make it back to the hut, the rain had found weak points, beginning usually at the neck. It made a drab world in which what wasn't muddy was sooner or later wet and covered with horsehair. The more fires that were built to dry things out, the worse the hut smelled and Isaac's world stank of scorched wool, so much so that his food tasted of it.

Wet through, unable to get dry, Isaac sat day after day in the hut, sulking and thinking about death. Rain thrummed on the tent roof and Jasper Coon slept in his bunk against the wall, his slumbers paced by a comfortable snore. He seemed as though he were gone into hibernation leaving Isaac to contemplate death and to wonder whether or not he should attempt somehow to dry the socks he was wearing and meanwhile search through his campaign chest to see if a dry pair could be located.

Before the rain, a century ago it seemed to Isaac now, Jasper Coon had gone wandering away at night, returning with chickens, a little pig just right for roasting, apples, sweet potatoes, and even a small cask of cider. Isaac, never one to bargain for stealing, had been shocked, but when Jasper served his plate and filled his cup Isaac's conscience went mute somehow. "Supplies," Jasper called these delectable fruits of crime and theft, and he not only had a nose for them, he knew how to prepare them too. A cook, as Isaac discovered, if he is a complete cook has a way of smelling things that ordinary noses miss. And he hears things. A real cook has a way with him of making mental notes and calculations, of computing distances and watching out the way when he rides along a road. A sour smell five miles ago that made the average soldier turn up his nose, that said *Pigs!* to a cook. And the clucking and crowing everyone else forgot when they passed it (oblivious to anything but the beauty of fields and woods in a dry, clean autumn), that clucking was not lost on a cook.

Thus had delicious aromas of cooking filled the hut once upon a time, in fair weather. When cooking, Jasper Coon didn't bother about sleep. Days in succession he might give sleep nothing but a nod or a brief doze here and there between his pots and his spits and his reflector ovens, tin sides popping before the fire. But when not cooking, Jasper evidenced great reverence for sleep. Wrapped in his blanket he would sleep all day — nevermind roll call. Isaac saw to it that his cook was marked present.

When working parties were wanted for felling trees and digging rifle pits, incessant tasks that fell on the men now the Negroes were gone, Isaac sent another in Jasper's place.

In citizen life before the war the man was shiftless, and seemed always headed for the stocks and the whipping post — or worse, a fine enough companion for growing boys, but the kind of fellow boys slough off in citizen life, when they become men.

Ugliness compounded, thinks Isaac with a glance at his sergeant's face across the way, his blanket beneath his chin, his nose wide, his brow a stack of creases, his ears standing away from his head like cups, his thin, long hair a strange sandy red. In a swearing contest he could shame the devil. A treasure he was, Jasper Coon — a gunner and a cook, but useless when it rained.

The tent flap door was drawn aside. "Isaac?" Tug Chambers's beefy head appeared. "Isaac?"

"Yes?"

"Boat on the river."

"Boat?"

"Yankee transport, looks like."

Isaac sprang up. He shouted at the sleeping Jasper and a moment later was dashing into rain and mud. Sliding and stumbling he scrambled down the steep slope to the ambush. Silently his men materialized and with Jasper Coon in charge prepared to serve the gun.

Above on the bluff a drum beat the long roll. Elias himself appeared answering *yes* to this, saying *no* to that, speaking in a quiet voice. His gray eyes were dark and there was a hawklike quality about him. Pettecasockee said something and Elias, the old man, nodded.

Following the direction of their gaze Isaac looked out upon the river as the boat came in sight. Though still a mile downstream it looked enormous. Its dark sides were sloped and sinister. Its wheels were covered. It seemed already dangerously close and on and on it came: they could hear the churn and chunk of her engines and the muffled splash of her wheels. And not a man in sight, not a man anywhere about her decks. On and on she came steering straight for the deep channel, coming straight for the gun.

"All right, let her have it," Elias said, speaking quietly.

Jasper Coon grinned and yanked the lanyard. With a buck and a roar the four-pounder delivered itself of a white belch of smoke. Rifles let go up and down the line with a rippling crack of heavy gunsound made ponderous by the proximity of water. The gun was served again. Again Jasper Coon showed his teeth and yanked . . .

As the smoke thinned and went drifting upward Isaac's throat was swollen with a sudden yell. His voice joined that of myriad voices up and down the lines of the ambuscade, for the boat, very close now, showed white cloth waving from her wrecked pilothouse, a shirt it was, in the hand of a man with a streak of black on his forehead — soot, grease or gore — it didn't matter. The boat came in slowly alongside the gravel bar. Men appeared on her decks and threw lines ashore into the eager hands of the Confederates who had swarmed over the log barricade, racing over the gravel to the river's edge. They hauled her in and made her fast. White water ceased to race from beneath her covered wheels. Beyond her in the current a tree came drifting, roots standing wild and yellow. As the drifting tree went by, the gangplank was thrown down, the tree spinning beyond the yellow wash of rain-swelled current.

Hands in the air, a file of soldiers in spanking blue uniforms appeared on deck and came down the gangplank into the damp crescent of waiting Confederates ashore, men in drab gray and butternut, wearing slouch hats, some holding shotguns for lack of muskets enough to go around, and some barefooted, a thing Isaac had really never noticed very much before, the barefooted fellows, and the boys in tattered butternut, and their old shotguns. The prisoners in spanking blue, wearing new boots and smart caps and shining insignia — was it a sign of something, that homespun would go it over factory looms?

A stir of good-natured contempt swept through the ranks of the Confederates. They'd seen the elephant, they had. Looked the son of a bitch straight in the eye and discovered to their surprise that he was mortal and fallible and easily scared and didn't want to mess up his fine clothes. Braggart warriors, that's all they were.

Prisoners and crew ashore, the captors swarmed aboard, opened the hatches, and began trotting her cargo ashore. Blankets, dark blue and thick and new from the looms of the North. Crates were cracked open and out came rifles, new rifles resplendent with brown gun grease; and pistols by the hundreds, and a supply of boots in every size, and sabers and cloaked overcoats, saddles, harness, horseshoes, portable forges and food stores, including hams and beef, sugar and coffee, flour, lard, hard biscuits, canned oysters, whiskey, wines, cordials, cigars . . .

Isaac went aboard and quietly helped himself to a steel scabbard saber, an overcoat, a pair of cavalry boots, riding gauntlets and a tin of English smoking tobacco.

In his mind he saw Jasper Coon again, lanyard in hand, the swift yank; he heard the sharp thundercrack, saw the dense blurt of white smoke plumed above the yellow surface of the river. In Isaac's chambered thoughts the rifles cracked again, up and down the line, slamming like triphammers.

Standing on her deck Isaac felt the fine, misting rain on his face. Steam hissed from the boilers; he smelled hemp and fresh paint.

In a commotion of swearing the teamsters snaked their mule-drawn freight wagons down the narrow, uncertain trail in the steep bank, wheeling to a halt on the gravel bar there to be loaded for the return trip.

Isaac carried his booty ashore. Meanwhile as early dark settled, first dense smoke and afterward fire boiled out of the little transport amidships, whether by accident or from malicious act no one seemed to know. She was emptied by then, anyhow, and Isaac went back down to the gravel bar and stood for a long time watching. The heat of her destruction was cast on the men and wagons and struggling mules, on the heavy struggle up the impossible, muddy bank. Finally she began to settle. Beneath a hissing cloud of steam she rolled down upon her side, her lines long since parted by the flames, her hull rumbling and groaning down the slope of the gravel now, where it gave into deep water. A few spars, still glowing red, drifted downstream.

When he returned to the hut Isaac found it bright with captured candles. The scorched wool smell had disappeared. Jasper Coon was smoking a cigar and cooking in the crude fireplace. The chimney, an arrangement of kegs with their bottoms knocked out, wasn't drawing well. Jasper left his pots and tied the tent flap back to let the smoke out, whereupon the chimney began to draw. One after another Jasper buttered a dozen biscuits, just baked.

The rain had ceased without Isaac's knowing just when. Thinking to look outside again he saw a thin moon and stars and the last frail patches of cloud moving as though to polish the heavens, like remnants of lace.

While he watched the dissolving clouds a banjo began to ring on the bluff above, soon joined by the high, clear voice of a tenor which was, in turn, joined by others . . .

My love lies a-dreaming . . .

The melodious tenor wended on and on, leading the rest. Never, thought Isaac, never was anything more beautiful . . .

Chapter 4

Defeat . . .

With a rapidity no one in the district could have anticipated in light of the proud speeches, the recruiting, the Confederate proclamations that the "Sacred Soil" must be protected from the heel of the Northern invader, West Tennessee was quietly occupied by a Northern army.

The Yankee troops at first made little difference. Except for a shortage of sugar, tea and coffee the days went by as they had before — only the menfolk were missing. The distant wall of trees at the edge of the cleared land was like a barrier that protected Oakleigh. "Stay at home, see to the management of the plantation. Everything will turn out right, you'll see," says a voice in Jane's heart.

A Yankee colonel called at Oakleigh. He had himself announced — Colonel Ennis Dalton. It was a rare warm day, unseasonably warm. Nervously Jane drew the silk patch over the maimed side of her face. The colonel was shown up to her porch and she asked him to sit down. He thanked her and took a rocking chair — very proper, and very polite. He was, he said, himself a Tennesseean — from the east section of the state. And this, he said, made him feel a special consideration for the residents of this occupied territory. He had come to pay his respects and, more than that, to assure Mrs. McCutcheon that though her sons and her husband might be fighting on the other side, their property would not be molested. He was hoping, however, that Jane might understand that his troops, in the near future, might be needing some horses . . . Pause.

"As officer-in-charge it is not my purpose to make war on the citizen population. Yet if we are to get along together as we should, the citizen population must not cooperate with the rebellion. The presence of Rebel soldiers in the district will be reported to me at once and they will be arrested. Have I your word of honor, Mrs. McCutcheon, that you will support the government of the United States?"

"No, sir," says Jane in a quiet voice.

"Then you have Rebel sentiments, Mrs. McCutcheon?"

"Of course I have," says Jane.

"I have the power to have you sent south, beyond the Rebel lines."

If they did send her south, she thought, she'd see Elias — and Isaac and Willy. They were there in Mississippi waiting, and expecting to ride north again. They wrote in their letters: "Almost any day now . . ."

She knew it would mean big fighting when that happened.

"I know you have the power," she says. "To send me south."

"So long as you realize that. I want to make myself plainly understood, should any Rebels return."

"Yes, you've made yourself plain."

"Then, with your permission I will take my leave." He

stood gazing out at the land, his hand on the balustrade of the porch. "What a beautiful place."

"Thank you, Colonel."

"I have heard that your husband wasn't in sympathy with the Rebel cause."

"That's correct."

"Yet he owns slaves. Was he willing to give them up?"

"He was and is. He opposes the war."

"Yet he's fighting on the Rebel side."

"In the Confederate army, yes."

"It would be hard to give such as this up without a fight. He must be a very rich man."

"He's worked hard all his life. I don't know what you'd call very rich."

"Compared, I mean, to how we live in East Tennessee," says Ennis Dalton. "I see why he would fight. To save his property, to protect his home."

"My husband went to war because his neighbors asked him to go. He could not refuse them for the reason that he asked them once to go with him, and they went."

"On the raid against the Horse Pens."

"Then you've heard about it."

"You hear a lot of things," says Ennis Dalton. "I know of your misfortune and the raid."

"It isn't worth mentioning," says Jane.

"But the raid brought law and order and helped build the district. I hope I may someday have the pleasure of meeting your husband in person, under peaceful circumstances."

She looked at him. He stood with his back to her. He was a strange man but these were strange times. If the forts on the rivers had held he would not be standing here, she thought. It was those forts that could not be defended, or were surrendered too easily — either way those defeats had pushed the Confederate lines south into Mississippi and here stood

Ennis Dalton, a Yankee colonel, with his hand on the rail of her high porch, talking one minute about sending her away below the lines, and in the next breath expressing admiration for Elias.

"Perhaps it will turn out that you shall meet him," she said at last.

"What can you tell me about Mrs. Ellen Ashe?" He was still gazing out over the land.

"She's widowed, I believe. Her son and her brothers are gone to the war."

"Quite a beautiful lady. She offered to shoot me dead if I should set foot on her property again. And Shokotee McNeilly, isn't he your father?"

"My adopted father, yes."

"He made me a gift of a coil of rope. Indian, isn't he?"

"He is."

"It's my responsibility to know as much about the people hereabouts as is possible."

"Of course."

Did this blue-clad creature imagine the territory would all be given over to the United States without a fight? Was he all so dense and oblivious? To judge his demeanor, Ennis Dalton felt the war was practically at a close. Why? Jane wondered. Couldn't he feel as she could the impatience of the men who were waiting at Corinth to come north again and strike this foe?

Jane saw again the line of the trees that had, until now, kept her safe, that wilderness wall. This man had somehow come over it.

"Goodbye, Mrs. McCutcheon."

"Goodbye."

He left, but she knew he would be back.

Leola came to the porch. "So, as though I didn't know all along they'd be coming here! What did *he* want?"

"To frighten us, I suppose. I don't know, Leola."

"He was tall. I saw that much. Sits his horse like a gentleman. Didn't offer him any refreshments."

Jane shook her head.

"He didn't seem like such a bad fellow," says Leola. "It's not the officers we have to worry about."

Jane shut her mind to Leola's prattle. So long as Elias and the boys were encamped about Corinth they were safe. It was springtime she must worry about, for in the spring they would come north again and try to retake the ground they had lost. She wondered what they might be doing now — Elias and the boys and Pettecasockee. She hoped they were not cold nor hungry and that they were not sick. Camp fever was killing so many. Death was crowding about, trying to touch every household in the district, it seemed. Hubert Wray and Lem Alson and Simon Musgrove and others more and more, were listed with the dead.

The sick and wounded that the army tried to send home had to be brought past the Union checkpoints under loads of hay, or carried through the swamps on secret trails and pathways. Once home they were to be hidden in attics, slave cabins, and smokehouses, always with the fear that some neighbor or slave with a long held grudge might betray them. Then it was arrest and imprisonment in the North. Those taken in that way would probably never again be seen alive . . .

Chapter

5

Fancy Callister had the comfort of her home and her children about her. Nevermind if the Callisters weren't slave-owners. It didn't bother her. The Callisters managed, even with Dutt gone away and two of her boys getting ready to leave shortly. They'd have to slip out past the Union guards, the boys would, but that wasn't any trouble, no. West Tennessee was too wide a territory for so few Union troops to guard.

Fancy saw to her chores and supervised the children at their reading and arithmetic. Adele, the oldest, was acting strange. She'd asked Fancy's permission to let one of the little Yankee soldiers call on her. How on earth young folk *met* under conditions and in times such as these was a mystery, but they managed. Maybe Adele had talked to him on the street in Somerton. A mama couldn't watch her daughter *all* the time.

Adele, with her father's narrow nose and long face, but with pretty features for all that, Adele had said: "Private Billy Mulligan wants to come calling, Mama. Mayn't he come calling, Mama?"

"Mulligan? A little Yankee? Irish too, isn't he? Mulligan?"

"Mama!"

"You should know better than to ask such a thing. I'll not have you see or speak to anything in a blue uniform. Your father already gone away, your brothers nigh ready to go and you — be ashamed Adele Callister. Mulligan!"

Fancy spat out the name like it was poison on her tongue and Adele had looked stricken, just the way Dutt sometimes looked, hurt and stricken and like her father always wanting to do something so damn-foolish it was downright silly. Likely get the house burned down over their heads, should Adele let a Yankee come calling.

Older women had set the example, though, as Fancy was well aware. Yankee officers had been *seen*. That tall one, Colonel Dalton, for example, leaving Ellen Ashe's house; and a certain major, dressed in *his* blue monkey suit, and entering Mrs. Fanny Parham's, and the poor doctor, her husband, long since gone away to war with the mounted rifles. They said the Union major was a Dutchman and that he was seen leaving the Parham home quite late of an evening and it was said he drank overmuch, moreover. And . . .

Consorting with the enemy, thinks Fancy Callister. And a special place would be set aside in hell for those women that spread their legs for a Yankee, thank you, that spread their legs, yes ma'am, and dropped their hoops and petticoats, stooping and offering themselves to anything in a blue uniform.

No sooner were the Union soldiers in the territory than some stole slave girls from the plantations to launder for them and share their beds, and what recourse had the poor plantation owner but to keep his mouth shut?

None, thinks Fancy Callister, busy with her winter sewing. She made what flannel she had go as far as it would and stuck to her knitting and scrubbing and cooking. So long as she cut her cloth snug to fit the pattern they'd survive. Main thing was to get in a corn crop and once it was pulled hide it good. When the Confederates came north again she had sense enough to know that nothing in the way of forage would be safe. Any horse not hidden would be taken. She knew that for Dutt had told her how it was sure to be. Both sides would prey upon the citizen populace, no way around it, no doubt about it, sure as death and taxes, Dutt had said. Fool though he was he had a head on his shoulders, Dutt had.

Adele came in the room where Fancy sat sewing with her table drawn near the fire.

"Mama?"

"Yes?"

Pause. The fire popped. Silence.

"Yes?"

"Oh — nothing!" the girl said. She sighed. She was acting awful strange.

"Anything you want to tell your mama, Adele? Child? Look at me."

"Oh, it's nothing, Mama. It's only that all the boys are gone away and some are dead already. Edward Ashe, he's home and has his hand ruined for life and they've got to hide him or the Yankees might arrest him and send him to prison in Ohio."

"But the war will end," says Fancy.

"And I'll be an old woman and the men will all be dead. That's what I keep thinking. They'll all be dead and I'll be old and won't have had any fun . . ."

Fancy sighed. "Adele . . ."

"Yes, Mama?"

"You were not put on this earth to enjoy yourself. How many times must I remind you of that?"

The child broke into silent weeping. Her thin shoulders shook. Child? Maybe. Yet at *her* age, thinks Fancy, *I* was married and had a babe of my own at my breast. Yet she's only a child . . .

"Now," says Fancy. "Now!" She put her sewing down and went to Adele, where she stood so forlornly weeping, as though the world were all at an end. Fancy put her arms about her. "Now!"

"Oh, *Mama!*" the child wept.

Chapter *6*

Willy came home, thinner now, and outgrowing his uniform.

He had been wounded below the knee. The household at Oakleigh nursed him and as he regained his health he related something of his adventures to Jane, and something more to Leola, but more still to Rance and Jake. He told grim stories to the menservants. And all those who had stayed at home were eager for every tidbit he could tell.

"We've seen the thick of it," he would say speaking vaguely. There was much he *couldn't* tell. For example, the rumbling of supply wagons and the jingling of horses in harness, a seemingly endless train of men in a column all wending in a single direction through open countryside. How the mass halted, then how it started marching again.

How to tell of that cold wind cutting over the bitter, barren hill? How to describe thickets and bluffs that you ride past wondering every second if a Yankee ambush is there or not? You ride with a strange sensation in your behind where it rests against the saddle, never knowing whether or not some hidden sharpshooter may already have you in his sights and be about to empty your saddle. You see it happen all around you. You see the dead beside the road, face down, pockets turned out, boots stolen, haversack and knapsack missing, letters and papers scattered all around. Amazing, so it was, how many letters the average soldier carried and how they got scattered when he died . . .

When waiting, the cold had been like a mask on your face. The wind brought the distant thump of artillery. You thought of yourself as a floating speck amid thousands, a single speck that was part of the giant, serpentine critter that made up an army marching in the field. The wind died somewhat; the sun rose higher. An end to waiting and you were climbing, riding up towards the crest of a ridge where, spread out below, you saw what it was that had called you here. Above the floor of the valley huge white rings of smoke marked the bursting of shells in the air. At ground level white blurts marked the location of the opposing batteries. The pace quickened downhill. The road leveled. The infantry moved ahead of you at the double-quick. Shells whispered overhead. Units held in reserve stood quiet and pale; others, ordered to attack, fanned out eagerly, two hundred abreast. Cannonballs bounced up and sailed overhead. Fused shells came in, hissing first, bursting next. Outgoing shells thrown from the Confederate batteries made a mournful whimper.

How to describe the clattering storm of steel when the soldier boys on foot, a thousand strong, fix bayonets? Or the demeanor of a lonely subaltern, quietly erect upon his horse, inspecting the enemy through field glasses one moment, and atomized the next by the burst of a Yankee shell?

The field is dotted with wounded. Some hold their arms crooked as though to shield their faces from the pallid sun. Others look gray-faced and lie very still. Some seem to be trying to recall something. Others lie face down as though praying or asleep . . .

Comes the cavalry's moment. The charge sounds and the distance begins to close over a field now so thick with the fallen it is impossible not to ride straight over some. Six hundred, five hundred, four hundred — three hundred yards — the distance goes, rapidly eaten away by the steady advance of the Confederate horse. A dragon tongue, winking flame, flickers along the dark snake fence where the Yankee defenders stand.

In the air all about you bullet swarms have begun buzzing like bees. Two hundred yards from the fence you can see the flash of the Union ramrods. The gray-uniformed Confederate infantry stand and load methodically, blazing away as you pass through.

The cavalry reaches the fence and pours over it, firing at the backs of the broken lines of the retreating enemy. Fence rails splinter and explode beside you. You ride for the nearest gun where the Union gunners seem too busy loading double-shotted canister to notice you.

Drawing a pistol you fire away, dropping one blue belly just ready to yank the lanyard. You drop a second one who is trying to unhorse you by striking with a ramrod. Your third shot misses. Your fourth shot breaks a man's arm. Leaping down from your horse you and your companions turn the gun, train it, and fire point-blank into the fleeing teams of the Union artillery. More cavalry meanwhile comes pouring through the gaps in the fence. Sabers aloft, the gray and butternut riders stretch forward. Like a harvest scythe they rake into the flanks of retreating lines.

Taking your reins again from the companion who held

your horse, you try to mount. Something strikes your leg. You reel, you fall, and almost faint. The bone goes numb below your knee . . .

Gunsmoke dilutes the thin sunlight. A band is playing "The Girl I Left Behind Me." First sounds of cheering, then more infantry comes, moving up briskly. You are dragged a little distance and propped up against the wheel of a captured gun. You faint and are waked by random shots. Men go about shooting the crippled horses. Ammunition wagons rattle by you. Rails taken from the snake fence are stacked over the carcasses of the dead horses and set fire to. The smoke from such fires blows black and bitter.

Now, at long last, litter bearers. Taken up you faint again, but pain brings you around. Two weeks in the hospital and then the slow agony of the journey home for convalescent leave. In spite of your crutches officers in new uniforms stop you and ask to see your papers. Others demand that you salute them. "None of your front-line manners here!" they say.

None of it matters, though. For headed home those last secret miles through the bottoms you lie in the back of a jolt wagon and witness strings of ducks and geese climbing the gray sky.

In dreams you will sometimes see the company flags and the regimental colors fluttering. You hear "The Girl I Left Behind Me."

Wall Stuart discovered Willy was home and came to Oakleigh and demanded to see him; Wall wouldn't take no. Scared Jane and Rance and Leola half to death for their thinking no one in Somerton knew their soldier boy was home, and here comes Wall, driving one of his own hired buggies from the livery stable, right to the front door and demands to see Willy.

Nevermind, Willy saw him. Wall only wanted to know about the fight Willy was in and how he got wounded.

"Big fight, wasn't it?"

"Yessir."

"Hurt your leg, did you?"

"Yessir."

"I see others that come back and they say it ain't all it's cracked up to be, the army ain't. Through for good, are you?"

"Nossir. Just on convalescent leave."

"You mean you got *permission* to come home?"

"Yessir."

"Well, that's *good.* I didn't know. Some I know come home without permission. You were in a fight, eh?"

Yes, Willy says. He was. Yes, it was a win for the Confederate side. Yes, the field was cluttered with dead Yankees. He says all that from a feeling that this is what Wall Stuart expects and wants him to say.

"Don't you hate 'em?" says Wall.

"Who?"

"The Yankees! Trampling our Sacred Soil."

But no, Willy doesn't hate them. Still he believes it's better not to tell Wall he doesn't hate them. Silence. Wall can't understand why Willy can't tell him anything more.

Wall says he's thinking of joining himself. Might ought to volunteer. Believes, yes, he will volunteer, by God. He's by God *gonna* volunteer, he says.

At long last Wall took his leave. The buggy rolled out of the drive and over the frozen road and Willy goes into the house and finds Rance in the hall, Rance saying:

"Hope he don't go in town and tell dem Yankee sojers what he found hid out here! Don't trust him nohow!" A scowl comes into his dark handsome face.

"Nevermind about Wall Stuart," says Willy. But he's uneasy, still and all. He wonders a bit himself about Wall Stuart.

He struggles upstairs. Jane calls him from above.

"Willy?"

He goes into the darkened room. She's in bed.

"He left," says Willy, going to the bed and laying his crutches aside. She puts out her arms to him and hugs him a long hug. Then pushing back she holds his hands.

"Can't get over how you've grown!" she says. "Willy?"

"Ma'am?"

"The war, is it bad?" She hadn't asked before, for fear maybe of hearing my answer, thinks Willy. "Tell the truth," she says.

"No, Mama," says the soldier. And thinks: *How to tell you? You would never understand it for I don't understand it myself. No one does and if I were to try to tell you I'm afraid my voice might fail me. It can't be told.* "No, Mama, it isn't so bad . . ."

"Not bad as they say then, Willy? I want to know . . ."

"No, Mama. Not all so bad." *No, worse! Worse than any can tell. Worse than dreams. It's all the dread there ever was in the world and it turns your blood to ice water . . .*

"Your father and your brother. Are they all right? I've asked before, but now I want the truth."

"They're fine." *No, they are not all right, Mama. They are in danger of being killed any instant, or of being smashed in a way that would hold more horror for them alive than death could offer. No, Mama, I fear for them all the time, every moment, for knowing they may either or both of them be dead. It happens. It happens quick as thought, Mama . . .* "Father and Isaac are fine, Mama."

Leola comes in and interrupts. "Best lie down now and rest, Willy!" says the old Indian.

Rance comes in after her and without saying anything

builds up the fire. The lamps are lit. Leola brings Jane's dressing gown and her slippers and helps her out of bed. Jake appears, as he has every day at this time since the soldier has been home.

"Um," says Jake. "He a lot taller. Thinner too." He speaks as though Willy cannot hear, as though Willy may be still gone away. Then stepping close he says to Willy in a low voice that if he feels like it maybe he'd like to come visit out in the cabin later. "Somethin' to tell you I ain't mentioned before. Somethin' sort of secret?"

Willy nods. Yes, he will come to the cabin later.

Jake leaves and Leola sends a hateful look after him. Things are the same as ever at Oakleigh.

"I can't understand why you didn't get your box," says Jane. "We sent your new jacket and your boots and some socks, not to mention cookies and poundcake and fruitcake."

"It may reach me in time," says Willy.

"But it was sent before the occupation! Before the forts on the rivers fell," says Jane.

"It will get to me in time," says Willy, the whole while knowing in his heart that that box, like most boxes, somehow got itself dropped and broken open. No doubt a pasty-faced clerk was wearing the boots and the jacket and had long since finished eating the sweets . . .

He recalls what Christmas was like, a day like any other for the Mounted Rifles. They had ridden out on patrol . . .

For Jane is saying: "We had a lonesome Christmas here, but a good many fireworks. Roman candles and wheels. We brought the children up from the quarters. Leola passed out the presents and we had a lot of shouting. But without you, without Isaac and your father — the firecrackers didn't sound the same, Willy."

"We had lonesome eggnog," says Leola. "Yet I knew this would happen and tried to tell you. Nobody listens to Leola.

I'd best go stir about the kitchen. Come along, Rance. And the rest of you," she says to the other servants who've a way of gathering now just to look at Willy and share their wonder at his having been wounded, and to sense for themselves something of the adventures he's endured.

Willy and his mother are alone. The little clock on her mantel ticks. Leaving her bed again Jane goes to the music box and winds it and puts on the new wheel. It's "Dixie" and then "The Yellow Rose of Texas," and next "The Bonnie Blue Flag," and last of all "The Girl I Left Behind Me." The tinkling medley winds down; it stops.

They went downstairs, mother and son. They ate in the dining room. Willy felt as though Isaac and his father might walk in at any moment. He drank milk by the pitcher, asked for more potatoes and more bread, more butter and more beef.

"You've been starved," says Jane. "You seem better already."

"I'm getting well, I can feel it," says Willy.

"Was it so bad?"

"No, ma'am."

Supper over they went back upstairs to her bedroom where the little clock ticked as before. Sitting on the rose-colored sofa Willy answered her questions. Every evening was the same. "Tell me the truth, Willy," she would say from time to time.

And he always told her Isaac and his father were in no particular danger.

Before falling asleep she rarely failed to say she did not believe the South would win the war. She had been going to church, she said, and it was a great strain on her to go about in public, but she had gone to church and had tried to believe what the preacher had said, yet she could not believe him and it seemed to her the cause was lost. "Is it lost, Willy?"

"No, ma'am," said Willy. "We're winning, Mama."

Perhaps that satisfied her, for she fell asleep then. Willy went quietly about the room, snuffing candles. Finally the firelight and the little mantel lamp by the clock were all that illuminated the room. His mother lay quietly snoring on her high bed.

He went out. At the foot of the backstairs he heard talk from the kitchen. He found Leola and Rance at the kitchen table. ". . . and when they do come they gonna take everything in sight and burn us out, you'll see," Leola was saying.

"I know it," said Rance.

They looked up. "She need anything?" says Leola.

"Asleep," Willy said. "I'm going to see Jake."

"Don't know why you must waste time with him," says Leola.

Willy went out into the night. Water was pouring over the milldam. There was a bright moon. The ground was hard and the air was frosty. Each fence, barn and building was clearly delineated. There was a fragrance of woodsmoke in the cold air. The giant sycamore stood lonely guard down beside the river.

Willy knocked at the cabin door. Jake opened it. Willy entered. Jake's family were all asleep.

"Lemme stir dat fire, Sonny. Set where you be comfortable." He took Willy's crutches.

"Were you asleep, Jake?"

"Maybe my eyes was at rest. Dreams and snitches — but I wadn't *asleep*, Sonny. Naw."

They sat before the fire. Willy had always been comfortable here. Jake had always treated him as a grown-up. Willy had drunk coffee here when he was considered too little to have coffee at the big house. And while Jake and his wife had treated Willy like a grown-up, they had also treated him like a son. Here was the place he had missed, this house that his father had built. Willy's spirit found rest here. Here the fires were warmer, the chairs more comfortable. The dog that slept upon the hearth was a hunting hound. Jake struck a match and was lighting his pipe. His gun was in the corner. His coat and his hunting horn were on a wall peg above it. The boots he wore and now propped towards the fire set him apart from other servants. They were hunting boots laced to the knee, the same as Isaac and Willy and Elias himself wore, with a red wool sock turned down over the tops.

Since "the blow fell," which was Jake's term for the war, there was news and news, he said. His life had been a series of blows. This last was but another. Everyman's life was a series of blows, as Jake saw it. They fell one after the other until finally they beat him down into his grave, six feet under where the grass could grow over him and birds could fly above as before and the animals make their tracks.

"A thang happened," Jake said. "It was some of Mister Edward's business. He's been brought back home wid two fingers shot off an' his left arm broke in two places. They nursed him three months. Well, he's on his feet again and ain't doin' but one thang, ain't lookin' fer but one thang. That gal."

"Gal?"

"Betsy. Because he got to her and his mama, Miss Ellen, she had to trade her off. Sho. So that blow fell here. Marse Elias took her on here and we married her wid one of my boys on dis place. Now Mister Edward's located her. He's found her again and won't be happy till he has her back wid him. So that blow fell and we had to pack her up an' send her to Marse Shokotee an' let him see if he can hide her good enough."

"Edward came here?"

"Sho! An' tole me outta his own mouth that didn't I find that gal and bring her to him he gonna *hang me* and burn dis house and what all. Sho."

"We'll see about that," Willy said.

"Mister Edward rides in here on us every day or two nursin' his arm and dem missin' fingers."

"Does my mother know this?"

"Naw, Sonny. What will you do?"

"Go see him," said Willy. "First thing tomorrow."

"Jus' be careful, Sonny. Mister Edward seems like he's half a crazyman to me. Don't let him harm you. They tell it he killed a lot of Yankees."

Here was an example of the very thing soldiers more and more heard was happening at home. With so many men gone and so many more soon to leave, strange things were happening. It strikes Willy that those tales are true! All along till now he's taken them with a grain of salt! Here's Edward Ashe showing his butt, thinks Willy.

"Edward's a bastard," Willy said. "That rumor's gone around far back as I can remember. She claims she was married to a man named Ashe but that he abandoned her before the Poes moved here and settled. This Ashe is supposed to have come for a visit, only to walk off again. That's too thick for me."

"Well, we hear things and more things. But it was your daddy that made them just about everything they have and are down there. He felt sorry fer 'em."

Not even his anger nor his plans for Edward Ashe could hold back the weariness Willy began to feel. Jake, of course, would have sat up all night. Willy decided he must leave now and go to bed. With a final promise to see about Edward Ashe tomorrow, Willy said goodnight. He made his way back through the cold to the big house and let himself in the kitchen door.

Going up the backstairs and down the hall to his room, he found Rance there, dozing by the fire. The Negro woke up and stirred the fire. Willy's bed was turned down for him and a clean nightshirt was laid out. Rance helped him put off his boots and slip out of his uniform. He climbed into the feather bed. Rance blew out the candles. The tired soldier slept.

Chapter 7

Willy's body made a fool of him. Woke him before daylight as usual when he could have slept the sleep of the just in a feather bed. Try as he would he could not go back to sleep.

He got up, sent Rance for a horse and had Leola feed him breakfast. He dressed in a suit of old clothes in place of his uniform, threw on a heavy cape and in spite of the fact that it had snowed during the night and was still snowing, making the pond and the river black and capping the black fences with white, he rode out on a little black mare. He set a good pace on the snowy, trackless road, and went south in search of Edward Ashe, his crutches tied to the saddle.

Nevermind where he was going, he had told Leola. Nevermind when he would be back. Tell his mother he had gone on a little errand he said. And:

"Expect me back when you see me."

The old squaw had straightened in alarm. She wasn't accustomed to such mystery. And besides, this was her own Willy. She had rocked him and nursed him and told him little stories — how the rabbit lost his tail, and all. She didn't expect such short shrift from her baby. And she said,

"Now what kind of talk is that, Willy? All dressed up so early and snow everywhere, and yourself crippled! Why the animals won't make tracks as early as this. They'll lie close and warm all day in the thickets. You'll risk your death in such weather. Now answer me, Will McCutcheon! What's got into you?"

But Willy had only made a stern face and pulled his broad hat down tight.

Now the mare kicked the snow at a muffled pace on the road winding south and the world all about was a shimmering white that made his eyes almost blind with the glare of it, and here and there was shiny, mysterious, wet-looking black, under logs and against tree trunks. Big snowflakes came at him and touched his face and broke against his eyes and he pulled the hat down lower still. For a long unbroken distance he rode through the wonder and beauty of the snow, entranced by the mere riding, transfixed by the muted sounds and soft progressions of distance unfolding upon strange vistas. He was so beguiled that he almost passed the Poe plantation.

He dismounted in the drive, hitched his horse, took his crutches, and went boldly to the door. He seized the brass door knocker and let it fall several times.

To the servant who opened the door he said: "It's me, Willy McCutcheon. Edward here?"

"Go right on up, it's all right."

Willy thumped briskly up the stairs. He entered Edward's room without knocking or ceremony. His friend was in bed, half sitting up. The curtains had been drawn aside. A book lay face down on the nightstand. The glaring brightness of the snow was reflected inside and when Willy looked beyond the wide windows he could see the river, a ribbon of black laid in the snowy landscape.

"Willy — by God! It's really you!"

"Hello, Edward. Was Virginia as rough as we hear?"

Edward nodded. He looked more pale than Willy remembered him. Edward's left arm was hidden beneath the covers. His right arm lay upon the coverlet.

Willy put his crutches aside with his cape and his hat and his riding crop.

"Edward, what's going on between you and Jake?"

"Why?"

"You told Jake you were going to hang him. Did you really say that, Edward?"

"That was just talk," says Edward. And so saying he drew the hidden hand from beneath the covers and held it up. It was terribly raw-looking. The middle and fourth fingers were missing. And as he spoke again his voice fell away, him saying:

"This is all I got, Willy." He thrust the ruined hand away out of sight again. "All I got," he said.

Wounds in the field were so common that not much was thought of them. Death was the same. In the field there wasn't time to think. But here, on the home ground, Edward's hand somehow seemed to fill the room entirely. Here upon his bed with the snowlight glare pouring through the windows, it was exceedingly clear to Willy that something terrible had happened to Edward Ashe. If he were in uniform riding the cars through Alabama with that hand in a sling nobody would give Edward a second look. But here, as Willy discovered, here it was all different. Willy struggled to get hold of himself. He said, "A lot more will get a lot worse than that before it's over."

Edward smiled a weary smile. He looked toward the balcony and said, "It's over for me."

"But you can ride again, can't you?"

"I can. But the arm's weak and I've got no grip in the hand. The leaders are torn and scarred and drawn up and . . .

for a while I thought I'd lose the arm." Edward's voice was quiet and hard, and had no fall in it, and he said, "If I don't get her back, if I don't, if they've sent her somewhere —"

"By God, sir, she's married to another slave — *married*. Edward, you're *crazy!*"

"Willy, what nobody wants to understand, what nobody can *let* themselves understand is that I love her . . ." Edward spoke in such a strange way, in a voice so much older than he seemed, and he said such a terrible thing but again he said, "I love her!"

"Good God a'mighty," said Willy. "But you *can't*."

Edward was breathing as though he had just run a long distance. Outside snow was falling again. The little flakes seemed to fly upwards and spit against the windowpanes.

Forgetting his crutches Willy got up and limped to the balcony doors and back to Edward. Speaking slowly he said. "Maybe you better tell me about it, Edward."

"God," Edward groaned. "God help me."

"And let's us see what we can do," said Willy.

"You believe me then."

Willy drew a breath. "I believe you. And I never before believed anything as awful in my life. Yes, I b'lieve you. Yes, damn it . . ."

Edward told his story. Because it was something nobody wanted to hear, perhaps he hadn't told it before. There was a house servant, Betsy by name. What was she like? An ordinary slave, born on the place, and brought to the house like any other because one of the house servants had passed on to her reward. Just at that time Edward had been calling on one of Doctor Parham's pretty daughters. She had other beaux. Edward was jealous. Sallie Parham was fickle and faithless. She loved another, maybe! Edward woke late at night and walked the lawn in his nightshirt and lay face down in the dew and let it wet his hair. In the daytime he rode past the Parham house as fast as his horse would carry him and never looked that way. He got drunk at the Steamboat and Majestic where everyone could see and go tell her about it. His friends could go tell Sallie Parham that he was throwing his life away, drinking himself to death for the sake of her; so drunk by noon he couldn't see the spots on his cards but continued to play anyhow.

"It was what you might call a regular ordinary run-of-the-mill love affair," Edward said.

In three or four months, he couldn't exactly remember which, he got tired of it and realized he was eighteen and getting too old for that sort of horseshit. And he had come home and been sick then for a while. Doctor Parham had come to bleed him and dose him with calomel.

And then, while still sick with his fever, he had spoken to Betsy. She did him little kindnesses. They had long visits in which they spoke of life and slavery and of what she thought and of what he felt and of the prospects of war and whether or not it would last very long if there were war. Betsy was fresh, she was honest. Perhaps it was no different, that little seduction. Betsy didn't make a great fuss. She seemed happy to help Edward get over Sallie.

But Ellen had got wind of it. And meanwhile Edward had discovered to his dismay that he wanted Betsy — and her baby. Honor bound to defy Ellen and get into the army as soon as he could (for Ellen was against his having any part in the war), he was no sooner out of training camp than his unit, while scouting, met a squadron of Yankees on the road and flew into them with their sabers. None of them knew, so early, that sabers were damned near worthless and a last resort after pistols and carbines and even — bless God — poor lowly shotguns. No, Edward and his messmates flew into the Yankee squadron with sabers and Edward got his arm broken in two places, his horse killed, and his two fingers shot off. His friends on either side of him were killed. He recalled with a shudder the awful *thug* of a bullet when it struck the man nearest him in the head.

And after the disaster Edward had three months of pain. And when he came home, too weak and much crippled, he had known there was only one happiness for him — Betsy and that child.

Listening, Willy felt the last vestige of his rancor turn to pity.

Edward's eyes had tears. He said, "There is nothing else I want in this life."

"Then by God," Willy said, "we'll get her and we'll get the kid and . . . but where will you go?"

Edward shook his head. He sighed. "Canada, perhaps."

Willy wondered if he were doing right. Maybe, later on, he would be sorry. He was going against everything he had been taught. And he could guess what Isaac would say. Isaac wouldn't understand any of this. Neither would the law understand it. And the Confederacy certainly couldn't be expected to understand it.

"How can *you* help?" Edward was saying.

"I know where she is," said Willy. "Get dressed."

"You know?"

"Sure. Get your clothes on. Let's get this damned business over with. I don't want to use all my leave foolin' with *this*. Will you need — can you get?" Willy stopped.

Edward was laying his clothes out. "What?" he said.

"Money," said Willy. "I've got some I can let you have. So you told old Jake you'd hang him? What'd he say to that?"

"Scared billy hell out of him," said Edward. "I've got money, yes."

With no more explanation than that they were going for a ride in the snow, the two young soldiers took the road north.

As they rode north by the river Edward continued:

"They put us in a tent, all the wounded together. When gangrene ate through some poor devil's artery his blood would spurt to the roof of the tent — a fountain! The doctors couldn't get the gangrene smell off their hands. You enter another world when you're hurt, don't you? When they think a man is dying they take him to a separate tent. They took me. Took me to the dying tent."

Willy knew those horrors, yes. He had seen piles of arms and legs behind the surgical tents. He had heard the moans and screams of the shattered creatures brought from the field in litters and the ambulances. And this built up in him, as he and Edward made their way north to Shokotee's plantation, a dread that he had never felt till now — the realization that he must go back to the fighting. He wanted to say something about it to Edward but he was afraid.

He said, "How still snow makes everything." Each time Edward brought up the war, Willy tried to turn him away from that subject.

Edward carried his red, injured hand drawn back into his coat sleeve. He managed the reins entirely with his right hand.

They had ridden the last few miles in silence when Edward said, "I should have known they'd send her to your grandfather's place."

They stopped in the road and sat looking at Shokotee's mansion which lay across the bridge on the other side. Only the smoke above the chimneys gave any indication of life. Now they were here Willy wasn't sure how to proceed.

"I suppose we'll have to steal her," he said. "Are you sure she's willing, Edward?"

What Willy really wanted to ask was whether Edward was sure this was what he wanted — a Negro wife and a Negro baby and God knows what sort of awful existence in Canada, leagues from home, and in such exile as would make sure he'd never lay eyes on the South again. He would break his mother's heart. Willy was embarked upon a high crime and the more he looked at what he was doing the more he wondered. What the hell has got you in so deep? he asked himself.

Edward had lit a cigar and sat smoking, gazing at the mansion. Then, with excitement in his voice, he said,

"Get word to her to bring the baby and meet me on this side of the bridge at dark. The snow will make light enough to take her into Somerton. I'll go to the woods and wait."

Willy shook his head. "You'll freeze to death before dark. With that arm you couldn't take her on your horse even if she didn't have the baby. No, you can't get her there alone. The three of you could die in weather like this. Let's see my grandfather. I'll do the talking. Come on!"

They headed their horses over the bridge, rode up to the big house at a canter and dismounted and drew their reins through the hitching rings. Willy knocked on the front door and was greeted by Anda who shouted for Belle. The young men were drawn inside, their coats and hats taken, and Shokotee, looking no different to Willy than he looked when he had seen him the last time, to tell him goodbye, took them both in by the fire and called for eggnog. He admired Edward's injured hand and congratulated him for having the courage to stop the surgeons from taking his arm.

"Soak it every day in warm water," he said, "and rub it afterward with a little oil to make it loose. It will be strong again, you'll see."

Shokotee had a long acquaintance with wounds and the injured. He was moved to tell of an action he had seen in Alabama. Edward's hand was a reminder for he told the story with relish, smiling now and then at the memory.

"Speaking of close engagements. I had a good friend, Jack Sherrill, who was a major and had a temper about like your daddy, Elias. Jack was a gouger when it came to a fight. A big old Indian buck came at him. First they clubbed their guns and broke them swinging at each other and then they dropped their guns and laid hold. Wasn't anytime until Jack got both thumbs in that big buck's eyes and the Indian begins hollering *Canally nacuah! Canally nacuah!* They've had enough when they holler that. But Jack says 'Damn you, you can never have enough while you're alive!' Then he picked up one of the broken guns and knocked his brains out — ah, it was a funny sight! That buck Indian bit off Jack's little finger. I had a good laugh over it. *Canally nacuah!*"

Edward no longer tried to tuck his hand out of sight, but let it lie carelessly on his leg. Presently he used it to take his cigar from his mouth. For the first time that day he laughed.

"Oh, yes!" said Shokotee. And looking at Willy he said, "And what about you, nothing to show for it? Let's see your leg! Did you get a look at him or did they keep you back behind where you couldn't see anything."

"I got a look at him," Willy said. "We turned one of his cannons around on him."

"That's good for him," said Shokotee. "God *damn* him!"

"Jake sent a girl up here, Grandpa," said Willy.

"Um. He did. She's got a baby. Leola paired her off with a fellow but there was trouble and they sent them here. She's like as not to run away first chance she gets. That kind of thing makes all your other servants unhappy. Um."

"I want you to give her to me," said Willy.

"She's not mine to give. She's from the Poes, property of Mrs. Ashe."

"I'm Mrs. Ashe's son," Edward said.

"Ho-ho!" said Shokotee. "Then it's all arranged."

"Edward's going to take her with him," Willy said. "All right?"

"Um. Anda! Anda?"

Anda came in and stood silent while Shokotee appeared to think. Finally he said,

"That girl Jake sent up here? Have her brought here to me with her baby. Nevermind her husband. Start him back to Oakleigh."

Anda nodded and left. Shokotee smiled. He turned to Edward and said,

"There, ain't as difficult as you thought, eh? These things happen and the best way is to let people have their way. Now where will you go?"

Edward blushed. He looked at the fire and said, "Canada."

Shokotee looked at Willy as if to say Canada might be more difficult than Edward imagined.

"T. Laird and the widow, Mrs. Parham," he said. "Tell them I said it would be a favor to me if they would help. Snail, he's dealing in stolen slaves and betraying them just lately for reward money. Just say I'd deem it a favor. Tell him I said mind and no slips. You'll have to pay him of course, but he and the Parham widow, they've got the connections with other agents. They deal in everything, those two. She was a whore before she married the doctor."

"Widow?" said Willy.

"Parham was killed last week I heard," said Shokotee. "Pity. Now let's have something to eat. You can't leave before dark."

"I'm very grateful, sir," said Edward.

"These things happen. But Willy — if he don't get a move on he may wind up an old bachelor with dogs in front of his fire and no thought but what he will hunt next."

Because he could not think beyond the war, nor imagine that the war would ever really be over, Willy found the old man's words strange.

They had set off at nightfall with a servant to drive the closed buggy with Betsy and the baby bundled up inside with charcoal warmers. The snow, though it was deeper, made the way bright enough to travel without lights, as Edward had predicted it would. Riding ahead into Somerton, wary of Union pickets, Willy scouted the place. He found not a soul stirring abroad, no sentries; the cold had driven everyone indoors. Edward was waiting in the shade of a thicket at the edge of town and the two young Confederates escorted the closed buggy to the Snail's.

After some knocking they were received by T. Laird and his servant, Aunt Tio. Then, warming himself in front of T. Laird's fire, Willy delivered Shokotee's message, that it would be a favor to help Edward and Betsy on their way to Canada — and be sure there were no slips! As he spoke he had his first opportunity to observe the woman Edward Ashe was forsaking all else to possess.

He saw a girl of dark ivory complexion with delicate features. Though she had nothing to say, her happiness was manifest when she smiled; she was beautiful, the more so as she was experiencing the realization of a dream that, until now, must have seemed an utter impossibility. With one slender hand, she held the baby to her breast, a fat, yellow-brown little infant with golden looks and dark hair, a round face, and a tiny spread-out nose. It was obvious that the two gave Edward Ashe a feeling of happiness when he looked at them. Something very different than what Willy had first imagined must have taken place between Edward and this girl; this was no mere rogering in a slave cabin. "Here it is," thought Willy. "The Abolitionists have written about it, yet I never believed it could be true. Yet here it is and I'm a party to it."

There were things Willy felt he ought to say to Edward. They were all the things which anyone in his right mind *would* say, were he to confront the very thing the South hated most. *Look, friend, what you're doing is a betrayal of what we've been fighting for. And how the hell will you make out in a strange white community?* He could say all that and more. Yet he didn't. He warmed himself by the fire trying to look pleasant and act as though this were something that happened every day. Just as the God damned Abolitionists claimed it did. Why sure, he was just Willy McCutcheon and probably rogered darkies himself for all anybody knew.

Then there was Shokotee. None of this appeared to surprise him. If anything the old man had seemed amused.

At that moment Mrs. Parham came in with one of her servants. Her hair was jet black, her eyes had a dark fire, something dangerous about them, when she looked at a man, and her skin was beautifully soft and creamy white, as though her debaucheries and now this Negro-stealing only served to keep her young and beautiful.

"How do you do, Mister McCutcheon?"

The way she looked at him when she spoke made Willy blush. Certainly he had never imagined that a whore could make him blush.

"How do you do, ma'am," and when he spoke he politely bowed and smiled.

Mrs. Parham turned to Edward and took the baby to look at it. She said how very happy she was for the three of them. And she said how noble it was of Mister Willy McCutcheon to bring this little family together again.

Willy looked at the fire. Aunt Tio brought him a cup of coffee though he said three times already that he didn't want anything. It had seemed that it would be better if he didn't eat or drink anything here. He was half a mind to put the cup and saucer down, but then he saw Mrs. Parham was looking at him and he looked down into his cup, raised it and took a sip.

"Is your grandfather, Mister McNeilly, well?" she said softly.

"Yes, ma'am. Thank you. He sends . . . he sends . . ."

"My best wishes to him when you see him," she murmured. "Your mother, how is she?"

"Very well, ma'am. I was sorry to hear . . ."

"Have you heard from Isaac or your father recently? There was an ambush in which my husband the doctor lost his life." She bit the edge of her lower lip and tucked her head, showing how much she missed the doctor.

The Snail, a grizzled little brown man, bent forward at the waist in a permanent stoop, as though something heavy had sat itself on his shoulders long ago, was smiling at Willy and at Mrs. Parham, as though nothing pleased him so much as having these two guests under his roof. Now and then he took his hands out of his coat pockets and rubbed them together. Now he said,

"Let's get business out of the way so we can have our supper, eh?"

Willy wondered what his father would say to all this. He knew what Isaac would do. Isaac would have the sheriff and two constables here by now. Willy took the money he had with him — some three hundred dollars in notes — and pressed it into the Snail's hands. He spoke quietly into the Snail's ear,

"For Edward, give it to him for me. If anything should happen to him Grandpa will kill you — or I will. Understand me?"

The Snail smiled as if he had received a compliment. "Of course," he said. "We'll take the very best care of them. I know your grandfather, sir. I know him well. In good health I hope."

Willy wondered if T. Laird had heard him. Then he decided that he must have. And here was how men acted, that is to say half-breeds. You couldn't insult them.

Willy handed his coffee cup to Aunt Tio and asked for his coat. She brought it and held it while Willy put it on and fastened his buttons. She handed him his broad hat and his riding crop and his crutches. Willy looked at Edward and said,

"I'm on short leave and will be leaving soon. So this is goodbye, Edward. I wish you all the luck." He put his arm around Edward's shoulder.

"Stay! Stay, sir!" the Snail cried. And in that same bent posture he turned his head and smiled first at Edward and then at Willy.

Mrs. Parham had joined them and Willy was aware of her perfume. She looked at him with her dark eyes.

"Before you go back to the war," she said, "do please call on me at home?"

Willy said he would. Edward went outside into the snow with him and waited while his mare was brought around. P'-nache came leading the horse. Edward was wishing Willy luck, wishing him well, thanking him for what he had done.

As Willy rode away, he was troubled but conscious above everything of Mrs. Parham's dark beauty, the perfume she had been wearing, and that tempting invitation. The moon had risen and the world all about him shone and the mare went willingly.

Chapter 8

In time you heal. Bone mends; a scar covers your left leg where the bullet flew in and downed you. Older men don't get well so quickly. The young are lucky. Willy discards his crutches. He's well enough to go back to war and has been dreaming these last days at home, dreaming of a woman with white skin and dark eyes . . .

He has arranged with Jake to have himself smuggled into Somerton for a visit with the Widow Parham, to call on her as he had promised he would. As he washed that last morning, shaved, and put on his uniform, it was with a feeling of sadness.

The soldier says goodbye to boyhood, going about the room that once was his.

Well, time for a last look at some things — squirrel rifle, powder horn, skinning knife, rabbit's foot, eagle feathers. On the floor in the corner near the chest there's a toy coach drawn by strong little iron horses managed with wire reins. Nearby is the dusty small iron cannon, and beside it five lead soldiers, five where once had stood twoscore, but soldiers are made to be lost.

Farewell to a mother wearing a black silk patch on her

cheek. She's been counting the minutes. Something tells the soldier she must have lain awake all night.

"Now mind you don't forget the letters," says she. Those letters for Isaac and Elias from herself, and the letters from Shokotee for Pettecasockee, and from Fancy Callister and her children for Dutt. They serve to keep Jane's mind off the dangers Willy must pass just getting beyond occupied territory. "Don't forget the letters."

"No, ma'am."

"I don't like your smuggling yourself into Somerton just to call on poor Mrs. Parham. I suppose with the doctor dead and all . . ."

"Never you mind about *dat*," says Jake, who has come to help Rance and Leola with Willy's packing. Suddenly the soldier's room is full of servants getting each in the other's way. "I'll git him into town and out agin, Miss Jane."

"I suppose he must call on her. Tell your father, tell Isaac . . ."

She said the same things over again.

"When will you be home next?"

"Depends how things go," says Willy.

"Yes," says Jane bitterly. "Now run down and eat your breakfast."

He went down and sat at his father's place at the long table in the dining room. He fed the cats on the stand tidbits from his plate, just as Elias would have. Leola's old fyce wandered stiffly into the dining room from the kitchen. She barked three times at the cats, sniffed at Willy's boots, and waddled away back to the kitchen. Jane appeared just as Willy finished a final cup of what passed for coffee nowadays at Oakleigh. Burnt field corn was ground up and hot water poured through the powder to make a dark drink which was sweetened with sorghum molasses, for there was no sugar anymore. But there was milk, there were eggs, there was bread, and meat in plenty.

"Tell your father . . ."

She said the same things. She gave him money, three gold coins. She was sending socks to Elias and Isaac, packed among his things. He'd find them. And a shirt for Petteca-sockee, a hunting shirt such as her brother favored, sewn with her own hands. "Tell him, tell Isaac, tell your father . . ."

She shuddered and began to weep.

There was a sound in the hall. Shokotee came into the dining room. "Just thought I'd come this way. Passing the house and thought to stop in — is it today you leave, Willy? Is it?" As though he weren't aware all along it was today. The old man coughs. "Coffee? Yes, thanks. I don't mind. Crying doesn't help!" he snaps. "Hush!"

Jane tries to hush. And Shokotee: "I have more letters here. You may as well take them long as you're going that way. And tell my son . . ."

Willy tries to remember it all. Surely he will remember everything. He must try to listen and he must try not to let himself think that the very worst part about military leave and coming home is that you must go back again knowing now what it is that waits for you out there . . .

"So long as you're calling on Fanny Parham tell her there's a subscription for new pews in the Presbyterian Church as a memorial to her husband. Jake drives back and forth to Fort Hill so often you'll get in and out all right. Just don't take a fool's risk. Eh?"

"Yes, Grandpa."

"I half suspect they know our boys come home. It's better for the Yankees if they overlook some things. A soldier never knows when the tables may turn and he may want a little mercy himself. Ennis Dalton's not a bad fellow."

"You gave him rope!" So saying Jane smiled. Her face twisted grotesquely. "Ha-ha!" says Jane. "He told me."

"I gave him rope, yes." The old man smiled. "Well?"

They went out. On the porch Willy kissed his mother. Jake brought the spring buggy around. Behind the seat was a large packing crate, large enough to hide a soldier.

Willy climbed up on the seat beside Jake. Leola, surprisingly spry, came after him, and gathering her dress to keep it from dragging, climbed up and gave Willy a kiss and stepped down again into the snow. Her eyes seemed to bother her. "My baby . . ." she muttered in her cracked old voice.

Jake took the whip from the socket and slapped the reins. "Step out dar!" the Negro ordered. The matched pair sprang into a trot. Down the drive they went. Willy waved a last goodbye.

As they turned into the road the river was black between its snowy banks. A flock of wild ducks which had rafted up on the dark surface rose at the buggy's approach. Wild wings flashing in thin, red sunlight, the mallards circled low, passing just above the leafless treetops, quacking raucously. The milldam whispered on the left. The horses thumped smartly over the plank bridge. Willy did not look back.

Helped out of the packing crate by Jake at the rear entrance of the Parham house, Willy went limping inside when the back door was answered by a young lady.

"Your mother home?"

"Mama's not here. She wanted to be but — you must be Willy McCutcheon."

"Yes."

"She had an errand. Will you come sit in the parlor?"

He couldn't take his eyes off the girl. Going ahead of him into the parlor she sat across from him on a love seat. She had her mother's eyes and her mother's mouth and the same white skin and the same raven hair. She wore a black gown, a mourning dress, with buttons on the sleeves. Her hands were long and graceful. So he was going back to war? He said yes. Was it very frightening? He said no. He had served with the same troop so he must have known her father? Yes, he had known him and had been very sorry to hear of his death.

"Thank you," she said. Then after a silence: "I know some of the boys who *don't* like it. When they couldn't get permission to come home after their enlistment was up, some came anyway and —" She broke off and picked up a little ivory elephant from the round table beside the love seat. Looking at the elephant, never taking her eyes from it, she said: "I've seen you before."

"You have?"

"Tearing up Fort Hill on your horse."

He blushed. His tight soldier's collar felt warm at the neck. "What's your name?"

"Sallie Parham and I'm seventeen." She said it quickly, in a small voice, still looking at the elephant in her hand.

Willy felt strange. He could take women or leave them, couldn't he? He had a few daguerreotypes to prove it and he had gotten several letters from the Callister girl. He liked girls like Adele Callister because they were tomboys, sort of, and didn't go in for white fingernails, nor for wearing their hair in curls upon their temples. But now, sitting opposite Sallie Parham, he wasn't sure.

"It's a long journey," he said, "and I'd best be going. It's late . . ."

"But won't you have some cake and wine?" she asked.

He would, he said, if she were having some too. In that case she was, she said, and for the first time she laughed. The sound spoke to his heart. It told him something . . .

She brought him a large slice of cake and a stem glass filled with wine. For herself she took only the barest sliver of cake and put only a touch of wine in her own glass. She mentioned that it was lonesome with all the older boys gone away. She and her friends had a party last week. Some had dressed up like young men so they could dance at least.

"What are the girls in other places like?"

The cake was poundcake, his favorite, and his mouth was full. He took a sip of wine. The cake was every bit good as Leola's! After wondering how he would answer he said:

"None near so pretty as Somerton girls." And then, suddenly: "Do you have a sweetheart?"

She gave him a look and a certain light came into her eyes. She bit her lower lip, trying not to smile. Then she laughed in a way that made him laugh with her and she said:

"I wonder if I should tell?"

She fetched her writing paper and wrote down Willy's address. They were quiet for a while after he had finished his cake and drunk his wine and refused a second helping.

"Is it so hateful to go back?" she said softly.

"Ah, no," he said. "Not hateful . . ."

She fetched a letter from the mantel and handed it to Willy. He knew his father's handwriting and guessed what it was, unfolding it meanwhile.

"It's a beautiful letter. I read it over and over," she said.

After a polite interval during which he scanned the words ". . . pen in hand . . . leaden heart . . . brave husband and father . . . faithful comrade in arms . . . defense of his country . . . reconnaissance upon the Ohio River . . ." he handed it back to her. It was time to leave and he stood up. Looking at the girl Willy wondered why it was that he had discovered her only now. There was one last glimpse of her waving to him through the window, before Jake helped him back into the crate.

When he could get out of the crate and ride on the buggy seat with Jake again they had reached the bottoms. Water stood on either side of the lonely road. Snow powdered logs and stumps. It was a backroad and the horses went but poorly. "Come up dar!" said Jake from time to time.

Two alone on the backroads. South they went, picking their way. Master and servant, and friends for all that, willing to die for one another if need arose. They carried pistols primed and loaded and a packet of mail and a basket of cold fried chicken and a compass for just in case. On such roads in such country it would be easy to get lost — or worse yet, robbed and murdered.

"Mind the winter the river froze hard as your headbone, Sonny-boy — remember?"

Willy remembers.

"We had us some fine times," says Jake. He sighs as though to admit once and for all that those times are over. "Gone and done."

Chapter *9*

Losing Tennessee and Kentucky so soon was a blow. Elias knew it was not just land lost, not mere territory, no; not just homes and hills and valleys and dirt, which would be bad enough; no, it was horses. Horses would be missed most of all if Tennessee and Kentucky, which the Confederate army, with the fall of the river forts had been forced to abandon, were not retaken.

Lost horse country meant lost raiders and riders. Strip an army of cavalry? It stood no chance. True it was that infantry might be the queen of battle, but it was cavalry that fell upon his rear and raked him with catclaws. Cavalry tore in upon his baggage trains, setting all afire. Cavalry could circle him and throw him into a panic. Cavalry raiders could chase him day and night until he surrendered for sheer lack of sleep. Run him far enough and long enough — he would throw down his arms in exchange for a nap . . .

Elias made no claim to understand the grand strategy. He was a raider; and getting tougher. Fighting and killing and riding; capturing what was needed to supply his raiders. Recruiting where he could, he'd been joined by like-minded volunteers, mostly young fellows, who, combined with what he thought of now as his "old guard," fellows from the Fort Hill district itself, made a troop that would dare anything.

Aye — they were into it now.

Before the forts fell Elias had been searching for the Yankee cavalry the captured Union transport had been trying to supply.

The thin notes of the bugle had scattered upon the breeze. Drums had beat the devil's tattoo. The regiment had wakened to the sound, uncoiling from its bed. In a long, sinuous column the regiment came pouring out of camp from the white tents, taut and looking as though ironed to attention. The camp gave off smells of canvas and paraffin, of leather and beeswax and brass polish.

Further along in open country the wind burnished the sky; the woods smelled of wet leaves. The clean rot of autumn obtained here and the wide land stretched far away. The road was spliced by wet plank bridges spanning deep ravines. Rich fields of corn stood yellow and ready for harvest; autumn pastures were dotted with stumps, silver-gray rail fences ran endlessly, sun-bleached and enduring; plump haystacks, full barns, neat houses; cattle, heads down, slowly grazing. In the distances, on wooded hillsides, the maples showed saffron leaves and the gum trees showed crimson and the cedars made dark shadows and looked almost black, like dried blood.

Weakened by winter's approach the butterflies had struggled, fluttering south across the road. Their summer colors were various as the autumn leaves and the wildflowers and many fell in the road. Now and then amid these fallen legions a wing moved. . .

In a village of white clapboard houses where stood a line of shops and general stores and from the midst of which a railroad passed, curved track slanting away over a brown timbered trestle, the gray regiment paused for a rest.

Sullen inhabitants stood on porches or stayed indoors. These were border people with men in both armies. When Elias questioned a constable wearing a string tie, his shirt collar soiled, his black suit frayed, the man had hitched at his suspenders. Spitting tobacco juice he said:

"Soldiers? Seen no sign of soldiers 'cept you fellows."

And he spat again. On the far side of the village the land all about was quiet. The raiders spoke quietly and moved quickly. Elias ordered the advance and rear guards doubled. He sent Pettecasockee and Willy to scan the woods and the ridges and sent the Shelton boys to scour the roads running parallel through that wide country. Halt to listen; hear your ears ringing. A death calm and no breeze and a day too warm for autumn. Thus it was, a pervading quiet as though someone were watching. The blood beats in your face. Your pulse tells that here is Indian summer again.

Sundown. Camped on a hillock with open land all about, they chose a campsite removed from the road. From the hill was a good view of things in every direction.

There were no fires. The pickets were posted. A double

guard was set upon the road. Waking, Elias saw the sky and sensed the movement of the stars. In dreams he saw the attacking horse of the enemy. He heard the tumult of the clash and sounds of killing. In his dreams the regiment was cut to pieces. When he woke the stars had wheeled upon the face of the heavens. At last he smelled a cool rising scent from the creek which told the approach of day. Going down to the bridge upon the road he spoke to the guards. He was there, waiting when the sky came pink. Two riders came up the road giving the password. Elias recognized Willy and Pettecasockee.

Dismounting, the scouts crossed the bridge, leading their horses, fine figures they were, wild and lithe, and full of daring . . .

"Over here," said Elias.

"Found them," says Willy.

"Clymer's Landing, ten miles," says Pettecasockee.

"What kind?" says Elias.

"Cavalry, Kentucky and Ohio boys," says Willy.

Hell drew a breath, as the saying is, and the devil's bitter risen bread was baked. The regiment rose from its bed upon the hill and like a thing with yellow eyes and leathern wings it skimmed the autumn road to Clymer's Landing, curved beak of steel thrust forward, thunder in its iron-shod feet. A cry burst from its red throat as the raiders drove in with a cheer amidst the tents and the breakfast fires of the Kentucky and Ohio boys until the dead lay on every side butchered and shot to death and the last of the living finally herded down to the river's edge where they tried to make a stand, but couldn't, for the raiding gray riders rode through and over them back and forth, cutting them to pieces.

No time for the Yankee bugle to blow. No time for the Yankee drums to beat, as their pickets were driven in and ridden down.

In less time than the telling the fight was over. Pistols and shotguns and carbines did the work.

"Ho!" from the Kentuckians on the Confederate side. A border fight is always bloodiest, for border-state boys see brimstone and boil to kill their kin. Combatants on both sides hailed from the same state and district. No quarter asked and none given until very awful near the end when truce and surrender were forced upon the blue soldiers. "Ho!"

Slashing and shooting, stabbing and clubbing, enough to make the devil grin. Thus had the smell of war finally fixed itself in the nostrils of the regiment, in man and beast.

Thirty-six raiders dead and fifty wounded. Nineteen horses lost. The Yankee lads had exacted their toll.

The wounded and the prisoners were set on the road south and the dead were consigned to marked graves. Isaac himself saw to the records, for a family would want their boy's bones brought home. They'd send and want to know upon what spot he lay and would ask how he died and what he said if anything and just how the fighting went and what the day was like, whether fair or raining. Everything — they wanted to know everything afterwards, the families did.

Elias wrote the slow, painful letters that went home. "*Dear Sir and Madam . . .*"

Chapter 10

He was small, Confederate gray, and had been freezing and starving beside the road, hidden in a brush pile, and waiting for death. A man and a horse came to rest nearby, and other men and other horses, such that the little creature was frightened at first. Then hunger made him bold and he wobbled out from beneath the brush and made for the man's boots and rubbed against them, mewing.

"By God," said the bearded fellow. "Well, by God."

"Sir?"

"A kitten."

"Sir?"

"Here's a kitten just walked from under that brushpile." So saying Elias picked up the gray foundling. "Poor devil." He was reminded of his cats at home, at rest on the stand in the dining room, fed by hand every mealtime, "Wish I had some milk for you."

"Sir?" said a private.

"Yes?"

"Sir, Malcolm Turner's mare still had some milk yesterday."

And not a moment later, or so it seemed to Elias, that

wonder which any sane man resting in the desolation and snow between Nashville and Dover, Tennessee, would have known to be impossible, happened. Private Turner produced a tin cup of milk from the teats of his sorrel mare and the gray cat took the nourishment, still warm from the mare's body, still steaming in the cold air.

Seemed a pity to leave the little critter, for while he might have stood a chance to fend for himself in mild weather, he would surely die if left in freezing weather.

Elias put him in his haversack. Might be as he'd find a home for the little critter in Nashville, he said, for it was a fact well known that cats can't go to war. The mounted rifles had a fighting *chicken* that lived in the knapsack of a Tennessean and fared very well, crowing at daybreak even while on the march, but a cat . . .

At Nashville the disorder was such that men could not consider cats. The Yankees were on the way, due to arrive any moment. The citizen population was breaking into the supply warehouses of the Confederate army. A railroad official had commandeered an entire train to transport himself and his family and a few wealthy friends south over the rails to safety.

Between leading forays against the citizen mobs and cracking them on their heads with the flats of their sabers, and seeing to the shipping of as many supplies as possible south to safe depots, there was not time to worry about the kitten. He slept in his haversack, mewed when hungry, lapped up his mare's milk, accepted a piece of bacon now and then, and managed somehow to sleep with Elias, against him and upon him and under his blanket, without getting crushed. It was never the man's intention that a cat would become a fixture in *his* life.

The cat, for a cat he soon became, never let Elias out of his sight, the men saying of it that at least Tom, for so he came to be called, was the right color. He was dead gray and had a rebel look and could eat just about anything. He was death on mice and rats. It was a known fact, of course, that a cat couldn't stand the sound of guns and wouldn't stay in a bag with a man on horseback during a fight. He'd spook. He'd jump out and run away and never be seen again. He'd go wild in the woods somewhere, for cats are born deserters. They rarely volunteer and they never enlist and the minute the going gets tough the cat's gone. So it was said . . .

But he lasted through Nashville and was still around, sticking to Elias like wallpaper, when the mare's milk gave out and he had to be satisfied with an occasional *sup* of milk — bought, borrowed, or stolen — instead of his daily ration.

He survived the first fight at Richland Creek, just west of Nashville, on the outskirts, where some Yankee pickets disputed a bridge and got themselves laid low. Tom McCutcheon, for such he had come to be called, stayed in his bag, though Elias emptied four pistols in that fighting and engaged a Yankee major in single combat with his saber and cut the fellow out of his saddle with a swipe that nearly took his head off — aye, would have taken it off with a little more swing to the stroke had the man's hand not been in the way to take part of the lick. The major's head was left hanging and he went backwards out of his saddle and Elias took the man's horse.

It was said that in that first engagement the cat, Tom McCutcheon, had been too frightened to move, what with all the yelling and the guns popping. Elias said insofar as he knew Tom had slept through the entire business. And that as far as cutting the major went, Elias would never have cut him so hard had the major not seemed to aim a lick at the haversack where Tom was sleeping, as though he somehow knew a cat was in there and hated cats maybe. "When he acted that way I saw red," says Elias.

Tom McCutcheon would leap out sure and run away in the next fight, the men said.

And said Pettecasockee, admiring the horse that had been the Yankee major's mount: "Are you glad now I sharpened your saber?"

"The edge does help," says Elias. "Let Isaac write an order that all sabers will be sharpened. Officers will check the cutting edge of sabers during inspection.The fine will be two dollars for any man carrying a dull saber."

Isaac objected, but he wrote the order. A sharp saber would likely cause a man to cut his horse or another's horse, to sever reins, to cut one's own companions in arms. The list of objections to the practice was apparently endless and had been the subject of treatises by scholars writing upon the art of cavalry warfare.

The cat was still with Elias when the Mounted Rifles went into camp at Corinth, Mississippi. Winter camp, it was; the usual lice and boredom and rats, and the yearning to be once again in action and the wondering how Willy, sent home with that hole in his leg, might be faring, especially now the Yankees had occupied the Fort Hill district.

Elias wrote letters to Jane and letters to Ellen and letters to Shokotee. He steered the pen but slowly, nothing like Isaac and his quick, fancy penmanship. A pen felt strange to the hand of this raider. Pen and paper and ink and wafers hadn't been part of his tools nor his weaponry in life, not till now when a new necessity pushed him.

Tom McCutcheon lazed about the tent. He'd fall in love presently, Tom would, and wander away and not be seen anymore, it was said. He was a tom, after all. His balls were visible when his tail was high. He'd get the hots presently, wait and see. Goodbye Tom, when that happened. He still went for rides with Elias, but his size was such that when the going got hard the man would have to toss him aside, haversack and all. Man couldn't tote a cat and everything else he must have for campaigning — carbine and pistols and forty rounds of ammunition and forage and rations and a shotgun maybe, loaded twelve buck balls to the barrel, powder and caps and lead and a comb and a scrap of mirror, and a teethbrush stuck in your buttonhole; spare shirt and dry socks, and blanket rolled behind your saddle. No, a cat, a grown cat like Tom McCutcheon, he would be too much even for a man the size and heft of Elias.

And besides whoever heard of a cat going to war? For it would be war this time, real war when they went north again as they were bound to go, with the entire army this time, ten thousand strong at least. It would be soon now that they would be hunting Yankees. It was our time to attack in force.

Elias was wondering if Willy would be back in time to take part in the move north when it came. He was in his tent, stretched out upon his cot, with the cat asleep at his feet and himself in a half-doze, just wondering about Willy, when the lad walked in with hardly a limp to show for his wound.

"Well, I'm back," says Willy.

"How are things at home? How's the leg?"

"I brought some letters. They're fine, I guess. My leg's well."

"You were just this instant in my thoughts."

"When do we leave here? Any word?"

"None as yet, but it can't be long now."

"So this is the cat!"

BOOK FIVE

The Raider

Chapter 1

Rain — days of water dripping down from a dark sky; dawns that grow out of gloom, clammy bedclothes and musty closets, and the air like damp oil against your skin; days without sunsets and Jane must listen to a deal of groaning and complaining at Oakleigh.

For Rufe, Jake's oldest son, has walked out of the woods not a few weeks back making tracks from Redleaves. Tracks in the snow, coming all that distance down on foot so ordered by Shokotee, and Rufe has complained to Jake and Jake has complained to Jane Nail McCutcheon. It seems that Rufe's wife, Betsy, was taken from him and he was told to walk home to Oakleigh. And more, and more, and more . . .

Gloomy as the rain, Rufe says it was not just Master Edward Ashe, no. Rufe says it was Master Willy McCutcheon himself that brought this thing about. Shokotee sent Betsy into Somerton with her baby, the two of them in a closed spring buggy with foot warmers and a lantern under the laprobe. But they sent him, Rufe, home through the snow afoot. For all they seemed to care Rufe could have frozen to death or been eaten by wolves.

Taking such chances with a servant! For Rufe's a fine big,

black lad, ever so much bigger and stronger than Jake, and it was Leola herself that married the pair and Jane herself that sanctioned the match to help Mrs. Ellen Poe Ashe, that owned Betsy and needed to get her off her own plantation and so sent her to Oakleigh.

And Jane Nail McCutcheon can hardly believe the homecoming soldier could have done such a thing. She says it's out of character that Willy would have helped Edward Ashe, that lost his fingers and nearly lost his arm and was sent straight home; and why would Edward Ashe interfere? Why indeed? And Jane smells something.

Then Jake says Master Edward was the papa of that baby.

Jane says no such thing could be, for Miss Ellen would have told her and wouldn't have sent Betsy to Oakleigh knowing it would cause trouble.

Jake says things may not always be as they seem, and besides, it's the Master himself that allowed Betsy to be sent here and the Master himself had to know what it was, that it was Edward's baby the gal carried. And the Master had always looked kindly on those Poe brothers and their sister, from the first that Jake remembered; the Master had looked on them kindly and always tried to help them any way he could, whereas he didn't seem to care as much for the Callisters or other neighbors close about, no, he more or less seemed not to trouble himself about *them,* but where the Poes were concerned he seemed to put himself out and to send them what they needed from time to time so as to help them get a start there in the woods, and now they were rich and had sent the Master back trouble to repay him for all his goodness and Jake's Rufe was ruined in reputation and wounded in spirit and had been separated from the little wife he loved and the little baby he cherished and Willy McCutcheon was a party to the stealing of two slaves belonging to Miss Ellen Poe Ashe.

Leola tells Jake he's about to get himself some stripes should the Master hear of such backtalk.

Jake says be damned to stripes for his Rufe is wounded in spirit and in reputation and has had his wife and that baby he loved taken from him and has been sent to walk home through the snow and that the skin of his feet peeled off from the cold and the humiliation; and that Rufe will not be the same again, damaged in his feet and in his spirit . . .

It's such a scene and a scandal and so much fussing and fuming that Jane hasn't time even to think of her own affliction and some days even forgets to tie a silk patch on her face to hide that hole in her cheek with its constant leak of spittle.

For Jake allows that if folks intended to run all their servants away they could not contrive it better than to let a blow such as this fall upon the son of the man on whom all depended now for the running of Oakleigh.

And if all of this were not bad enough, Mrs. Ellen Poe Ashe appears, demands an interview with Jane McCutcheon and says her son, Edward, is missing and was last seen in the company of Willy McCutcheon, and the two of them said only they were going off riding in the snow, and what had Jane to say about it and what on earth had happened to Edward? Hadn't Edward gone away and almost got his death in defense of the Sacred Cause?

"Um," says Jane. "Who was the father of that little baby?"

"What little baby?" says Ellen.

"Black Betsy's child," says Jane. "For when it was born here it came out yellow. Who was the father?"

"I wouldn't have any idea," says Ellen. "They all come out yellow and get darker as they grow up, don't think I don't know that much. I only asked your husband to take her because she made trouble between my servants. I didn't expect you'd send her off and let her be stolen."

Silence. "But never mind that, I want to know what Willy McCutcheon has done with my Edward."

"Ho!" says Jane quietly. "Ho!"

"What would you mean by that?" says Ellen.

"Maybe you didn't let Edward have some money?"

"Maybe I did," says Ellen. "Mothers let their sons have money if they are mothers."

"How much had he with him when he left home, I wonder?" says Jane. "For a ride in the snow? Willy had three hundred and more, came home with it and said he didn't need more. Yet before he went back to the army he said he'd had to make a loan to a friend, to Edward Ashe, he told me. 'Edward has gone on a trip,' was what Willy said. 'And I let him have my three hundred dollars.' So I gave Willy more and he went back to the army. How much money did Edward have with him?"

"Well —"

"Enough for a ride in the snow, maybe?"

Ellen seems to crumple a bit. Poor Ellen, whom can she blame after all? She takes a handkerchief out of her sleeve. She says, "He had some thousands with him."

"If you *want* to know," says Jane, "maybe you could write him a letter and ask him where he is? You know where he is and you know what he's done, Ellen Poe Ashe. But you never thought it worth my while to tell me about it, no! Let Jane Scarface stay in the dark, you thought."

"I never thought that!"

"Coming to me, blaming Willy. Ho!"

Silence. Jane takes a certain cruel satisfaction in seeing Ellen, that had a cow before she did, and a bull calf besides and was once the envy of the whole neighborhood not so many years ago, has come to this. And Jane says,

"Who was the father of that little baby, Ellen Poe Ashe?"

"It came out yellow?" Ellen asks in a weak little voice.

"Bright yellow," says Jane. "And we had Betsy jump over the broomstick with Jake's Rufe and got the child a daddy. And we baked cakes and gave them a wedding supper here in my own dining room. And we loaned Betsy a gown and I knitted the baby a hat for his little head and sent them both to my father's house when there was trouble here about them."

"Trouble? What trouble? A little boy," says Ellen, with a distracted look. "Did he have his fingers and toes?"

Ellen Poe Ashe has fallen a long way from that time when people spoke about her cow and envied the Poes because they had butter on their table every meal and had brought some fine things with them from back east. Oh, fine-mannered people, the Poes. That was before other people had things and Jane has lived all this time with her scar and suffered and stayed in a shuttered room with her sorrows while Ellen went about and was the beauty of the neighborhood and had that wild son she was so proud of and gave everything. And Jane says,

"Yes, and it was I that knitted him a little cap. He had his fingers and toes but no one came and asked about him. And I gave him a daddy, Jake's Rufe, that was the finest boy on this place until the blow fell on him. For it seems a certain white man came here one day and said if Betsy were not found and given to him he'd hang Jake. That's Jake McCutcheon, and was the first *servant* in this district if you'll remember. Not the first cow, no. Others may have had a cow and a bull calf and butter on the table before we did —"

"You can't forgive me that, can you?" cries Ellen. "Well, here's something else, I'm not a savage Indian either!"

"Um," says Jane. "Do you know who it was came here and said he would hang Jake?"

Ellen shakes her head. She doesn't want to know. She's had enough but Jane won't let her off and says,

"Master Edward Ashe."

"I don't believe that."

"Master Edward Ashe. Shall I call Jake?"

Edward's mother shakes her pretty head. She's got a scar now, an invisible scar, but a scar that she will want to hide the rest of her life. But people will know about it and they will hear about it and they will see it just as plainly as if it were real and on her cheek and running spittle day and night.

Ellen's shoulders begin to shake. And Jane says,

"Don't blame my Willy. The wonder is he didn't horsewhip Edward Ashe. Instead he took pity on him. Maybe Willy saw it more clearly than some of that baby's own kin could see it. And maybe that's why he helped. And where is Edward, by the way?"

"In Canada."

"Um. Jake's Rufe has lost his wife and got his feet frozen and the skin slipped off like they'd been boiled and Master Edward's gone to Canada. My Rufe's feet are worth something. So is my Rufe's spirit and his reputation!"

Ellen tosses her head. "Indians never forgive, do they! Savages never forget! My son was all I had. Oh, Edward! Edward!"

"Nevermind. Who's to know if it's kept quiet-like? My *Willy* hasn't even told me. I had to drag it out of Jake."

"Yes, and his Rufe, you can sell him down to Louisiana," says Ellen. "Get rid of him."

Jane shakes her head. "Rufe needs a wife. Otherwise his spirit can't return, nor his reputation. You'll send him a wife, won't you? One as fine as Betsy, but not so fat, maybe? Then Jake's Rufe wouldn't feel so bad. A new wife will make his feet well. That is if you want it all kept quiet-like, Ellen Ashe!"

Ellen's agreeable. What can she say but yes? She's a fallen, beaten woman and says,

"Yes. I'll send him another wife."

"And deed her over to *me*," says Jane. "Make her over to *me* so the two *won't* be separated."

Ellen looks daggers at Jane. But then she crumples again and sighs and says,

"I would do that anyway. In your name, yes."

"And be quick about it," says Jane. "For the quicker a crime is covered up the sooner it's forgotten." Jane can't resist saying everything she can and Ellen goes away with her head bent and her handkerchief in her hand and looking like she's got a mouth full of buckwheat.

As soon as the road dried a little and the weather warmed a mite, Jane had to go pay Fancy Callister a visit, and that was strange, for Jane McCutcheon never went visiting, but waited for Fancy Callister to come to see her so that Fancy could elaborate on whatever bright ray of news she had from the battlefronts.

Fancy's news was always to the effect that the North was suffering such terrible losses that folk in the North were staging riots and burning whole cities rather than see their men sent off to fight a war they could not believe was right.

And Fancy said secret delegations from the South were making treaties with England. Europe, she promised, would enter the war on the side of the Confederacy. She said Federal armies had no more fight in them they had been so soundly whipped. They didn't dare stand and fight anymore, but ran from the soldiers of the South.

And Fancy Callister said all of this in spite of those Yankee troops in Somerton. She said this in spite of the fact that the war dragged on week after week. More and more men and boys went away to it and more and more were coming back from it sick and mangled, without arms, without legs, blind . . .

Certain others didn't come back at all . . . and Jane could

not bear to think about those others. And during the coldest days of winter Jane had wondered if Elias and the boys were cold. Now while it rained she saw them wet to the bone and shivering. During the hot summer she had wondered if they ever got a cool drink of water.

And secretly from time to time she asked herself if all of this could be some kind of punishment decreed upon the South by God. She halfway feared it was and told Fancy as much when she went to visit her. Maybe she told Fancy some other things, some juicy things about a certain woman who had thought she was better than other folks for years and years and had had the first cow and a bull calf when others hadn't gotten butter on their tables as yet — maybe she had to tell Fancy that, for Jane was only human after all. And Fancy promised *she* wouldn't tell anyone — cross her heart and die if she could bring herself to breathe such a secret. Fancy was a woman to be trusted with a secret and what did she care besides, if Edward Ashe had run off with his mother's black Betsy and a little yellow baby to Canada? Fancy said she always knew that Edward would come to harm with his wild ways and his gambling.

As for Jane's fears about God, Fancy said Jane should go with her to that church Isaac had attended every Sunday because the preacher, Brother Holmes, was certain God was on the side of the Confederacy and had all the reasons why and could prove them by the Scriptures.

Thus after Jane's visit to Fancy, Jake had to get up at daylight on Sundays, rain or shine, and put the horses in and drive Miss Jane down to pick up Miss Fancy so the two of them could go all that distance into Somerton to church. Jane bought Jake some white gloves to wear and a stovepipe hat, and thus made an appearance Isaac would have been proud to see.

But Jane never quite understood what it was Brother

Holmes said, no. For she no sooner had sat in the pew with Fancy Callister than the singing began and then the special announcements about the death of this husband and father and the wounding of that cherished son and the departure of the following beloved members of this fellowship and congregation to the defense of the Sacred Cause.

It made Jane's ears buzz and upset her so that by the time the sermon came around and Brother Holmes began giving his proof from the Scriptures she couldn't think of anything but that terrible roll call of names. Her mind froze when it came to her that next Sunday Elias McCutcheon, or Willy, or Isaac could be on that list . . .

And certain days an inner voice seemed to tell Jane that if she did not eat meat that day, her men would be safe. Another day the voice might say "bread," or on another day "milk." And on every such day she would not touch that thing the voice had forbidden.

At night, sometimes, she would wake and see the little mantel clock. It was illuminated by a tiny self-filling lamp so that she could see what time it was at any hour. And every time she woke thus and saw the time she got up and sat herself in a chair and kept herself awake the rest of the night, for she knew if she went back to sleep something would happen. The enemy would creep up and surprise Elias, or Willy, or Isaac . . . She sat up those nights when she woke, and kept watch, and she knew Leola did the same . . .

And who should come traveling in a fine closed spring buggy drawn by a matched pair of jetty black horses driven by a wizened but dignified little servant wearing white gloves and a tall hat? None other than Gabe French, and he's as close to Jane as an uncle.

When she spies that buggy approaching from alongside the river which she's been watching from her window high above, when she sees who it is (guessing who it must be, knowing in her heart who it is before she sees him even), she runs down to meet him.

Gabe, he's never been better and he's glad to see her so much improved, but first off before anything else, he says, he must have a few words with her in privacy, and together they go into the library.

He closes the door. He wears a dove-gray swallowtail coat, a mauve and yellow silk vest with a heavy gold watch chain showing, and dark pistol-leg trousers pulled smartly down over his shiny black boots and held with an elastic strap under the heels. Laying aside his gold-headed cane he puts a small morocco leather travel case on the table and takes from it a fancy rosewood workbox. This he opens with a show of care and deliberate preoccupation, as is proper with weighty matters and serious business. Slipping on English steel-framed spectacles he takes out a little notebook and opens it.

"First, I owe Elias for some trifles. Hm. Nineteen hundred in cash and assorted items . . . clothing, boots, gloves, that whalebone riding crop, horse and saddle." He makes a swift calculation with his pencil.

Putting aside the notebook he takes out a purse, opens it, and counts out three thousand in gold, easily as one-two-three. Taking up his pencil again he writes something, looks at Jane, studies his notes again, and says,

"Yes, that covers it, I believe. Yes."

The mystery of him! One minute threadbare; rich the next, and never any end to him. He asks about the men.

Jane knocks wood on the tabletop with her knuckles. "Only Willy has been home wounded and he's gone back again." She knocks wood again.

Gabe nods. "Wounded but well again." Clearing his throat, he removes his spectacles. The years have treated him kindly where looks go. His square, sturdy frame, his comfortable belly, the freckled hand with which he fondles his watch chain, and the serene look in his eyes. "You converted everything you could to gold, did you?"

"Yes, I took your suggestion."

"And hid it here on the place?"

"Yes," says Jane.

"Don't mention it to anyone. Now at least if the war goes against the South, as I fear it inevitably will, you've been sure to salvage something."

"But," says Jane. "If our boys in the field go hungry and we've saved something back . . . if they were to lose because we failed them, then what?"

"The boys are giving enough. Elias has given enough. Mustn't we look to the day when this war, win or lose, will be over? What then?"

"I think sometimes it will never be over for me," says Jane.

"Now, now . . ." says Gabe French, in his comforting voice.

"At least I took your advice about the gold. I acted before the banks were captured. You've always known what was best."

Jane went to the window and sat down on the arm of a chair and folded her hands in her lap. Beyond the window was the lawn, the curving drive with its border of shrubbery, and further down lay the riverside and the trees beyond on the far bank where the shadow of winter had withdrawn and spring was just touching.

"It's precaution, preparation only," says Gabe, behind her. "We must look to eventualities. Elias will understand."

Jane looked through the window trying to think how it was here long ago. Something was wrong with the view. Then she realized that it was the big hollow sycamore that was missing — the sycamore and the wagon shed built on, the place where Elias had lived alone with his dog when he came here. And behind her Gabe clears his throat and says,

"Coming this way I thought of the forest that stood here all about, back when the river ran clear at all seasons. I hadn't a gray hair in my head and everything always seemed to be just beginning. We dreamed then of the day when this land would lie under cultivation and be squared by fences and the roads would be wide enough for wagons — when a traveler wouldn't have to find his way by blazed trees. When I thought of the future I saw an empire of agriculture and commerce walking hand in hand into the bright promise of the future." He paused. "The big sycamore — what happened?"

"Lightning tore it to pieces," says Jane in her slurring voice. "Jake and the hands broke it up and hauled it away. They blasted the stump and made the ground smooth again."

"Seems a pity. I slept there once. Once long ago . . ." A pause. And then: "I hadn't a gray hair in my head."

Far down on the road Jane saw horses and blue uniforms. They came on into the drive at a walk. Nine horses — she counted them. Federal uniforms — she turned to Gabe.

"Hadn't looked for this. Not so soon," says Gabe. "Figured it would take a few days, maybe."

"Leola!" Jane calls. "Leola!"

The old woman came at once, Jane handed her the gold pieces. *Chink* — deep in the folds of Leola's gown — *chink!* And she hurried into the hall again and disappeared.

Meanwhile outside, the soldiers dismount, an officer comes up the walk. Loud knocking at the front door and Rance answering the door and talking in the hallway, and coming then into the library.

"The lieutenant — he wants Mister Gabe?" says Rance.

"Show him in," says Gabe. "How the *deuce* they've come so soon," he muttered to himself.

The young man walked in, slender, resplendently military. Rance stood in the hall.

"I'm Lieutenant Kerrigan, West Tennessee Command. You must be Mrs. McCutcheon?"

"Yes," says Jane.

"Are you Gabriel French, sir?"

"I am, sir."

"I have an order for your arrest."

"I'll just have my things brought around if you don't mind?"

"Not at all, sir. Madam?" And the young man bowed and then turned on his heel and walked out, lean and tall and proper. Jane could hear him outside giving orders to his men.

Gabe clears his throat. Jane looks around at him.

"Apparently this is goodbye," he says.

Jane felt frozen. "What have you done?"

"Dealing, speculating. What have I always done?"

"But you haven't dealt with *them*?"

"Afraid I have." He cleared his throat. "They were all there was."

"What will they do with you?"

"Jail me on some charge or other. I have friends though."

"Friends — you mean among *them*?"

"Yes, influential friends. Nevermind worrying about me. No, it was a risk. They have all that confiscated cotton and . . ."

"I see," Jane said.

"Well, you don't see, but what is there to explain? I didn't make the war. Nobody made it, really. How the deuce they got here so soon? Well, there's always jealousy and always someone who thinks he didn't get his fair cut when time comes to divide profits. They complain to higher headquarters. What can they do but make a show of arresting me?"

Rance came in. "They ready for you, Mister Gabe."

"Yes, yes." Gabe took a gold piece from his pocket. He handed it to Rance. "Forgot to give this to you last time I was here, Rance. Token of my appreciation for your many kindnesses, eh?"

"Yes, sah. Thank you, sah."

Gabe turned to Jane. "Goodbye," he said. He was very pale but very erect and he went out slowly and she saw him then beyond the window, climbing into the buggy, and the buggy beginning to move down the drive flanked by the Yankee patrol, more like an escort for some noble person than soldiers with a prisoner. It had gone so swiftly, so politely, so calmly, Gabe's arrest. Rance came back to the library window and stood watching.

"Lord, Lord," he whispered. She heard his breathing and knew he had been frightened.

Leola came in. "So — Gabe French was trading with them, was he?"

"Yes."

"I heard it a month ago and more. Gabe French is doing business with them. Supping with the devil. But maybe his spoon wasn't long enough."

"They're gone at least," says Jane. She was trembling.

"But they'll be back, and nevermind," says Leola.

Chapter 2

When springtide warmed the land again, Elias, the raider, found called to mind a warm day (long ago it was now) when his seed sprang against the woman's thigh and dropped into the dark, fecund earth, and he heard again as it were, in dreams of half-sleeping, the falling sound of their hoes afterward chopping and chopping in the wide stumpfield.

In the midst of these, his dreaming ruminations, came the word so long awaited. The Southern army that had lain camped by Corinth, Mississippi, was ordered to take the march north again. The gray army moved, towards Tennessee . . .

And you are floating now, part of an endless, undulating ribbon composed of men upon horses and men upon foot, and of freight wagons, guns, caissons, ammunition trains, ambulances — of all manner of horse- and mule-drawn conveyances, trundling the narrow roads, wending north.

And above, north of your moving gray column, camped by thousands upon the banks of the Tennessee River at Pittsburg Landing, a blue army waits. In reaches of inner vision while on the march you see the neat tents and the clean company streets of that blue and distant enemy. You sense those distant lives — bodies, bellies, spleens, livers, brains — you know the small concerns of every day which surround and encompass them, each man a breathing, living speck; and taken together they compose a mass of men held there upon that riverbank by the timeless admixtures of fear and patriotic inspiration and pride, by resignation, and by hoped-for grace and by the wished-for means to glory.

Thus it is the same for blue as for gray. The most and highest that can be wished is that you may avoid disgrace and miss your death, all the while realizing that, ofttimes as it falls out, a man must embrace the one to avoid the other. He must walk upon the narrow choice, live with it, sup with it, drink with it, ponder it and pray to Almighty God about it, and debate inside himself upon that greatest of all battlefields, the human heart, no less. No less . . .

At the head of his regiment, Elias, a man: and in his heart the woeful work of war, and his eyes watch woods not entirely leafed as yet. His outer vision takes in the rolling warming land, the seedtime fields waiting to be broken.

Fruit orchards lie beside the way and a south wind comes, breathing upon the new grass. A sun, no longer wintry and thin of light, shines with new and welcome warmth. Bees bumble in the white and pink of the blooming orchards. They cast down a soft ring of petals about the foot of each orchard tree.

Night. The gray army settled for a brief spell of uneasy rest. Dawn pales. Before the birds are full awake the gray army is moving again, marching through a ground fog in air so still, so still . . . At such times we move like a scentless ghost of armies, shoulders and muskets upon shoulders and slouch hats, and all floating forward steady as thought, floating upon a shoreless sea of fog. A mist, as it were to hide us, to keep our advent from the eyes of the blue enemy. We move, gray upon gray . . .

And moving thus Willy McCutcheon has his morning thoughts. The sun burns the mist away.

See us on the roads in wending columns, Mother? Twenty thousand of us on the march all at once. Marching — that's just appearance, marching; no, Mother, we're waiting.

After camp fever and smallpox and unmentionable things, after so much sickness and dying and so many graves beside Corinth, battle holds no more terrors. We welcome a fight now, Mother. No, it's waiting we dread most of all. It's waiting, thinks Willy, inside himself speaking to Jane, his mother . . .

And Tug Chambers thinks as how when this war is over he'll be back about Somerton again and will ask Ellen Ashe again for her hand in marriage, and then he'd be a planter, so he would. Meanwhile there was but a bit of killing between. He has a sharp saber, pistols loaded and capped in good order, and a willing horse between his legs.

Get on with it, have it over with, Tug thinks. Dew and spider webs, and the quiet woods dripping on either side . . .

Camp is pitched that night above the sloping banks of a creek. "Tomorrow," a voice seems to say. "Tomorrow . . ."

Awakened at midnight Elias goes to the outpost. Seems the enemy is moving his infantry about on the opposite bank of the creek.

The sound comes closer. "A horse," says Elias. "It's a wandering horse, that's all." Tug Chambers wades the creek and comes back with a horse sure enough.

"One of their artillery nags," Tug says in a cheerful voice, climbing the bank.

Going back again to his tent Elias puts off his saber and stretches out again, almost drifting back into sleep, but Isaac comes. Isaac is chewing tobacco. The sweetness can be smelled in the darkness. Father and son go outside and sit down. Isaac spits and spits again and after a silence wants to know if Elias finished reading the artillery manual.

"Yes." Elias rode down Jasper Coon and beat him with the flat of his saber during an artillery exercise not a week past in Mississippi. Beat him thoroughly and Jasper was only performing a movement with the ammunition wagons while Isaac watched.

"Well?" says Isaac. "Well, sir?"

"By your *book* the movement was correct, but when fighting you can't run away with the ammunition," says Elias. "And guns need to be rolled forward as close as possible."

Isaac heaves a sigh. "If you read the manual then you know the guns are placed well back so as not to be captured."

"Yes, but the manual is wrong. Guns need to be drawn up to the line where they can do the greatest damage — to point-blank range."

"Then he captures your guns," says Isaac. "Don't you *believe* the manual of tactics?"

"Guns are made to be captured," says Elias.

Their talks always go the same way lately. Isaac quotes the book. Elias has his own notions, some that agree with the book, some that don't.

But it's friendly talk, all the same.

Jasper Coon left off trying to sleep and went to look about the horses, for he knew it was they, the beasts, that must draw the guns into battle and it was they that must bring them off again. The beast-critters. He passed up the line, speaking to the animals one after another, rubbing a hand of reassurance over each.

Aye, God, he thought. He saw the thousands of men and

horses in opposition, he sensed the restlessness in the Confederate camps. He saw someone, a shadow.

"Who's there?"

"Isaac. Is it you, Jasper?"

"Seeing to the horses. Aye, God."

"Is anybody sleeping, I wonder?"

"Pretending to sleep, maybe. How is the old man?"

"He was awake."

Jasper sighed. "Do me a favor, Isaac?"

"What's that?"

"Pin m'name and address on m'back tomorrow. Don't forget."

"All right. But why?"

"Case I get it, hurt real bad, or . . ." He stopped. "As many as will be out there a body could get easy lost this time, lost and put underground without they'd never know who or what he was. I want the old woman and the kids to know it was me. Otherwise they might think I'd just walked off and left 'em for good and never gave a shit about 'em."

"I see. Very well," says Isaac.

"It's going to be a hell of a big God damn fight, Isaac. The biggest God damn thing any of us ever seen yet. Thousands upon thousands of 'em there on the other side. And they got better guns. And they got gunboats on the river to shell us. We don't have nothin' to compare with what they've got, Isaac. The North is too big and they're too many for us. They got foreigners coming from over the sea by the thousands to join up against us. We're fightin' the whole God damn world, Isaac. I never wanted none of it."

"Nor I," says Isaac. "Nor I."

"But I hate 'em. Seen too many of our own dead not to hate 'em. And they're down here on our land, our soil, where they got no business being. Funny — we never wanted it, yet we hate 'em now so bad we fight 'em with everything. Are we too proud or too dumb, I wonder? Or what?"

"I don't hate them. They're under orders same as you and me, Jasper. Hate them —? No."

"Then how can *you* fight?"

"Because I have to fight. It's my duty — our duty."

"I'm a Free-Soiler and should be over there on that other side, Isaac. So should you, only we can't none of us fight against our own kind nor invade our own soil, can we?"

"No," says Isaac.

"Want an apple?"

"Where'd you get an apple?"

"There was a cellar. Behind a house we passed. You never noticed? This is fruit country. I slipped back after dark and filled my haversack. The people must of left home to get away from the fight. Didn't see a soul about nor any livestock. Found a can of cream in the well."

"Wonder you didn't get shot crossing the picket lines."

"Pretty good apples."

"Wonder you didn't get shot," says Isaac, admiration in his voice. They walked back, passing the caissons and the guns. Jasper ducked into the tent and fetched four apples from the haversack. The friends sat on the ground. The apples were grainy and had soft spots, but they were sweet.

"Fruit country," says Jasper, chewing. "Had more time I'd find some peach brandy. Had more time, I would. Aye, God." He was full but he was hungry. If he could have found a pig, he thought, or a chicken, just a scrawny chicken — wouldn't matter how tough, he'd have a little fire by now, hidden so no one could see it, and he'd be making broth, sitting with Isaac and enjoying the smell of the broth, waiting for it to be ready so they could sip it down.

"Maybe we'll get into their supply wagons and take their officers' tents," says Jasper.

"Always thinking of plunder?" says Isaac.

"Well, I say shit, what more can the common soldier expect to have out of it unless it's plunder? What's wrong with plunder?"

"Nothing," says Isaac. "Apples are good."

"Yeah," says Jasper. "I'll get some more."

Tug Chambers had put on dry breeches. He sat with his back against a tree. His messmates were long since rolled up asleep in their blankets.

Earlier Tug had gone among the men, speaking to this one, slapping that one on the shoulder, always ready with a joke and a cheerful word, ready to share his tobacco. Earlier he had felt brave, or had he?

Ever since his patrol in Kentucky when others had run away, Tug was well thought of because he had remained behind to fight and had helped get his men through the Yankee skirmishers blocking the road. He had handled himself well in that little fight. It had happened so suddenly there wasn't time to think. But he had had time now to see what had not been so apparent in that first skirmish, and what he had seen in himself since nightfall had made him fearful. Thus all the earlier joking and backslapping and tobacco sharing was nothing but pretense. Now that he was alone his mouth was dry.

There was talk in the army of releasing overseers from their enlistments to send them back to see to the management of the plantations they had come from, to make grain crops and keep the slaves from starting a rebellion behind the lines. He thought of going back to Somerton, of finding Ellen again and sitting at the table with her when they took meals. Would she be grateful to him if he got out of the army and went back to see after the place and protect her, or would she think him a coward and spurn him?

Tug wiped his hands on the ground, trying to wipe away fear, trying to rub some sense into himself through his palms; hands in contact with the soil, the earth from which good things grew. He never bargained for this clank and rumble and tramping. He'd prefer to be on his plantation horse again with his whip and his knife and his pistol, seeing to the drivers who in turn would be seeing to the slaves, to their health and their work and their discipline. *Dangerous* was the word for overseeing a plantation large as the Poes' with so many Negroes. Overseer never knew when a nigger might be waiting his chance, lying awake nights and plotting in his mind how he'd do it — one slash with a cane knife. Overseers got murdered in bed sometimes. Slaves poisoned them, ambushed them, ganged up on them and tortured them to death. A man could never be sure if he chose that life. Yet bad as it was it was nothing to compare with this — no. He'd go back now if he could, Tug decided, and again he saw Ellen — her bosom, the shape of her arms. He had thought earlier today that if he became a hero in the war she'd marry him when he came home again afterwards. He'd ask her and she'd accept him and he'd be a planter and his neighbors would call him "Colonel." His children would grow up and be planters themselves and the Chambers line would be famous throughout the Southland — aristocrats. So it all had seemed, in daylight . . .

He closed his eyes. Have I by God struggled my whole life long just to be killed here on this field?

He moved his lips, shaping the words: "God Almighty, don't let me die tomorrow. In the name of Jesus Christ, thy son, don't let me die tomorrow. All I ever wanted was to work hard, to get a little land of my own and a few slaves and I was almost there when this all happened. So in the name of thy son, Jesus Christ, I pray, let me live. Amen. And please make the South win. Amen. We never any of us did anything to deserve to lose. Amen. The children of Israel had slaves and treated their slaves one terrible lot worse than we treat our hands, as thou dost well know. Amen."

Opening his eyes he saw a paleness through the trees. Surely it wasn't yet daylight? But it is, he thought, and he felt a heaviness in his chest, a weight that seemed as though it would pull him and bend him forward and crook his back. Day paleness, right enough; he could almost see the shapes of things. Wearily he got to his feet and walked to his tent. Pushing the flap aside he stepped into the warm darkness.

Dutt woke. He had chosen to take his blanket outside, to sleep on the ground, and he had dreamed he was in the west, asleep beside his campfire while buffalo grazed nearby. In his dream he was not married, yet he knew he was in fact married, but the dream modified it somehow, someway, as dreams will, to make his mind easy about the fact of his having crossed the river into the west to live his life in freedom as he pleased, to follow the buffalo.

It took him a moment to know where he was, so real was the dream. He sat up and saw that it was nearly day. His mind was at ease. They'd move in a little and once they began to move any nervousness that had built up in the men would melt.

After so much waiting and so much riding and moving about the country actual engagement came as a relief. It broke up the boredom of army life and made a man feel younger. It let him see everything all new again, as happens sometimes after a rain when the air has been cleared of dust and the sun has not quite come out again. Something about that light and that clearness makes the whole world appear as though newly created.

Not bothering to fold his blanket he walked to the latrine ditch, dropped his pants, and sat down on the cool, morning-moist slats. He took a leisurely crap. Riding a horse so much had a way of packing a man's shit inside him. It was best to wake up early and take time and empty your bowels, this day especially. Others passed to and fro between the ditch and the tents of the regiment, some smoking pipes, some chewing tobacco, nothing boisterous, but all quiet and polite and soft-spoken. There was an almost Sunday reverence. Men readied for battle quietly. In the line nearby the horses were being fed and watered and taken out to be saddled. The troopers inspected their horses, careful to look about everything, rubbing and petting the beasts, talking to them.

Every fourth man in the regiment had the designation of horse holder, such that when the order was given to dismount and advance into a fight on foot, the horse holders could be counted on to take the animals back a distance and to keep them safe, to hold and comfort them; nobody begrudged the holders. It took more courage sometimes to stand still in the rear than it did to go forward with the main body. A man wanted to be sure his horse was safe and ready to carry him if needed. It was the way of Elias McCutcheon to protect the horses and to conserve them as much as possible, and Dutt saw there was wisdom in that.

It came to him how once on a time he had begrudged the holders, long ago now it seemed, when they raided the Horse Pens; yet not so long ago as that, still and all. Time. Time . . .

He took a bit of paper from his shirt pocket and wiped himself and stood and drew up his pants and buttoned them. He was hard and as fit as ever he had been in his life; more fit, perhaps. He hadn't a spare ounce of fat on him. His service with the regiment had trimmed that extra flesh away such that his uniforms had had to be taken up again and again. He was muscle and bone now, and his face and his hands were weathered to the shade of brown earth. He could sit a horse all day and all night if need be. He could even sleep in the saddle while riding, napping and never losing his balance. He was nothing like the Dutt Callister who rode away from a fight in Kentucky, nothing like the green asshole he was then, dashing off and dropping his gear. Elias had given him hell and demoted him for that episode.

Never again would Tug Chambers show Dutt up and shame him! What made men like Chambers so brave from the first? Maybe, Dutt decided, maybe they're born with it.

Heading back to his tent he saw Tug's big red face, his wide neck, his huge arms. The sergeant wasn't scared, no, not in the least. Tug smiled and saluted, calm as salt, a man's man, a soldier's soldier, Tug Chambers.

Private Willy McCutcheon tied his horse and went slowly forward until he saw what he had been looking for; the Yankee picket stood with his back to a beech tree, not twenty paces off, facing Willy's direction.

Drawing himself erect, Willy began whistling. He walked boldly in the Yankee soldier's direction as though not seeing him.

"Hey!"

Willy stopped. "Hey yourself."

"What the hell you doing?"

"Just walking, that's all. Seen anything?"

"Naw," said the other. "Better be keerful how you walk around. Feller could get shot that way. You miss roll call you'll git on th' report."

"Uh-huh."

Walking on, leaving the man, Willy felt a queer tingling in the middle of his back. Whistling as before he presently came to the company streets, neat rows of tents. They'd been here a while. If this army expected trouble they showed no sign. From the tents came sounds of snoring.

Unhooking his cup from his belt Willy approached a still-smoldering fire. He tested the coffeepot handle for heat before tipping his cup full without removing the pot from the tripod. The coffee was warm. He drank greedily, tipped himself another cup, swigged it down and dumped the dregs into the ashes. Hooking his cup back on his belt he strolled down for a look at their horses. Everything seemed brand-new — from tents to halters to horses. It made him envious.

Heading back the way he had come he entered the woods and steered for the beech tree. The same Yank was there. Willy went towards him as before.

"You again? Don't you sleep? Hoped you was my relief. Got the time?"

"Naw," says Willy.

"Hell," said the other.

Willy walked on, whistling until he was out of sight of the beech tree. Finding his horse he rode back to his own lines and went to his father's tent.

He was in awe of the old man lately. For Elias, with his iron beard, had about him a quiet and deadly purposefulness, as when he sat now, still as stone, to hear what Willy told, touching his beard at the chin and nodding and staring at his two hands, curled at rest on his thighs.

"Anything else?" said his father.

"No, sir. What will we do?"

"Orders are to guard this creek."

Going to his tent Willy felt the restlessness of the army.

Just after daybreak it begins — a chattering of rifle fire far down on the left wing of the Confederate line.

Elias, at the head of his regiment, standing on the creek bank with his horse's bridle in one hand and the other hand resting on the butt of a Navy six revolver holstered at his side, waits, ready to advance awaiting the moment, the order.

Small-arms fire tears at the fabric of the sky. It increases to a roar, it swells to an iron growl. Like some surly beast, some creature surely larger than the very firmament, has been discovered, galled, inflamed, and raging blinded and berserk, mighty and ravening. Such is the din and the echo. The creature heaves about creating storms and lulls, but the roar and the iron growl grows steadily. The footfalls of its thousand hooves are brass. They crash in volleys more terrible than thunder; a hard sound is there, a steel crash and satan roar of flames and sulphur. The mother earth herself is jarred, violated, wounded in her bowels . . .

Aye, the man thinks. It's but destiny there in the woods, striving to seek us out; but a destiny not like any other, no mere common destiny, but a beast-thing more terrible, deeper than mere thought.

Battle, engagement, skirmish-line, development, bombardment — words only and no more meaningful than *sacred soil, honor, valor, independence.* Now the words are blown aside and the woods and the clouds and the wind are witnesses.

A man, waiting for orders — words again; they don't come! Suddenly his existence is no longer ordered by words, no, he is ordered rather by blind notions and by forces that make his eyes dark, that flare his nostrils and bare his gritted teeth and set hairs at the back of his neck on edge, raising his hackles. "Forward!"

The regiment passes over the creek.

Dutt Callister, looking stiff somehow, as though moss were stuffed behind his eyes, opens his mouth: "Wonder should we wait a bit?"

The raider only glares at him and spurs his horse to a gallop. He lets earth flow under the steed's belly. The woods unfold on either side. He goes guided by the thickest of those heavy sounds, does Elias.

A moment later, rewarded, he sees everything — the lines of the enemy, the blue lines wavering, men in blue swarms and myriads falling back in the direction of the river — aye, driven. No need of help here and Elias reins down to the right, hunting now, seeking, then finding the scent, and suddenly uttering a cry. Just yonder see a line of Confederate skirmishers meeting total resistance. The smoke is heavy, the death cloud is dense and unmoving, a stubborn rakish stand of smoke. He rides straight for that place, into the smoke and through the remnants of a gray division of infantry turned back, shattered as though by steel tongs.

The raider takes his regiment in, breasting upon a human tide, leaping through eddies of broken units and breathless men, hard upon the line, hard into the fragile dividing place, passing like wind over the middle distance and driving into the wedged jaw of the resistance, shooting and sabering.

The man saw wonderful things. He saw a fertile field and beyond that a blackjack thicket flanked on the other by the pink and tremulous miracle of a peach orchard full in the brave brilliance of bloom. Beauty it was, sheer beauty in standing defiance of so much death. A slashing, daring, majestic thing, that massy slash of damsel pink and perfume. To the edge of the orchard, the Union batteries draw up and calmly unlimber, training their guns on the regiment, guns in a line like squatting bulldogs drawn up to bark.

As that enemy work is progressing Elias sees, at one and the same time, a brigadier general down on the right. Spurring that way and reining in beside the gray lord of battle, Elias yells:

"Can't stay where I am! Must move up or back!"

"How so, sir?" says the gray general.

A salvo from the Union batteries. Down go men and horses

of the regiment, knocked down and thrown backwards in a tangle of dismounted troopers and prostrate horses. "Order me to charge!" cries the raider.

"Impossible, sir. To give such an order."

"What?"

"If you order a charge it must be on your own responsibility, sir!" says the gray lord of battle.

Reining, turning back, drawing his saber, Elias dashes to his regiment. Seeing that saber the bugler sounds the charge. The regiment bunches, coils to a gallop and rams full speed into the tilt and the twilight smoke.

Union gunners materialize in the gloom, standing to their pieces. The raider leans into their blue midst and begins killing. Leaning and swinging with the might of muscles formed in labors of wilderness, with ax muscles and maul muscles, he bends to the work, swinging and hacking again and again. One at a time, and he cuts men down. To the right and left of him Union batteries limber as magically as they appeared. They dash for safety. Blue gunners not shot or sabered run scattering like rabbits for the blackjack thicket, a copse so dense that horses can't follow. A mass of gray infantry meanwhile forms behind. It licks forward and envelops the captured Yankee guns.

Foam flecks the withers of the raider's horse. In the orchard blossoms are falling. A courier slumps, shot through the breast; he leans, clinging a moment more to nothingness before he slides from saddle to earth, holding to thin air but a moment longer before he lets go, a youth with April bloom in his cheeks, a bright being in his springtide of life. A dismounted trooper takes the boy's place on that glistening saddle, none other than Tug Chambers it is, springing up from nowhere to take that good horse.

Moving the regiment up the line again the raider rides slicing into a Union division. The blue ranks give way. The raiders pass through and cut back upon the flanks of the unit, pinching off escape, isolating the desperate fighters, and driving the subdued soldiers straight into the stubborn, clubbed muskets of the Confederate infantry.

A surrender, the first he's seen today. Muskets drop to the ground; arms raised, the prisoners begin trudging back through the gray lines — a captured column marching to the rear.

"*Dis-mount* — advance on foot!" cries the raider. Horse holders spring down to take the reins of the rearing beasts. The raider leads his regiment forward on foot.

Isaac's guns, unlimbered at last, begin shelling the woods. Entering that shade and gloom the regiment dislodges a ghostlike enemy and drives him. The blue lines fall back, the gray troopers drive forward.

At five o'clock a courier finds the raider, bringing orders to fall back with the brigade and prepare to camp on the battlefield.

Elias frowns. Quit *now*?

He sends to know if this order is not in error. A mistake, surely, just when all is going well. "Another shove and we'll drive him into the river!" Elias says. "Surely they see that all we have to do is push him in and drown him!" Anyone could see as much, couldn't they?

Here comes the courier back again. Order repeated. "Fall back with the brigade and camp upon the field." A written command . . .

"Um. Well."

"Commanding general lost his life, sir."

"Our general?"

"Yes — our general, sir."

A deep cough, as though from the mouth of a furnace, followed by an explosion in the woods; another cough, another explosion. The Federal gunboats are firing from the river, blind shelling; it explodes harmlessly in the woods.

Elias reluctantly gives the order to cease pursuit, to fall back and camp. The day ends in a quiet falling of rain through which litter bearers slip and stumble, and the wounded, revived by the wet, begin their scattered cries from woods and the fields, ditches and ravines.

In the cover of rain and night Elias rides close to the Union lines, so close that he can see the beaten troops massed along the bank of the river. Lights appear moving into the landing. Gangplanks rattle down and fresh troops march ashore and muster while the wounded are taken aboard. One after another the Federal transports back out into the stream to make way for others. He had seen enough. Elias rides to Confederate field headquarters. "Unless we attack immediately . . ."

But what does he, Elias, know of West Point — of tactics — nothing! Of fighting — only what he learned in the backwoods.

Still he ventures his opinion — strike now, he says. And says again. Otherwise the gray army will take a hell of a whipping in the morning.

Not so say the staff officers. Not so says the gray general. "We'll be ready for them in the morning," says the general, speaking kindly.

Returning to his regiment Elias passes more wounded men. The Yankee gunboats continue to cough shells into the woods. The rain falls drumming on the Confederate tents. Lamps show inside the surgical tents where, amid scents of carbolic and with sleeves rolled up, the surgeons work, arms bloody, tables slick with blood. Their saws bite live bone. Brisk and businesslike, the doctors pause now and then for a swallow of whiskey. The wounded cry for water. The litter bearers pass and repass. "Mother!" groans a young voice. "Mother!"

Back in his tent at last, Elias lies down. He cannot sleep.

At dawn "Boots and Saddles" broke the morning air like a silver cascade. The bugle stirred Isaac's men to action. His cannoneers and drivers went to work, seeing to the transfer of limber chests. The six cannon with their six caissons, put in motion by seventy-two horses, moved forward at a trot. Months of battery drill had schooled man and horse to that unity and precision required to move the guns (each of which weighed nine hundred pounds) over the roughest terrain.

Dismounted cannoneers strung along behind, following on the run; the men mounted on the limber chests, clung to the handles as the carriages plunged and pitched over the rocks, grazing stumps and shaking the ammunition in the chests. Their faces showed their strain and their confidence in those rattling, hard-riding vehicles. Nothing else in the regiment could compare with Isaac's batteries for bristle and dash.

Forgotten now the awkwardness of the standing-gun drill and the petty rivalry between drivers and cannoneers. Here was action and Isaac's men were ready to estimate distance, cut fuses and become a part of the war machine.

"Fire to the rear! *Caissons*! Pass your pieces! Trot-march! In battery —!"

The columns break and wheel and with a sudden clanking the guns are unlimbered in line, the cannoneers spring to their posts, and the caissons align to their positions at a proper distance rearward. Now in battery — the guns belch and boom.

Two companies of blue cavalry appear, form a distant line, and sweep forward, sabers flashing. They close the intervening distance at a gallop.

At Isaac's urging, the guns are reloaded; the cannoneers stand rigid, and when the blue riders are but a few rods away the lanyards are yanked. The burst envelops cannoneers and the charging enemy in boiling smoke.

As the mist thins; the blue cavalry is discovered in bloody

recoil, like a bird dragging a broken wing. The rattle-roar of musketry intervenes, subsides, bursts out again, like a creature of iron. Fountains of fire and dirt vomit skyward. A solid shot has dismounted number 3 battery, three men are wounded, the piece-wheel is disabled. Quickly the gun crew sets to work, mounting thc spare wheel.

But with dismay Isaac sees that the Confederate line has begun to give way . . . A vast, cheering surge of blue is pushing slowly over the field.

"Limber up!" Isaac shouted. The bugle sounded, they prepared to move to the rear when suddenly a white burst of flame caught Isaac unawares and whirled him. He heard a cracking and felt his head whipped as though by the blunt edge of a huge, fiery knife. He fell face down, struggling to be up again. Rising to his knees he saw the bloody wheel spoke that had hit him; he saw the disabled gun, and the dying cannoneers . . . and his blood.

The day went against the Confederates as Elias had known it would. The ground was wet and the plunder of yesterday had to be abandoned. The men were tired and the horses were tired; the Union artillery began to get the range and explode caissons and dismount guns and disable teams of horses.

The wreckage and the confusion, the death and the butchery, Elias saw, had ignited fear. It was an all-pervasive fear, like a bad smell, that turned the day into a series of disasters, small and large, and it was Elias's duty to watch and to stay behind with it while the main body of the gray army funneled into the narrow road and for a time jammed there, where it might have been shot to pieces had the Federal artillery been able to move quickly, but the blue army held off for some reason and seemed satisfied, just at the strategic moment, to rest a bit, and the gray troops finally cleared the road. Shoving wagons and wreckage into the woods and ditches on either side, the retreating columns began to move south, away from the field where, only yesterday, they had been victorious.

Rain gave uniforms a rank, unwashed odor. Rain made the tired bodies of the troopers leaden and it made the smell of wet horses heavy and persistent. A man could feel how the mud made heavy going, how it punished his horse. Not keeping to the road, Elias instead took to the side of a low hill where the going was better. The rise of ground put his troopers above the confusion of the road and let them see how it was with things below on the muddy flat.

The portion of road that had jammed the Confederate withdrawal lay just below, straight down the ridge. There the road passed through a large field of felled trees. The trunks lay scattered like matchsticks, more than a hundred acres of timber that had been cut and left to lie where it had fallen. War had walked in on that logging operation and from its appearance the men who had been about the work had left suddenly. The road through that section was miry and narrow.

A few miles to the south the troopers could see the rear vans of the Confederate army. In that direction columns of smoke like rows of sooty fingers marked the destruction of stores and ammunition. Wrecked field ambulances and freight wagons and abandoned hind-limber boxes framed the sides of the road.

The advance columns of the blue army appeared. They came four abreast until they reached the neck of the road where it mired and passed between the field of fallen timber. Here they fanned out in a skirmish line, their cautious officers perhaps thinking sharpshooters would be lying concealed among the fallen trunks. The skirmish line went clumsily, like a crippled snake. The infantry found tough going, for the ground was wet and the fallen trees were constantly in the way and had to be climbed over, one after another. Behind meanwhile came fresh thousands in blue uniforms, guns at the ready.

When the advance guard of the Federal cavalry began to move up it was flanked by two massed divisions coming down the road behind.

"Mount!" says Elias. The Federal cavalry, in confusion now, was just entering the field of the fallen trees, as though trying to unravel that matchwork and to pick their way through and beyond, while the infantry skirmishers, hopelessly bothered now, began to pile up . . .

"Sound the charge!"

Down the ridge they rode. Saber in hand Elias, the raider, stood up in the stirrups and felt the fingertips of the wind in his beard and in his knees the bunched spring of his horse's muscles and sinews.

Spurring ahead, Elias rode into the blue mass. He felt its panic and recoil. In shock and surprise and without room to maneuver, without time to react, the blue infantry began dropping muskets. The Kentuckians began firing their shotguns. The Texans rode in with drawn revolvers blazing.

In his eagerness Elias had ridden too far. In his thirst for hacking and sabering he had, he saw, cut a trail that was now closed in behind him. He heard cries close by:

"Shoot that one! Kill the somebitch! Shoot him — there's one! Pull him off his horse!"

Something exploded against his side. Wheeling his horse about furiously he looked down into the face of the soldier who had shot him. The man still held the musket and would have raised it to fend the blow away, but it came too swiftly. The blade bit the Yankee's neck below the ear and his head craned and his knees bent double. Elias felt the shock of his own wound in a hot, spreading jolt of pain that transversed his back between shoulder and hip before it went numb.

It came to him as the horse spun that he would be captured or killed and it occurred to him at the same instant that if he were to come out of it he must have a shield. He saw a soldier below him. He grabbed the man by the collar and heaved him up behind, holding him there while he drove the spurs home and headed out of the mass, bolting suddenly away while the back burden struggled helplessly. A moment later his own troopers closed in about him and together they bucketed back up the ridge. Elias dropped his prisoner and stuck his finger in a spurting hole that had appeared in his horse's neck. Holding the wound thus staunched he trailed in between a thick stand of cedars and slid down and stood on the slanting ground, swaying and uncertain. His horse slumped down, stretched out its head and was still.

They helped him up on a fresh horse and rode on either side to keep him in the saddle. It seemed a long way down the ridge but they kept riding and came then to that part of the road which passed the swamp and he smelled the rotting essences and the mud and the drowning trees and it was cooler there in that passage.

"We turned them. We turned them back," says Dutt's voice. "But you rode into the midst of them like a fool."

"Hush," says Tug Chambers.

"But he did — he rode like a fool."

"He killed nine of them," says Tug, speaking as though Elias were nowhere about.

"How is he?" It was the artillery sergeant, Jasper Coon.

After what seemed to Elias an interminable time they took him down, and stretched him full length on the ground. A bandage was passed about him and pinned and he was placed on a stretcher, then in an ambulance that moved and stopped, jerked ahead and stopped, and finally, began moving at a regular pace. The ruts brought him back to life, the pain began to quicken.

The ambulance stopped during the early dark and a soldier

who had died was taken out and another was put in his place. Someone gave Elias a drink of water and fed him a cup of soup. It had beans and ham in it and was steaming hot. "Who is it?" Elias asked.

"Compliments of Sergeant Coon," says Jasper's voice. "The Yankees ain't following."

"Then we did stop them after all."

When the halt was finally called a tent was pitched for the wounded and Elias was put on a cot and Jasper stuck a bayonet in the ground beside him, put a candle in the socket of the bayonet and lit it. He brought the surgeon who looked at the wound and then wrapped it up again and said that in his opinion it was not fatal.

"You must be sent home to recover," says the surgeon, and he went away.

Home. He had not known until now how much he missed that clearing in the woods. Home . . .

"Sir?" It was Jasper again.

"Yes?"

"Isaac was hit. So was Willy. Don't worry; they'll make it. . ."

Isaac, on that second day, had undergone the most deadly disappointment of his life. Himself wounded, he had seen his guns captured. He had watched his gunners waver between the wish to fire one more round and the impulse to limber the guns and take them to safety off the field. He had seen his men shot, clubbed down, stabbed with bayonets, sabered, and captured. Had not Jasper Coon appeared with a horse and urged him on it Isaac himself might have been captured. As it fell out the victorious Yankees were too elated to bother with a forlorn, bloodied captain and a dogged gray sergeant riding away while their adversaries were cheering and back-pounding.

Isaac was groggy. Jasper Coon had had to drag him away

saying, "What's wrong — don't you want to live? If I wouldn't shoot Jeff Davis; he caused th' whole mess he did by God . . ."

And having begun to swear Jasper Coon continued to swear until they found a unit of Texans and then two companies of Morgan's cavalry and so made the distance back, first to Lick Creek and now into the woods and along the ridge with what cavalry was left in the rear guard. There Jasper bandaged Isaac's wound with a piece of shirting and staunched the bleeding.

Everywhere Isaac looked he saw the wreckage of exploded caissons and the spare wheels of abandoned hind-limber boxes. Straying artillery nags went galloping sideways, kicking hind legs at the sky.

Massed divisions came pouring down the road behind the advance guard of the Federal cavalry. What a beautiful target for guns if only he still had them. From the height he could see the vast field of fallen trees. He watched the advance guard of blue cavalry entering that matchwork confusion. They were trying to pick their way through it, when the infantry skirmishers, confused by the tree trunks, began to pile up.

"*Charge! Charge!*" A bugle blared.

Isaac was carried away over the ridge and straight down the slope with a mass of mixed riders and uniforms. In the lead and pulling away from the rest, with his sword raised, standing in the stirrups, was Elias. The Texans had their revolvers drawn. Morgan's troopers began firing shotguns. The blue soldiers, separated upon that field of fallen timber as effectively as if they had been under the fire of Isaac's guns, threw down their muskets and tried to scramble back the way they had come. Isaac managed to draw his pistol. He snapped two caps, knew his powder was wet then, and put the pistol away. He drew his saber, entangled it in his reins and nearly lost his seat before he dropped the weapon and began working to regain his balance and bring his horse under rein.

Isaac saw his father spurring into the Federals, riding beyond the fight, waving his saber, closing with a solid mass of Yankee troops that began to surround him, trying to pull him off his horse while he hacked them with the saber, his horse whirling about.

Isaac grabbed at the reins of a Kentuckian who was aiming a shotgun. Without looking at Isaac the man shot down a Yankee beneath him, thrust the shotgun into the scabbard beneath his leg, and drew his pistols, cocking and taking aim first with one hand and then the other regardless how his horse behaved. Then seeing Isaac, he paused at his work.

"The Colonel!" Isaac was yelling, "He's surrounded!"

The Kentuckian's face was smeared, black with powder. The wrinkles about his eyes showed white. He looked in the direction Isaac pointed, yelled something to the men on the other side of him, and spurred through the mass of men and horses and smoke. Isaac followed him.

Elias's horse turned a half circle again as Isaac watched. Behind him a foot soldier ran up, pressed his musket against Elias's side, shot him, and leaped back. Elias swayed for a drunken instant, then wheeled about again, bent forward on the neck of his horse. He had put his saber away and was holding his pistol. He dropped it and grabbed the nearest soldier, lifted him bodily and flung the fellow across his back. Still holding him like a spare coat or a sack of straw, he ripped away from the foot soldiers who were clawing at him and headed straight back. He passed Isaac. As Isaac and the Kentuckians turned to follow, Elias flung his prisoner away and headed back up the ridge with his riders closing behind him.

The Federal divisions were stopped short in confusion. The

blue mass began to buckle back upon itself. The Federal cavalry, until now boxed in by the fallen timbers, made a flying stampede rearward through the ranks of their infantry skirmishers, riding over them and heading through the massed division which could be seen parting to let the riders through.

Pursuit was checked. Temporarily the Federal army was thrown back on itself, and Isaac knew Elias must be mortally shot.

Inwardly, as he rode back up the slope of the wooded ridge, he began to pray. The faces of all about him were covered with mud. The uniforms were spattered with it, the saddle girths were hidden under it. The stuff flew up from every hoof to strike eyes and spatter reins.

The officers were bawling commands, trying to collect and reassemble troopers by squadrons.

Reaching the brow of the ridge Isaac's horse sagged. Isaac had just time to leap before the creature rolled down, thrashing and kicking its way into death.

Isaac looked back. The dead and the dying made a solid mass there below where Elias McCutcheon's men had ridden back and forth among them on that killing ground.

An Alabamian reached down for him and Isaac leaped up behind and was carried away. The man said,

"I think the Colonel is shot. I heard he was shot."

Further on a way they turned down the ridge and took the road south. Isaac asked everywhere about Elias and could only discover that he had been taken on ahead to be looked at by the surgeons, that he was in great pain, but that he was alive. When he was able to get another horse he rode on ahead, but it was not until nightfall that he found the surgical headquarters and finally, nearby, the tent where Elias lay. The place was heavy with the odor of carbolic acid.

Here and there a bayonet had been stuck in the ground in

the narrow spaces between cots and a candle stuck in the socket and lit — but for all this the tent seemed very dark. Two men with a stretcher came past Isaac. They were removing a corpse.

"Over here, here's a place," said a voice. A soldier, groaning monotonously, was placed on the cot from which the dead man had just been removed.

There was barely room to stand between the cot on which Elias lay and the cot beside him. Isaac knelt. His back touched the next cot and he could feel behind him the poor fellow's violent trembling. The man breathed as though snoring.

"They probed but didn't find anything," Elias was saying, his voice weak. "I fixed several before they got me. Hit in the head, eh?"

"Yes," said Isaac. "You'd best be going home to get well."

"Home? Yes, home I suppose. They've brought Willy in a while ago."

"Willy's hurt?"

"Yes, he's there somewhere. Hit in the legs again."

"Willy!" Isaac called.

"He's over here," says Jasper. "Want some soup?"

Making his way to Willy's cot Isaac saw that his brother was suffering. He looked pale and seemed too weary to talk.

When Isaac finally stepped outside the tent, his head was throbbing. He tried to breathe the odors of bile and blood and carbolic out of his lungs. Taking a plug of tobacco from his pocket, he cut himself a chew. The tobacco's dark, musty taste took away that awful smell of suffering. Walking down a way he saw soldiers crowded in a disordered mass about a field kitchen.

Dreading what he knew awaited him, most of all dreading the smell, Isaac turned back towards the hospital tent. The ground was churned to mud.

They woke Willy at daylight and carried him to one of the freight wagons and put him inside and put blankets over him.

The wagon had a smell of salt meat. He lay very still. His legs felt as though a grass rope had been pulled through both thighs and when the wagon moved that rope seemed to pull and when the wagon jolted the rope gave a jerk which caused a red blossoming at the edges of his vision and he tried to think of something else, and then tried not to think.

When the pain began to feel as though it would bite him in two he reached for the canteen a doctor had put beside him and took a swallow of whiskey and closed the canteen and put it down again and waited for the whiskey to wear itself against the edge of the pain that cut now clean across his hips and seemed to return to its proper place in his thighs only when the wagon paused. The teamsters swore at the mules now and then. They were in mud and Willy could hear the mud sucking the wheelspokes and slapping the sideboards. The smell of salt meat put him in mind of the smokehouses back home at Oakleigh, full of hams and shoulders.

He longed to be at home again. In his mind's eye he saw the land. It would be spring and things all about would begin greening.

He reached for the canteen and took another swig. "Shot and drunk and being hauled about in a wagon," he thought. "Shit oh shit!"

Then he began by intervals to doze. He could adjust to anything, after all. There was in Willy an animal self that could finally accept whatever it was that came to him with a slow but sure composure.

"I'll not die, God damn it!" he thought, upon waking, when the snorts of the animals and the slap of reins and the crack of cowhide whips seemed to ride out of sleep into his waking and hover about him and mingle with the salt and the smoke smell of the meat.

The journey was sliding away beneath him into miles and more miles. He did not die the next day nor the next. They reached Corinth and he was not dead. He had drunk a lot of whiskey, but he would not die. And the surgeons day to day wavered between wanting to take out the shell fragments or allowing maybe it would be best to amputate.

Chapter 3

Elias was sent home with orders to return to duty as soon as he was able. And with his orders came notification that he was advanced to the rank of brigadier general. There was also included a recommendation that on his return to active duty he should organize a bodyguard to remain with him at all times while on the field of action.

It seems Dutt Callister made a report to the commanding general which was forwarded to Montgomery and thereafter investigated, remanded to the headquarters at Corinth, revised, written again, verified, forwarded again to Montgomery with additional recommendations, meanwhile, with every revision and emendation gaining a certain loftiness of language which more and more removed it from the realm of Dutt's simple, straightforward account. The newspapers made much of Colonel McCutcheon's exploits at Shiloh Church, or Pittsburg Landing, especially the delaying action upon the Field of the Fallen Timbers.

McCutcheon, so it seems, has fought the successful rear-guard action, nevermind whether it was at what now came to be called Shiloh, or what was once Pittsburg Landing — Elias, the raider, who ended the second day getting himself shot for "going too far."

Shiloh! The news of that fight went ahead of him into West Tennessee. *Shiloh!*

And, taking Willy, whose legs were still attached in spite of so much talk of amputation, Elias went home. Not by rail, however. Not to the depot, to be met as befits a hero by the Somerton Band and a crowd of citizens, no. Not by Jane Nail wearing a silk patch on her cheek and by Jake and Rance nor by Madam Fanny Parham, the doctor's widow, and Wall Stuart, who as Mayor of Somerton would surely have made a brave and patriotic speech in which General Elias McCutcheon would be hailed as a proud conqueror from the far-flung fields of glorious war. None of that, for the sad reality was that the district was still held by the Yankees, and it was necessary for Elias to smuggle himself and his son home through the swamps and the backroads.

Elias comes home wounded and sick, passed from hand to hand by loyal Confederate families, moving only at night. Even so, his return has great effect, for the young men appear anxious to serve in McCutcheon's Brigade. Preachers offer prayers for the swift return to health of the General and his son.

Jane touches that place on his side where the ball entered. "Should the Yankee colonel find you they'd take you both to prison. I'm afraid, Elias. Was it so awful? Willy's legs look bad."

"We'll heal, nevermind," says Elias. "It was awful, yes, awful because we could have whipped them good and we quit!"

"Never fancied I'd be married to a general," says Jane.

"Neither did I."

"Is Isaac recovered?"

"Yes, almost, with a scar on the side of his head, red as a rooster's comb. He was hit by a spoke from the wheel of the number three gun. Bled a great deal."

Elias was home, but his thoughts were with his men, and upon forming the new brigade, and upon the fighting to come.

"Red, did you say, Isaac's scar? *Red* . . .?"

And by the look of her Elias knew she was grieving for Isaac, her firstborn, and wanting Isaac home as well.

"Isn't so bad, Isaac's scar," says Elias, speaking kindly.

"Your cat, Tom, what about him? Was he lost?"

"Tom? No — I left him in Corinth, with a family there. They promised to feed him. Isaac has got him back again and is seeing after him for me."

"But you must give him away — give him up. You can't take him *everywhere*," says Jane. "Generals don't carry cats about."

"Well . . ." says Elias. "He's Confederate gray, did I write that?" Pause. "He's lucky too, I believe."

"Yes," says Jane. "I read your letter to the servants. It made us all laugh."

Elias was not sure he wanted to give up Tom. Not all the way. For it seemed to him if Tom was safe then the safety of himself and Isaac and Willy was sure. Had he taken the cat with him north to that fight it might have gone better, thinks Elias.

Odd thoughts, peculiar notions — but soldiers have a way of becoming superstitious.

Chapter 4

Sitting in his father's tent, on the edge of his father's cot, Isaac passed his fingers over the livid scar on the side of his head and gazed into his pocket looking glass. The cat purred beside him on the cot, dozing. Another inch, that spoke would have taken my ear, thinks Isaac.

The scar and the area about it on either side have no feeling, and thus it is like touching the face of a stranger, a queer, rubbery face. But his eye was not affected. And Isaac had no hole in *his* cheek to show. He'd seen what a *bad* scar could be like, Isaac had. He'd grown up with it.

I'm lucky, he thought. Lucky I wasn't killed . . . lucky.

The mail orderly came with a letter for him. Isaac saw Jane's handwriting. Home seemed ten thousand miles away. He hoped Elias and Willy were safe.

Though he put his mirror away he let the new mail be a while, the more to savor the anticipation of this pleasure in reading news from home.

Sitting thus, quite still, with his hands clasped between his knees and the stir of the camp and of Corinth going on all about and beyond him where he waited, he was wondering when curiosity would overcome him and make him open the letter, when Jasper Coon walked into the tent.

"Ha!" says Jasper. The sergeant's tired, weathered hands twitched beside the seams of his frayed artilleryman's britches. Jasper was suffering from chronic diarrhea, like so many others, for the fact of the army's drinking water being taken just lately from contaminated pools. Isaac had avoided that plague by boiling his own water before he drank it. "If I owned twenty niggers you'd have to send me home," says Jasper, in his slurring backwoods voice.

"How is that, sir?" says Isaac, not pleased at the interruption.

"I just heard the order read! Any rich planter bastard owns twenty of them black jack-apes gits *his* freedom to go home. *Leave* the God damn army, yes he can and go home and dine on the God damn fat of the land! Let him go pet and curry-comb his slaves. Yet what of a poor bastard like me, Isaac? Answer me that? Couldn't I have a whole fambly of twenty kids back home starvin' to death and what am I told when I want a furlough? 'No!' that's what. 'No!' Now account for that, by God."

"You'll do well to contain yourself," says Isaac, cool as springwater. He gives Coon a look. "If such is the law, it's unfair. And no doubt such a law has been passed if you've heard the order read. Under those terms I could go home myself and stay."

"You're a damn fool if you don't go. I can tell you, was it not for the fact I'd be shot or have my head shaved and a *D* branded on both my hips and walked through the whole army to the 'Rogue's March,' for a deserter, I'd be gone *tonight*. You'd not have Jasper Coon for roll call tomorrer —" Silence. "Is that mail?"

"Yes."

"From our district?"

"From my mother, yes."

"Well. What's the news?"

"I've not as yet opened it to read."

"Will you go home, Isaac?"

"To Yankee-occupied territory? I won't go home . . ."

"Some will, wait and see. Some will leave."

"Let them," says Isaac.

What Jasper said had truth in it. Beyond the tent entrance Isaac could see the company streets. Dust now, they had been mud when the army returned from Shiloh. Dawn after dawn bugles summoned the men from sleep. They fell in for roll call while the officers, Isaac included, looked at their watches. Half-rations then for breakfast, and a lag time after during which buttons were shined, buckles polished, boots rubbed, worn uniforms brushed. Then they fell into ranks again. *Right shoulder arms, for-wwarrd!* The command springs from company to company to company throughout the army, *Ha-aarch!*

Afterwards the routine is the same. Formed up in squares on the dusty parade grounds they dress their lines.

They stand in the heat. They wait. Inspections and more inspections . . .

Waiting thus, the men begin to sway. Then the weakest of them faint. Falling, muskets clattering to the ground, they lie prostrate while on all sides no one stirs a muscle.

Heat devils dance on the parade ground. *At-ten-shun!*

A staff lieutenant is reading the sentence of the court-martial. His voice falls. His words are lost in the dust; the army, after all, is indifferent.

When the staff lieutenant has folded the document away the drums begin to beat. The condemned man is taken to the death post by two privates in the provost marshal's corps.

The victim, for such he becomes in the minds of the witnesses — the victim kneels, blindfolded beside his coffin.

Out marches the firing squad, forming up before the death post. A lieutenant, not the one who read the sentence, draws his sword. The drums, which have gone temporarily silent, begin to beat again. The muskets are raised to firing position. The executioners take aim. The order to fire is given.

The impersonal volley hardly echoes. The massed press of so many witnesses sops up the sound. It seems to fall upon felt or cotton wool.

In the presence of so many thousands the limp body is placed in the coffin, the coffin is nailed shut, loaded on a caisson, and hauled from the field behind a pair of languid, nodding horses.

Next comes the reading of more orders, more regulations, more promises, and more promises of punishments.

What Jasper said had some truth in it . . . thinks Isaac.

"When you gonna read your letter?" says Jasper. Anxious for news from home, is Jasper.

Isaac looks at him, speaking kindly,

"Why now, of course. I'll read aloud if you like."

"Thanks," says Jasper, not without some dignity. "Thanks," he says, in a softer voice. A look of reverence comes to his face as he watches Isaac open the letter.

Mail, more coveted than gold . . . Isaac slowly unfolds the letter. He savors the handwriting, the stoic quality of her thought as Jane tells him that Willy is going about a little now, though his legs have been terribly mangled, or so it seems, but his youth gives him an ability to heal quickly. Her Willy, shot in both legs, and oh, yes, he seems to be in love with the Widow Parham's daughter.

And this time Jane does not write as in previous letters that the Widow Parham was "*thet hore wyth al thoze chilrun thet married the doctor.*"

No, she omitted that line in this letter. She writes that the girl's name is Sallie and that it looks as though the preacher may be called before Willy and his father return to the fight.

"*Yore father is but mending slowly . . .*"

And Jake and Rance and Jake's boy all three were begging to be allowed to go to the front and help their masters. Many servants in the neighborhood had gone away to help. The Negroes at Oakleigh began to feel ashamed for that they were not in the fighting too, but wrong it would be of them, writes Jane, to fight to defend their own bondage . . .

And at the end some sad news. Fancy Callister has lost two of her boys killed and just this week is packing up the next oldest to send *him* to the fighting. How was Dutt taking it — two sons killed?

"What news — can you read me any?" says Jasper.

"Yes," says Isaac. "Bad news for Dutt." And beginning from the first, Isaac reads his letter to Jasper aloud.

At the news about Dutt's boys Jasper bows his head . . .

Chapter 5

Dutt Callister had found his life's career. He was out of that shouting, screeching, complaining bedlam back in Sligo County, Tennessee. He is a soldier now and it seemed to be all he had ever needed or desired.

The whippings and executions left Dutt pleased. His subordinates seemed scoured and polished after each such ceremony. The world was a bit brighter, the air a bit fresher. He felt as though his own spirit had been scrubbed with lye soap.

The army was beginning to look like an army again, and less like a rabble. Short rations had the effect of reminding the plain soldiers of what they were and the conscription act had put spine in them. They knew they were in for the duration now. They had no choice but to be soldiers and fight.

But when a man got the notion that he would be sent home in a week or a month he began to be fearful. It started him brooding upon death. It made him put a sudden senseless value on his life out of all reason and proportion. The son of a bitch wanted to live more than he wanted to be a good soldier. All that was changed now.

Dutt saw, waiting for him on his cot, a letter from Fancy. She would want to know why he had not written. She would wonder again why he had not been able to get a furlough. And she would tell him again, perhaps, about Edward Ashe leaving the country with a slave girl and a little yellow baby, and of Willy McCutcheon's complicity in the business of Edward Ashe stealing those same servants from his mother.

This Ashe business was perhaps the only thing of interest that had been in any of Fancy's letters. He remembered a certain day in the woods when he had heard voices. And he had crept up close enough to see two people — Elias and Ellen Poe Ashe — and no doubt as to why they were there and what they were doing.

It had made him bold, about a month afterwards, to ride down that way and visit Miss Ellen himself, but she had spurned him, and he had guessed that she was probably in love with Elias. Then her baby had come along and she had put out that unlikely story about her husband. Dutt would let whoever would believe it, but as for himself, he felt, in an odd way, richer for the fact of his having known the truth all these years and kept it strictly to himself.

He fetched out his jug from under his cot and had himself half a glass of whiskey. A drink now and then served to cut the heat and ease the boredom and let him have a comfortable nap with his boots off and a handkerchief over his face to keep the flies from being a worry.

He was just having half a glass of that good red whiskey when someone called "Hello" outside his tent. It was Isaac. Dutt answered and Isaac came in, looking strange and Dutt thought maybe the lad was sick. He pulled out the jug again and got a tumbler for Isaac but Isaac said thanks but he didn't believe he wanted a drink just now.

"Got the Corinth quickstep, eh?" Dutt said and laughed. "Well, many have it!" Isaac was strange and quiet and just now he seemed flustered. He spoke about having gotten a letter from home, from his mother, with the terrible news.

"Oh?" Dutt wondered how long Isaac would stay. He wanted to finish his whiskey and stretch out and unfold his handkerchief and feel the sweet approach of sleep. Tonight he would call at a certain address in the residential district of Corinth with a package of rations under his arm. He would be freshly shaved. He would have combed a few drops of sweet oil into his hair and his sweetheart would play some songs upon the piano. She was a widow and wasn't shy about turning back the bed covers after supper and pretending to swoon and faint and not to know what was happening while she wrapped those legs about him and hugged his neck hard enough to break it. Dutt was dedicated to trying to give her all she wanted and she was dedicated to never getting enough of his hard nerve. Her husband had been killed in Kentucky and she had moved to Mississippi to be out of the way of the war. The thought of her made him draw a breath.

Isaac meanwhile was saying how it was such a terrible loss. He said he hardly knew what else to say. He stumbled-like, in mid-sentence.

"Yes, well," said Dutt. The whiskey was taking hold. He was sorry Isaac wouldn't join him in a drink. But again the stuff was getting more and more expensive and rich as Isaac was he could certainly buy *his* own. Dutt looked at Isaac and wondered what the young man would say if he were to be told he had a half brother named Edward Ashe. Isaac was apparently grieving over the recent losses at Shiloh. Younger officers were prone to be affected that way. "That's the way of war, Isaac. Doesn't do to brood and look back, eh?" Silence from Isaac. "You won't join me in a slosh of good old Kentucky painkiller?"

Isaac shook his head. He had taken a letter from his pocket and was about to unfold it when he spotted Fancy's envelope on the cot. Dutt picked it up, as though just discovering it, and remarked,

"This just came from Fancy. Let's see what she says."

And still acting, Dutt tore the thing open, unfolded it, and began to read . . . he felt a catch, his throat was awful God damn dry. His voice cracked as he said,

"Seems I've lost my two eldest boys in two days of fighting. Lost. And now she's sending Lester. Our third."And he felt another throb. "Had you heard?" Silence.

"Just now," Isaac said. "In the same mail . . ."

Dutt finished his drink. "I'm going to lie down. I — you never know how it will feel to lose a grown son. You know how you hate it when a baby dies, but this . . . is what you can't anticipate." He unfolded the handkerchief and put it over his face.

"I want you to know how terribly, terribly sorry I am," said Isaac. The boy was weeping.

Dutt seemed to feel that he had swallowed a word. Down somewhere in his throat a word was stuck. His throat began to hurt. He moved his head slowly.

Chapter 6

As soon as ever Sallie Parham heard of it, after Willy was home again and had begun to live day after day in his room, lying abed most of the day while Leola and his mother changed his dressings; trying to act as if his legs didn't stink and keeping the pus wiped away and the place covered with pledgets soaked in turpentine, Sallie Parham came to Oakleigh.

Willy had been embarrassed. His legs — they stunk awfully much. Did she notice? She smiled. Tears filled those lovely eyes. And she touched his hand.

Sallie Parham was so faithful that Leola began to notice and say things and look wise.

Then Mrs. Fanny Parham called and after a brief bedside talk with Willy went downstairs to the library with Jane and they had a visit behind closed doors. Leola had gone down to listen and had come up afterwards to say she had heard some mention of Brother Holmes and the First Presbyterian Church. Leola couldn't be sure there was anything meant by that, she said.

Willie ordered his crutches brought and went into his father's room and sat down at his bedside.

Elias was changed. The man Willy saw nowadays was both older and younger than the man he remembered as his father. He was much thinner and his hands were like weathered, brown pieces of wood. His beard was longer than he had ever worn it before, and there was command in his voice. Elias asked:

"Love is it?"

Willy, too overcome to speak only nodded.

Elias said, "Well, I've walked the same path! It's all right — you'll see."

And Elias adds, "I halfway like being wounded, eh? We can drink all the whiskey we want and your mama won't holler at us. Eh? I don't mind some scratches."

Willy smiled. They were only scratched after all. If his father sees wounds as scratches, then so does Willy. And Elias clears his throat and looks wise.

They had a good laugh. They laughed because they were still in one piece.

"Leola!" says Elias, calling her.

She might have been listening in the hall, for she came right in and wondered if anything were wanted.

"Whiskey," said Elias.

Days pass like whispers against the high ceilings of those upper chambers where Willy and his father lie hidden at Oakleigh. And the river chuckles at night and the wind blows and the leaves speak of summer and the only one missing is Isaac.

Leola thrives upon the secret excitement in the household at Oakleigh, with two menfolk home wounded, and the widow Mrs. Parham and Sallie, her daughter, here all the time!

In the settlements people are quick to condemn, but they are just as quick to forgive sometimes and forget, and Leola, without quite giving it a thought, now refers to the widow as "Madam Fanny," and leaves off the rest of her name, which has been for many years "the-whore-that-married-the-doctor." Strangers to the settlements might think such a name hatefully applied, but it was not. It only referred to the facts as simple people knew them and even to a certain pride in progress measured, as when a genuine high-class whore thinks well enough of a place to migrate there from New Orleans.

More and more Madam Fanny brings her servant, Aunt Tio, with her and Aunt Tio visits with Leola in the kitchen. She's a stately yellow woman belonging to T. Laird, the free Negro, but hired out now to Madam Fanny.

Leola begins to notice that often as Aunt Tio comes to visit, dressed in calico and wearing a hat, and bringing a smell of perfume to the kitchen, Jake somehow seems to find a reason for being present when there is really no reason at all. Jake should by rights be elsewhere about his business upon the place, and especially now it's spring again.

On a day when the kitchen is in a scurry of preparation for the noon meal and Leola has her hands full with her kitchen help and her household help, with pots on the stove and bread baking in the oven, and pots on the hearth, with turkey and venison being turned on the spit and basted so that the drippings now and then raise a smoke from the hickory coals, the smoke puffing into the room like steam to make folk hungry, who should walk in but Aunt Tio again, wearing white cotton gloves this trip, yes, and with a little parasol and a tiny purse and she no sooner sits down than she opens a little ivory fan and starts it fluttering very ladylike. No sooner the fan opens, it seems, than here is Jake McCutcheon, dressed in *his* best, just as quick as that. Like flies to shit, thinks Leola, noting his clean, brand-new hunting boots and that fine black broadcloth coat with tails, no less, and that briar-eating jackass grin on his face, making his howdy-do to Aunt Tio as though the world didn't know he had a wife and a cabin full of children nearby and grandchildren besides.

In the midst of so much work he sits down at the kitchen table with Aunt Tio and calls for coffee and makes a show of thanking Ponselle's Dotty, his own daughter, and saying he'd like a little poundcake — oh, he's playing the master!

"Like flies to shit!" Leola mutters, and allows herself an extra dram of whiskey, but she's Indian pure and simple, through and through, and has hated Jake all these years for a reading slave and hasn't forgiven him for that book she found among his things in the tree. Now he's at it again, making his latest boast, that he will be gone to war soon as Marse Elias has his health again. "I am needed," says Jake, putting on what he must think is a brave look. "Yes, I am needed. You Dotty! Gal! Warm my coffee just a drop? Yes, needed to look and see after him and that's how the blow fell."

"Needed and you have to go to war," says Aunt Tio in a dreamy voice. "Who will go with Master Willy when he returns, I wonder?"

"I may send my boy, Rufe," says Jake. "That's another blow, but I may send him and let Rance go see after Mister Isaac. That's a blow for Rance."

"Another blow." Aunt Tio flutters that little ivory fan. "Another blow," she says in a singsong voice.

And Leola eyes one of the boiling pots on the hearth and eyes Jake sitting reared back in the way like a regular gentlemen and eyes the pot again, a good black pot with a full two quarts of water and going a rapid boil and has done service since it was brought home by the Master himself with other goods in exchange for those loads of shingles he used to split by firelight in the early days.

"Oh, yes," says Jake.

Leola takes up two quilted pads and stoops to fetch the pot from the glaring blaze of the hearth. Her little fyce dog, Trish, is peacefully asleep in the basket beneath the stove with the cats that doze there most of the day, and find their kittens there and nurse them all in that same basket. She lifts the pot and turns with it as though to set it on the stove and then — like a poor old helpless woman — she trips and the scalding water strikes Jake first on the neck and next on the shoulders and finally wets him down his back and he leaps up with a scream and overturns the chair and the pot falls and rolls on the bricks and the dog begins to bark and Jake does a dance and starts tearing those fine clothes off to rid himself of the burn, while Leola lies fallen and helpless and hardly able to know what it is that has happened, and not even able to regain her feet by herself.

Jake continues to bellow and rend his garments. Aunt Tio's purse drops, her parasol is somehow kicked, her hat comes off and her chair clatters over backwards as she leaps up and tries to draw up her skirts and get out of Jake's way.

Finally Dotty manages to catch him.

"Hush! Hush!" Leola cries at the dog. "Ah — thank you," she says to Aunt Tio, who helps her up. And: "What's wrong with Jake?"

"You've scalded him," says Aunt Tio.

"*I* scalded him? No, it wasn't *I*, it was just that I tripped — is he scalded? Wait, rub on some bear fleece!" She totters around to fetch the fleece, knocks the top off the old churn she keeps it in, and scoops out a handful and presses it into Aunt Tio's white glove, saying, "There, Tio, rub this on him — is he scalded?" And the fleece drips on Aunt Tio's gown. In her excitement Leola scoops up another gob from the churn and runs at Jake and slaps it on top of his head. "There — this will help. Are you scalded? Rub this on, Dotty. Oh — his coat, that good coat. Is his shirt torn? Augh! Augh!"

"Now she gonna vomit on me," says Jake. "Watch her — you ole squaw!"

"Augh!"

"She's scalded me lack a hog!"

"I — no — I only turned like this and tripped. So many in the way here — are you scalded, Jake? Why would I scald a servant?" And: "Ah, Tio, look at your gown. That's bear fleece. Wait, I'll fetch some ashes — Oh —" Leola clutches her side. "Ah —" She barely makes it to the settle. Her little dog leaps in her lap and licks her. "Augh! Dotty — a dram! Dotty!"

Dotty brings her a dram of whiskey. Leola closes her eyes and lets it slosh back and forth a few times over her tongue, getting warmer and warmer, before she swallows it.

"Just one more, Dotty! Augh!" And then: "Rub soap and ashes on Aunt Tio's gown — be quick about it!" And then, to the dog: "Yes, it's all right, Trish! It's just poor Jake that tripped me — but I'm only bruised. Yes, did it scare my poor baby almost to death?"

Jake's neck meanwhile has a fine blister and there are little blisters on his shoulders and some down his back and he can't bear to wear a shirt.

"Why, Jake. Whatever? Are those scars on his back?"

"Yes'm, Miss Leola. He was bad whipped before he come here," says Dotty.

"Did you ever see such, Tio?" says Leola.

"Oh, yes. Jake's had those from the first I knew him," she says and then she looks strange. "Yes, those scars — he *told* me about them."

"But he never *told* me," says Leola. "*He! He! He!*"

"I'll kill her!" says Jake.

But Leola thrives on excitement and makes such a point of limping and groaning when she finally begins to move about again that she gets more sympathy than Jake.

And of course it comes to light that Jake was in the kitchen wearing Sunday clothes on a weekday and was drinking coffee instead of seeing to the plowing and the planting, and was eating poundcake instead of minding the plantation as was his duty, when Leola tripped and scalded him, which was an act of God and all he deserved.

Chapter 7

Because Yankee troops held the district, the wedding must be a bootleg affair. Otherwise, did the Yankee colonel get wind of it, he might appear, might he not? With a hundred or so blue bellies he'd arrest the groom and the groom's father and any other furloughed Confederates he might find, and ship them north into Ohio, to prison . . .

Madam Fanny paid the colonel a visit. Wasn't her first time to see him, no.

He received her in his private chambers upstairs in the hotel. He served her a glass of sherry. She spoke of this and that, but more and more of the necessity for life's going on, even if war were upon us. The colonel seemed to understand.

"If, for example, a young lady's young man were to come home from the army to take her hand in marriage," says Madam Fanny.

"Yes?" said the colonel. "A young man, you say? But of what persuasion?"

"A Confederate soldier, of course. But it could as well be a U.S. soldier boy if the circumstances were reversed."

"He's a Rebel then."

"You may say so — yes."

"And the young miss is your daughter?"

"You may say so, yes."

"Young Miss Sallie?"

"Yes."

"On what day would the wedding take place?"

"Thursday next."

"Where?"

"At Oakleigh."

"Oakleigh!"

"— just so, Colonel."

"My duty —"

"But it isn't your duty I'm here to inquire about. It's your sense of honor, your notion of what is decent and good. Many would be grateful to you."

"I'll give them seventy-two hours from Thursday, daybreak, to be out of my district. No patrol of mine shall be in the vicinity of Oakleigh during that time, and guests going and coming shall not be stopped. Who is the lad, Madam Fanny?"

"Willy McCutcheon," says Madam Fanny. "God bless you, Colonel."

"Please don't mention it. Let this be our secret, till death — or the cessation of hostilities. Shall we drink to the bridal pair."

"The bridal pair."

They drank.

"One thing more, Colonel?"

"Madam?"

"You have a prisoner in the jail, Mister Gabe French."

"I do, Madam." The colonel looked pained. "He's accused of dealing in government cotton."

"Could you parole him — just for the wedding?" Madam Fanny looked her sweetest look upon him.

"I'll see what I may be able to do," said the colonel.

Early on the day of the wedding wagons began to roll into the drive at Oakleigh. The passengers, some of whom had gotten up before daylight and dressed in the dark, jumped down and stretched. The men and boys, a few in uniform, some showing wounds, threw off their coats and helped drive the wagons into the shade where they took the horses out. The animals were taken to the barn to be rubbed and fed.

These early arrivals wore their best clean blouses. The women might even have brought extra dresses for the dancing. Now and then, a farmer with a fiddle under his arm.

All came through the front doors and looked about and said their "How-d'-ye" to Jane and went in to speak to Elias. He was buttoned into his best uniform and remained sitting down in deference to his wound. Willy, who was able to stand a bit without his crutches, had posted himself beside his father's chair, and was so shy and smiling that it seemed hardly possible he was old enough for war and just before being married. After speaking to Elias and shaking hands with Willy the guests went upstairs for a look at the gifts that were set out for display upon all the beds and tables and settees in the upstairs chambers. Gabe French, mysteriously out of jail, had never looked more distinguished. He circulated everywhere, bowing and smiling and offering his arm to the older ladies to help them on the stairs. He wore a cornflower blue coat, a white vest, black silk gloves, dark, trim stovepipe trousers, and black pumps with gold buckles on them. He winked a certain way to the men who followed him into the dining room where punch was being made. He took them straight through into the kitchen and when they came back they were talking into their handkerchiefs and laughing and looking wise and showed red spots above their cheekbones. The children ran everywhere about the lawn outside playing wood-tag and hide-'n-seek and London Bridge. The older boys went to the river and got stones from the road and skipped them on the surface. Those with pistols soon commenced firing at snags, sawyers, turtles — anything they could see to blaze away at — and further up, in a deep, grassy swale, those with the fastest quarter horses were rubbing them down and beginning to brag. A Negro servant was cutting stakes and driving them in the ground to mark off a race course.

Presently fiddles began to scratch. The first breakdowns started up in the horse barn beside the threshing floor. Then the group at the big house, who were somewhat timid at first, began a Virginia reel, tuning a bit and scraping at first as though to get accustomed to themselves in the large drawing room at the south end of the house. All the rugs had been taken out and all the furniture but a few chairs ranged along the walls had been removed to make a ballroom.

At noon came the first buggies. These were driven by their owners. Some of these were in mourning . . . These guests got down more slowly, but they threw off their coats, nonetheless, and went to the barn with their horses. Returning to the house they began serious conversations about the progress of the war and then stepped into the dining room after a polite interval and judged the punch. Then each took a plate and passed around the long table loaded with platters of stuffed eggs, potato salad, fried chicken, quail, venison, turkey, bear, baked hams, fish, pork chops, and hot breads — spoon bread and egg bread, light bread and corn bread, biscuits, muffins — not a moment passed it seemed but a woman in a bonnet came in with a cake basket under her arm or a lady in silks appeared with a fresh layer cake on a plate; these delicacies were ranged along the sideboard with the apple pies and peach cobblers and the platters of pralines. Leola filled the silver coffeepots. Servants passed to and fro from the kitchen.

The fiddlers in the "ballroom" began to stomp. The reels began in earnest. The young folk danced at first — only the best dancers leading off, and after a few minutes the first lot of girls, faces glowing red as apples, went upstairs to change their dresses. The fiddlers had been furnished a jug by Gabe French, who also sent them a large cedar pail of whiskey punch with a tin dipper and a lump of ice in it. Rance had no sooner served the ballroom musicians than Gabe dispatched him to the threshing floor with a pail and a jug. The dancing launched into full swing. What had begun as a quiet murmur swelled to a roar.

Towards two o'clock the carriages and the closed coaches driven by servants wearing tall hats and white gloves, and some with grooms seated behind, began to arrive. These gentlemen, either in uniform or in civilian attire, stepped down and made a stately procession to the porch behind their wives and daughters, whose silks hung from their waists in folds — here and there a black mantilla, a grandmother clutching a gold snuffbox, a great aunt, austere and erect, her shoulders covered with a pale brown silk fichu. One and all these guests paused on the porch for a brief deliberate stare at the river in order that everyone might see them, while their stiff-necked servants drove the coaches and carriages away to be parked. Some too, of these, were in mourning . . .

Brother Holmes arrived in one such coach with a planter and his wife. Brother and Mrs. Holmes went in and saw the presents and Brother Holmes somehow lost his Bible which he had carried all the way from Somerton in his left hand. Nevermind, he took another plate of food and went back to the kitchen with Gabe, remarking that Our Lord's first miracle had taken place at a wedding where He had made wine. "But I'm not opposed to temperance societies either." Like the rest, Brother Holmes emerged from the kitchen talking into his handkerchief and after a word with Jane and Willy and Elias he finally drifted down to the threshing floor to watch the dancing there. He was not needed until four o'clock after all.

Yet he was no sooner gone than Mrs. Holmes began searching for him and calling him in a shrill voice and asking if anyone had seen her husband. She had found his Bible, where he must have left it she said. She had discovered it on the sideboard beside the cakes.

The best-dressed guests meanwhile gathered out on the verandas in the shade and took mint juleps from the huge silver tray that Rance passed around with, and soon the talking and laughter on the verandas got louder. Elias and Willy decided to move out with that company so as not to see the bride when she arrived. They no sooner stepped out than they were met with rebel yells. Willy was congratulated upon his legs; someone said none but a fool would think it ill of a young man to shoot himself for the likes of a beauty such as Sallie Parham. But even in the midst of so much foolishness as this the war never seemed very far away . . .

Shokotee walked into the company. They all stood, including Elias, as though greeting the governor, for the old man was far and away the richest soul in the district and was nowadays erroneously referred to as the "last chief of the Chickasaws."

And Fancy Callister, in deep mourning, arrived with her children.

Ellen was ill, and had sent her regrets . . .

Brother Holmes was sent for; Willy, even though he knew better, was solemnly told the bride-to-be had not arrived. The shrieks from the girls on the front porch and in the front hall had told him that she was in the house now. The instant those sounds reached him his young heart had begun to fill. He felt the most intense happiness he had ever known.

Someone handed him a note purportedly from Sallie, saying the wedding was cancelled. He was too preoccupied, almost to read it. The smoke and the noise of firecrackers and pinwheels enveloped the verandas, drifting up through the shrubbery with the happy shrieks of the children. Gabe French went about asking the guests to gather in the hall. "In the hall, please ladies and gentlemen? In the hall! It's time, please!" Servants ran to the barn. A former district judge fell over the porch rail backwards into the shrubbery. He was not even scratched. Jane Nail and Fancy Parham embraced in the hall, both weeping. Brother Holmes had lost his Bible again and this time it was located in the kitchen.

Then, at last, quiet fell upon Oakleigh. Only the baying of the hunting hounds from the kennels broke the stillness. Down the high spiral staircase came the bride on the arm of Gabriel French. The bride wore a white silk gown with lace about it. The short sleeves were adorned with lappets which were attached to a delicate sheathing of French lace which extended to her wrists and set off the shape and beauty of her arms. Her veil was held by a wreath of white roses, and white ribbons trailed from her bouquet. The fresh outlines of her radiant face were revealed as though in a cameo and her bodice swelled ever so gently and modestly with each breath she drew through half-opened lips. Gabe French conducted her slowly into the main room, and soon there she stood beside Willy, a ramrod straight young horse soldier, at stiff attention. The pair faced Brother Holmes. The preacher intoned in such a low voice that almost nothing of what he said could be heard even though the ladies held their breaths to listen.

"... *pr'nounce you man 'n' wife, amen!*"

Champagne then, *captured* champagne, as it turns out, and all the more appreciated therefore by the gentlemen crowding about to kiss the bride. The couple drank a toast. Leading now, playing at a more leisurely pace, two fiddlers take the young folk across the lawn in a procession down the green and velvet way to the threshing floor; the older folks soon began to pat their feet in the ballroom. After a little more wine and a little more, even the oldest dowagers took a few turns and seemed, as they moved across the floor, to light up, each one, in her inner face, and to remember something ... save those who sat veiled, wearing black.

Every eye was on the bride, wherever she might go. Whatever she did and said attracted attention and approval. She was like a dark jewel dressed in white and was the ideal of all who saw her. Her glowing young happiness made it plain how deeply in love she was with her soldier. He was surely a hero; for just this, it seemed, the South would fight on, to very death.

The celebration continued and the guests slept by order of rank and dined the same way, and seemed to be everywhere at once in the barns, on the porches, at the banquet table, or at picnic boards set up on the lawn.

Willy and Sallie were alone together but briefly at night. Someone put a chicken in the room with them. The young guests stood below their windows on the lawn and sang songs that had double meanings. The second night Elias happened into the hall and discovered a keyhole peeper at Willy's door. Wound and all, the raider dragged the young man downstairs, took him straight out, and threw him in the pond — the son of the former district judge who had fallen off the porch.

After two days it was over at last. The third morning Leola took the young folk their breakfast, not forgetting plenty of biscuits and butter and a pot of wild honey. Sallie and Willy stayed that day in their room and didn't appear until nearly noon, she in fresh calico, Willy in uniform, and although it was sprinkling rain the pair walked to the river. As young folk will they walked in the rain, in the sprinkling rain, holding hands.

That same evening Elias and Willy left home, to ride secretly out of the district and return to the brigade.

Chapter 8

In command of his own brigade, Elias, the raider, is ordered to scour Middle Tennessee and break up supply lines and destroy the railroads.

Hot summer it is. By night they move and by day hide in deep woods until, having reached their objective, they strike.

Finding a bridge they burn it. The day after, following upon the railroad, they come on a bridge guarded by a blockhouse, a bridge on a lazy limestone creek west of Nashville. The blue soldiers in the brown blockhouse shout that they will not surrender. Their sharpshooters cover the bridge, ready to pick off the Confederate incendiaries who, with rags and tar and turpentine wait hidden, buckets and matches ready.

"Roll up Isaac's guns," says the raider.

"How near, sir?"

"Point-blank range, roll them up by hand." Here come the guns . . .

"Load!"

After three shells have been thrown a white flag appears above the blockhouse. It and the eighty souls inside are surrendered. The incendiaries move, climbing like squirrels into the timbers of the bridge. Odors of tar and turpentine and black smoke reach the raider's flaring nostrils. The brigade is four miles from Nashville . . .

The telegraph begins to click. The enemy can't decide whether the raider has twelve hundred or four thousand with him.

The brigade meets a wagon train accompanied by four hundred stalwarts of the Thirty-sixth Indiana. The swift clash roils to destruction swifter still — more paroled prisoners go marching back into Nashville to tell the Yankee commander how they were set upon by McCutcheon's troopers.

As Nashville is surrounded by burned bridges and charred trestlework, Elias sends a note to the Yankee inviting him to come out and fight. But the Yankee has orders to hold Nashville. He will not be lured out. He remains where he is, only sending out a squadron of cavalry with orders, two words: "Destroy McCutcheon."

But if something is to be destroyed it must first be found. Elias, the raider, makes warfare into hide-and-seek. Willy and Pettecasockee and the Musgrove boys stay on the Union squadron's flank, watching and reporting every move.

And if McCutcheon was before Nashville yesterday, then he's attacked Manchester today, killing half a dozen and capturing twenty. Now McMinnville clatters on the wire. "Four killed. Two sentries shot. McCutcheon is here. Cavalry sent to capture him."

More clattering: "Where is McCutcheon? He gathers our men up as easily as he would herd cattle. Train of the Fourth Division captured yesterday. Has McCutcheon got infantry with him? Urgent."

McCutcheon is at Woodbury. No, he's back before Nashville again.

This is July, mind you, when the sky flames like a haystack and horses and men alike fall down in a dead faint with so much riding in the heat of the Southern day. Northern soldiers are not used to such; it is more than the Northern constitution can take.

The Yankee cavalry commander, General Nelson, finally has all he can bear and on July thirtieth he sends a wire to headquarters:

"Task hopeless. Chased to and fro across Middle Tennessee. The effort is vain. No one can come up with these Confederates. In this hot weather it is a hopeless task to chase McCutcheon's command. They are demons mounted on racehorses. Request further orders."

And this reply:

"Proceed at once to McMinnville. Destroy McCutcheon."

Nelson wires from McMinnville:

"The condition of this country is as bad as possible. McCutcheon has it in arms almost to a man. We are fired on from every bush and tree. My wagons are lost. Request further orders."

Answer: "Find McCutcheon and destroy him."

More Federal columns ride out from Nashville to join the search. The infantry begins marching and countermarching. McCutcheon's troopers trot ahead of them just out of range. They stop and dismount just long enough to cut down twenty or thirty bluecoats before mounting again and trotting — again just beyond range of the Yankee muskets.

Union infantry, collars buttoned, collapse beside the road, felled by the heat, choked by the dust.

So long as summer lasted the chase continued, to and fro, back and forth. Elias recruits a telegrapher, a clever fellow who can ape the style of another sender as readily as some fellows whistle a tune.

The raider's telegrapher taps into the wire to add to the confusion of the Federal commanders who begin to believe that Elias has an army of thousands and that he is some kind of wizard.

"That devil McCutcheon was here. My guns are lost. I despair of ever catching him. Nineteen killed. Seventy of my best men captured. Hundred-and-fifty horses stolen. My ammunition all carried away, my stores burned. We are fired on all night long. No sleep. Men exhausted. Request relief at once."

September. The main body of McCutcheon's brigade is assigned to Bragg's army. Keeping four companies of veterans the raider sets about recruiting a new command in "occupied territory," in Middle Tennessee.

The brigade is so popular with the people now that the gray troopers are cheered as they ride the roads. Elias, the raider, is spoken of as the rock and foundation of the South's hope for victory here in this far-flung territory which the enemy has occupied. The young recruits flock in and soon Elias will have numbers enough to go raiding again . . .

Summer goes away. Cold weather comes again.

A fiddler joined the brigade, fiddle and all. Of an evening

strolling by the campfires he plays "Take Me Back to Georgia," slow tune; he follows that with "Old Tom Pussycat Died in the Corner," fast; then "Billy in the Lowlands," haunting and stirring; and "The Soldier's Joy," also called "The Song That Lost the Corn Crop" (no one knows just why).

He's a clever fiddler and can play "The Eighth of January," holding the fiddle behind his back like they do at contests. His final tune of an evening is usually "Peeky Boo Waltz," and brings a tear to the eye. Reminds the boys of something lovely-like; makes a man turn his face to the shadows . . .

After one such serenade Elias woke deep in the night. No warm cat purring beside him, no sign of Tom. He called him. No answering meow. Elias never laid eyes on Tom again.

Chapter 9

Encircling hosts of enemies no longer had the power to bother Willy. He was a young veteran now, part of a brave old army. So much so that he took everything calmly and slept whenever and however opportunity offered.

Returning late, making his report to Tug Chambers, he

was stiff from cold and from riding over icy roads. Searching a bit in the darkness away from the fires he found a bedding place in the leaves. Rolling himself in his two Massachusetts blankets, with his haversack and his canteen for a pillow, he composed himself for sleep.

He was wakened the first time by the rumbling of artillery and ammunition trains passing on the frozen road some miles away. The forlorn and lonesome sound died so gradually it seemed almost never to stop. Some men, wearing blue or gray, some poor devils of whatever loyalty were out there struggling in the dark, fighting to stay awake.

Willy dreamed. In his dreams he ate apples and bologna sausages, cheese and canned oysters, and citron candy. He drank fresh pitchers of milk. In reality, in the cold world of everyday, he lived on a few handfuls of parched corn, a cold turnip taken from an abandoned field and downed raw . . . a cold drink of water from an icy stream, his horse drinking beside him . . .

Waked the second time by talking he sat up and knew that it came from the direction of the quartermaster's tent nearby. "Forty gallons of good old apple brandy," said a voice through the tent wall. "Litter and forage?"

A low voice muttered something in reply. Then: "Hams, beans, sugar, vinegar, soap, candles, salt, rice, meal, peas, flour, lard, beef," said the first voice. Another mumbled reply. Willy pushed his blankets off and stumbled his way to the tent and looked inside.

"Line blue foolscap. Paper? Brown ink? Now, George, that's ninety-six salt pork — no, salt *beef,* hundred tallow candles. Was there any mess pork? All right. Bushels of corn — thirty-five. Bundles of fodder, five hundred. Corn meal rations, two-eighty-eight."

Silence: "Five gallons turpentine to burn the bridge. Five gallons."

"Supplies?" Willy asked.

"Just in not an hour ago," said the clerk, not looking up. "From a captured depot. The old man sent 'em along."

"Litter and forage?" says Willy, thinking of his horse.

"Aren't you a scout?"

"Yes," says Willy.

"That would be Tug Chambers. He drew rations. See him . . ."

It was a dream come true.

Just after daybreak, his horse fed and rubbed, and himself stuffed with hot-water corn bread and salt beef and beans, Willy rode out again upon instructions from Dutt Callister and Tug Chambers.

After a ride of two hours he stopped beside a bridge on one of the parallel roads, marking its location on his map. He returned his map to his dispatch case and snapped shut the leather pouch slung about his shoulder. Looking down at the water he was thinking that the fish would likely bite here. A good place to fish, thinks Willy. Beside a bridge such as this where the water ran cold. The low sun, without much success, was trying to warm the world. Though not hungry anymore the boy was still lonely, thinking of Sallie. Those contemplations of fishing helped.

Riders. They came for the bridge, seeming not to see him nor his horse. Only when the foremost of them leaped down did Willy realize they were Yankees. Drawing his pistol Willy killed the dismounted trooper without aiming and vaulted into the saddle, riding away and yelling as though calling to a regiment nearby for assistance. It was a ruse he had practiced many times, calling for nonexistent help as he rode away. Bullets splintered the railing.

Looking back, satisfied that he was not pursued, he heard drums. Bugles called. He reined about and stopped to look more closely. Puffs of smoke popped out from the slopes of the farthest ridge he could see. A shell exploded in the woods beside the bridge. The *thrumm-thrumm!* from the big guns rolled down the valley.

In the road just beyond the bridge the body of the dead man lay where it had fallen.

Here is the territory between the armies — scout's ground. He went back, intending to cross the bridge again and find an observation point on the high ground beyond.

Thrumm! again from the guns hidden upon that farthest ridge. He paused, taking care to reload his Navy six. While he was about this a company of Confederate cavalry came trotting into view, emerging from a trampled cornfield down to the left. Entering the road, the cavalry clattered over the bridge and beneath a bursting shell. Just emerging from the woods into the path of the cavalry, came three companies of Confederate infantry, swinging along at a steady march.

As he rode for the bridge Willy heard a shell looping overhead. Then another and another. They cracked into the trees knocking limbs to earth and cutting white scars in the live wood . . .

Reaching the bridge Willy saw a trooper in gray lying close beside the rails. The man was groaning. His legs were moving. Leaping down Willy saw a frayed sleeve. Bending closer he saw the man's naked lungs and the pulsing of his heart.

"Help me!" said the fallen man.

Reaching for him Willy somehow brought the victim to his feet, getting blood on his hands and boots and feeling the other's bearded cheek graze his own.

"Nevermind, I can make it," said the wounded soldier. As Willy released him the man took two steps, coughed and fell dead.

Mounting again Willy rode over the bridge, thinking how it was with himself the last time he was wounded.

The first surgeon to see him had said his legs must be amputated at once, but at that Willy had shown the surgeon a little derringer. That started the surgeon swearing, yet he went ahead, cleaned the wounds and dressed them, the whole while telling Willy he would die of gangrene. "But if that's how you will have it — pointing a pistol at me — you little son of a bitch!"

"That's how I want it," Willy had said, never lowering his derringer, not once until he was safely out of the surgical tent, never once lowering the little pistol until, as it happened, he fainted.

The surgeon had shouted after Willy as he was carried out of the tent, that were he not so busy saving lives he would have Willy on report and see him shot for insubordination. Hollering back Willy had told him to wipe his chin. Ten days later the wounded boy had been on the way home to Oakleigh with his father.

Finding his way through the woods, riding up the slope of the ridge, Willy thought again of Sallie.

As he reached the edge of the brow of bluff that formed the highest promontory he swiftly counted two brigades of Union soldiers and four batteries of limbered guns moving forward at the trot.

He noted the direction of the movement and calculated the distance and the expected time of the attack (for an attack it surely was); now he must reach the Confederate encampment, and he turned about and rode down the slope again, making for the bridge, when he saw smoke. He was struck by something and hurled down, suspecting even before he hit the hard earth that he was shot by his own men, by nervous boys in some company of green recruits.

They ran to him and were swift about carrying him towards the rear. Though in pain Willy had presence enough of mind, meanwhile, to give warning of the attack, its strength and direction. They saw he was thirsty, coming in and going out of himself. Thirst overpowered him.

The interior of the tent in which he came awake was dim.

"Shot by accident. Scout. Willy McCutcheon," said a voice.

"Any messages?"

"Letters here — from his wife."

"Any message for your wife?"

A surgeon examines him. "You are seriously wounded."

"Tell her — tell her," says Willy, trying to think what it is his Sallie must be told. "Water —" he says.

"It would only hasten the end," says a voice.

"Please tell her —"

"Speak louder if you can."

"Yes," says Willy. "Yes."

He was out of himself again. Someone is kneeling beside his cot. His hands are in a warm grasp. By candlelight he sees the face of his father, tears in those gray eyes, from that wolf gaze that has seen the death of so many thousands.

"Is it bad, Father?"

Elias nods.

"I'm cold, Father."

Closing his eyes it seems to Willy that he is just passing the cabin of the laundress at Oakleigh. So real is the vision that he can smell the ironing. He feels something gathering at the back of his throat. He opens his eyes and sees his father again. Elias is kneeling and holding his hands as though to keep him from something.

"Will we meet again, Father?"

Did Willy speak, or did he imagine the words? The gray eyes turned aside for an instant, then the stern face turned a trifle. Elias nodded. "Aye," he whispers.

Willy knew what it was in his throat. It was the formation of a thought, a *word* that was the containment of that thought; and he closed his eyes that he might, while riding as now he saw that he was, while riding through flat and rolling country with the sun upon it so splendidly bright and the fields everywhere green, and the sun, the sun of morning-tide — oh; land such as this was surely worth dying to preserve, was it not?

No longer riding now, he is writing a letter.

my dearest, looked at your daguerreotype by firelight and thought of meeting you soon and talking over the dangers which I am now passing through. saw a great many unburied skeletons yesterday presenting a most horrid appearance, the site of one of our skirmishes last year. counted forty-nine skulls in one little ditch, where the heaviest fighting of that sortie took place. My dearest love . . .

And again he sees the cabin of the laundress. Again he smells the ironing. A gentle cough, long gathering behind him, comes suddenly forward now. A burst, a vision of dark sunlight. Then . . . nothing.

Chapter 10

Grief.

In the mountains about Chattanooga, at the bloody passes

and in the narrow defiles of the road through north Alabama leading into Georgia — Elias lives with grief. His uniform grows loose on him; his complexion, darkened by winter and sadness puts his gray eyes in sharper contrast. His beak nose gives a hawk's look to his haggard face.

He lives with sorrow and by the saber; butchering and shooting enemies in raid and battle, assault and pursuit, pushing himself always to the forefront. He is there, towards the thick, always standing in his stirrups and slashing . . .

After Willy's death Elias turned with the brigade upon Murfreesboro which was held by units of the Eighth Kentucky Cavalry. Like an iron storm the horse soldiers swept into the city just before daylight, whirling straight to the courthouse square, breaking down the doors to the hotel and riding into the dining room and swarming on foot into the upper chambers where the Union officers were quartered.

The sky no sooner paled than the slashing and stabbing and shooting indoors were almost done, staining linens and carpets and featherticks and nightshirts, smashing china and night tables.

Taking the Union commander prisoner they moved upon the jail and the courthouse next. Fetching a log the Confederates swung it between them butt foremost by means of ropes, staggering up the walk under a hail of savage musketry from the windows above, some falling as though tripped by invisible wires, only to be instantly replaced by others; they moved the ram on, so on up the steps and on beneath the overhang and *crack!* into the double doors, and *crack!* again, this time so furiously that the spine of the building seemed to give. The doors burst. Gray attackers swarmed through the opening, hacking with sabers and firing away, and yelling the shrill, keening Rebel yell.

Prisoners are mustered, the dead buried, supplies seized, the depot set afire.

Then *wham!* from Federal batteries not accounted for, and on inquiry among the prisoners discovered to be elements of the Third Minnesota camped west aways on the edge of town. *Wham!* from those batteries — four guns.

Forming up and making in that direction Elias discovers that the Minnesota boys, given ample time and warning, have fortified, turned over freight wagons, and taken cover behind them. Elias draws his pistol and makes a quiet gallop through the wide fields, a silent sweeping encirclement that brings him upon the flank of those guns and overturned wagons so swiftly that the Union encampment scarcely knows what it is that has overtaken them before they are captured too, flushed from behind their barricade and forced to stack arms.

The day hardly begun, the sky just beginning to pale, and the brigade's gamecock just thrusting up to crow, the blaze of his head and comb thrust out of his master's knapsack where he has ridden this whole while till now, sleeping in the midst of so much tumult, roosting the roost of the just . . .

Elias remembers the cat, Tom McCutcheon, and wonders what must have become of the warm, purring Tom, and he thinks that mayhap it had been a sign, an omen of Willy's death, Tom's disappearance . . . Were *Tom* not lost *Willy* might not have died?

Aye, Willy, the man thinks. *Willy.* A cradle, a packing crate with strings at the corners, strings tied to bare rafters. *Willy*, that seemed the bravest child in all the west . . . Aye, Willy.

And the gamecock crowing and units of the Ninth Michigan Infantry and two companies of the Seventh Pennsylvania Cavalry, and four guns of the Third Minnesota — all captured; and Tug Chambers cautioning a new recruit, saying:

"Hold your fire till you see the other man's fingers. Don't pull a trigger sooner than that. Otherwise your foe is out of range."

"Yessir, Sergeant," in a young voice so much like Willy's own that Elias must turn and look at the lad to be sure . . . "When I can see his *fingers*."

"That's it," says Tug. It's the older men that gentle a boy along and try to keep him alive until he is seasoned and can fend his way on his own.

Tug blows on his hands and rubs them together. Captured horses are brought around, and mounts swapped and saddled . . .

Isaac and Pettecasockee approach. And Willy would be with them were he alive, thinks Elias.

Chapter 11

After some days of recruiting Elias received orders he had long awaited —

"Advance into West Tennessee . . ."

Sending word back, he asks to be supplied fifteen hundred muskets to replace the shotguns and squirrel rifles his recruits carry. "Six hundred new recruits have no weapons at all. Urgent."

Back comes the reply: "Not available."

Yet the brigade would cross the Tennessee River, three-fourths of a mile wide and patroled by gunboats placed there just to prevent any such crossing. Strong contingents of Union troops waited on the other side, to catch and destroy any invading Confederates that should succeed in passing the impassable river.

Cold weather, December and dead winter and Elias faces west at last. He begins the march with two thousand and fifty-three men.

Pettecasockee has gone ahead to see to the building of boats and to take Isaac's guns over.

"Blood on the hands of General Bragg!" the men are muttering.

Many more write last letters of farewell to their loved ones, realizing that the wounded will be left to die and the dead will be abandoned, unburied.

Says Tug Chambers to Elias: "If you are ready to die then we are ready, I reckon."

"I'm ready to kill Yankees," says Elias, speaking quietly.

Dutt Callister, urging and gentling his horse along in the cold, knew why it was they were being sent into West Tennessee. To be trapped and killed that's why. It was the same reason his two sons were dead and buried. They had been trapped and killed in Virginia. Trapped and killed . . .

Here, Dutt knew, was God's way of punishing him just a little more. For years he had tried to figure out what it was God really wanted of him. Was God trying to tell him something and Dutt just couldn't get the message? Had he, Dutt, no business calling on that widow down in Mississippi and fucking her? Otherwise his two boys would still be alive?

"I'll cut off my God damn pecker if that's what you want from me," Dutt thought. *"If you never had given me a pecker in the first place I'd be on the prairie now, setting by a nice little campfire."*

In spite of everything, Dutt Callister knew he was happier here, facing a river he was not sure could be crossed, than ever he could be at home.

When they had reached this place and dismounted Dutt had moved off by himself to avoid that slope-jawed, slack-gallused, baggy-britches white-trash artillery butthole that dogged around with Isaac day and night. Dutt had walked down the bank to the gravel bar to look at the boats that were supposed to take twenty-five horses and men each. Seeing the boats Dutt had felt his heart sink like lead shot. The boats were new and drawn in behind a low spit of trees in a cut-off that gave on to the main river.

In a clearing up to the right at the head of the slough was a village. It was a bleak collection of shacks flanked on all sides with fishing boats turned hull up to the cold weather and barrel nets and fish traps all in a clutter here and there. What people as remained there must surely all be indoors, locked up tight as pussy. Such settlements had a way of coming down wholesale with the "fever" whenever soldiers came along. Dutt knew the whole routine. Knock on any door you choose. A weak voice answers and says there is no food in the house, no whiskey, no females under seventy-one, and they've *all* got a terrible contagious killing, deadly ass fever and can't come to the door, no. They're dying of assbite fever, whereas if you saw them from a distance five minutes ago they were all playing the fiddle and jumping and farting and dancing and cracking their heels together and fucking each other and running footraces and lifting anvils. But now the village was shut up tight as a sulled box turtle. Even the chimney smoke looked timid.

Elias, meanwhile, after a look at the boats, said they had best do the ferrying at night. And a line of sentinels must be spaced to stand north and south along the bank to warn well in advance against gunboats.

"There are plenty of gunboats," says Isaac. "They've got a heavy patrol up and down the river. Thick as bumblebees in clover. Plenty of turtles, all right," says Isaac.

Elias didn't say anything. He never did say much before, and with Willy dead he spoke even more seldom. Unless he was riled, Dutt estimated, he got by on ten or eleven words a day. It was enough to wonder sometimes if Elias had clean down forgotten how to talk. He would ride in silence, as though he were totally alone. Just Elias, maybe, and his horse, that's all. It got so you yourself thought of him that way, as if nobody else were around, as if it was only him, that heft of him carved out of red oak maybe, and going it all alone and the horse a mechanical something. Looking for a fate that only him and maybe God, between them, knew anything about. For all Elias had to say for himself you found it hard to realize that two thousand others were alone here with him, and that six hundred of those didn't carry anything more dangerous than switches and would be about as much use in the next fight God damn as a thumb growing out your asshole.

Elias, somehow, had gotten hold of four kettledrums. He let those drums be beaten on desolate stretches of the road, maybe to give courage, maybe just to give the six hundred something to do besides worry about what everybody else was worried about, worried about six hundred of us that must go to the bushes and cut a fucking switch when the fight starts and use *that* for a weapon because General Bragg don't have any muskets to spare us. Too busy having his orderly wipe his chin and light his cigars, maybe; too busy figuring how he was going to make sure the South, no matter what, lost whatever small advantage it had left, and thus lost the God damned war.

Dutt was put in mind of another crossing he once made. No matter that it was a long time ago. He saw that crossing again as clear as yesterday. *That* had been a time, sure enough. Thinking back to the Horse Pens raid he knew how little they all had to worry about back then. Yet every heart back then was jammed up into every throat like a wedge of iron.

There being nothing for it but to wait until dark, the horses were put to graze. Dutt took his pone of corn bread and his slab of cold, fried fatback, and sat on a bleached drift log and started eating. He was tired, he was cold; he knew God was down on him. The water beyond the gravel was black. Past where the slough opened on the main river was an island, serene and alone. It gave something to look at and took a man's mind off his worries. The cold meat had a good, strong salt taste. The yellow hot-water cornmeal hoecake mixed with the meat and left a man feeling satisfied, full and comfortable below and back of his belt. It didn't do for a soldier to look to the past very much and it was the worst of all God damn mistakes for him to look ahead. His best bet was to live right here and now, to enjoy it when he could rest for an hour or take a shit, to find pleasure in the smallest of tiny little things. To get by, a soldier had to go awful easy. Was it so much a sin if he called at a certain address and took a package of food to a widow? Would God be so awful cruel as to set his face against a poor unhappy soldier for doing a charity such as that? Because the balance might be that a soldier would have his two oldest boys taken from him, and that he would, after that loss in death, somehow decide that whippings and brandings and firing squad killings weren't such great guns by God wonderful as he had thought they were at first. For it was someone's children they were treating so, and it was a terrible wrong that was done them.

For you take boys, and especially brothers, they might get it in their heads to slip off from camp at night and go foraging, might they not? And what if they found a smoked shoulder and a couple of chickens and brought back these little treasures to share with their hungry comrades? Was this a reason to take them out and shoot them and write their mother and break her heart? Was the South so far gone that it had to murder children in such a style, just as an example to other children?

Seen another way that lonely island yonder could give somebody a heavy heart if he were not damned careful. He wiped his hands on his britches and had a cold swig of water from his canteen. Then he wiped his eyes and saw Jasper Coon's approach, that sloping walk. He was such a sad-faced son of a bitch, Jasper was, so inelegant; he was like a rusty plow dipped in shit. He had the criminal's face, a sloven's tongue, and his voice had a bray in it. If that shithead didn't burn barns and poison wells Dutt misjudged him badly. Dutt frowned, but Jasper Coon came on, undaunted. Hoecake crumbs clung to the edges of Sergeant Coon's mouth and lodged in his stringy chin whiskers. He stared at Dutt a moment before he spoke with a whine. He said,

"Them boats won't do. We'll all God damn be drown-ded, and whatever for?"

When Dutt wouldn't answer him Jasper turned away shaking his head. He went sloping and shuffling off in the direction of the village, as if he had business *there!* His long arms swung at his sides, his red hands were stuck out of his frayed sleeves.

We've finally arrived at the jumping-off place for sure, Dutt thought.

Jasper was right about one thing. He was right about those boats, Dutt decided.

Elias sent the men over to the island first with orders to hide themselves and their horses deep in the canebrakes. No fires would be allowed. The work went forward at night and was slow. They moved the boats with poles and oars and the brigade lay hidden upon the island in the canebrakes the next day. The Yankee gunboats pushed by that day and threw up waves against the shore of the island.

On the opposite shore the Confederates could see men on horseback riding the bank in small groups — the enemy. Billy Yank was there, damn him, watchful and waiting. He well knew Elias's brigade was coming and he knew where the raider would cross. And the Yankee was sending his patrols, and his slope-sided gunboats were laboring up and down the stream. Pettecasockee and his scouts were already over there in his territory, hiding from him and watching him.

Elias asked Dutt to wake him when the last boatload was ready to cross. Then he wrapped himself in a blanket and lay down to a cold, uncomfortable sleep. When Dutt woke him it was dark. He had been dreaming of Willy. Elias stretched, rolled his blanket, and stood up.

"Hold the boat while I make one last check," he said.

"We've looked," says Dutt.

"Nevermind. Now I'll look."

Taking his time Elias made his way along the shore to the far end of the island. He went slowly, listening. Hearing something he turned in through the cane and found what he sought — someone snoring.

"Wake up," said the raider.

"Huh?"

"How many of you here?"

"Four — who are you?"

"Elias McCutcheon. The last boat is about to leave. You want to spend the winter here?"

"No, sir!"

"Let's go then."

They followed him. Again he went deliberately, taking his

time. They reached the boat and got aboard. Elias took up a pole and pushed hard against the gravel shore. Others pushed, and they began to move away into the slow current.

In the breaking light of winter dawn they found themselves in the middle of the river.

"Swap up! Swap up!" Dutt said. "Fresh men on the oars. Hand your pole to the next man."

A lone figure stood in the bow of the boat, with his blanket about his shoulders. He was offered a pole. He turned his face aside. He said he was a lieutenant.

"Take your turn," Elias said. "Take your turn, sir!"

"I don't see why I should. There are private soldiers here," said the lieutenant.

Elias made his way forward. Shifting the pole into his left hand he swung with his right. With his open hand he slapped the lieutenant. No ordinary slap. The man flipped like a pancake. Overboard he went and splashed. Elias pushed the pole to him and hauled him back aboard. The fellow lay, shivering and gasping like his lungs would burst. The raider's voice was hoarse in his throat. He said,

"Now God damn you take a pole and push! Or so help me God I'll drown you! Too good to work? Too good to get your hands dirty?"

The dripping, shivering lieutenant got up and manned a pole.

With the final boatload safely over they began to move west. When sunup found them at last, the soldiers stretched as though they had just come awake, as though they had slept the night through and had not spent it toiling over the river.

The little gamecock began to crow. The men with kettledrums began to beat them. Infantry on the march, the sound and bustle of a great army on the move. The rooster crowed again. The men began to sing to the throb of the drums; they sang "The Girl I Left Behind Me."

Pettecasockee meanwhile had ridden ahead of the brigade during the night. He had sent his scouts to villages and farmhouses where they knocked on doors and passed the word. McCutcheon was on the way with ten thousand men!

They went thus unmolested until they fell upon the approaches of Lexington, Tennessee, that afternoon, driving in pickets, chasing down a squadron of cavalry and capturing a colonel who had just managed to telegraph his commanding general to the west at Jackson to inform him that General McCutcheon had attacked him with an army numbering between ten and twenty thousand, that his cavalry was whipped, and that unless something could be done, all was lost. Then the key went dead.

Elias had captured two pieces of artillery, fresh horses to replace his jaded ones, and several hundred stand of rifles. And by daylight of the day following, when the gamecock began to crow and the kettledrums to crash, Dutt took a detail of twenty-six forward and drove in the pickets before Jackson.

Thus begins destruction of the Mobile and Ohio Railroad. Elias, dogged and single-minded, orders fences pulled down and piled upon the tracks.

Meanwhile the horse soldiers locate one by one the trestle bridges. Isaac's guns are rolled up to shell the blockhouses. The white flag appears. Prisoners are marched out; the trestles are burned.

And the rails twist and buckle under the consuming heat of a hundred fence-rail fires.

Embarrassed, with so much weight of prisoners and spoil, the brigade continues to move. Prisoners, in lots of one hundred and fifty, are paroled and sent marching into Jackson, carrying the wounded on litters, driving the message home.

Whipped by a madman, McCutcheon the invincible. The raider offered no choice. Either a garrison surrendered or it was stormed. In the event a garrison had to be stormed, no quarter was given. Thus the raider left officers and gentlemen no choice but to show the white flag. There was grumbling. Some said the rebel McCutcheon was not a gentleman.

Soldiers talk. If an army has secrets, best not entrust them to soldiers. Elias McCutcheon's own men tell it on him that the General knocked one of his officers overboard while taking his command over the river. And the poor young fellow, who had come from a good family, was drowned!

They tell citizens and they tell prisoners before they are paroled. And as they seem fond of saying, if Elias would do that to his own, what *might* he do to his enemies?

Days fall one upon another moving towards Christmas. The fury of the brigade is such that they oversee destruction of every bridge and trestle on the railroad. It seems a hard thing to folk round about as know the awful expense and terrible trial it was for men to build those fragile, spindling spans in this midst of so much swamp and wilderness. How many years did people wait and dream about the wonder of a railroad? A long time, and the graves of the Irish are still here and there along the way and show how much death there was in all that building.

And it seems to folk that God himself must punish men as would treat the railroad thus and they are not backward about telling the soldiers that winding blue columns of infantry are tramping this way on the roads from Memphis and a reliable man in Kentucky during the course of a cold ten hours' vigil counted no less than two hundred steamers on the river, troop transports jam-packed to the rails with General Grant's soldiers. Keep on at burning the railroad, they say, and see if more winding columns of blue don't come down after you from Kentucky. Not as folk were so much for the Union, nor against the Confederacy, no; but burning the railroad seemed to them a hard thing. And maybe they draw a little cold comfort and satisfaction from telling the soldiers that the Yankees are building fires too, east a way on all the creeks and rivers. The Yankees have burned the ferries and the bridges so that when Elias McCutcheon's men try to break out and make their way east again, they'll find themselves trapped and hemmed up and at the mercy of those tramping columns of infantry.

Chapter 12

It was said, through all those furious days, that Somerton at least, was safe. The General, after all, hailed from Sligo County, and had his home there, near Somerton. He'd not foul his nest. The blue soldiers in Somerton that guarded the depot and saluted their officers on the street in front of the hotel, and marched about up and down Fort Hill just as soldiers had done there once long ago, could be sure they had nothing to worry about. Elias was a friend to Somerton. He'd not clatter up his horses in that direction and shell the stockade and burn the depot and destroy those nice archways there by the station tracks, for that waiting room with those archways was brand-new, spanking new, and just saw itself completed before the war began and was connected to the old depot that was still yellow, whereas the new building was alabaster white and made passengers sit up and take notice. Even the blue soldiers said those arches were as remarkable as anything in Illinois or Iowa or even Wisconsin and Minnesota.

And it seems the proportion of officers to enlisted men is remarkable too, just at this glorious season. The hotel is full of officers. T. Laird's got officers. Madam Fanny Parham's got officers. It's more than Somerton can do just to keep up with so much laundering and cooking and barbering. Somerton, it seems, is a sort of winter spa lately. Lieutenants and majors and colonels everywhere . . .

But the blow fell. Was it one of those terrible mistakes? Could it have been an oversight? Were those gray furies Confederates that stormed in from two directions, west and east?

It's hardly daylight. Yesternight was Christmas. The rattle of small arms is angry. The blue soldiers are furious. Citizens crawl under their beds. Officers leap out of windows and try to leave by the back way only to be chased down by men on horseback that have no respect for kitchen gardens and fences and the persons of gentlemen in blue britches and nightshirts.

The stockade, the warehouse, the depot, the supply wagons — all are so quickly and expertly gutted and ripped and set fire to — that some can't halfway realize so much destruction could befall a community of peaceable citizens, much less those nice gentleman soldiers that seemed to be living here like guests and bothered nobody.

So they said it was all a mistake. It's some grievous error.

That big fellow with the muscles of a young man, and his skin all red-brown with winter tan, himself all sad and scarred and scratched-like, and smells of whiskey and tobacco and gunpowder and dried blood — not unpleasant at all, mind — but he looks like a regular ruffian, and has a powerful, forlorn look and sends men bucketing in every direction with a look or a nod, or a frown. Some say it's Elias — the General himself.

And a thing happens in front of the hotel. One of the blue soldiers unholsters his pistol and cracks down on that burly fellow while others with more sense than he are trying to surrender. The Confederate turns his horse aside just a hair and kills that blue soldier, shoots him stone dead with a pistol ball through the neck no less, outright as murder. And some say it's Elias himself.

Yet when people wear uniforms and stay so much in the saddle that they live outdoors, their appearance changes. They don't look like themselves. They seem to be something else, and the difference is fearful sometimes. The difference can come as an awful surprise.

Citizens that had all along carried it in their heads that if ever they saw Elias they'd caution him not to burn the depot and give him what for about such wanton destruction of the railroad and ask him by God *why*, when West Tennessee was so peacefully and even in some instances *profitably* occupied with nice neat fellows in blue uniforms, *why* he'd come this way and stir up trouble? They have thought all along that they would let him try to talk his way out of that one. Now that they've got the chance the cat's got their tongue.

Yet a couple of blacksmiths at Wall Stuart's livery stable aren't so backward as their whitefolks. They've heard things. For one, they'll be free men as soon as ever the first day of January comes, for Mister Linkum has signed a paper that makes it so. For another, they've been treated well by the blue soldiers that have told them they were as good as free.

Now these men in brown butternut and gray and every sort of clothes, all ratty and muddy like something wild out of the woods, they've come and they want horses shod right away. It seems they have not heard of that paper signed by Mister Linkum.

The blacksmiths fold their arms. And one, braver than the other, speaks up. He says,

"See all of you in hell before I'll shoe a Rebel horse."

"Best not let the General hear you've said that.'

"General? General *who*? General *what*?"

Someone has to go tell the General that they've got trouble with Wall Stuart's servants. And it's no secret what servants are worth, especially expert farriers. Two and a half thousand wouldn't buy even one of them and Wall owns a pair of them, a matched brace, as it were; they're the pride of Somerton. Folks stand a little in awe of black men with so much skill and always will stand aside for them a little bit.

"Hang them."

Have they heard right?

Back they go to the stable. And Wall Stuart himself, who's the mayor and has been on the verge of going off to war *himself* all this while but hasn't quite been able, not just yet, to get his business in order so he can leave it, has got wind of something. Where has Wall been all this while? Nobody knows, but he appears now and countermands the order. Maybe Wall's been in his own loft and fell asleep up there and is such a sound sleeper he hasn't heard a thing until now. He's got a little hay in his hair at any rate and he stares the poor little soldiers down and says nobody will hang *his* servants. Go tell *Elias* that. Hasn't he known *Elias* all these years?

"Better if you told him," says a little private.

"Well, by God, so I will!" And people get a look at Wall Stuart with little bits of hay sticking to him, walking down to the hotel and wanting a *word* with Elias McCutcheon. Wall goes straight inside the hotel, by God.

Silence.

Wall Stuart comes out of the hotel, but not alone. He's under guard and looks strangely pale. The first citizen of Somerton, marched like a rogue, his depot in flames, Somerton's hospitality violated and a servant money can't buy hanged dead by the neck . . .

The remaining one, however, got to work and began shoeing Rebel horses. Not only that, but Wall himself decided to put on an apron. It isn't so long ago that he's forgotten his trade, it seems. Besides, he's pleased to do anything he can to help the General.

Elias?

Why no, he'd not say *Elias*. He's the General, says Wall, and anybody as knows the first thing about military etiquette must be aware of the proper way to speak of a general when he comes to visit.

Yet it may be as Wall is somewhat disappointed. It may be as all of Somerton feels as though it's been failed by its hero.

As someone remarks, it's a strange fellow that will burn his own cotton. Doesn't he know that's some of his own money tied up in those bales? Hasn't someone surely whispered that fact to Elias?

T. Laird and Madam Fanny Parham both take to their beds. Just when all was going so well for them, just when the sting of these strange hostilities had begun to abate for them somewhat, Elias appears and sends all of it, thousands and thousands, straight up in smoke.

Then, as suddenly as he had come, he went away again and never so much as told anyone goodbye, no. He didn't make apologies. He didn't leave them with any comfortable words. He marched seven hundred humiliated prisoners away and took all their horses. And he's got a great list of captured officers entirely disproportionate to so small a garrison.

He's got to get out to Pinoak, it seems, and burn their cotton and kill their blue soldiers and set their little depot on fire. That's his work for that afternoon. Just look a bit east in the right direction and you can see the smoke and be sure that Pinoak hasn't got it any better than Somerton.

On the next day, which was the twenty-seventh, Wall Stuart called together his Vigilance Committee and packed off nearly a dozen skulkers and cowards with orders to get straightway through the lines and join the Confederate army. He was tired of seeing so many slackers and laggards, he said, and he hinted again that he would go himself just as soon as he could, but he was shorthanded just now, and was having to wear an apron himself, since "the accident."

Chapter 13

Heavy work for Elias, but there was heavier work yet ahead. Putting Dutt in temporary charge of the brigade and giving Tug Chambers orders as to how the prisoners must be paroled, Elias had ridden out on the cold road, heading for Oakleigh, burdened with what he must tell when he got there.

Coming into the yard before Jake's house Elias shouted and sprang down. Jake appeared in the cabin doorway. "Hoped it was you!" says Jake, and took the horse. "Miss Jane most likely in her room."

"We're on the march east. I haven't much time. Jake?"

"Sah?"

"Willy — he was killed."

"How? God, no —"

"By our own troops, as he approached a bridge."

"Naw!" cried Jake. "Naw!" He reeled and bent over with weeping. Startled, the horse shied.

Elias turned and sprinted for the house, up the wide front stairs. He pushed open the front door and hurried into the hall.

"Jane?"

He saw Leola.

"It's the Master," says Leola. "The Master!"

"Where's Jane?"

"Upstairs of course, in her own room. What's wrong? What is it? Jake?"

But Elias was on the stairs, running up them. In the hall he stopped and then made himself walk to Jane's door.

"Come in," came her voice, answering his knock.

He saw her scar. Her hair was down. She was sitting up in bed.

"Who is it?"

"Elias," he said. His voice was unsure. Going to the bed he took both her hands in his own and kissed her. "We've lost Willy," he said.

"Willy's hurt?"

"Killed."

From the hall below came Leola's shrill grief-cries. Leola appeared with Jake and Sallie.

Jane's hands trembled and went icy cold. She held to Elias, drawing him down against her, as though wanting him to shield her from something.

"How and where," she said at last. "Leave nothing out." And she pushed him back that she might see his face as he told her.

"Had he anything to say?"

"He sent his love to Sallie."

Sallie gave a choked cry. "He won't see his baby!"

So she's expecting — Elias bethought himself then to lie. "And to you —" he said to Jane. "And Leola."

Leola's shrill wailing rose again, muffled now. The old woman had stuffed her skirt in her mouth.

"Naw!" Jake wept. "*Naw!*"

In the hall more servants were gathering and weeping.

"And what else," said Jane. "You saw him buried?"

"Yes. We'll fetch him home after the war."

"Fetch him here, yes," says Jane. "But where was he struck?"

"In the chest, the side, the stomach, and in his leg, here," and Elias showed the place on his own leg, taking his hand from Jane's grip.

"His poor leg again," says Jane. Her body was trembling. She picked up a towel and damped the spittle on her cheek.

"I told you this would happen," says Leola.

"Bring me his letters," says Jane. "I want to read them again. Have we any laudanum? Some of that, if we have any."

Sallie, almost a stranger here, Sallie who knew Willy the least of anyone here, but who was closest to him after all, came forward. Elias put his arm about her. "What will I do now?" says Sallie.

"You'll go on living," says Jane in her flat voice.

"Have your baby here," says Elias.

Looking to Elias Jane said: "How long can you stay?"

"I must leave now and go back to the brigade."

"Have you killed a great many?"

"Yes."

"Good," says Jane.

"Well, goodbye."

"Just kiss me goodbye," says Jane. "It's bad enough without a hard leave-taking. Just a kiss, Elias. Kill as many of them as you can."

When he kissed her he felt the coldness of her lips. Dotty was at the foot of the bed with a tray. "The laudanum and whiskey?" said Dotty.

"Here!" cried Leola. "Let me have that and get back in the hall where you belong!" With quavery hands Leola mixed the potion in a silver cup. She handed it to Jane, who, taking the cup, drank down the contents without once lowering it.

"Goodbye." Elias kissed her again.

"Farewell," said Jane in a dull voice. "Farewell, my Elias. Leola, you and Sallie remain until I'm asleep."

"Yes-yes," said Leola. And then: "I'll fetch the letters."

Elias went out. The weeping servants stepped aside. Jake was ahead of him and held his horse. Bleak weather and a bleak season at Oakleigh. It all seemed strange, like a house belonging to someone else. Sounds of weeping came from the house. The dogs were howling in the kennels. Across the river a hawk went hunting over dun-colored fields.

"I hope you luck," said Jake.

"Look after them for me," says Elias, and he went galloping away.

Chapter 14

Hiding by day, riding by night, Dutt calculated it was twelve days straight in the saddle for the brigade, twelve days of hiding and dodging and working east again, making for the Tennessee River.

Tuesday, bright and clear, the General gave Dutt his instructions. He would take two companies and scout a parallel road angling through the half-flooded bottoms.

Elias meanwhile would push forward with the brigade on the main road.

As Dutt put his foot in the stirrup Elias stepped in beside his horse. "Find a bridge. Look for shallows we can ford."

Dutt raised his hand and rode out at the head of his column. The road went straight at first and then began winding and uneventful, skirting horseshoe lakes and letting then into higher land. Here lonely farms lay.

At noon the patrol reached a crossroads village. They passed white clapboard houses and a line of shops and two general stores that faced a railroad line that slanted away over a timbered trestle spanning a deep, narrow creekbed.

Dutt ordered his incendiaries to fire the trestle. He set one company to work laying fence rails on the track to fire and buckle the rails while the other company stood guard.

Looking about he saw that although the inhabitants here had Confederate flags and waved them, they still and all stayed on their porches and soon went back indoors again. They were plainly borderers; some doubtless had men in both armies. Looking about, Dutt could see in the faces of his men that they shared his own uncomfortable feeling.

Dutt questioned a constable. He was defaced by moles and wore a string tie with a soiled white shirt and a stovepipe hat. His long overcoat had buttons missing. His homespun trousers were frayed. He reached inside his coat and hitched at his suspenders.

"Naw, sir. Ain't seen a sign of no soldiers 'cept you fellows," he said. The thin sunlight made his blue eyes watery. "Hope you good luck," said the constable. Dutt and his troopers mounted again and passed on through town. On the other side of it they stopped at the creek, took saddles off, and watered and rested their horses and ate their cold noon rations. Dutt kept to himself.

"And I thought," said the boy nearby, who did not look to be sixteen years old, "— all the damn fightin' would be done by now!"

"Where's your mule?" his buddy replied.

"Shit," said the first one.

Dutt sighed. What would the main column be encountering now? he wondered.

In midafternoon Dutt had heard dull sounds of bombardment just south aways and guessed what it must be. He called a halt, and filled his pipe. The ominous thudding sounds gave him pause.

He saw the strange look in other faces and knew it must be

like the one he was wearing himself. The temptation was to saddle up and head straight back to the brigade, but he had three days' cooked rations. It didn't do to disobey Elias.

The captains and the lieutenants gathered around him. The enlisted ranks stood apart at a little distance, listening.

When the firing stopped Dutt waited a while before he called for saddles. How many were dead by now? How many had lost arms and legs? Would the living be prisoners now? Would an escaped remnant be pushing out this way, maybe?

They took the road again.

A private reined in beside him and asked permission to return to the brigade. His brother was back there, he said. He could ride back and see what had happened, switch horses, and rejoin the column by nightfall.

Dutt wanted to say yes. The complete silence after such a stretch of dull thudding had begun filling him with a morbid tincture of dread. He felt as though a thousand little poison tongues were lapping and drinking from his bloodstream. Yet if he needlessly used up a horse there would be hell to pay. There was no way of estimating what Elias McCutcheon might do, for Elias maintained that the welfare of the riding stock was the difference between life and death, between whipping the enemy and getting whipped by him.

Even as he sat weltered by indecision, Dutt knew a squadron of blue cavalry could be on his trail. Indeed, the more he thought about it, the more real those pursuers became. He felt as though guns were already pointed at him. He found himself gazing about, and looking down the ridge behind, in the full expectation that the last rays of the sun would catch the glint of drawn sabers.

"Be back t'night," said the private, taking Dutt's silence for assent. "Captain said it was *fine* with him if you didn't object."

"Bring a complete report," Dutt heard himself say. "But mind and don't ruin your horse . . ."

The boy had already turned and was dashing away down the length of the column as fast as his horse would go.

Dutt doubled the number of vedettes riding behind and in advance of the column. He put six riders in the woods on each side of the road to scan the low ridges and keep a sharp lookout; but he was still uneasy.

He didn't stop to rest until well after sundown.

Then he lay down with his saddle for a pillow, fully clothed. He woke and untangled the blanket which had caught on his spurs, and lying back down again he saw that the stars had moved since he was last awake. His mouth was dry and his bladder was full. When he stood up his head began to throb. He unbuttoned his trousers and pissed against a tree trunk, a long, painful process. With so much riding it didn't do to drink a great deal of water before lying down, but his fear had increased his thirst. He found the canteen, opened it, and took a mouthful of water and swished it around in his mouth. It had a stale, woody taste. He spat it out and stuck one pistol in his holster, one in the belt, and thrust two inside his blouse. Then he made his way to the road and asked the men on guard about the private.

"No sir. Not a sign of him, Major."

Dutt sat down beside the road. He dozed off and didn't know anything until he heard voices and opened his eyes and saw that the sky was red and that the guards were talking to a man on horseback. It was the private.

"Over here," Dutt said. "What happened?"

The boy approached. He was leading his horse. He leaned forward peering at Dutt. His face was indistinct.

"Major? That you?"

"Yes. What took you so long?"

"You said not to ruin a horse."

"Well, what happened?"

"Aw, just a sorta ambush. Some Yanks threw a few shells is all and then left."

"Anybody hurt?"

"Nossir. Nobody got a scratch. We kilt some of theirs though."

"Just what I figured," Dutt said. "I knew it was wasted effort to send you back there. Could tell by the sound of things it wasn't serious. Well, you saw your brother at least. Anything else?"

"Orders from General McCutcheon. Nearly forgot."

He handed the paper to Dutt. "Much obliged," Dutt said, taking it. He felt quivery inside from lack of sleep. He stood up slowly and stretched.

"Major. Just want to say thanks. For lettin' me go back, I mean. It's relieved my mind."

"Well, I knew there wasn't anything to it. When there's something to it it has a different sound. No mistaking the real thing. Didn't hurt for you to go back though. Didn't lame the horse, did you?"

"No, sir!"

A captain approached and asked if the men would be allowed fires so as to have a warm breakfast.

"Fires? Yes now that it's light. But tell them mind and not make a lot of smoke. Small fires, yes . . ."

"Thank you, sir." The captain saluted and turned away and a moment later it was shouted around that small fires were permitted. The camp began to stir. Smells of frying bacon brought Dutt back to himself. Two hoecakes were stuck on his saber and propped over the coals.

Remembering the dispatch he took it out of his blouse and opened it. "Proceed at once to original crossing. Way is open."

"Boots and saddles!" he called. "Let's get it!"

There was just time to eat his hoecakes. A trooper brought his horse around and put on the saddle. Dutt stood up and dusted the seat of his britches.

"Mount up and move out!" Down the slope he rode at the head of the column. He reached behind him to check the neat roll of his blanket.

When they entered the Titus Road that afternoon he put out his flankers and his advance guard. His scouts turned off the road on either side and soon disappeared. He kept a slow pace. Sensing that the direction was east, his horse had to be held in; Dutt felt him straining to be let out, he danced along sideways now and then.

They had gone five miles at a slow walk when the road curved upward through a cut in a thickly wooded hill. Dutt was almost to the gap when the woods on both sides of him, just at the dark edges, flashed red and belched smoke. A ripple of gunfire smacked in from both sides and smote horses and men. The column reeled and while horses collided and saddles were emptied the murderous flashes continued to wink up and down like a series of slumberous eyes, blood-red. The gelding spun. A black, riderless horse backed into him and then went to its knees and rolled slowly down as though sagging beneath invisible weight. As the gelding continued to turn Dutt saw a string of riders sweeping towards him down the road from the gap — the advance guard. On they came, crashing past him into the confused mass. The column swayed and squirmed, trampling back and forth, and milling in upon itself. The woods seemed to turn slowly around. There was a rumbling, like grindstones and the air all about whispered and popped with the sound of a thousand little whips crackety-cracking and it swelled to a roar, like fine gravel pouring against taut canvas . . .

Tug Chambers rode in beside him. "Dismount us so we can fight!" he cried.

All around meanwhile the column took losses. Dead, dying and wounded lay in the road. Dutt's horse began to buck. He hauled back on the reins. The gelding reared up and walked on two legs. Dutt raked his spurs down the gelding's sides and brought him down to four legs again. Driving spurs into him he headed him up the sloping road and felt his black-plumed hat fall away. He had lost his right stirrup meanwhile. He leaned down against the horse's neck, caught the flailing stirrup and jammed his foot firmly into it again. When he looked up he was rounding out of the cut. As he crested the hill he saw what first appeared to be a fence barring the road. As the distance closed what he had taken for posts became men in blue uniforms — a Yankee skirmish line. He drew a pistol. It snapped and snapped again, popping caps, failing to ignite the powder and at the same moment it came that the men in front waiting for him would shoot him dead, for he rode straight for them armed with four pistols each primed with damp gunpowder.

So this, he thought, was how death came. The line ahead of him parted like a ribbon. There was a flash, then a series of flashes. Heat seared the side of his face and singed his hair. Yet he was not hit and when he finally dared turn in the saddle for a glance back of him he saw remnants of his column stringing down the slope, coming after him.

He didn't look back again. He set spurs to the gelding's sides and rode for dear life. His heart pounded so hard it felt sucked up into his throat.

Chapter 15

October. The winds that blow in that month had begun, those strong and steady gales that bring no rain with them, but seem rather to burnish the skies. And the geese had started coming down by night. Jane heard them in her sleep. During those bright, burnished days she sat on her own high porch sometimes and watched the long strings of mallards sailing down out of the northern reaches of the sky, and the hawks came sweeping and circling on the wind, coming by pairs and scaling to great heights.

She was there, sitting at midmorning one day when she saw eight soldiers on horseback coming up the road beside the river. She had gotten a letter from Isaac that day, brought down by a wounded soldier. And the letter only said that there had been fighting about Chattanooga and that in the fighting Elias had lost one man of every four from his command, but that Isaac and their father had not been hurt, all in a letter written in September. And seeing those soldiers she thought of Isaac's letter. The cavalcade rode in beside the creek, past the millpond and disappeared in the vicinity of the slave cabins.

Wondering what it meant, she stood up and shaded her eyes. She heard faint shouting. The hunting hounds began to bay from the kennels. When at long last the soldiers reappeared, they were galloping, going back the way they had come, and raising a racket as they poured back into the road and disappeared in the direction from which she had first seen them.

She heard running then, on the stairs, and voices beyond in the halls. Then Rance and Leola appeared on the porch and began to shout. The soldiers had taken the meat from the smokehouse down by the quarters and had run into the cabins snatching up things and breaking them. She must come right away and see for herself what they had done.

"You don't do something about it and they'll be here next!" Leola said.

They waked Sallie with so much commotion. She came to the porch and asked what it was. She had plaited her hair into a single dark braid and her face wore the soft expression that sleep always brought to it.

Jane put her hand to her cheek . . . to that silk patch.

"They'll be here next," Leola said, but there was no savagery in her voice now. She spoke, instead, in a low, husky tone and shaded her eyes for a look at the road.

"But why would they rob the servants?" Sallie said. She wore a little gray gown with lace at her collar and lace about her sleeves which stopped just at the elbows. Her gray gown was hiked up in the front and showed her soft little black slippers when she walked and she was very pretty, and the baby in her was carried high as though the girl were proud of it, as indeed she was, and she wore a little necklace of white pearls about her neck, a gift from her dead husband, Willy.

"They don't dare come here quite yet," said Jane, holding her cheek. "They must work up to it."

Rance had been polishing brass. He wore his black butler's

apron over his clean white shirt which he had turned up at the cuffs. The apron came almost to his knees and he had on his second-best black trousers and his second-best black shoes and he smelled of vinegar and gripped the cloth he had been using, in his left hand, as though he didn't know it was there. He was staring at Jane and he said,

"What must we do? Miss Jane?"

He was a house servant, nothing else. His life was given over to the care of the house and to the people and the things in it. His voice and his manner seemed to say: "Instruct me and I will protect everything."

"Find Jake and Rufe and fetch them to the kitchen."

Rance nodded. *Now,* said this nod, *something is being done!* And he left the porch.

"Ho!" says Leola. "What can they do?" She gave a sniff. "With the men all gone away to war, didn't I know it would come to this? Can Jake do anything? Didn't I know what *he* was the day we found that book!"

"Hush," said Jane. She was wondering how it could be that Elias was gone. For hadn't he, always and always it seemed, been by her when she needed him? No fright was too awful and no hurt was too much if only she had him here to help. A silent voice inside her was calling him to come in from the dusk, to leave the field and come along and wash up, to rinse his face and his arms there by the barrel outside, to come in and see what a neat design she had drawn on the dirt floor with a pointed stick, and to see what a nice dinner she had cooked for just the two of them, as she knelt at her own hearth, before the firelight . . .

She went down to the kitchen. When she got there Rufe and Jake, who had been in the fields where the hands were picking cotton, were waiting. Their faces were without expression. Their clothes were stained with work and they smelled of it. They didn't look at her but sat where they were, on those chairs Elias himself had built and made, and they had their hands in their laps and were looking down. Rance stood with his arms folded across the chest of his apron, and was leaning against the cupboard door. He was staring at the floor. He still held that polishing cloth. His hand was trembling.

Jake spoke without looking up. He said,

"They trampled over the turnip patches. Broke in the smokehouse fer hams and shoulders. Then the next blow fell. They went in the cabins, busted doors, knocked panes out the windows, emptied the flour and the meal on the floors and tracked through it and turned the sick from they beds. Ripped open the mattresses."

"Did they touch your house?" she asked Jake.

"No, ma'am. Just in the cabins."

"They slapped my wife," Rufe said. "Called her a black bitch and slapped her so her mouth is bleedin' and her sick. Dumped her on the floor. Broke ever'thing in my cabin. Took my weddin' watch and chain and all our spoons."

"Who were they and where from?" Jane waited.

"Yankees outta that bunch in Somerton," said Jake, finally. "From Somerton and no place else." He paused. "And another thing."

"What else?" said Jane.

"They took and busted every gun they could find. So they got nothin' down there to hunt with and here it is almost time for them to hunt. So there went meat this winter — every gun busted."

And Rufe said: "Told my wife if they come back next time and found a gun that whatever place it was in they would burn that place to the ground. Then they busted my shotgun all to pieces." Rufe shook his head sadly.

"Jake?"

"Ma'am?"

"Leave the women to work at the picking with the children. Bring in your grown men, hitch wagons enough, and empty what's left in the smokehouse and take the meat and wrap it and hide it in the hay. Cull the livestock. Leave a few old cows, old mules, old horses. Drive the rest away into the bottoms. Hide them and leave men to watch them."

"Put 'em in the canebrakes," said Rufe.

"Yes." Jake and Rufe left.

Jane turned to Rance. "Put the silver and the best china underground — you and Leola and Dolly. And then come down to the cabins and help. I'll be there with Miss Sallie. And hide our guns and fetch Jake's guns and hide them."

"Yes'm. But if we hide the guns what will we shoot them with to drive them away if they try to come into this house and harm it? How can we kill them?"

"They have too many. We could never kill them all."

"Then what's to become of us, Miss Jane?"

Leola walked in with Dotty behind her. They had put the table silver in cotton baskets which they carried in front of them against their stomachs. They gripped the hand holds, leaning back away from their burdens and swaying from side to side as they struggled through and eased the baskets down side by side upon the brick floor, near the stove. They turned and looked at Jane, as though waiting to hear what answer she might make. Jane put her hand to the silk patch. It was soaked through and had begun to drip saliva on the bodice of her gown. She took a handkerchief from her sleeve and she felt a dark wave trying to rise inside of her. She tried to push it down.

"You sick?" It was Leola. "Sit down here . . ."

"No . . . I'll manage. We'll all manage. We've always managed somehow."

She sat down. The dark wave tried to rise again. Leola put vinegar on a handkerchief and wet her temples. Jane closed her eyes.

"There now," says Leola, speaking kindly, in a husky voice. "I'm here, yes. Leola's here!"

Jane smelled the vinegar. It was like a taste in her mouth. She mustn't be weak. She mustn't show fear. She must not set a wrong example for others. All the years of her life were calling on her to be strong, to struggle. She wondered how long she could bear up. She gritted her teeth and felt a burning sensation in her lungs. That inner voice was calling Elias again, a voice crying into dusk, a sound swallowed in twilight, in years and memories. God help, hadn't she had enough? Must there be more? *Elias . . . Elias . . . Elias.* She must stand up and go down to the quarters now and hearten the sick and the children. She must set everything right and tell one and all that this was only what was to be expected in war.

Chapter 16

When Jane woke the next morning the wind was blowing as it had the day before, and again she had heard geese passing low over the house. Leola brought her breakfast and Jane ate but little. Instead of coffee there was only hot water which had been boiled with burnt corn kernels. She could not drink it and when she asked Leola about Jake the old woman said that he must have stayed overnight at Shokotee's plantation. He had not returned as yet. Sallie was still sleeping, Leola said.

When Jane listened she could hear the wind. When she looked out she saw the same hard, blue burnished sky. Beyond the river some of the trees shone yellow, like dull brass. The little packet steamer no longer came now and the river had a wild look. The landing was deserted and on the shore willows and grass and cattails had grown up, and the wind came bending them all in a single direction. Looking at Leola, who had helped her bathe, and who had brushed her hair and tied a clean patch on her face, Jane said,

"I think sometimes I hear the packet steamer."

"No, no. It was taken at Memphis and was burned. You know it was burned." And Leola coughed a nervous cough.

"But I think I hear it. Listen. Do you hear it, Leola?"

"It's the wind only," says Leola. And she put away the ivory-handled brush.

"I wish it would come. We need coffee. We could walk down that way and go on board."

"Nevermind," says Leola. "It will come again. They will build another one, you'll see. The new one will be prettier."

"Seems to me I hear it now and then."

"You hear your memory of it," says the old woman. And she went to the doors leading out upon the high porch and opened them. The hinges made a moan. "Come and sit out here and try not to let your mind worry," says Leola.

And Jane went out and she sat down and saw how the leaves all flew spinning in one direction and Leola stood by her for a while and held her hand. "Try not to worry your mind," says Leola.

"I see a hawk," Jane said. And she shaded her eyes with her left hand. She could not see the mate. There seemed to be but one bird, only one scaling the wind. She looked for a long time but could not see a second hawk riding the wind south. "One alone, all by itself," she said. The dark wave was trying to rise inside her. She bent forward and closed her eyes and pushed that darkness down again until she could breathe.

"What day is it?"

"Wednesday," says Leola.

Thursday.

And the wind which has been blowing all in one direction has stopped during the night and this still day seems to take a step backwards into summer.

Soldiers, blue-clad, on foot and soldiers on horseback and they have a supply wagon with them, drawn by four horses and they turn first and go down past the millpond to the slave quarters and begin the work there.

While going about the work a cabin is set on fire. Three soldiers walk out on the milldam with their rifles and begin firing at the geese. The geese swim in a line upon the still surface of the millpond. When a goose is hit its white wings fan out on either side and the long neck stretches out and rests upon the water. The wings flutter a moment, and the bird is still.

When they are finished in the quarters the soldiers come to Jake's house and drag out the furniture and the bedding. They break out the windows.

Jane stands on the porch at Oakleigh with Sallie. Leola stands in the hall, just inside. Rance, who asked about guns and spoke of driving the soldiers away, cannot be found anywhere. Rance is gone since morning. There are no servants at Oakleigh but Leola, standing just there in the hall.

The soldiers cross the lawn and trample the flowerbeds and stand in a bunch below the porch steps. Then their wagon comes and is drawn up below the steps in the driveway.

Jane puts her hand to her cheek. Two soldiers with bayonets on the ends of their rifles climb the steps. The boldest one is no bigger than Willy and no older than Willy, her lost Willy . . . Jane can smell his heat and the sour-sweet of whiskey on his young breath. His cheeks are red and his face has a stiff, swollen look to it. His eyes roll a little and he says,

"Inside. Place hasta be searched. Inside!"

Sallie goes in the house ahead of Jane and her heels make a sound as she runs up the stairs.

Following those first two the other soldiers come now and walk in boldly and seem not to notice Jane and Leola. Soldiers enter the library and begin taking down books. At first they merely look at them. Then one decides he will take the books and he goes out to the wagon with an armload. The books are thrown down. There is a scuffle in the library. The tables are overturned. Two soldiers come into the hall dragging a rug . . .

The first young soldier, the same bold one no bigger than Willy, finds Jane again. "Upstairs!" he says, and motions with that gun and that long bayonet. Jane and Leola climb the stairs ahead of him. Below then in the hall something is smashed. Pieces of something scatter on the floor. Jane looks down into the hall. Two soldiers are carrying the hall clock between them. Held thus, longways, it looks like a coffin. Through the front doors comes a soldier leading a horse. The horse stamps nervously. Soldier and horse disappear into the dining room.

Jane goes to her own room with Leola. The young soldier follows, and when Jane sits down he goes to the dressing table and begins opening drawers and rummaging. Leola stands beside Jane's chair, watching.

"Thieves," says Leola.

"Hush, Leola."

"Thieves," says the old woman again.

The young soldier wears a look of dreaming preoccupation. He takes the ivory-handled brush in his hand, drops it on the floor and picks up the comb. He puts the comb in his pocket, goes to the chest of drawers in the corner and pulls open the drawer at the bottom and begins pushing and probing with his right hand while he grips the rifle with his left, propping the gun butt on the floor beside his dusty shoe. He stands up with something.

Jane looks. He holds a packet of letters, old letters tied with a faded ribbon.

"No!" says Jane. Leaping up she runs to him and snatches the letters away from him and holds them with both hands. "These are my husband's!"

"Give 'em here," says the boy. Still holding the gun he lunges, grabs her wrist, and then lets go suddenly and tries to fend Leola away. The old woman is flogging him with a brass poker. He raises the gun butt and strikes Leola squarely in the chest with it and staggers her backwards. Then he turns on Jane. "That's money," he says. "I know what that is! Drop it!"

"No!" says Jane. The boy seems to duck. She sees blood on his forehead and something strikes her in the side. She lets the packet fall and looks down and he jerks the blade backwards out of her and is down, reaching for the letters again, when Leola, old and dark, and wraithlike in her black dress, strikes again with the poker, at the back of the neck this time, holding the heavy brass rod as though it were an ax. He slumps down flat. The rifle clatters beside him. Leola strikes again and again. "*No!*" Jane whispers.

"*Ai-ai-ai!*" Leola yells. "Ho! Now hit me! Thief? Are you sleeping? This thief is asleep."

She drops the poker beside the boy and gathers up her

dress and picks up the packet of letters and looks down at the boy and says,

"Read our Master's mail, would you? Pry after him, eh?" And she turns to Jane. "Here," she says. Then she sees something. "What? Hurt?"

Jane nods, holding her side with both hands now, still standing somehow. Leola reaches for her. Jane feels a terrible ripping, a tearing through her insides. She screams and Leola begins to drag her, dragging her into the hallway while she screams. She begs Leola to let go. Leola drags her, mumbling, and pauses at the top of the stairs. Smells of smoke!

"Soldier! Soldier!" cries the old woman. "You, soldier! Come here!"

"Just let me lie still," says Jane. "Put me on my bed, Leola."

"And let the place burn down around the both of us?" says Leola. And then: "Soldier! Help!"

Hands grab Jane on all sides. A blue brightness, as burnished almost as the October sky, flashes from her side and spreads suddenly upwards before her eyes and something very heavy pushes her out of herself and she is suddenly riding on a dark wave and the crash of it becomes a steady roar in her ears. Then she hears the cry of the wild geese, passing high above, from beyond that darkness . . .

Chapter

17

Nightfall. The soldiers have gone. Oakleigh is still burning, but it has long since fallen in upon itself and the nearest trees have exploded in flames, those that shaded the porches. The heat is such that it reaches the whole way to Jake's cabin.

Leola has managed. All by herself she's gotten an old bed inside against the wall where Elias and Jane once had a bed before, and she's dragged Jane in and put her upon it. All by herself Leola, who was surely so old she could not count all her years, had set the bed up and gotten Jane upon it and had packed a damp cloth against that dark puncture in Jane's side.

But it was death that was coming to Jane anyway. Leola knew. She felt it coming. She sat beside the bed and watched Oakleigh burning down to dust beyond the broken window.

Once she thought she saw the evil spirit. She saw eyes and horns and a head and her blood had seemed to freeze. But when she could finally look away and then look back she saw it was only a cow come to look at the fire, curious-like, and to poke her head through the smashed window to see what she could smell.

"Git!" Leola had cried. "Git!" And the cow had wandered away and was no sooner gone than Leola was sorry she had not gone out and tried to catch it and pen it up somehow or tie it, for today had told her that cows would be scarce again . . .

Jane stirred. She muttered something. Then in a clear, sudden voice she called,

"Elias?"

"It's only me, Leola," said the old woman. "The Master, he's away."

"Where is Elias? Elias?"

"No, it's only me. He's at the wars, gone away just as I said would happen."

Jane groaned and stirred again. "His food will get cold," she said. "If he doesn't come soon, it will."

"The wars take them and they never return again," Leola said. "There was a cow just here but I never thought to catch her. Then we could have had some milk."

"Elias?"

Leola couldn't push her tears back any longer. She took Jane's hand in both of her old and knobby ones. And Jane said:

"There you are . . . where have you been? At the fence — you work too hard. Do sit down. Hold my hand, Elias."

Jane breathed a long sigh. Her hand tightened in Leola's hands, and she died.

Chapter 18

Sallie had gone straight up the front stairs, down the long hall, and down the backstairs to the kitchen. Finding no place there to hide, she went through the back porch and down the steps into the yard and then walked straightaway from the house, past the icehouse and into the fields.

She had no thought other than to protect the life she carried inside her. She knew nothing else but to flee, and like a creature of the wilds she ran until she reached the oak. There she hid herself for a while and rested on a mass of honeysuckle vines.

When she saw smoke rising from the house she began to tremble. Scrambling up, she began to cross the long series of cleared fields that fell away north towards the bottoms. She ran and walked by turns and each time she stopped to look back the smoke above the big house was darker than before. When she had crossed the last field and entered the edge of the woods she turned for one last look. The smoke was a towering column now, black and seemingly motionless. It was like a dead thing painted upon the horizon. She promised herself that she would not look back. Imagining that someone must have seen her and that the soldiers would soon be following, she went straight into the woods. The leaves made a crisp autumn carpet. She walked on and on; she must take herself safely beyond reach of those horrors.

And at last it seemed that nothing and no one could follow and find her and she stopped by a fallen tree and sat down on the trunk and began pulling the cockleburs from the skirts of her gray dress. She searched until she had found and pulled away and thrown down the last burr. Next she unbuckled her slippers and took them off and emptied them and brushed off the bottoms of her stockings before putting the slippers on again. Then, feeling rested, she began to walk again. She went slowly and when she stopped she held her breath to listen.

There was nothing but the sound of birds. Nothing else. "I'm lost," she said. And she felt that she ought to pray. Her voice seemed small and strange to her and she wished Willy were here. She thought of her mother and of Jane and Leola, and she wished for them. It seemed every time she stopped to listen that she would surely hear someone calling her. It wouldn't be like them to let her be lost for long. She went thus walking and listening.

She thought of Adele Callister. Adele had two brothers dead in two days of fighting and her father was gone away with Elias McCutcheon. Sallie had envied Adele because she still had her father living, Adele did. But things had been evened up. Adele went walking with Yankee soldiers, thinking she was so smart she could get away with it. More than once while visiting Sallie at Oakleigh, after the wedding, Adele had said that while it must be nice to be married, still it was also nice not being married too, for an unmarried girl could slip into Somerton when she pleased and go walking with soldier boys from Michigan and Minnesota. And she had made Sallie envious telling how two little Yankee boys risked their lives coming to the Callisters' clearing at night.

More than once Adele slipped out to meet them. It was a shame, said Adele, that some girls were promised and others were married and couldn't take moonlight walks by the river. She had said such to Sallie to even things up between them and make Sallie unhappy.

Then not a week ago it had been Sallie's turn to go see Adele. For Adele, it seems, had come down sick. And Rance had driven Sallie down to the Callisters' in Jane's best carriage to see about Adele.

Adele, poor thing. She had been a fright to see. She seemed half wasted away and Sallie had said, "Adele, why what on earth?"

"Fever," says Adele.

They talk of this and that until Adele hints that it may not be fever after all, but something else — a dark hint.

"Why, what on earth?"

"Oh," says Adele. "They gave me turpentine and sat me in hot water and tied a rope about me here." She points at her middle and gives Sallie a wise look.

"A *rope?*"

"Shhh! Not so *loud!* A rope — yes. Tight enough to cut me in two. And sat me all night long in water hot enough to boil eggs and heating more water all the time. Mamma fetched that old squaw down from your house and they sat up with me all night."

"Leola came *here?*"

"That's who came and you never had a hint of it, did you?" Adele starts to cry. "Never, never tell, Sallie. Oh, *promise!*"

"I promise, Adele," says Sallie. She feels weak and knows a sudden dread.

"Sunday, all night," Adele whispers. "Then Monday before daylight — they held the funeral."

"*What?*"

Adele nods. Her lips starts to tremble. "It was a little girl and had her fingers!"

Sallie feels weak and knows that dread all over again just to think of it. She's walked such a long way . . . But here's a fallen tree nearby. Going to it she's sure she can't be far from the edge of the fields now. She stops and sits down to push away that awful thought of poor Adele Callister. Adele, made to walk between Leola and Fancy Callister; made to walk and carry something wrapped in a newspaper; Fancy with a lantern and a Bible, Leola with a digging spade; and those three walking down by the river and holding a funeral on Monday before daylight.

Sallie was hungry. Her mouth felt dry as cotton. She saw something on the ground. Cockleburs were on the leaves about her feet. She picks one up and sees gray lint caught in its spines. It can't be; it is. Lost . . .

She decides now to do what she feels she should have done here the first time she reached this place.

She kneels down. She's somewhat clumsy. Her back aches. She rests her belly against the log and props her elbows on it. She clasps her hands and bows her head. A cocklebur is pricking her left knee through her dress.

"*Holy Mary, mother of God . . .*"

Wishing for her father, calling Willy even though she well knew both were dead, Sallie finally lay down on the leaves. She fell asleep.

Waking, she knew herself to be alone in the bottoms. It was dark now. Looking upward she saw a red glow against the sky and walked that way, towards that red cloud, and thus found herself, after a little while, at the edge of the fields. In the distance she saw Oakleigh, still burning, and she set off walking that way. She found Leola in the cabin and saw that Jane Nail McCutcheon was dead. "Killed by a soldier's bayonet," says Leola.

Sallie was too exhausted to do otherwise than sit in a rocking chair while Leola was busy with washing Jane's body and laying it out nicely, with the small hands properly closed. Leola made a fire in the hearth, set the kettle to boil, and taking meal from the barrel she made a large pone of bread which she set to bake before the fire on a johnnycake board.

She had found Jake's whiskey. She put the jug out on the table and took a dram for herself now and then. When the bread was done and had cooled she put it on Jane's breast, then removed it, and brought it to the table.

"Why did you do that?" says Sallie. "Leola?"

Leola had made a pot of coffee and she passed this back and forth above the corpse. "What?" says Leola, her old voice cracking a little.

"Why are you doing that?"

"The sin offering. Here, have some coffee and cake. This way we take Jane's sins to ourselves. Come, sit at the table here."

Sallie moved to the table, thinking she could not eat, but when she smelled the warm bread and took the coffee cup in her hand she began to eat the bread and sip the hot coffee. Leola ate slowly . . .

"Hear that?" says Leola.

"What — the owls you mean?" says Sallie.

"They only sound like owls. They're the soul birds calling Jane's spirit to come away with them."

"Heathen nonsense," says Sallie, but the owls did sound strange, come to think of it.

They sat thus, just the two of them and watched the night through until dawn began to streak the sky. Leola stood up at last and snuffed out the candles.

Sallie's eyes filled then, and she began to cry.

Jake appeared.

"Where have you been?" says Leola. "While your mistress lay dying? Eh?"

"Hid," says Jake. "Miss Jane — dead?"

"Fetch a mule."

"Mule?" says Jake. "Miss Jane — *dead?*"

"Saddle a mule. Go find your master and tell him."

"Dead," says Jake. "How?"

"Stuck through, stabbed by a soldier," said the old woman. "Tell him Leola killed the soldier that did it."

"I wonder where will I find him?"

"Go south. Ask and keep asking. Say why. You have news for him. Go now."

Jake stood a moment, very still. "When she needed me, I run off and hid. Had I been by her nobody would of touched a hair in her head." He approached the bed, stood a moment quietly, hat in hand. And then: "I'm sorry, Miss Jane."

Sallie stirred. "It wasn't your fault, Jake. Find the General and tell him. Say Leola and I are well and will stay here."

"Yes, Mistress." Shaking his head slowly, Jake turned away and made for the door.

A moment later Sallie saw him outside with the mule. He came in and Leola handed him a sack of meal and some bacon. Wordless, he went out again, mounted the brown mule, and rode away.

Springtime. No sign of Jake, though many months have gone by while the river murmured and the moon rose — many and many months such as the pairing month and the month of the wild plums; no sign of Jake, though Leola has looked for him.

Leola steps outside the cabin and shades her eyes. Her brown hand is tremulous. She's looking for Willy's return. Just lately she's old and forgetful. She has a merciful memory now and mutters aloud that if only Willy were here he could see his wife and admire this first son of his and maybe start another; but Willy's a scout, and like Pettecasockee, his uncle, must be always gone killing behind the lines like a hunter . . .

Any day it seems she must see her men again. Come back they will, in a single troop, from all those wars they've gone away to fight, and when they return each will have two extra gunstocks tied to his saddle and his tin cup hooked behind to his belt . . .

Meanwhile Leola's had her satisfaction. Twice she's killed her man. Once when Jane's face was cut and afterwards when she bagged herself a soldier using that heavy brass rod that was the poker to Jane's fireplace, and wasn't made for killing.

She hears far off thunder. Or guns, it could be. Whatever the sound it mutters and mutters again, behind her. Her old eyes search the sky. Towards the north, and high above, she sees clouds piling.

Jane and Willy, she thinks. She thinks of life and how it's a ragged net that folks walk on; and now and then some fall through and are seen no more. Below the net is no bottom; below there it's all bottomless. God puts others on to replace those that fall through and the world goes on somehow, with a lot of thinking and talking and gossiping between, and with folk like Isaac who claim to make sense of it.

Chapter 19

Isaac was dreaming. His mother stood on the lawn at Oakleigh plain as day. There was no scar on her face. There was no war . . .

Jasper was shaking him. Isaac came awake hearing Jasper's whisper: "*Women!*"

Isaac was tired. He preferred the dream world he had just been living in to the world Jasper's hard hand was dragging him towards, the world in which his mother's face was scarred, in which his brother was dead and his father in the sort of grief that runs so deep it shows no sign of itself on the surface.

One by one the sorrows of the real world were tolled into existence, held together by the all-encompassing fact of the war itself.

At least, thought Isaac, the dead sleep. No one wakes them.

"*Women!*"

In darkness Isaac fumbled into his clothes, following Jasper to the horses then, worrying. Last night it had all seemed so appealing. Jasper Coon was welcome at a certain house not too far distant in the North Alabama countryside. There were two women — Jasper's woman and her younger sister. The sister would be Isaac's. At one in the morning, at the risk of being shot by your own sentries, and in the face of violating the most sacred of military regulations, the notion went stale for Isaac. Still and all he went along. For one thing he had reached the point now where he realized, in spite of his youth, that he could be killed at any given moment on any given day. It was only reasonable therefore to partake of any pleasure that offered, or so it had seemed last night when the plans were made.

In a furious attack on a Yankee supply train the brigade had taken a vast spoil of mostly useless things. The green troopers in their new and Northern uniforms had fought back bravely, killing and wounding many more raiders than the spoil, at least in Isaac's estimation, was worth.

The fight had settled into a sort of siege. The Yank's quotient of bravery when he was shipped into the bloody South as a replacement was a sort of stubborn and totally unyielding frame of mind.

The lads in blue had refused an offer of peaceful surrender. The ragged veterans of McCutcheon's brigade had finally stormed in to make an end of it at close range, with shotguns and pistol. It was all the more senseless because the Northern lads had been defending cases of wine and demijohns of whiskey, and a myriad supply of citron candy and enough perfumed soap and canned oysters to supply a large officers' mess for a year at least.

No saddles, no blankets, no weapons, no munitions, no uniforms. Wasn't it plain to everyone that the tired end of the sanguinary madness was close at hand when men who wanted corn for themselves and their horses took lives and lost their own for a thousand pounds of citron candy?

Isaac felt a twinge of shuddering uneasiness between his shoulder blades at the memory of the enemy dead. They had resembled so many children. In the long and blurred memories of so much fighting, this last one stood in Isaac's mind. There had been one other like it sometime back — a long time back, and below Memphis. They had stormed a fortress defended mostly by Negro troops and the same thing had happened. No terms for a reasonable surrender could be arrived at, for even surrender requires a degree of courage. The fight had gone out of hand, beyond the control of Elias, even. The shooting had dragged on and on at close range. Afterwards someone called that fight "the slaughter pen" and the name stuck.

Mounting his horse in the dark Isaac followed Jasper who took the way along a thicket below a sand bluff. It was a path none but a forager like Jasper could ever guess was there. They rode single file through a dense convocation of honeysuckle vines. The cool, sandy earth gave back no sound of hoof or passage.

"Here's the road," Jasper said.

They let their horses out into a slow canter. The road was a gray-brown ghost. Like a scent trail it lay between woods on the one hand and ditches on the other. Like all the future it promised Isaac nothing but uncertainty.

The captured supplies bounced in the captured haversack tied to Jasper Coon's saddle and the war itself reduced to a horse chase. Since the armies back east lost at Gettysburg it's been downhill this way, thought Isaac. Would the time ever come, he wondered, when his life would cease to be a series of mindless, running fights? I'd welcome a real battle for a change . . .

Jasper found the lane. They turned their horses into it and rode the last waning mile to the small white house. It gave an impression of live, exposed bone, in the darkness. While the dog barked his weary, dutiful bark, they went behind the house to the barn and put their horses in and wired shut the ramshackled doors.

When they crossed the front porch a lance of yellow light fell at their feet from the cracked door. "Come in!" cried a woman's voice. They went in and Isaac met Jasper's woman first and next the fox-faced younger sister. She would be his. He knew a sort of resignation. The excitement he had wanted was nowhere to be felt. War drags us down to this, he thought. He took a kiss from her narrow mouth and felt how cold his own lips were against her warm ones. He felt the touch of her small white teeth.

The men from this little hill farm had gone away to fight on the Northern side and while they were gone away these, their women, left behind, consorted with the Confederates in return for soap and sweets. Nevermind how awful it all seemed in contemplation; in truth and fact the bargain was like a pact between children. It was all too innocently done to be sordid.

"Married?" she asked.

"No." Isaac saw that she didn't care. It was as innocent as playing at mudpies. The haversack was emptied. The wine was opened, the soap smelled, the oysters sampled straight from the tin, the candy nibbled. Jasper and his woman had already stepped into a nearby room and shut the door.

"My bed's in here," she said. Isaac followed her, bringing two glasses and a bottle of wine. She put the candle on her bedside table and slipped out of her clothes. Her breasts were small and pointed. "My name is Ruth," she said.

"And mine is Isaac."

He laid his pistols beside the candle and undressed. She poured wine in the two glasses meanwhile. When he climbed in the bed and they kissed for the second time he knew what it was that her breath had reminded him of — wild honey, the dark honey of wilderness and azaleas and bending goldenrod, full barns and shuck silence, and a pellucid luster of days.

"Git some!" she cried, trying to hurry him. "Git some! Oh!"

Wanting it or wanting it over with — Isaac could never be sure. Even while thrusting that engorged part of himself straight up inside her between-thighs narrowness he ignored her, he took his own secret sweetness of time.

An instant afterward, it seemed, the candle was guttering and he was hurriedly hauling himself into his britches and boots, calling out to wake Jasper. He took up his pistols last of all and kissed his bedmate one final kiss. She mumbled something from her sleep and turned away and left him wondering if a Yankee patrol would even now be on the road between this place and the camped brigade.

Now that pleasure was satisfied conscience returned, hardscrabble Southern conscience strongly tinctured with guilt, and laced with fear like the taste of brandy in milk. What if the brigade should have saddled up and moved out quietly? What if Isaac and Jasper should return to the ground to discover cold ashes and abandoned latrine ditches, cold horse turds on the picket line and a rotten flung-away glove with the fingers worn through? No sentry would be left behind to instruct them as to the whereabouts or the destination of their comrades. The prospect of disgrace has always been the penalty for dishonorable acts and it is after the fact, always, as Isaac had discovered,that the consequences enter a man's head. Setting out, seeking pleasure and cunt, a man never gave the consequences a thought. It was always the aftermath of his pleasure which made him a coward and left him feeling numb. Tempt fate and it would be your luck to be in the wrong place when *who-who-whoo-whoosh!* and *bloom!* and your body was sausage, seasoned with shrapnel and stuffed in your uniform.

Sausage. They smelled bacon frying long before they reached camp again. Isaac rode dozing in the saddle; awake he smells the cookfires of the brigade; asleep he smells the cornfields about Oakleigh. He has glimpse-dreams of his mother, the river, the sycamore-tree shed, the warm land, the green corn, and Leola, a strange and wrinkled priestess with dark braids and shadowy eyes . . .

Slipping back into camp they passed a Negro on muleback. Hitching his mount back in the line and dragging the saddle off, hoping he won't be noticed, and thinking of the fox-faced girl, Isaac turned and saw the Negro again, astride the mule, and approaching him.

"Sah?"

"Yes?" said Isaac.

"Seeking Gen'l McCutcheon? This be his bunch?"

"Yes —" Isaac was about to ask what business the man had with the General. Sometimes they had reports, intelligence of real value. Other times they were only a nuisance, bent upon wheedling and begging. It were best not to bother the General with trifles. Isaac felt an awakening recognition and said: "Is it you? Jake?"

"Sah?"

"Isaac, Jake. Don't you know me?"

"Been so long on this road I can't hardly believe I've made it at last," said Jake, slipping down. He advanced upon Isaac and the two embraced, each patting the other's back.

"Your mammy's dead, Sonny," said Jake.

"Oh, no."

"Miss Jane's gone."

"But how —?"

"Stobbed by a Yankee. Killed by a Yankee bayonet."

They went to find Elias and Jake told his story again, weeping as he spoke, and dragging out the words as though he feared for himself. His eyes rolled.

Elias stood with his head bowed. "Where will it end?" he said, before he broke and wept.

Robbed of his weariness, made fresh by this fresh grief, Isaac stood hollow and empty. *When I kissed that whore*, he thought, *my mother was dead.*

Chapter 20

When the word, so long expected, came at last, that Lee, weeks earlier, had surrendered in the east at Appomattox Courthouse, the brigade stacked arms and the menace of the encircling hosts of the enemy was ended, not with a shout, but with a long sigh. The fighting was over; the Sacred Cause was lost.

They were deep in Alabama, far to the south in the black belt, when the tidings that signified the South's total prostration and exhaustion, reached the fighters in Elias McCutcheon's brigade. Some climbed down from their horses and stretched out and straightway fell asleep on the ground.

Isaac was one. It rained and he slept through the downpour. The next dawn the battered bugle sounded and the drums beat the roll to assembly for the last time and Elias made his farewell. It rained again.

Tug Chambers was the last man wounded, shot in the foot by a Yankee bullet, stung by the final angry bee of lead: "My luck — my God damn luck!" And he shook his fist at the fates. It was a bad wound and gave him agonies day after following day as those few from among the many who had left West Tennessee at the war's beginning, headed back that way again with sidearms and haversacks and a forage bag hanging from the saddle of each tired horse.

Pettecasockee hardly looked about him. He was pressed low by the coppery taste of defeat. He sat his horse and gave back daggered looks to any who spoke to him.

Jake spoke to his mule. "See there, just look yonder," said Jake. "More chimneys than houses. See how they had to burn down ever'thang they couldn't tote away." The mule went nodding northward as though, through some deeper wisdom, it understood what Jake told it, how it was on this endless unwinding of roads day in and day out, dawn upon the right hand, sunset upon the left hand, summer to the rearward, and springtime straight ahead. "Fences all tore down and burnt up — no pride, no hope. Shit and ashes, that's all." Amid the marks of so much destruction even Jake, for long stretches, was taken speechless. He muttered to himself. He whispered. The rain came at intervals traveling over the open fields from great distances away, raising and driving and scenting and finally settling dust as it scattered over and beat itself down upon them and was gone. Each swift attack, soon ended, left behind it a chuckle of red water in the ditches. The sun broke through afterwards and raised a steam from the flanks of the horses.

Presently they crossed into West Tennessee and now destruction took on familiarity as they encountered the charred stumps of bridges they had burned themselves, swimming their mounts over, and Jake, who could not swim, hanging to his mule for life as it swam and snorted and moaned.

It was after the crossing of the south fork of the Forked Deer River, where it was incumbent on them to swim over, as though the nearer they came to home the more obstacles were offered, that Jake spoke again, this time not to the mule, but to everyone in hearing.

"I see some more niggers," Jake said.

And there were, sure enough, a whole band of them, two hundred and more sitting by the roadside like a resting flock of tired, migratory birds. All sizes, all ages, all colors from blue pitch black to creamy yellow, some had bundles on the ground beside them. The smoldering from their cookfires made a still haze on the air. A child was crying. Here and there a mother jiggled an infant at her breast.

Elias reined up beside one of the old men nearest the road. The Negro was so thin he looked like an assemblage of sticks with the black skin stretched loosely over the disorderly framing of his body. His hair was white. He stared upward at the figure on horseback.

"Where do you belong?" said Elias, speaking to all of them, but addressing this nearest one.

"Free now," croaked the old man. His arms shifted like the featherless wings of a bird, nervously. "Don't b'long nowhere."

"You'd best go back — all of you — to whoever it was that owned you."

"We ain't gone *never* do that," said a woman's voice. It rang from the midst of so many sprawled figures that it was impossible to know who had spoken.

Jake rode in beside Elias and reined up as though summoned to the white man's side by the sass in that female retort.

"Ha!" said Jake. He looked them over and smiled, imperious as a black pharaoh. “Free are you? You look hungry to me!”

“We hongry,” said the old man, nodding. And then: “But we free.”

“Shit,” said Jake. He spat. The rest of the column had filed past without stopping, without looking most of them, for flocks of displaced Negroes were nothing uncommon, and no more unusual than the silent chimneys standing to mark the places where houses had been. The ex-slaves were no less a reminder of the magnitude of the South’s defeat than the chimneys.

“You must be a driver,” said a voice. “He acks like a driver. He must be a driver.” And the flock nodded a silent *amen* and made a rustling noise.

“I was a driver,” said Jake. He kicked the mule and turned away up the road, showing them his back, sitting ramrod-straight.

“Go back home where you belong,” said Elias.

“We hongry. You got any food fer us, Marster?”

Jake wheeled his mule around. “He ain’t your master! You got no masters and that’s your trouble!” He rode down on them and stopped. “Half sick, half starved, and none fit to be killed!”

“You a driver all right.”

“I was!” Jake turned again and rode away.

Elias untied his forage bag. Leaning down he handed it to the old Negro who reached out his skinny arm and snatched it. The nubbin ears of dry corn, protected, held above the flood at each crossing, rationed a grain at a time for parching, made a muffled rattling of seeds. The starved horse thrust its head forward, reaching at the bag. Elias reined the animal about.

When he had caught up with the rest Jake noticed at once that the bag was missing. “I know what I’d give ’em,” said

Jake, speaking to the mule. "They'd remember me after I got through with 'em."

A few miles further along Jasper Coon halted his nag at the dog path leading to his cabin. They were just north of the old military road, with the river on their left.

"Well," said Jasper. "Well." His Adam's apple was moving. In a moment now he'd see his old lady again, the same woman that he'd taken for a portion of his spoil from the raid on the Horse Pens. He'd see his children and his cabin. He had gone away against his will and he had somehow lived through it. "Well," he said. "God dang if I ain't about to cry and I don't —" He didn't finish, but rode away into the dog path and out of sight. Whooping sounds came lofting from the direction of his clearing a moment later.

It was Dutt's turn next. Time and again Dutt had vowed he'd not go home again when the war was ended, no. He'd strike out into the West, alone. "So long boys," he said, and rode towards his house, his sadness, his wayworn boredom. The war was really done.

Chapter 21

The war was done, but the peace was reluctant and there were seven years of strife and of night-riding. Just as the war itself had been slow in coming, so it was that the return of peace to the district was gradual and like a river that will not be hurried but takes its own way and its own time.

Elias saw how it was. Lincoln dead of a murderer's bullet and Johnson, the Tennessean, impeached and almost removed from the office of the presidency, and the veterans of the gray army disfranchised until seven springtimes had swelled the river at Elias's doorstep.

He pondered what might have been, had Willy lived, had Jane not been stabbed and killed, had Isaac remained in the district to become a planter instead of leaving to go east to Virginia to make a life for himself as a scholar at the university.

What might have been, had Ellen Ashe not married the Yankee colonel, Ennis Dalton, and moved north with him to St. Louis; what might have been?

There were surprises, meanwhile. Edward Ashe, like a prodigal, returned from Canada one autumn. Alone and prosperous, he appeared, took up his residence at Riverside with the Poe brothers, his uncles, and never told anyone what had become of the slave girl and the child he had taken north with him when he left.

And Jake's wife, that was his spoil from the raid on the Horse Pens, she ran away with a Yankee soldier and was not heard from again.

Elias lived in the cabin he had built by himself, in that room wherein his sons had been conceived and delivered of Jane Nail, and it seemed to him, from time to time, when just waking, that she was beside him again and would stir any instant now and climb over him, heavy and warm with child, and slip her gown on from where it had fallen beside the bed and stir up the fire beneath the kettle. Any moment, now, Dog would scratch at the door and whine to be let inside. Old Rattler was standing in his pen, impatient to be fed.

It was a sweet dream, all in all, and so real to him that the spell of it lasted longer and longer into the day as he grew older, and the iron in his hair and beard turned more and more to white.

In fine weather, sometimes, when Sallie drove out from Somerton to bring her son, Tom, to visit his grandfather, the old man would be restless and of a mind to pull up stakes from here and make his way west into Texas to take up new ground. His mind perfectly clear . . .

Other times, and especially during the bright days of autumn when the geese were flying, he was as serene as the river itself; but forgetful, more and more. He might call Sallie "Jane" from time to time and address Tom as "Willy" and wonder why Leola was so long about the milking.

"Dotes on that cow, Leola does," he would mutter. Then, going to the mantel he'd find his pipe and tobacco, loading the pipe and lighting it and puffing up a cloud of smoke. "And what of my old friend, Gabe French, how is he? When have you seen him last?"

It was no use telling him Gabe French was long since buried. Not a moment later he would have forgotten it and would ask the question again, such that Sallie had learned to humor him and to report that Gabe was happy and well as ever.

The day came when Tom took his bride to the cabin to visit. Coming away afterward, driving south again alongside the river she asked who Leola was.

"An Indian, an old squaw," the young man replied.

"What was she like?"

"I wouldn't know. I never saw her to remember."

The leaves fell down in lazy spirals into the road just ahead. Beyond a bend Riverside came into view. A cool breeze rose from the river, a wind of autumn, and the road entered upon a stretch of high forest which set the couple pondering what it must have been like hereabouts, in the beginning . . .

Author's Note

The Raider is the story passed down to me through my father, my mother, and my grandparents; it is the story of my people and of the land as it was in the Old Southwest, that territory which we know today as the South; but it was the Old Southwest back then, long ago, a hundred years and more, when whites and blacks and Indians all worked at the same thing, at building a nation where nothing but wilderness was before.

Fortunately for my story, West Tennessee, where Elias McCutcheon and his family and his servants and his neighbors lived, was settled late. Chickasaws held the territory and ruled it well into the last century, thus holding out a pocket of virgin wilderness until young wanderers such as Elias walked in alone, leading a horse, with a dog following . . .

Formal history has much to say about the "purchase" of West Tennessee from the Indians, a work done by a Colonel Shelby and no less a personage than Andrew Jackson; but historical personages do not concern Elias, the Hedgepaths, the Poes and the Musgroves and the McNeillys and the Callisters, and the others . . . Day to day their involvement with the land and with family and animals and growth — for it was a growth that was ongoing, a wondrous growth — it was this growth that took and held *their* attention, and not historical personages.

The writing of this story took two years of reading and six years of writing, a great lot of time for a story so simple. I had to get it right, though. It had to be authentic, or I had been untrue to those who came on the land before me. More could have been given to the fighting, but fighting is repetitious and so many forays and onslaughts finally pall and blur. The horror is too much. I make no case for having told it all.

I wish to thank Dewey Pruett, Curator of the Mississippi Valley Collection, Memphis State University; Edwin Folsom, Patricia Browner, and Phyllis Bateman. I offer special thanks to the many who let me read letters and diaries left to them by ancestors who fought in the War for Southern Independence, and to Edward Weeks, my friend and editor.

J.H.F.